ISBN 978-0-483-97725-9
PIBN 10200316

# THE HOME LIBRARY.

# BLACK AND WHITE.

## *MISSION STORIES.*

BY

# H. A. FORDE,

AUTHOR OF "LASSIE'S SHOES."

PUBLISHED UNDER THE DIRECTION OF THE TRACT COMMITTEE.

LONDON:

SOCIETY FOR PROMOTING CHRISTIAN KNOWLEDGE;

NORTHUMBERLAND AVENUE, CHARING CROSS;

43, QUEEN VICTORIA STREET; 48, PICCADILLY;

AND 135, NORTH STREET, BRIGHTON.

NEW YORK: E. & J. B. YOUNG AND CO.

# CONTENTS.

iv                    CONTENTS.

# BLACK AND WHITE.

<hr>

## THE WHITE MAN'S GRAVE.

### SIERRA LEONE.

You all know something about missionaries and mission work ; if *you* have not time for much reading, your children come home from schools and classes with strange tales of heathen idols, and the efforts of Christian men to replace them with the image of a greater, more loving God, and you are called upon to look at sundry little green and pink covered books whereon are pictures of black children and strangely feathered warriors listening meekly to the white man's teaching. Sometimes, too, you hear a missionary sermon, and give your alms to help on the good work, remembering that the first great Missioner said, " Go ye into all the world, and preach the gospel to every creature." But all the same, you do not go very fully into the subject, and between times, till the children begin upon it again, or the special collection is once more made in

B

church, you almost forget that there is any other country in the world but Christian England, and any other souls to be cared for save yours or your neighbours' in the next street or cottage.

This is a pity, inasmuch as it deprives you of a great interest, and others of a great comfort; for, let me tell you, nothing lightens the labours and soothes the spirit of a hard-worked man, and especially a missionary, be he in India, China, the African deserts, or the islands of the great Pacific, as the feeling that his countrymen and countrywomen at home are watching his toilsome steps, and stretching out over land and sea to help him, if only by kindly thoughts and prayers. So, as probably you have neither the time nor the power to collect for yourselves the story of mission work in this great wide world, I shall try in these papers to give you at any rate a peep at those distant fields where so much work is to be done, and where, alas! as yet the labourers are so few and so hard-pressed; while, at the same time, I shall also direct your notice to many a corner of our own England, where the sick, the ignorant, and the sorrowful are being quietly yet efficiently cared for by many a faithful disciple of the great Master.

There are two names for the part of the world to which I am going to take you first: one is the map name, by which your biggest boy or girl will easily find it in the school atlas—Sierra Leone; the other is a name we shall all understand, but at the speaking of which we keep silence a moment in awe and pity—The White Man's Grave. Yes, that is the name this country on the west coast of Africa has earned for itself; the burning heats, the moist vapours, the sudden rains, and their following chills, all cherish disease and death for its white visitors. Who would venture there, then, knowing this fact so well? I will tell you.

The soldier goes when duty calls him there with his regiment; the sailor goes when his ship is needed to guard that deadly coast; they are serving their queen and their country; and though their friends wish them good-bye with sad hearts, fearing never to see their faces more, they quit themselves like men, and hope for the best.

But who else would face the dangers of that African coast? I will tell you again. Other soldiers, the soldiers of Christ, who deem His command of "Go ye into *all* the world, and preach the gospel to every creature," as laid upon them to obey to the letter.

Their Commanding Officer has not said, "Go ye to the pleasant places of My earth, and tell the people there My message of love and life." That would have been easy enough to obey; but the order comes in unmistakably plain language, and takes in lands hot and cold, people savage and dangerous, ay, even this fever-breeding and death-breathing country of Sierra Leone.

Almost the first missionaries ever sent from England alighted on these shores, and I will tell

you why good men at home felt that here their
labours were almost owed to the wretched black
people of the district.

You have all heard of the slave-trade, but perhaps
you hardly have been told that not so very long
ago England itself joined in that flesh-and-blood
traffic, dragging the poor negro from his hut in
Africa, loading him with chains, and shipping him
off with a crowd of other wretched creatures to work
in plantations hundreds of miles across the seas.

A prosperous English merchant thought no shame
then to have his slave-ships on the ocean—packed,
these wretched creatures, more like herrings than
men, between the decks of the vessel, and dying by
tens and twenties on the voyage.    Some were
kinder masters than others, better men, as it were,
and went to church, and heard that new command-
ment to love one another, with full intention of
keeping it, yet never thinking it might include the
poor despised negro slave.    But just at the end of
the last century England seemed to rouse itself to
the conviction of the wickedness of this buying and
selling of human creatures, and an Act of Parliament was passed some time afterwards abolishing
slavery entirely throughout the whole of the
British empire.

Then arose a new difficulty.    What was to be done
with all the poor negroes who were suddenly loosed
from their chains ?    And when a slave-ship was
seized in mid-ocean, where was the live cargo to be
landed and made at home ?    In Sierra Leone, was

the answer to this; and, convinced of the suitability
of the place, England collected the destitute negroes
shivering in her streets, put them on board vessels
to the number of four hundred to begin with, and
sent them to the west coast of Africa, where they
were joined in time by a multitude of other liberated
slaves, all thankful to settle down in a free country,
guarded by British power. Poor neglected heathen
they were indeed still, none the better perhaps for
their wrongs and misfortunes, but greatly to be
pitied.

So when England woke up, after hundreds of
years of dull sloth and neglect of our Lord's plainest
command, to feel she must do something for the
world lying in darkness around her, she chose
Sierra Leone as the first field for such work. Yet
there were many difficulties in the way. First, as
regarded the missionaries to be sent out. Though
the need of these was made clearly known in England, not one man stood forth to fill up the gap, so
hopeless was it thought to be to attempt to instruct
the wretched negro, and so terrible were the fears
of the deadly climate of Africa. It was left to
Germany to provide the earliest missionaries to our
new colony, though the English Church Missionary
Society, then just organized, took them under its
care, and sent them out to their field of labour. They
worked well and heartily, gathering round them
children and grown men, the latter even more
curious than the former to be taught out of the
"white man's book."

And much they needed to be taught its gentle lessons, for this mixed multitude of people, snatched cruelly from different tribes and districts of Africa, had no law by which to live save the law of force. The stronger among them robbed the weaker; they lied and stole; they made offerings to the devil; while in their outward appearance it was long before Christian teaching could effect improvement.

Clothes they did not understand, and would not wear; they threw them away, or changed them for drink or gay trifles, as beads and looking-glasses; and not till one of the missionaries dressed his servant up as an example could even the well-disposed be induced to cover themselves in any way.

No one dare cultivate the ground either, lest the lazier people around him should rob him of his crops; and as to keeping pigs and fowls, it was an almost impossibility—they were stolen and eaten almost before they could be housed.

Think what a hopeless people to labour among; but missionaries must never be hopeless, and our painstaking Germans toiled and taught, prayed and worked, till light dawned on the settlement.

Freetown, the capital, and Regentstown began to grow in importance. Houses were built, gardens fenced in; here sprang up a Government house, there a hospital, school-house, parsonage, ay, even a church.

Did I tell you that when the missionaries first came there was no such thing as marriage known

amongst the people, and no two, man and woman,
chose out a little home in which to live quietly and
rear their children?  Instead of that, from ten to
twenty people would crowd into a wretched hut,
quarrelsome and riotous, the feebler often dying of
starvation in their midst.

Besides this sad state of affairs, the missionaries
had other troubles to contend with; the slave-dealers
of different nations were all their enemies, of course,
often inciting unruly negroes to attack their houses,
and once even burning down their church.

But such hindrances were not suffered to stand
long in the way, and fifteen years after the arrival
of the first missionary upon these shores the state
of affairs in Regentstown—a settlement under the
care of Mr. Johnson, also a German missionary
—was this: a full church half an hour before
service was to begin, nicely clothed boys and girls
marching two and two to the service, the black
people listening eagerly to the teaching.  On Easter
Sunday 120 baptisms, two marriages, and 253 black
people kneeling at the Holy Table; all this, though
as some may think but the outward form of religion,
yet a comfortable promise to those interested in the
mission that the inward life was there.

Shortly after this Easter gathering, Mr. Johnson
had need to pay a short visit to England, when his
faithful negroes accompanied him as far as Freetown,
saying good-bye to him there with many tears.
They even desired to accompany him further on his
journey, had that been possible, saying, "Massa,

suppose no water here," pointing to the sea, "we go with you all the way, till no feet more." Mr. Johnson was spared to return to his people, to win still more of their love, and then he too fell a victim to the climate, dying on board ship, three days from land, when paying another visit to England to see his sick wife. Only seven years a worker among his poor black flock, only thirty-seven years of age, this man had made his mark in the world. He died thanking God for giving him the opportunity of sowing the seed of eternal life in Africa, and looking forward to his own happier, brighter life with God.

How many missionaries and missionaries' wives in these twenty years had been laid quietly down in the "White Man's Grave" I have not told you; but they were not a few. Wives lost their husbands, husbands their wives, and the tender little Northern children drooped and died one after another on their parents' knees, to those parents' bitter anguish.

One great comfort at these times must have been the love and sympathy of their people. The poor negro is very affectionate, and attaches himself most strongly to those who are kind to him.

One missionary's wife endeared herself very much to her husband's flock, helping and teaching the women, not merely how to read—not preaching to them, as was her husband's duty—but showing them how ω cook and sew, to nurse this sick child, to contrive that strange but much-desired garment. She must have been a clever woman as well as a good one, she managed to do so much and to make so little fuss over it, and so she was doubly useful. But she died, too, in the summer of her days; and speaking of her loss a poor African said years after, "Oh! had you only been see her funeral, de crowds of people dat follow, crying and weeping and wailing, you would have said it was dat of one great queen."

You must see, if you think of it, that the colony of Sierra Leone was likely for a long time to be a source of constant anxiety to its rulers and teachers for this reason: fresh cargoes of liberated slaves were constantly being landed on its shores, and they, all miserable and ignorant as they were, had to be provided for, instructed, and civilized. No more stealing from one another, no more religion of drum-beating and wild dancing and devil-worshipping could be permitted, but clothed, and with the dawning of a right mind within them, these poor souls were shown the church and the schools, with the happy black babies in their gay pinafores, till they wondered to what strange paradise they had been brought.

I do not think I have told you much about the sort of land this Sierra Leone is; you have only heard of it as yet as hurtful, nay, deadly to Europeans; but to the black man it is very different. His body is framed to bear the hot sun and the chill damps, and he finds all he wants in the fertile soil, out of which in one day a plant will spring a foot out of the earth!

All sorts of strange fruits and gay flowers make beautiful this spot of earth; of those we know at home, I may mention the pine-apple and the orange. Coffee, too, grows here, and so does the palm tree, from which the oil is made so much used for greasing the wheels of railroad carriages. But the country is so overrun with lovely foliage and flowers that it would be useless attempting to describe them. The forests and uncultivated grounds are called "Bush;" but the word sounded strange from the lips of a little black nurse sailing with her mistress to England, on sighting the Isle of Wight: "Please, ma'am, I see Bush." There is not much "Bush" left in any part of England now—it is so thickly populated. Then the animals of Sierra Leone. To begin with, there should be lions, as the name tells us, but I expect they have long taken themselves into the recesses of the mountains, for where people gather they object to stay. But monkeys still chatter and gambol in the trees, very pretty and amusing to watch, while very tiresome and destructive to gardens and houses. Lizards, snakes, and ants abound. But the ants are the terrible plague of the country, at least to housekeepers; nothing keeps them away from food. They crawl in a thick, irrepressible stream into cupboards, up walls and tables, devouring everything before them, and are hardly checked by planting table-legs in basins of salt water and guarding all precious food in tin cases. Sometimes a colony of ants will try to take possession of a house, and then boiling water must be poured on them, or everything would be devoured in a very short time. Yet people who think of such things do not needlessly kill even these troublesome insects, as they are very useful scavengers, devouring every sort of rubbish and castaway food. So greedy are they that a lady in Africa has to reflect, before she rubs her needles with oil to prevent them rusting in the dry season, what sort of grease the ants most dislike, or all her care would be in vain.

But perhaps of all the things which render Sierra Leone terrible and objectionable, next to the unhealthiness, it is the storms; they are most awful. The sky darkens, the grasshoppers and insects cease their noisy chatter. There is a fearful silence; then heaven and earth seem to break loose in violent rain, hail, thunder, lightning, and wind. Houses and trees are blown down, and unhappy wayfarers crushed beneath them. After a while the storm ceases as suddenly as it came on, and people tremblingly unbar their doors and shutters, repair damages, and again rejoice in the cool air and refreshed earth.

Of late years the ground has been more cultivated, and the country rendered somewhat less dangerous to white men, but the records of death among missionary annals are pitiful to read.

In the course of the first twenty years fifty-three missionaries or missionaries' wives died at their post.

And now that we have seen Sierra Leone gather-

ing in its midst a Christian population, with churches
and endowed schools, is it to be considered that
mission work and the spread of the gospel is necessarily at a standstill there?   Not at all.   When
you hear good news, of whatever kind, what is
your first thought?   To tell it to some one else.
Yes, surely; and these poor liberated slaves, rescued
from traders' vessels, and placed in a free country,
no sooner woke up to a real sense of who it was
that put mercy into men's hearts, and gave them
life and freedom and hopes of heaven, than they,
too, longed to be messengers of such good tidings
to others.

Think a moment of what sort of people Sierra
Leone was filled—with waifs and strays from
all parts of Western Africa, poor black souls torn
from mountain fastnesses, from sandy plains, from
seaside villages.   They were thankful for the peace
and liberty of Freetown, it is true, but far away
they had homes of their own, where brothers and
sisters, fathers and mothers yet lingered, wondering
perhaps still where was the curly-headed boy who
had been so rudely torn from their arms long ago.

So when church bells rang, and the gospel story
sank into their easily touched hearts, they came
out into the sunshine with tearful eyes, and looked
longingly into the distance, where perchance their
own land might be.

And presently one and another could not be
hindered, but set out in all faith for their own dear
home, here or there, by the great river Niger, or

southward towards the Gold and Ivory Coasts. Ay,
and reached home too, and fell on the neck of some
old father or mother, or were welcomed by a whole
tribe, perhaps, who remembered them long ago. And
then there was joy all around, and shouting and
dancing, and offerings to their god. No, stop there.
That could not be; or at least the Christian wayfarer
would spread out his hands in remonstrance. He
worshipped the true God, and could bow to no
other, and the dear old father and mother, or the
rejoicing friends, must be shown the new faith too.

So into the Yoruba country and the Niger district,
and hither and thither went the gospel tidings, not
cleverly told by wise men, but falling, perhaps awk-
wardly, from the lips of those who had it but in
their hearts. Seed grows, though, even if infants
throw it on the ground, and the true God began to
be worshipped up and down, here and there, in
strange corners of this Western Africa.

And then, later on, came messages from the
Yoruba country, to which region many freed slaves
had struggled back, and the message was this—

"Send us a missionary to our land; many want
to hear of the great God, and the English can best
teach us; they are a people nearer to God than any
other." You see they had been told how kindly
their countrymen had been treated by British ships
and British people, and they longed to know more
of their customs, to live under the care of their God.

So a missionary was sent to Yoruba land, and
a settlement formed there. I dare say you think

when England gave up the slave-trade, and refused
to let it be carried on under shelter of its flag, it
was pretty nearly at an end in the neighbourhood
of a British settlement; but it was not so. Not
only did other white nations still prey on the poor
defenceless negroes, but the very black men themselves bought and sold their own fellows. If one
tribe went to war with another, slaves were cap-
tured on either side; if a man offended his kinsmen,
and they were stronger than he, they sold him for
a slave. Even such a sight as this might be seen
in the streets of Yoruba: a little child cowering by
the roadside, exposed for sale, cold and hungry, and
crying pitifully to the passers-by, "Buy me! buy
me! take me home with you!"

Sierra Leone might be rejoicing in a streak of
daylight, but there was great darkness and superstition in the neighbouring districts.

A race of Mohammedans living near the Yoruba
country have been cruel neighbours to them, continually overrunning their land, and carrying off
men, women, and children as slaves. One little
lad of eleven years old, torn from his mother and
sisters, was sold for a slave, and after several
changes fell into the hands of the Portuguese, who
were great slave-buyers. This poor child, with a
chain round his neck, fastened to a crowd of other
miserable creatures, was happily shipped on board
a vessel which was pursued and taken by English
men-of-war. Little Adjai and six of his companions
were taken at once on board the *Myrmidon*, but

the trembling, ignorant children could not at first believe what good fortune had befallen them. Their eyes fell first on a dead pig hung on the deck of the vessel, and their hearts failed them. This was surely human flesh, and their turn to be eaten might come next. Then a fresh shiver ran through them. In a great heap at the further end of the ship were surely a pile of negro heads, neatly arranged, but meaning without doubt instant destruction to poor black folk. You will smile when you hear that on closer examination the terrible objects turned out to be cannon-balls. After this discovery little Adjai and his fellows must have taken courage, especially as they had decent clothes given them, and were kindly treated till their landing at Sierra Leone. Here the children were sent to a Church mission school; and a missionary's wife, finding the boy earnest and wishful to learn, gave him further teaching after school hours with a little girl of the same tribe, called Asano.

Adjai and Asano were happy little people now. They presently changed their heathen names for Christian ones; Adjai was baptized "Samuel Crowther," and Asano became "Susanna." Then the boy went to England once, twice, three times, always with the intention of advancing his desire to become a missionary to his own people. The first time he only looked around him, wondering at the strange land, and longing to make Africa more like it; the second time he studied in the Church Missionary College at Islington, receiving ordination there, and

going back to his country the Rev. Samuel Crowther.
On his third visit, his usefulness then being tried
and acknowledged, he was consecrated Africa's
first black bishop in our cathedral of Canterbury.
In the cathedral was that very missionary's wife
who had taught little slave Adjai his letters, and
his helpmeet as Missionary Bishop of the Niger was
Susanna, the fellow-learner of his boyhood. Here
it cannot be told how the slave-boy worked his way
to such a post, but work he did eagerly, earnestly,
and thoroughly. One interesting story in his life-
history must, however, find a place here. Twenty-
five years from the day that he was dragged from
his home by cruel men, a poor tried woman near
Abeokuta heard that a black clergyman had come to
bring good news to the Yoruba country. And rumour
said the clever, English-speaking, gospel-preaching
Mr. Crowther was her little long-lost Adjai. Could
it be possible? Up rose the poor woman and sought
her son. "When she saw me," wrote Mr. Crowther,
"she trembled. She could not believe her own
eyes. We grasped one another, looking at each
other with silence and great astonishment; big
tears rolled down her thin cheeks. She trembled
as she held me by the hand, and called me by
the familiar names by which I well remembered I
used to be called by my grandmother, who has
since died in slavery." The poor woman had long
been a slave too, but after a while her young
daughters had found her out and redeemed her, and
she was now living with them, taking care of their

children. Mr. Crowther had the happiness of seeing this affectionate mother renounce heathenism, and she received Christian baptism at his hands, being called by the name of the child Samuel's mother—Hannah.

The Niger Mission, over which Bishop Crowther rules, must necessarily be a mission of native workers, since the district is even more certainly fatal to white men than Sierra Leone. Every expedition that has made its way up the great river has come back sadly thinned in numbers. Now, with white men's prayers and white men's hopes, the country is left under entirely black care. For years the bishop has worked there unflaggingly; he has native clergymen under him, and when more are wanted he will ordain more. One of his own sons is a pastor at Bonny, a town on the Niger. There is also no lack of native teachers. Such is the present state of the Niger Mission.

There is much persecution of the Christians in that region, for the heathen dislike giving up their old gods, and try to prevent others doing so. We all grow to love our sins and the old guardians of our sins. But in time the poor Africans begin to grope their way out of the darkness, and to bring to their new teachers sticks and straws, lumps of iron and clay, their greatest treasures, the symbols of their heathen gods. And in return they carry back with them the One God in their hearts.

Such customs, too, as had to be done away with among the ignorant creatures! A rich woman's

c

young daughter died, and when the missionary
came, thinking to comfort her, the sorrowful mother
told him, quite as a matter of course, that at the
funeral ceremony a slave-girl would be killed, to go
with her young mistress to the other world and be
her slave there.  The Christian teacher was shocked,
and tried to convince the woman that such murder
was wicked and useless; but all to no avail.  "It
must be," said the heathen lips; "it is our custom;
I cannot help it."  And since Christians were few
and helpless then by the Niger river, the heathen
rites took place.  A little slave-girl was killed with
a club, and buried by the side of the rich woman's
daughter.  Crowds looked on and approved.  This
is the belief of the heathen.  Shall we refuse to
teach them better ?

I have told you here something about Sierra
Leone and the neighbouring countries in a very
hasty way, but still I hope you seem to know the
places a little better.  Can you think of Sierra
Leone now as a Christian country, with its own
clergy, its own churches, yes, and its own bishop
too, able to stand alone, and even to send out
missions to less favoured districts—a native Church,
after much persecution, strongly rooted in Yoruba
country, and the Niger Mission doing good work
under Bishop Crowther and his handful of clergy?

And taking in all this, will you say that the
white men, whose graves lie thick in Freetown
graveyard and in more out-of-the-way corners, have
died for nothing ?  I think not.  Sorrowful as their

seemingly wasted lives and early deaths appeared at the time, they were the foundation of all after-success in the building up of a Christian Church in these regions.

The sowing in tears we know was theirs; and if they did not live to see the reaping in joy, who shall say that at the resurrection day, when hidden things shall be made plain to them, the glad surprise will not be all the greater?

# TWELVE HUNDRED MILES FROM A NEIGHBOUR.

## TRISTAN D'ACUNHA.

HAVE you ever come upon a cluster of cottages far
from a town, far even from the nearest little village,
and talked to the inhabitants of such a spot, hearing
the tale of their secluded life, and pitying them for
the various inconveniences of it? Such a long way
to market, such a long way to the school, difficulties
in the way of selling the eggs and butter and garden
produce, difficulties in getting in the necessary
stores from the town—no doctor, no church!

You listen, and think the poor souls terribly out
of the world, and wonder that for the sake of fresh
air and cheap house-rent they can manage to exist
in so out-of-the-way a corner. But what will you
say when I tell you the story of just such a cluster
of cottages, inhabited most of them by your own
country-folks, but planted on a desolate little island
*twelve hundred miles* from the nearest neighbour,
from shop, from market, from doctor, from church!

I hardly know if the place is marked on the map
of the world, but there it lies, on the grey Atlantic
Ocean, the rocky islet of Tristau d'Acunha, with its

two sister isles near, one rightly named Inaccessible, the other strangely called Nightingale, after the first discoverer of it. Not from the songster of that name, for only screaming sea-birds build their nests in these barren islands.

Who, then, among us has dared to make a home in these solitary regions, tilling the little strips of land at the foot of the great wall of rock which almost crowds them into the sea, and bringing up children with English faces and English names who yet never may set foot on English soil ? I will tell you.

The story begins in the year immediately following the great battle of Waterloo, when the British Government thought fit to send a detachment of soldiers from the Cape of Good Hope to form a settlement on Tristan d'Acunha. They brought with them horses, cattle, sheep, pigs, and poultry, besides stores and seeds for planting, evidently meaning to stay there for good ; but just as they had built a few houses and cleared something of the lower land, an order came that the island was to be given up and the troops taken back to Africa. Perhaps they were not sorry, for the climate was not good ; howling winds tore down the rocky sides of the mountains and made melancholy music in the evenings, and there could be no pleasant stir of men coming and going, since the wide sea separated them from all other people, and only whaling vessels at times entered the difficult and not over-safe harbour.

So the ship *Julia* was soon filled with the troops,
and only waiting for the captain to come aboard,
when a terrible calamity occurred. The wind rose
to a violent extent very suddenly at midnight,
parted the poor *Julia* from her anchors, and then
beat her on to the cruel rocky shore till she became
a total wreck. More than sixty souls perished on
that inhospitable beach. But still, when the remnant
were collected and about to be borne away to a
safer station, one man stood forth and asked to be
allowed to remain behind with his wife and two
small children. He was a Scotchman, a corporal of
artillery, William Glass by name, a man of good
character, and well thought of by his officers.

His request was granted, and cattle, seeds, and
many other useful things were left for his benefit;
two other men also, Englishmen, Nankivel and
Barnell by name, volunteered to keep him company,
promising, however, to regard Glass as their chief,
and before the trooper sailed away an officer drew
up a form of agreement to that effect.

Now, stay a moment, and see if you can picture
to yourselves this little company waving their last
adieu to their comrades, as they stand on the shores
of their wild ocean home—Glass, Nankivel, and
Barnell, and two baby children of the corporal's.
One of these tiny things was a girl, and to give you
an idea of the utter solitude and out-of-the-wayness
of the place (to coin a word), Mrs. Glass for four
years saw no female face, save that of this infant
daughter. And yet she was happy. She had, of

course, plenty to do with her house, her children, her dairy, and a little sewing and mending. The men, too, were far from idle; trying the land with this crop and that, and finding out slowly that it would grow little else but potatoes, the fierce winds harrying more tender plants to their destruction.

Other work they had, too, work by which they meant to grow rich, the collecting of seal-skins and sea-elephant oil for exportation, for these creatures at certain times of the year visited the island in great numbers.

All day the three men were hard at work, and at night they collected round a blazing fire in Glass's house, either resting or chatting, or reading the few books the governor possessed. It is well to call him by that title, since he kept it all his life long. Every morning and every evening this little family prayed to God to watch and guard them, and each Sunday, as best they could, they went through the Church's services, thus linking themselves with the other members of Christ's Church throughout the world. If there were no Sunday bells for them, they had the Sunday heart of praise.

But Glass, while content with this narrow life for himself, desired something more for his children. He had not the time, and, perhaps, not the learning to teach them properly, so when the boy came to be five and the girl four he gave them up to the captain of a sealing ship to take to England and educate. The small things made the long journey safely, and were kindly treated, but in a year their protector failed, and, becoming very poor, was obliged to send the children back to their father in the same fashion of a sealing vessel, which, after a tremendous journey by Cape Horn, brought them once again to Tristan. The poor little things must have been weary of sea-voyages, and their father kept them four years at home till he had an opportunity of sending them to school at the Cape of Good Hope, another long sail. There they remained six years, learning a good deal, but I expect very much pleased when they were allowed to come *home* for good.

Meantime the colony had begun to increase. Two men were shipwrecked on the island, and chose to remain there; two others, old comrades of Glass's, had come to join him, and two sailors from a passing ship had chosen to cast in their lot with the islanders. Mrs. Glass was next to have companions, though hardly very pleasant ones. A large vessel, the *Blenden Hall*, was wrecked on one of the neighbouring uninhabited islets, and there for three months the passengers and crew were forced to drag out a wretched existence with scarcely any food but sea-birds' eggs. Only by accident did they discover that Tristan was inhabited and able to afford them shelter; and then, having made a sort of boat to carry them across, they all, forty in number, threw themselves on the hospitality of the Tristanites. Houses and beds, food and clothing were instantly provided for them, and the greatest

kindness shown to the poor creatures. They must
have presented a very strange appearance to the
islanders on their first arrival, for the ship had been
laden with white muslin and red and blue cloth for
India, and in these gay colours, a little soddened
by sea-water, men and women were dressed. Yes,
women at last! two English, two East Indians, and
one English maid. The *ladies,* as I suppose the four
first must be called, had been very quarrelsome on
board ship, and not much better on their desert
island, and now it seemed as if they were to bring
the strife of tongues to poor Tristan. But, luckily,
after two months a vessel touched at Tristan, and
gave the shipwrecked company a passage to the
Cape, and peace came back to the settlement. And
Mrs. Glass had still a companion left her, for the
servant-girl, Mary Riley, the nicest by far of the
five women visitors, remained behind with one
White, of the *Blenden Hall,* as her husband.

And now there began to be quite a colony on
the island, and the children had multiplied into a
healthy, happy little flock; more settlers landed,
hearing of the seal and whale oil trade, and run-
aways from ships, a bad sort of company, coming
now and then made a disagreeable stir in Tristan.
One new arrival, however, proved a pleasant friend
for Governor Glass—a Mr. Earle, a gentleman artist,
travelling about in search of subjects to sketch, was
detained by bad weather at the island, his ship
sailing away without him through stress of weather,
and leaving him without clothes or comforts of any

sort, an uninvited visitor. At first he was quite
melancholy at his fate, and he would have been
more so had he known that eight months would
elapse before he would be rescued, no ship touching
at Tristan in all that time. The wind roaring at
nights used to make him think of England and the
dear friends who were wondering where he was, and
as an aggravation of misery he felt as if he had
nothing to do—no books, no post to expect, and no
occupation. However, Glass and his wife were so
kind that he soon got over that stage, and almost
enjoyed his quiet, humble life, with milk and water
for drink, potatoes for food, and fish as a great treat,
if it could be caught. The chat over the fire at
night seems to have been his great pleasure; and
in the day he made himself clergyman and schoolmaster, teaching Glass's little boy and girl in the
gap between their English voyage and their African
one, and reading the service and a sermon every
Sunday to the whole population. He tells an
amusing story about his clothes wearing out at this
time, and Glass promising to make him some more
out of a Scotch plaid shawl he had happened to
bring to the island with him. Days, however, went
by and no new suit appeared. At last Glass came
to Mr. Earle with a long face to explain that he
had taken the scissors many times into his hands,
but "could not find it in his heart to cut the bonnie
tartan." He was a Scotchman, you see, and this
bit of his own country touched his heart. As you
may imagine, Mr. Earle at once gave him the cloak

for his own, only saying that he must contrive him some clothes out of some other material. And presently these were fashioned of sailcloth and goat-skin with the hair outwards, giving Mr. Earle a hearty laugh over the Robinson Crusoe garments, as he called them.

The next great event after Mr. Earle's departure was the desire of the five single men on the island to obtain wives. Glass and White were both so comfortable and happy with theirs that one cannot wonder at this. But the means employed were not what we should think likely to procure good wives—the captain of a vessel touching at Tristan was asked to bring back with him from St. Helena five women desirous of husbands.

Not the nicest women in the island would have gone on such a hazardous invitation, and when Captain Anson brought back his cargo, the men were not pleased with their bargain. A bad begin-ning this of domestic life, but as the Tristanites had made the arrangement they felt obliged to stick to it, and so were added five more families to the colony. From this time things began to change for the worse, though Glass still held Sunday service and taught the children, whose parents cared for them to learn. A godless population grew up in poor Tristan, and the visits of rough sailors from whaling vessels did not improve matters. What was to be done?

Thanks to Governor Glass, God had always been acknowledged in Tristan, and twice the islanders had seen the face and welcomed the ministrations of an English clergyman. Once it was a missionary bound for India, who had landed for a day and baptized all the children on the island, twenty-nine in number. Another time a chaplain going to Ceylon had baptized forty-one children and preached to the people while his ship took in water. Though on his way to a distant part of the world, and never likely to visit Tristan again, this Mr. Wise had a heart wide enough to take in the wants and troubles of another flock, and no sooner had he left the island than he wrote to England, asking the Society for the Promotion of Christian Knowledge to send out books, and, if they could, a teacher, to help Governor Glass, and giving an interesting account of the little English colony on their rocky home.

A good man, with wealth at his command, read this account, and desired the Society to find a clergyman for Tristan, and he would pay him.

Accordingly, a Mr. Taylor offered himself, and in due time was ordained and set sail for Tristan. You will understand what a difficult place it was to each when I tell you that no captain of a ship would actually promise to take him straight to his destination. It was only "wind and weather permitting" that they agreed to land him on his rocky islet; and so it happened that the weather being thick, Mr. Taylor's vessel searched for a whole week in vain for Tristan; and at last, in despair, the captain declared he could wait no longer, and must continue his journey to the Cape of Good Hope, taking Mr. Taylor on with him. So the ship was put about, and the poor clergyman, with a sigh, resigned himself to the disappointment.

One regretful look, however, at sunset he gave to the bank of clouds where Tristan ought to have been; and there, above the grey leaden mass, was a tiny jagged peak that neither changed its form nor melted away as he watched.

Surely that was Tristan! The captain was called, the sailors ran aloft, and still the peak kept its place. It *was* the island; the ship was put about, and at daybreak next morning they were close in shore, and Governor Glass was seen rowing out to meet them, little thinking who was on board. For no letters, or very few, you must remember, ever reached Tristan, and that a clergyman should willingly give up home and friends and hopes of advancement in life to come to this desolate corner of the world was never for a moment expected by Glass or his comrades. But here he was hastily collecting his clothes and books, and leaping into Glass's boat, since the sea was rising and presently it would be impossible to land. It was Sunday, and the beach was crowded with little children in their Sunday frocks (furnished by whaling ships in exchange for the potatoes and seal oil of Tristan). After these little ones came the fathers and mothers, all, even the godless ones, no doubt touched at the sight of one come to care alone for their souls. There were only nine families on the island, but, as I told you before, children flourished there, and there

were sixty-four of these little creatures—Glass alone
having fifteen to his share. With one or two waifs
and strays, Mr. Taylor had a congregation of eighty
people the next Sunday assembled in Governor
Glass's largest room. Only sixteen feet long and
twelve wide was this substitute for a church, for the
winds are so high in Tristan that the houses, though
built of stone, must crouch lowly under the rocks or
they would soon be blown down. At one end of
the room stood a seraphine, which Mr. Taylor had
brought with him, and which served for a reading-
desk, and a few planks stretched across for seats
was all the accommodation provided for the worshippers. Such Prayer-books as Mr. Taylor could
muster were handed round, and then the service
began.

But only one voice sounded in the responses—
Governor Glass's. This was not *common* prayer,
*common* to all, and Mr. Taylor paused before the
Psalms to try and mend matters. Many could read,
he knew, of those silent ones before him, but the
tongues were stiff and shy, and utterly unused to
move in praise of God in His sanctuary. So the
patient leader of the flock ordered the books to be
opened and the places found, and asked all that could
to read a verse of a psalm alternately with himself,
afterwards standing or kneeling as he led the way.
This they gladly did, and the hearts of the little
crowd in that bare room warmed at this fuller unaccustomed worship, and a happy Sunday dawned
once more on Tristan.

On the Monday Mr. Taylor began school-keeping, a day school for the little ones, an evening school for the elders, altogether embracing forty scholars. But now books were terribly wanted. The Society for Promoting Christian Knowledge had sent out a box a year ago, in answer to Mr. Wise's appeal, but it had never arrived, and to teach fidgety children without easy lesson-books seemed impossible. Luckily Mr. Taylor had brought slates and pencils, and the little ones could be set copies of A and B to keep them quiet. For four months Mr. Taylor had to manage with only two spelling-books, accidentally found in his luggage, and two reading-books, which Governor Glass produced; at the end of that time the precious long-delayed box of books really arrived, and Mr. Taylor says the opening of it was one of the pleasantest sights he ever witnessed. The box was large and heavy, and to save the trouble of dragging it up the steep beach, Mr. Taylor opened it where it was landed. It was a lovely evening, and the children clustered round, full of curiosity, and proud to carry the books to Mr. Taylor's house for him. Shouts of joy filled the air as heap after heap came forth—big books and little books, picture-books and lesson-books, more than any of the bright eyes present had ever seen in their small, shut-up lives. All, too, so new, so gay, so inviting.

Mr. Taylor was now very anxious to have a build-ing erected to serve as a church and school, as also a little room for himself, since, as yet, he was living in

the room where service was held in Governor Glass's
house.   The people gladly promised to build both,
and began on the tiny abode for their clergyman.
Building, however, is no joke in Tristan; heavy
stones have to be moved with great labour, and the
walls must be two feet thick and not more than
eight or nine feet high, to escape the great winds of
the place.   It took a month to set up Mr. Taylor's
prophet's chamber, and it was two years before
they managed to obtain a church.   Meantime the
governor's room was beautified by a little red cloth
and a few forms in preparation for Easter Day.   On
Easter Eve Mr. Taylor gathered his island flock
to join in the preparatory services, and when the
day dawned sweet young voices were raised to the
old words of "Christ the Lord is risen to-day."
The morning service at ten brought all the islanders
together, and there at noon was another gathering
for a sermon and the celebration of the Heavenly
Feast.   How strange and solemn it seemed to all!
On that lonely island in the middle of the vast
ocean, a little band obeying for the first time their
Lord's command, " Do this in remembrance of Me."
In the evening a grown man came to ask for
baptism; he had not been baptized in infancy, and
longed now to own himself a member of Christ's
Church.

Mr. Taylor admitted him to the sacrament in the
presence of the congregation.

Now came daily service in the small room; at
first, as everywhere, well attended, then falling off,

but Mr. Taylor persevered in the practice. Some women always came, a stray man or boy would drop in, and none might say but that all might be touched by the solemn daily acknowledgment of God as the Creator and Preserver of poor Tristan folk.

A schoolmistress came forward after a while, the daughter of an English fisherman; she could read well, and really liked her work, teaching the little flock pleasantly and carefully.

So matters went on prosperously, if without much stir, and Mr. Taylor was so busy, and so interested in his work, that he only now and then felt a pang of home-sickness or a desire for tidings from England.

On the 4th of August, 1853, he married the first couple on the island; an old man of eighty asked to have the Church's blessing on his union with the woman he had called wife for many a long year. Others followed his example later; up to this year, such as desired the offices of the Church when taking a wife had been married by Governor Glass. But the festivities of the first marriage in Mr. Taylor's annals were speedily followed by the gloom of the first death. It was a threatening day that of the wedding, but though a cold, bitter wind was blowing (August is winter in Tristan), some of the young people went up the mountain to hunt for gonies, as they call the beautiful white sea-bird known to us as the albatross. Towards noon the wind rose to a gale, and when evening came the

D

parents began to be anxious about their absent children. At length, just as evening service was ended, a child came running to say they were coming, bringing with them one little fellow—dead.

It was too true; a young man carried the lifeless body of a boy of eleven; the heavy rain had drenched the cotton clothes he wore early in the day, and then the bitter wind blowing upon him had chilled the life out of the poor child. He had struggled on while he could, and then a kind elder had picked him up and carried him in his arms, the feeble breath passing silently away. The little lad had been baptized, and was learning to know the Master to whose service he had vowed himself, and now there was good hope that he had gone from these chill regions to a brighter, happier world. He had spoken some words the Sunday before, which seemed to show that he had had a warning of his end.

The poor parents had lost another child just as grievously some years before; a sudden mountain storm had caught him and his father, and, in endeavouring to cross a torrent with the boy on his back, a gush of water swept both out to sea; the father struggled, and regained his footing, but the boy of seven years old was never seen again. Deaths, however, in Tristan were very rare, accident or old age alone carrying off the inhabitants.

One of the greatest excitements the island ever had was the arrival of a steamer. Ships in plenty had cast anchor in Tristan Harbour, but never a puffing, hissing creature like this; men and boys alike were entranced when her Majesty's steamer *Torch* visited the island, and the commander sent a general invitation to every one to come on board. Some of the oldest men in the colony had never seen such a sight (it was in the year 1852), and the boys fairly rushed out of the engine-room in terror when the great rods began to revolve, only, however, to come back and gaze again. Mr. Taylor and Governor Glass dined on board, and all enjoyed their day immensely.

It would be impossible here to relate fully all the incidents which occurred in Mr. Taylor's ministry —the opening of the new church, the marriage of the schoolmistress, with Tristan roses strewn on the church pathway by her scholars, the comings and goings of the colonists, and the visits of strange ships.

One event must, however, be noted down—the death of the patriarch Glass. For nearly forty years he had happily lived in the land of his choice, and it pleased God to remove him, after a painful illness, not long after Mr. Taylor's arrival. He had humbly and truly tried to serve God, and he was supported in his suffering by Christian hope. His sons raised a plain white marble stone over his grave, with his name and age and position written thereon, followed by these lines—

> "Asleep in Jesus! far from thee
> Thy kindred and their graves may bo;
> But thine is still a blessèd sleep,
> From which none ever wakes to weep."

Glass had read this verse in a magazine, and it pleased him so much that he had chosen it out for his headstone.

And now we must leave the little lone cluster of cottages on the rocky islet, with its one white-fronted house, higher than the rest by its bell tower, claiming the name of Church House—its rocky background, and its stunted crops—leave the small flock of sheep and cattle, and the larger flock of merry children and graver elders. Time and space will not let us linger on at Tristan d'Acunha, and only one more strange fact must be written down regarding it.

A few years later the whale-ships ceased to come to the island, their quest leading them elsewhere; the inhabitants consequently were unable to effect their little sales and exchanges, and living became even more troublesome and precarious in lone Tristan. The lads and young men left the place, and the fathers of large families of daughters talked of going too. Matters, from no fault of the islanders' own, became so unprosperous that a great move of the whole colony was meditated—to America, perhaps, at least somewhere into the great world.

While in this state of mind, the Bishop of Cape-town visited the settlement; he suggested the Cape as suitable for a new home, and there Mr. Taylor and his flock finally removed, only a very few remaining behind.

These few, however, have already had a dis-tinguished visitor—the Duke of Edinburgh landed

on Tristan in 1867, visiting the houses, and reading
the inscription on the good old governor's grave.
The church is, alas! closed, necessarily disused.
The duke's chaplain baptized the sixteen children
of the place—for of course there is now no resident
clergyman, and the old state of things has come
over again, as it was in the days before Mr. Taylor's
arrival. That any other pastor will feel drawn to
the flock on this lonely ocean islet is hardly
probable, and we cannot but think that in time
the remnant of the old colony will deem it best to
sail away, as their comrades have done, in search
of a wider sphere of daily work, a larger share of
Christian fellowship.

# A GIRL-MISSIONARY.

## YORUBA COUNTRY.

IT is not at all an unusual thing for a child to listen to stories of holy men and women till it longs to follow in their footsteps; some boy or girl, perhaps, of your own has come home to you with its heart full of such matters, and the cry, "Mother, I would like to be a missionary·" or yet more ambitious, "I would be a martyr."

And they mean it at the time; but by-and-by they find out that a martyr's or a missionary's life does not consist only of singing hymns,· or even dying nobly in the cause, but it means a great deal of real ugly pain and suffering, and much every-day hard work. And *that* they do not covet, so there is no more said about the desire for martyrdom or missionary work. And as perhaps God never meant them for missionaries or martyrs, but simply for good, obedient, ordinary children, there is not much harm done; perhaps even good comes out of the dying of this little flame of fervour, and the child goes back to school or into its little world the humbler, because it finds it has not even the strength to go on wishing to serve God in the midst of extraordinary dangers. But every now and then

there shines out amongst us a little soul whose
flame will *not* be quenched, and who goes on longing
and longing to tell the gospel story in strange
lands—to do something more for its Saviour than
the narrow limits of home permits. Such a one
was little Anna Martin. She did not speak her
wishes aloud, but at thirteen, or even younger, she
longed to give herself up to some holy work—to be
a missionary, in fact; and something within her
told her that this would eventually be her lot.
But a sensible girl of thirteen knows that years
must pass before such a thing can be, and so
Anna took the work nearest at hand and taught
little English girls in an English Sunday school.

And talking to the six little ones in her care
soon made her acquainted with their fathers and
mothers, this one's sick aunt and that one's lame
brother, till she was on visiting terms with them
all. After that, as she grew up, and her clergyman
found that she loved teaching and cared for the
poor, he gave her plenty to do, and she became his
greatest help in his parish, and the dear friend and
teacher of hundreds of children and their families.

And all this time she was so bright and happy
that you would have thought she was leading just
the life she desired. But it was not so; that came
later, when she told a friend in joyful tones: "It
is all settled; I am going to be married to Mr.
Hinderer (a missionary in Africa), and we are going
to Ibadan "—Ibadan in Western Africa—the Yoruba
country, in fact, of which I told you a little before.

And not long after the announcement the little
girl who had longed to serve God in dangers and
difficulties—now grown to be a woman, with even
stronger desires of the same nature—was sailing
over rough seas, past strange lands, to her husband's
African home.

He had been to Ibadan before; indeed, he was
the first white man that had ever trod the streets
of that great city, wherein dwelt one hundred
thousand men that had never even heard of the
true God, and he had come to England to find
helpers to be with him there and assist him in his
work of Christianizing the heathen.

It was well that he had found Anna Martin ready
to come, as a loving wife and earnest missionary. On
the way out in that tossing, rolling ship I expect
he told her all about their new home, how the
people had received him kindly, and asked him to
"sit down" with them; but how ignorant they
were, how foolish, how terribly in need of the
commonest teaching, with their many and cruel
gods, their upholding of slavery among each other,
and their horrible human sacrifices.

Brave Mrs. Hinderer, however, was not afraid;
she had longed to be a missionary all her life, and
she was not going to shrink from the work. Fever,
however, was her first trial on landing; every one
suffers from that who visits Africa, and many die
under its attacks, while those who are spared have
their health weakened and broken by it. The first
attack over, however, she and her husband made

their way up the country towards what she afterwards called "dear Ibadan."

The first large place they stopped at was Abeokuta, where was a missionary settlement; here
both Mrs. Hinderer and her husband had fever
again, and were obliged to rest a while, till he was
well enough to go on to Ibadan and arrange about
the commencement of the mission there. Mrs.
Hinderer, in his absence, began to learn the Yoruba
language, and tried to make friends with the
natives, particularly the little children, whom she
always loved, whatever their colour.

It distressed her that she could only as yet speak
to them by signs. She longed to speak their tongue,
particularly to the Ibadan people, who had never
seen a white woman, and always thought of fair
skins and cruel slave-masters as one and the same.
Before, however, Mr. and Mrs. Hinderer could begin
their residence in Ibadan, one of the missionary's
greatest troubles overtook them—the loss of friends.
Mr. Paley, who had come out in their ship with
them, also as a missionary, took the fever and died;
and Mrs. Paley was so very ill that she had to be
sent back to the coast immediately and put on
board a home-bound vessel. But even that did not
save her; she died at sea, and was buried in its
depths, an untried labourer in the mission field.

After that the doctor died, likewise a fellow-
passenger from England. He was just going to
have taught Mrs. Hinderer a great many useful
things about medicine. To be able to doctor the

poor African is always a way to his heart; but
that was now all at an end, and with sorrowful
hearts the missionary and his wife set out for
Ibadan.

Their reception in that town must have cheered
them, if it was rather noisy. Such shouting and
screaming, "The white man is come! the white
mother is come!" Some were frightened, but all
were curious, and there was much pushing and
crowding to get a sight of the wonderful white
woman. At last they let them go to sleep in their
own little house, a sort of shed with a mud floor
and no ceiling, so that the insects often fell upon
them in bed—great spiders as big as your hand,
wriggling centipedes, and such like. Mrs. Hinderer
used to give a little scream at first when such
visitors came near her, but by-and-by she became
used to them. Mr. Hinderer one night, however,
heard a rustling by his bed, and jumping up to see
the cause, trod on a venomous serpent, which might
have killed them had it turned upon him.

Plenty of discomforts had our missionaries on
first settling down; but they were so pleased to
be in Ibadan, beginning their great work, that they
seemed light.

Mrs. Hinderer writes to a friend on the first of
her African Whit-Sundays—

"You should have seen a certain Anna to-day,
with a large mixed-up class of men and women on
the ground, with her four little boys (black), who
are with her every day, clinging to her, each trying

to be nearest at this afternoon school. You must remember they are cramped for room. As I sat on my chair, one little black fellow had clasped my arm with both his hands, another every now and then nearly resting his chin on my shoulder, the other two sitting close at my feet; and then such a burst of voices after me repeated the Lord's Prayer in Yoruba, and then two of the Commandments."

These little boys adored their mother-mistress; if a fly came near her they pushed it away, and when she lay ill of fever in her room all one day, they went about with tears in their eyes, mourning that they could not find "missis." The women, too, who came to visit her were gentle and tender, with all their curiosity. Mr. and Mrs. Hinderer were soon in full work: a day school with nine little boys, each in a blue shirt over their dark skins; Sunday services; every-day teaching of big and little; and last, and least perhaps, a boy of four and a girl of six taken to live in the house to teach and make Christian children of.

The first evening the girl of six dragged the boy of four by the hand, saying, "Akielle, you must not stay here; do you know that when it gets dark the white people kill and eat the black?" And off flew the poor little simpletons, trembling with terror. It was some time before tiny Akielle dared to stay the night with the kind lady he loved so in the day-time, but after a while he did, and to his sister's great joy and surprise she found him alive in the

morning.  The little children were the delight of
Mrs. Hinderer's heart; she had taught them to say
prayers, to repeat hymns, and to be good and quiet
in church.  Only one Sunday when Mr. Hinderer
was preaching about the foolishness of idols who
have mouths and speak not, the boys burst out
laughing and said aloud, "True, very true."  Not
quite our church fashion, but it showed they were
attending.  The school would have increased more
quickly, but the people got an idea that "book"
would make their children cowards; and as the
Ibadan folk are great fighters, always at war with
their neighbours, they were afraid of this.

A young black man called Olubi, who had been
with the Hinderers from the first as a servant, was
now given up to be a schoolmaster—a loss to his
master and mistress, but he made a capital teacher.
And then by-and-by came that solemn and joyful
day, when the first Ibadan converts were received
into the Church of Christ—two young men, two
young women, and one old man presenting themselves for baptism in white robes instead of their
usual blue ones, and fully understanding that the
waters of baptism were as a sign of that greater
washing, the washing away of their sins.

A little later came the first Christian wedding,
also an event in the mission life, followed by a
dinner and speeches!—for black men can make
grand speeches—the first wedding that was in
Ibadan at which He who turned water into wine
was asked to be present.

In Mrs. Hinderer's diary comes next a record of
eight little ones out of her house being received by
baptism into the fold; but these happy times were
succeeded by deep sorrow on account of the persecution which fell to the lot of many of the poor
heathen who attended the instruction of the white
people, and who showed a desire to know the true
God. Wives and daughters were beaten and tied
up by their heathen relatives; little scholars were
forcibly removed from Mrs. Hinderer's care, regardless of tears and entreaties; and threats of murder
were employed to terrify such as evinced a leaning
towards the new faith. But history has shown us
that persecution will never succeed in extinguishing
religious fervour; and the girls with the rope-marks
round necks and arms, the little children with the
angry menaces ringing in their ears, crept back to
the mission-house when the first tumult was over,
and clung once more to their kind teacher. Let
alone, and given enough to eat and drink, the
African child is a cheerful little creature, full of fun
and jokes, and Mrs. Hinderer would not have been
without her small body-guard for anything. They
amused her with their witty little sallies at times,
and she has noted one as specially clever. A little
girl coming to the Kudeti brook found it unexpectedly dry, and Mr. Hinderer riding by at the
same moment in a full suit of cool white clothing,
she playfully accused him of having caused the
drought, turning her words into a sort of poetry as
she spoke. Of course her rhyme was in the Yoruba

tongue, but I think you will understand it better
translated into English.   These were her words—

> " The white man of Kudeti's hill
> Has used the black child very ill;
> He washed his clothes so white, you see,
> That not a drop is left for me.
> Oh! tell him when he comes next day
> To wash his clothes some other way."

Mr. and Mrs. Hinderer paid a visit after a while
to the King of Oyo, to whose city Olubi had been
sent to make a beginning of teaching.   The king
received them very kindly; he had seen Mr. Hinderer before, and asked after "the good Queen of
England;" and on the next Sunday a real Church
service was held, which his Majesty greatly approved
of, telling the white men they might preach and
teach in his town.   And a little girl taking a fancy
to Mrs. Hinderer, and begging to return with her,
the king gave his permission, saying graciously he
wished he was a little girl and could go too.

The next event that stirred the home life of the
Hinderers was the desire of Olubi, their schoolmaster, to marry Susanna, a little Christian servant
of Mrs. Hinderer's; the match pleased her good
mistress, and she began to think of bridal clothes
in true English fashion.

You have not heard Olubi's early history, and it
is very remarkable.   His mother was an idol
priestess, and he was dedicated to a false god,
showing as a boy an angry hatred to the new doctrines of the white men.   "If I were a war chief,"

said the fiery black boy, "I would kill the missionary, who tells us to give up idols, and if he comes into my street, I will do it myself." But a mighty hand held back this little would-be murderer. When the missionary did come into Olubi's street, the boy was lying sick and helpless on his mat, powerless to do any harm. His ears were open, however, and he heard the preaching and praying, at first unwillingly, then curiously. "It is not anything so very bad he is saying," was his thought after a while; and when he got better, something prompted him to go to the mission school and church, and see how these white people worshipped.

He enjoyed the service, and notwithstanding that his priestess mother beat him for it, he learned the Lord's Prayer, and went to the school. After that he spent seventeen days with his mother in an idol house, worshipping and sacrificing, but on returning home he told his mother he should not do this next year, as he meant to follow the white man's fashion. This, of course, brought further ill treatment; but the boy's mind was made up. He joined the baptismal class for instruction, stood firm, and was in due time received into the little Christian Church by the name of Daniel. And then, with prayers and entreaties, he won over his bigoted mother, both she and his father in time forsaking the old gods, and turning to the once despised faith of the white man.

A short visit to England refreshed our poor hard-

working missionaries much, but Mrs. Hinderer soon
became anxious to return home to Ibadan. Their
people received them with rapture, and Daniel and
Susanna had another little Daniel to show them,
whom Mrs. Hinderer soon began to covet, to put
among her own thirty little ones! All sorts and
sizes of children were a delight to her, and her
ranks were sometimes strangely filled. Olubi
brought her one day from the beach a tiny baby
one week old, thrown away by some cruel mother.
A nice little child, Mrs. Hinderer thought it might
be a twin, as the heathen belief is that the gods do
not like twins. Poor little " Moses " had caught
cold from his cruel treatment, and only lived three
weeks, to his new mother's great sorrow. She was
glad, however, she had saved him to be buried
under a shady tree in the bush, rather than to fall
a prey to pigs or vultures.

By-and-by came another foundling to the kind
arms of the foster-mother. Another little babe, of
a few months old, lay shrieking and wailing on the
grass, a forsaken creature. For three days and
nights no one rescued it, but in the day-time every
mother passing took it up and fed it, not daring
to remove it, since an idol priest might have
ordered it to be left there. The wild beasts
would have thought it a tender morsel, but its
cries frightened them away. The news of this
little uncared-for passionate creature was brought
to the missionary's wife, and, as you may fancy, she
hastened to rescue the poor baby. It had a bad

cough, as was natural after the exposure, and gave much trouble and anxiety, but that did not prevent her becoming a great treasure and darling in the mission-house. "Eyila" she was named, which means "this has escaped," or "is saved." And little Eyila was indeed saved for this life and the one to come. She lived to twine loving black arms round the new mother's neck, to lisp her name, and the name of Him who loved little children. She lived to know what earthly care and earthly love meant, and then, still young, still a little lamb of the fold, she went to the heavenly keeping, carried off by small-pox, during an absence of Mrs. Hinderer in England.

How this baby's loss was felt appears in a letter of Mrs. Hinderer's—

"My sweet, my darling Eyila has left earth, and gone to her Saviour in heaven. She died of small-pox. Her last words to her faithful nurse were, 'Come, let us go home. I am going home; but too much thorn in the road, too much thorn.' Sweet little babe! the thorns are passed, and she is at rest and peace with Jesus, who will show me my babe again, my dear Eyila. But I do feel it exceedingly, and so does my husband." And then she winds up, "How grows in paradise our store!"

Mrs. Hinderer sometimes wrote home to English school-children of her cares and anxieties about her black flock. One of her little worries was the making them wash every morning. They thought this very troublesome and nonsensical,

and she had to say at last, "No wash, no breakfast," and then they went to the water as if they
were going to be whipped; but after a while they
actually got to take pleasure in the morning bath,
and to teach new-comers to do so also. Daniel
Olubi the second was a great darling of hers,
always in her company, even as a baby boy going
to church with her, and asking in a whisper when
tired, "Has not *dear* done talking yet?" *dear* being
Mr. Hinderer preaching to his flock.

With all the encouragement of a full church and
school, converts presenting themselves for baptism,
and the general confidence of the black population,
there was much still to make the heart faint within
them; witness this entry in Mrs. Hinderer's
journal—

"Our old friend the King of Oyo is dead. There
were not so many people put to death as is usual
on such occasions—not more than four men. But
forty-two of his wives poisoned themselves for the
honour of accompanying him to the other world!"
And later, when a general war was threatened, she
tells of a human sacrifice in Ibadan town. A strong
young man of five-and-twenty was chosen, all day
paraded through the town to be admired and
almost worshipped, and at night sacrificed. He
looked so proud of himself and his honours; poor
creature! he imagined that all sorts of glory awaited
him the moment after death. The priests told him
so, and he firmly believed them.

This was the beginning of war horrors. For

years after Mr. and Mrs. Hinderer lived in a be-
sieged city, the road to the coast shut up, no letters
reaching them, and all sorts of cruelties going on
around them.

Even the common necessaries of life failed them,
and they could hardly pray "Give us this day our
daily bread" for sheer weakness. If only they
could have sent to Abeokuta, the nearest town
where white men lived, relief would have come,
but the danger was so great of being seized by
some of the rival war parties that no messengers
would go. Clothes, too, wore out, and could not be
replaced, and Mrs. Hinderer was almost shoeless.

No wonder that fever visited them again and
again, and Mrs. Hinderer became so feeble that it
was feared she would die in her inland prison.

It was imperative that she should have change
and comfort as soon as possible. The kind English
Consul at the coast knew of this, and was always
trying to send for her, but the danger was too
great. Hope deferred made their hearts very sick
in those days. Even the school work suffered for
want of books, of paper to write on, of sewing
materials for the little girls; only two rusty needles
and one ball of cotton were left!

But still when one night a few brave men did
arrive from the coast, with a message from the
Consul that now Mrs. Hinderer might try to return
with them, her heart failed her. What, leave her
children, her schools, her dear Ibadan! Impossible!

But then she remembered how useless she should

be if weakness took still further possession of her,
and the desire to preserve life sprang up within
her. A visit to England might brace her up,
though, alas! not for Ibadan. So she went, leaving
Mr. Hinderer behind to put the mission affairs in
the best order before he followed her. His health,
too, had long been failing; the climate had all but
proved fatal to both labourers, and they could not
but feel that they had worked their last day's work
in their beloved Africa.

The wisest course was now to place the mission
affairs, as far as might be, in native hands. Olubi
was a host in himself, and there were other reliable
Christian teachers among the converts. Churches
and schools had been established, and the great
Head of the Church would not suffer it to be
extinguished in these troublous times. At the
same time, the white man's prospects were darkened; the European missionaries at Abeokuta had
been compelled to fly, and Mr. Hinderer, half dead
with repeated attacks of fever, gave up his charge
to his native helpers, and was carried to the coast,
following his wife to England shortly afterwards.

The story of Mrs. Hinderer's life is now all but
told. She revived a little on landing in her own
country; she visited friends and talked of old days,
always with the warmest corner of her heart for
Africa and "dear Ibadan;" then her husband had
an English charge given him, and she sat among
white folk in an English church, visiting neat
cottages on smiling greens, and talking to English

mothers at English mothers' meetings, her discourse often drifting back to black babies and black folk in far-off Africa.

But her days were numbered. In the sweet soft English summer following her arrival, she breathed her last, the missionary spirit of the child only quenched when the breath went out of the worn body.

The "dear and loving white mother," as the Ibadan people wrote of her afterwards, had gone to join the host in heaven, resting from her labours after the burden and heat of a long and weary day.

# PARIS IN TROUBLE.

### BELLEVILLE.

I AM going to take you back to troublous times to-day. Not far back, however—only to the year 1871 ; and the troubles then were not ours, but our neighbours'. Still, as was only natural, we took a great interest in them, and you can perhaps remember how the husbands and big sons used to return from work full of accounts of the war raging between France and Germany, of the Parisians getting the worst of it, and being shut up in their own city for months, reduced to feed on horses, dogs, and cats; of their being starved out in the end, and the Germans occupying Paris ; of the withdrawal of these unwelcome visitors ; and then, last but not least, of the inward disturbances of unhappy France, when the mob rose up against their lawful rulers, and would have things their own way,—a sad way, as might be expected. Mob law is never just law. These poor red-hot *Communists*, as they called themselves, were the authors of worse trouble than foreign invaders ever brought to Paris. I do not intend to tell you of their senseless rule, or rather misrule : I shall not describe their ravages in their once fair city, but I must, for sad truth's sake, bid you take one glimpse at their work, and that work was murder.

In Belleville, a suburb of Paris, one bright day in May, 1871, a group of pale, composed men were led through the streets to execution. What had they done wrong, these fifty or more poor creatures —clergy, soldiers, citizens? Nothing; they were honest and respectable men, and so chosen as the hostages of the Communists, and matters were now going against the mob, who, in revenge, would have the lives of their prisoners. Brave men die quietly, and there was just a whispered prayer here and there among the innocent victims—a priestly blessing, a glance to heaven, and then the sound of firing told the rest of the tale. No, not all the rest, the blackest part is to come. Women in Paris are as excitable, as easily led astray, as the men, and during that scene of butchery there were not wanting girls, and mothers with babes clinging to their skirts, to swell the crowd of gazers. No pity in their faces, only savage joy and cries of " Well done ! " to the executioners ; fair young girls rushing up to shake hands with the blood-stained officers of vengeance. Not the first time either that they had gloated over scenes of murder; not the first time the Communists had led out a batch of helpless hostages to die. Do you shudder at these Belleville women? I shall teach you to pity them next, for their days of anguish were close upon them, even as the shouts of fiendish triumph broke from their lips that May-day.

Fair Paris was not always to be in the hands of a cruel mob, and when the delirium of war and siege and revolution was past, and justice began to mete out punishment to wrong-doers, the Communists must needs be put down with a strong hand. We cannot tell whether the measures taken were too severe; peace and quiet for men at large had to be obtained at all costs; and the cost at this time was terrible. Five hundred Communists were conducted to the great cemetery of Paris, Père la Chaise, there shot, and buried in one common grave. We read of all this in the newspapers of the day, and groaned over our neighbours' miseries perhaps for a moment, afterwards sitting down peacefully in our own happy homes and forgetting all about them. It was only natural we should do so, powerless as we were to help in the crisis, but all the same we may be glad that one strong will and pitiful heart did not give all up in this fashion. At the very moment, perhaps, that people in England were reading in their rustling daily papers the account of the fearful though well-deserved punishment of the Communists, an English lady, Miss de Broen, was gazing with tearful eyes at a pitiful sight in the great Parisian cemetery. Only the night before the five hundred Communists had been executed, and here by the long covered trench, their common grave, stood a crowd of women and children—some weeping, some cursing, some uttering deep threats of revenge, some lying despairing on the earth, all lamenting the dead beneath that newly disturbed mound. Husbands, fathers, and brothers lay there, and bad and misguided as they might have been, these women had dearly loved them, and had now come with last offerings to their memory of little black crosses, and wreaths of immortelles to lay on the unmarked burial-place. One poor woman was so ungoverned in her grief that Miss de Broen could not but try to comfort her. " It is very sad for you to lose what you have loved," she whispered softly to her.

To which the poor creature answered wildly, " Ah ! but you do not know what it is. *I have lost all !*"

" You have not lost the love of God !" said the English lady in reply, and somehow these few words seemed to touch the poor bleeding heart, and others of the weeping crowd gathered round the speaker, hushing their sobs to listen to the quiet voice. Supposing even that these were the very women who had cried "Well done !" to the murderers of a few weeks past, were they not the more sadly in need of Christ-like pity and forgiveness in their own great griefs ?

Miss de Broen was so touched by the misery and wretchedness of that morning in Père la Chaise, that she went back to her hotel and to the friends with whom she was travelling, and told them that she *must* try to do something for these poor Belleville people. Naturally enough they were alarmed at her proposal, for though the Communists had been put down with a strong hand, it was not con-

sidered safe for decent people to venture into their
quarters, and for a young woman of gentle birth to
attempt such a thing seemed almost too daring.
But Miss de Broen was too much in earnest to be
daunted. The thoughts of the weeping widows
and children haunted her day and night—all in
deepest grief, many in bodily want, for, bad as they
might have been, these Communists had earned
bread for their families. And now the bread-win-
ners were gone, and no one went near the bereaved
wives and children—even good people shuddering
and turning their heads aside as they passed the
dwellings of law-breakers and murderers. For,
alas! the women themselves were not free from
such reproach. Tales were told, which were but
too true, of girls and women stabbing soldiers un-
awares, and pouring pitchers of burning oil into the
cellars of such as they deemed their enemies. No
wonder quiet people were afraid of them.

A new sight, however, was now to be seen in
Belleville. A lady briskly flitting here and there
among the poor houses, and bidding one and another
of the miserable women of the district come to a
certain room where sewing might be had and paid
for by the hour. Only fivepence for three hours'
stitching; but a French woman can make pence go
further than her English neighbour, and the tidings
were joyfully received. Eight came the first day—
poor, ignorant, dazed souls, to whom Miss de Broen
dealt out her work, and then read to them a few
words of a Bible story. They *were* ignorant indeed,

for when the reader asked them, "Do you know who wrote the Bible?" one answered, looking up confidently, "You did, ma'am." The sewing class was quickly followed up by a little evening service, which was open to men as well as women, and this was greatly enjoyed by the poor people, the hymns especially coming home to their hearts from the circumstance of their being in French.

It was not long before the sullen look of misery on all countenances changed into glad recognition of the kind missioner. Miss de Broen was accepted as a true friend, and into her ear was poured many a sad tale of past horrors : of the terrible days of the siege when the shells lighted here and there in the city, killing women and little babes as well as fighting men ; of the children who escaped this danger dying by hundreds of privation and bad food in their wretched homes; of the sick and old lying on the floor, because the bedstead and rickety chairs were wanted for firewood ; of the cold and hunger ; of the fallen hopes; of the last long despair. The Communist women, if they had been wicked, were sorely to be pitied, and no wonder when Miss de Broen came among them they should feel as if " God had sent an angel to them."

For a time Miss de Broen lived in Paris, and came daily to Belleville, three miles distant, to spend the day there; but when sewing classes and night schools, mission services and sick visiting, multiplied her cares, she found it impossible to live at such a distance from her work, so she took a

house in Belleville, and invited other ladies to come
over from England and assist her. These were not
wanting, and a little band of helpers soon gathered
round the first missioner. All had plenty of work.
The very cutting out for the sewers was one person's
business, for the women had increased to hundreds,
and the night schools and lending library required
heads and hands to manage them also.

Besides those offices, the poor and sick needed
visiting even more than in England, for in France
there are no workhouses, no last shelters for the
old and starving, save what the Church provides;
and these Belleville people had sinned so deeply
against order and religion, that even kindly in-
tentioned people turned from them. As one sign
of the misery of Paris at this time, it is reckoned
that in the year 1873 five thousand people committed suicide; and yet the French poor are
perhaps more thrifty, more managing than we
English: their very dress is neater as well as
prettier. The poor mother of a French family in
no way imitates the style of the day or the
fashion of the class above her, but keeps to her
nice dark skirt, loose jacket, and snow-white muslin
cap, frilled round her face and tied behind with
white strings. Nothing more on her head in
summer, but in winter a merino hood keeps her
warm; stout shoes and stockings of her own
knitting finish her costume. Of course, some women
are better dressed than others, but all have a respectable appearance. The children too look tidy,

with a large blue pinafore, fastened at the throat and wrists; no shabby straw hats on their heads, only their neatly plaited hair in summer for covering, and in winter a little hood like mother's.

The French poor are better off than ours in another way too; their little rooms are never crowded with steaming clothes, flapping on to the husband's head as he comes in tired from work. No, all their washing is done in public wash-houses or wash-boats anchored in the river, where a large tub of hot water may be had for a half-penny, and you pay twopence for six hours' use of all the appliances of the building. There is a drying-place too, so the clothes can be carried home quite ready for wear.

Then there is no large coal fire in a poor French woman's kitchen; instead of that, when cooking is to be done, a little wood or charcoal is lighted on a tripod, and when the soup or vegetable is ready out goes the fire again. This is a saving, though one misses the pleasant blaze of our fires. Miss de Broen was so sorry one day at the look of the chilly pinched faces of her poor sewers that, for a pleasant surprise, she got some hot coffee and bread ready for them to take when they had done work. They were told to put their sewing by half an hour earlier than usual; and so little used were they to kindness just then, that it came out afterwards that some thought they were to be searched for a reel of cotton lost the day before in the rooms. Poor creatures! one is glad to think of the pleasant surprise of that hot meal.

No wonder some looked starved, for they literally earned nothing save the fivepence twice a week at this sewing class, and when they went they took their money out in bread, because they had no fire to cook meat.

Once a week Miss de Broen gave a dinner to starving children. They really were accustomed to so little food that when they first came they could not take the basin of soup provided, but by-and-by appetite increased, and the little faces looked all the rounder for the good meal. Grace was taught them, and a hymn sung after dinner, the little ignorant creatures thus learning by pleasant experience that all good things come from God.

There is another means of good employed by Miss de Broen, which I must describe to you, and that is the Medical Mission. Since the siege of Paris there have been many more sad cases of illness among the poor, and the sick flock gladly to a room set apart for them where a doctor attends for their benefit. Four times a week he is there, and while one by one the patients enter his private room, Miss de Broen and her helpers go about among the rest, talking to them and hearing their sad stories. Their names and addresses are all written down, so that they may be visited if they wish it.

There is a little service held in the waiting-room at its first opening, which the sick people enjoy very much, and from this small beginning many learn to wish for more teaching, and so are led on to attend the Sunday services.

Such a number of pitiful tales come to the ears of the doctor and his helpers through the Medical Mission—this one dying of consumption from privations during the war-time, that one sick solely of hunger and poor food. Here is a pinch-faced child, not quite so bright as it ought to be in its poor mind—ah, that is a siege baby! Every one knows what that means: a little creature born amidst the terrors and troubles of the time when no one could get in or out of Paris, and milk was scarce and provisions bad and dear, and poor mothers must starve and their babies dwindle or die. One tiny creature shut up in a cellar with its parents actually did die of fright at the noise of the bombardment, and a child shot in the streets was no uncommon occurrence.

Poor little people! Tiny coffins carried through the streets hardly drew a sigh from bystanders in those days—at least the sight meant peace for some.

With sad tales, however, come cheering rays of comfort. Sorrow purifies as well as depresses, and but for the starvation and sickness of Belleville it might have been hard to get hold of these sullen Communist hearts.

A poor printer, sick, as he thought unto death, received so much benefit from the mission doctor that he was able to resume work. He was one who went from the consulting-room to the other religious services, and a text he heard at one of them woke up his sleeping conscience. This was it: "The fool hath said in his heart, There is no

God." Said the printer to himself, "I am a worse fool than this fool, for I know there is a God, yet I do not serve Him." Neither was he content with saying this; he set to work instantly to try and find out what God would have him do to serve Him, and as "far as lay in his power he tried ever after to carry out His will."

Another sick man and his wife were roused by the mission teaching to care for their souls; before that time they were living simply, as they said, "as the beasts that perish." *She* had only been to church twice in her life—once to make her first Communion and once to be married. Of a violent temper, she would rush all over the town, cursing and swearing if she could not get work; her mother had died when she was a baby, and no one had cared for her or told her that God cared for her. Her husband, of a quieter spirit than this, had been just an infidel all his life, neither thinking of God nor fearing Him. These poor creatures gladly listened to the new words of love spoken to them by the English missioners, and, as the woman joyfully reported, "ever since Christmas Day we have really believed in Jesus." Once the woman was missing from a Bible class, and on the visitor going to inquire for her in her house she was met by the cry, "I could not come to the meeting, for I was wicked, very wicked. We had no bread, and the pawnbroker would give me nothing on my husband's best coat, and I came home and was very rebellious. I could not pray, and that was why I did not go to the

Bible class." Evidently the old fierce temper had broken out at the cruel disappointment. People never become patient or perfect all at once, and all the more for that happy Christmas Day the devil would struggle to re-enter the swept and garnished chamber of these poor people's hearts.

These are the father and mother of the "siege baby." Poor little lad! they could get him no milk in his babyhood, only wine or coffee, and the bread was a sort of black stuff mixed with straw.

Another patient had been a monk in his youth, belonging to an order which enjoins perpetual silence; he did not take the vows, however, and finding the life different from what he expected, and the monastery he first entered being broken up, he gave up the religious life entirely, and became a marble-cutter in Paris. After a long illness he found himself too poor to pay the doctor any longer, and so made his way to the free Medical Mission. There, when one spoke to him about higher things than his sick body, he turned away, saying he "did not believe in God." But his sad face seemed so to need comfort that the speaker persevered, and at last he owned to wishing to read the Psalms in French. In his monkish days he had chanted the whole hundred and fifty in their turn in Latin, only comprehending a word here and there, and now, though he did not believe in the God of whom they spoke, he had a curiosity to understand more of them. And so from this small beginning came a desire for increased knowledge, and at last a craving for

F

Christ in His sacraments, and a wish to be a true member of His Church on earth.

I think I have told you enough by this time to show you that there are poor creatures in this wretched suburb of Paris sorely needing the helping hand stretched out to them by the kind English lady. Her first and greatest desire is, and has been, to care for their souls, but she remembers that the starved body was provided for also by the great Preacher and Teacher; therefore bodily tending and spiritual guidance are both included in her aim.

Money help, and the help of willing hearts and hands she has had from many friends during her ten years' labours, and in June, 1876, a great need was supplied, and an iron room put up capable of holding four hundred people. It cost £900, and is used for every purpose—schools, sermons, religious services, sewing classes, and so forth. Well lighted and comfortable, it tempts the poor outcasts of Belleville to peep in, to listen, to remain. Who knows what good may follow, without the necessity of noisy talk, or even of boastful announcements of a changed heart? Let me tell one simple story out of Miss de Broen's book to show what I mean.

A little Belleville girl in the school was so dull and stupid-looking that the mistress feared she was learning nothing, and fretted about her. This child, however, fell ill, and was visited in her own home. The mother told the mistress that the little dull one was always repeating the verses and hymns she learned in school, and was so good and easy to nurse. And so it may be with the elders; the iron room may see many unmoved countenances which yet may beam with the comfort of the good tidings heard there in God's own time.

Miss de Broen is also training little girls for service, hoping to send them to England as French nurserymaids by-and-by. They learn plain work and dressmaking, and household work, besides reading, writing, arithmetic, and the knowledge of holy things. One is an orphan. A visitor found her with a dying mother, who was so poor that she could afford herself no fire, but, sick unto death, had to creep to a neighbour's hearth when she wanted a warm. It was winter-time, and the poor soul said she should be glad to die if only some one would care for her child, little Bertha.

Bertha gained a few pence by leading about a blind man, but it was not a nice occupation for a little girl to be begging at street corners and public-houses with her blind master. So the poor mother was removed to a hospital, and Bertha made one of Miss de Broen's possible nurserymaids. The mother soon died, and the child set to work to save her money to buy a wreath of immortelles to put on her grave.

The last accounts of this mission received in 1880 speak of more work, more hope, and some success on Miss de Broen's part. She has taken a larger house in Paris, in which her helpers, and her children of the "Training Home," reside. The Medical Mission is greatly valued, and the patients are so increased in number that they have to be received in the iron room.

Besides regular teaching and visiting, such odd matters as keeping a Bible-stall at the "Gingerbread Fair," which lasts a month in each year, are taken up, and the many infidels in Paris are touched to admiration, if not belief, by the sight of such earnest work in their midst. One well-known infidel shook Miss de Broen by the hand, when she stood up for Christ, saying carelessly, "How happy you must be with such faith!"

What do you think now of this mission to the poor French in Belleville? Perhaps you wonder that an English lady has taken it up; but after all, when one comes to think of it, there is no English and French, no separation by tongue or country, in the followers of Christ. And we may humbly believe Miss de Broen heard the voice of God calling her to this special work when she stood among the sobbing crowd in the cemetery of Père la Chaise that sad May morning.

*You* would pick up a little foreign baby in the street and comfort it if it fell, and so feel all Christian folk for suffering men and women of every creed and nation. Of course, there are poor and sorrowful souls in England too, but they will be no whit the poorer or less cared for because of this effort for Paris. As the good old proverb says, "Charity begins at home, *but does not end there.*"

# RED INDIANS AT HOME.

## LAKE SUPERIOR.

I SHOULD like you to come with me to America now, a country so wide, so far-spreading, that it contains all varieties of human creatures, black, white, and brown, needing Christian help and teaching.

It is a gentle, I may say gentlemanly, race you are to visit—the Red Indian of the Western forests.

You know how our people have for years and years been emigrating to America. Well, they and others have disturbed these first inhabitants of the land, and pushed them, as it were, further and further back into the solitude of the mighty forests. At one time it was war to the knife between the new-comers and these feathered, blanketed Indians, and the red men got the worst of it; but now Government has come to the rescue, and, while allowing the white settler to use the bountiful resources of this great country, it yet has set aside for the Indians large tracts of forest-land where he can live, as his fathers did, by fishing and hunting. And so the red man and the white man have come to have a certain friendliness for each other, and, on the part of the quiet, reserved Indian, a certain

curiosity as to the habits and customs of these
wonderful new-comers.

There is a large and beautiful inland sea called
Lake Superior—the Indians call it the Chippeway
Lake—round which the Indian huts cluster, and
here from time to time good men have tried to
teach a little of Christian truth to the old inhabitants of the land.

A small mission existed at Garden River, when a
young English clergyman, the Rev. Edward Wilson,
passed by that way on a tour up the great lake.

Garden River is a pretty name, and in the sweet
summer-time it looked most inviting, with its little
white church, its parsonage with verandah and
flower garden, and its peaceable flock of about four
hundred Chippeway Indians.

It looked something like dear old England far
away. When the clergyman residing there, Mr.
whance, took his departure in the next year (1871),
Mr. Wilson and his wife gladly accepted the charge
of the little settlement for a month. The waters of
their river were not frozen then; they could come
by steamer, bringing their supplies with them, so it
was almost a holiday trip for them, and they
thoroughly enjoyed it. But wait a minute till I
tell you about the winter season in that part of
America. All lakes and rivers freeze, of course, and
deep snow falls. That is a usual and rather pleasant
state of things. Out come the snow-shoes and
the dog-sledges, and perhaps the rough pony harnessed to his sledge; bells jingle, and fur-wrapped

drivers crack their whips, and the scene looks cheerful and pleasant. The deep mud roads are hidden, and over the hard, white ground the farmer can take his grain to the mill, the timber merchant can convey his logs where he will, and the clergyman can visit his outlying parishioners without fear of being benighted on the road. But if a wind gets up all is changed. It is dangerous to go out in the drifting, blowing snow, which secretly steals even into the dwelling when it is tired of blocking up and darkening the windows. The very chairs in the kitchen are often frozen to the floor, and nothing can be done but huddle round the stove for warmth. Woe betide any poor missionary then trying to find his way back to his home and anxious wife! he runs a sad risk of perishing in the white bewilderment.

The Red Indians of Garden River were not un-instructed when Mr. Wilson came to them, or at least they knew so much of Christ's doctrine that they wanted to know more. They had already given Chippeway names to Mr. and Mrs. Wilson, calling the former " Clear Light," and the latter "A Lady of the Sky," which was intended as a great mark of friendship; and Mr. Wilson could speak their own tongue, so that was a good foundation to begin upon.

The month passed very happily with the mis-sionary pair, notwithstanding that Mr. Wilson had to make his own bread, and fresh meat could only twice be had in the time—once bear, and once a drake killed for a treat. Their one old duck laid an egg every day, too, which was a great luxury.

It was the Indians' sugar-making season, a grand business with them. They make a slit in the bark of a maple tree in the early spring, and, placing a vessel underneath, the sap drops into it. Each family taps from three hundred to six hundred trees in the season, and the sap, when boiled down, makes probably three hundred pounds of sugar, which they send to market. They camp out near their trees in the sugar season, and Mr. and Mrs. Wilson paid them a visit in the woods to watch the process, and to give them a little hymn-signing, and an evening prayer afterwards. It pleased Mr. Wilson to see how many a Chippeway Prayer-book came to light, even in those solitudes, when the rumour of an evening service went abroad.

But before the month was out the sad news that Mr. Chance was not returning to Garden River, and the mission must therefore hope for nothing from his supporters, caused great anxiety to the more enlightened of the poor Indians, especially to one old man of the name of " Little Pine." He already numbered three score years and ten, but he had made up his mind that, before he died, he must " see the Christian religion go on and increase." He had made a plan, too, he dearly longed to see realized—to build a house, and to gather in it the children of the flock, there teaching them white industries, farming, carpentering, etc., but, above all, the knowledge of the white man's God.

Little Pine thought of his scheme, and dreamt over it till it seemed to be alone what he lived for. Think, then, of his dismay when Mr. and Mrs. Wilson packed up, and only waited for the steamer to call for them, and no Mr. Chance was coming back! It was time Mr. and Mrs. Wilson did leave in one way, for they had come to the end of their provisions, and, if the Jesuit priest had not kindly sent them some butter and milk and a little cock to kill and boil with rice, they would have been much perplexed where to get food, since, kindly disposed as the Indians were, their food probably would hardly have been what white people are accustomed to.

But Little Pine probably knew nothing of this. Working in the lonely forest, and grieving over the probable famine of the Bread of Life coming upon the little settlement, he suddenly struck out a new idea. Why should not he go with the blackcoat— his name for missionary—and journey to the great blackcoat, the Bishop of Toronto, and ask him that Mr. Wilson might come again to Garden River and stay with the mission as its teacher? He felt as if the Great Spirit called him to do this, so he spoke to his wife, put a few dollars in his pocket, and, when the raspberry moon was fifteen days old, he stepped on board the great fireship, with the black-coat and his wife. You see, I am telling you this nearly in Little Pine's own words, and I dare say you can guess that "fireship" means "steamer" in his talk.

Well, to continue his story. He travelled afterwards in the fire-waggons, and reached Toronto, there attending a large meeting of blackcoats. To them he spoke forcibly and to the point, telling them that for forty years the gospel had been preached at Garden River, but that there it had halted, while the poor Indians of the Chippeway Lake had been left in their ignorance.

Was this always to be so? "I told the blackcoats," said Little Pine, relating the story, "I hoped that before I died I should see a big teaching wigwam built at Garden River, where children from the great Chippeway Lake would be received and clothed and fed, and taught how to read and to write, and also how to farm and build houses and make clothing, so that by-and-by they might go back and teach their own people. And the blackcoats listened to what I said, and they replied that their wish was the same as mine."

But this was only the beginning of Little Pine's exertions for his people. He stayed in Toronto as long as Mr. Wilson remained there, and saw much that amazed him :—the *speaking paper*, or newspaper, for one thing, printed, folded, and dispersed so speedily. Then on the day of prayer he visited a great teaching wigwam, and afterwards the great house of prayer or cathedral. " I could not understand the words of the service," said Little Pine, " but my heart was full of thoughts of God, and I thought how good a thing it was to be a Christian, and I rejoiced that I had heard of the love of Christ, who died for His red children as well as for the pale faces, for He is not ashamed, we know now, to call us brothers."

Mr. Wilson and Little Pine busied themselves in collecting money for the cause they had at heart, but Little Pine was dispirited at the small sums, and felt he did little good at this work. His cows at Garden River were needing hay cut for them, and the simple old man felt home duties press on him. But still Mr. Wilson took him on with him to other towns, and at last a larger sum was collected and Little Pine set out for home. You will be sorry to hear that the poor old man lost his way on the railroad, and the fire-waggon chief had to make signs to him that he must wait for a train coming from the sunsetting to go on in, which he did, and was allowed to sleep in a wire-house that night, probably a telegraph-office. In the morning he was beckoned out and put in another train, and so safely sent back to his quiet forest at dear Garden River.

This trial bore fruit, however. The Church Missionary Society promised to maintain the Garden River Mission for a year; and to the great delight of the Indians, Mr. and Mrs. Wilson came back to them. Little Pine was overjoyed, flourishing his crooked stick in the air, and shouting like any school-boy. The Christmas Day following, after the joyful service in church amid the fir and evergreen decorations, the Indians had a feast made for them: —a Christmas tree and a magic lantern!

Good times were come again to Garden River.

But a year is not long in speeding by, and Mr.
Wilson began to be anxious about the time to
come, unprovided for. When the winter broke he
determined to go to England to raise funds for
building the Industrial Home designed by Little
Pine, which also met the missionary's own views of
benefiting the poor Indian. The red men wished
to send one of their own tribe to help to plead the
cause, so Little Pine's brother, "Man of the Desert,"
was chosen. I do not tell you his Indian name,
because I cannot pronounce it myself, it is so long
and strange. For thirty-eight years this Indian
had been a Christian, and despite the distractions
of a new and wonderful country, he never forgot
the object of his visit. He was always addressing
meetings, asking help for his ignorant red brethren.

Mr. Wilson took him to Westminster Abbey,
Woolwich Arsenal, and the Zoological Gardens,
where to his great delight he saw one of his own
American thrushes, and took off his hat to it. And
he saw the Prince of Wales, and shook hands with
him.

But he longed for home, too, like his brother, and
a thousand pounds being collected for the mission,
he was allowed to depart laden with presents, and
greatly pleased with the kindness of the pale faces
in England. Each Sunday he had gone to church
at Islington, joining in the service with his Chippeway Prayer-book, and kneeling at the Lord's Table
to receive heavenly food with English worshippers.

It would make him feel the communion of saints

a real thing when he got back to the same services at Garden River, and brotherhood in Christ not only a name. It is pleasant to think how all over the world the same prayers rise up to heaven on Sunday mornings, whether from Indian forests or through the thickened atmosphere of smoky London.

Mr. Wilson followed Man of the Desert to his forests very soon after, to find his flock steadily endeavouring to keep up the little services at Garden River, even in the absence of their teacher.

Twice every Sunday the Indians had met together, one reading the Church service, the principal men afterwards addressing the people. Once in the week, also, this custom had been followed, and the day school well attended. There was much joy, however, at the return of their own pastor, and a large congregation flocked to his teaching on the ensuing Sunday.

Now all hearts were full of the new Children's Home that was to be; the land for the farm belonging to it had already been given over by the Indians, and the first pressing business was to clear it of tree stumps or logs, and prepare it for receiving crops. So Mr. Wilson summoned a logging bee. You know what a " bee " is. Perhaps you have heard of spelling bees; they have come over to England of late years. A " bee " in America is simply a gathering of people together for some useful purpose, whether for sewing, preserving, and such like household matters, or rooting up tree stumps, as in Mr. Wilson's case.

This was how he summoned his logging bee:
the church bell was rung, and the union jack
hoisted at half-past six on Monday morning, and
the signal was well understood, for the Indians
came trooping up, pipe in mouth, axe on shoulder,
ready for hard work. That day seven acres were
cleared, and the tree stumps burnt—not a bad
beginning. When the stern winter days were past,
the building of the Home was begun, and then Mr.
Wilson went about telling his flock of the purpose
for which it was destined, and asking one and
another if they wished their children to share the
benefits. There seemed to be a general feeling that
the little ones would be safe and happy with the
kind white people, and one of the first children
promised was Man of the Desert's little girl
Therese. The Home was to be called after her
grandfather, the chief of the tribe, the "Shingwauk"
Industrial Home.

On the 25th of September of that year the church
bell rang, flags were hoisted, and guns fired; the
Home was ready, and this was the opening day.
Fifteen children had arrived, and the Indians were
gathered for a dedication service—it was all joy
and rejoicing, Here at last was a place where little
ones could be trained for Christ, and in future days
go forth, missionaries themselves, to their less
fortunate brethren.

So thought hard-working Mr. Wilson, so thought
happy, heart-satisfied Little Pine, so thought every
one connected with the matter. But it was not to

be so. Only five days after this happy opening a
fire broke out in the Home, and though the children
were saved, all else perished—building, fittings,
clothes, books, everything. It was in the night,
too, to make the scene more alarming, a rainy
night, and through the downpour the missionary's
four little children had to be borne, all ill with
coughs, to the dwelling of the kind Jesuit priest.

What was to be done after the first shock ?
Absolutely nothing but to bow to the will of God.
The Indian scholars, in tears and disappointment,
were all sent home; the mission given in charge of
the catechist Mr. Wilson had brought with him
from England; and Mr. Wilson, his sick wife and
little children, prepared for a three days' journey to
Collingwood. But trouble did not end here ; one
tiny one was missing in the desolate group of the
missionary's family gathering on board the steamer
that was to bear them away. In the place of the
bright, merry baby of the flock, the bereaved
father carried a small coffin. The child had died in
the night—the exposure had been too much for its
tender frame. Can you fancy how Little Pine
wept as the steamer left the wharf, grieved for his
friends, but cut to the heart at the failure of his
darling project ?

Mr. Wilson, in all his trouble, had given a short
service in the church on the Sunday morning
following the terrible Saturday night of the fire,
preaching trust in God, and patient waiting in this
great and unforeseen misfortune; and some of the

Indians had asked him what he meant to do for the devastated Home, but it was too early times to decide. The houseless family must seek shelter elsewhere, to take breath after their great shock, and meantime Frost, the catechist, would keep the flock together for the winter.

So terrible a misfortune to the struggling mission could not but meet with sympathy. Across the great ocean the message had flashed—"All burnt down, nothing saved!"—and before the thrill of horror was past, the generous-hearted had unloosed their purse-strings to repair the damage. By the exertion of friends, £2000 was collected in the space of a few months, and Mr. Wilson saw his way towards building another and even more capacious Home. He had been working hard in his enforced leisure time at the Chippeway language, preparing a grammar and dictionary in that tongue—necessary helps towards Christian teaching. From his books, however, he gladly turned to the consideration of the new Shingwauk Home, to be built of stone instead of wood, on the banks of the Sainte Marie River, some nine miles distant from the dear old Garden River. This situation was chosen as being more in the midst of the Indians, and also further from the Roman Catholic Mission—a lovely spot, with forest-ground for the listless Indian children to ramble and hunt in, fishing-ground in the beautiful river, and space everywhere, since Mr. Wilson had been enabled to buy more land in this new spot. On the 2nd of August, 1875, the new

Home was formally opened by two bishops of our Church, and the great work of Christianizing the red children once again set on foot.

Fifty of them were admitted into the Home, half girls, half boys, varying in age from six to sixteen. It was a great change to them, this regular, cleanly, busy life, from their old free, careless way of living. It was hard to them to learn obedience even—to come when called, to obey bells, to do as they were bid. Some of them pined at first, as if in captivity, making unearthly noises, and even running away, but after a while they steadied down, and became happy and contented.

The intention is to keep the children in the Home for five years, and when the time arrives for them to leave, to find them work or land in the neighbourhood, and so by degrees build up a Christian settlement. The teaching in the school is simple, chiefly reading, rendering Indian into English, and such like. Every morning at prayers the children repeat a verse of Scripture; in the evening they are taught the Lord's Prayer, Collect, Catechism, and to sing hymns. Of all things these holy teachings are held most important. On Sunday mornings the children walk to the church in the town. No servants are kept in the Home, so everything has to be done by the children. On Saturday afternoon the arrangements for the week are made—so many cook-girls chosen, so many house-girls, so many laundry-girls; of the boys, wood-boys, water-boys, farm-boys, fish-boys, and so on. It is a little

G

difficult at first for the matron to rule her troop, since they understand but little English, but time mends that.

It is not a dull life. The fish-boys have plenty of excitement netting their fish; the water-boys have their grey pony that they call "Little Evil Spirit," because he has such a bad temper; the baker-boys bake all the bread for the community; two girls and two boys are learning medicine, and attend at the dispensary morning and evening to bind up wounds and administer doses to the sick; then the sailor-boys have charge of the boat, *The Missionary*, and do all the water commissions in their blue serge suits and straw hats, proud miniature sailors. Most of the children have long Indian names besides their English ones; here are a few translated to amuse you: "Child of the Wind," "Hole in the Sky," "Night Thunder"—these are girls; and of the boys, "Thunder in the South," "Canoe run Aground." Why such strange names were given to them we can only guess, probably owing to some circumstance attending their birth.

Hole in the Sky and Canoe run Aground, however, with their various schoolmates, are rapidly learning to talk English, not so much by tasks or set laws, but by a plan of Mr. Wilson's own.

On Saturday afternoons the boys form in line round the master's desk, and there is a great deal of fumbling in pockets, and counting up of little round things, which on closer inspection turn out

to be "buttons." All the buttons that come out of
the pockets are then changed for nuts; some have
many, some few.

The fact is, any red boy hearing another speak
Indian has liberty to say, "Give me a button," he
who gets most buttons getting most nuts; and so
those who like nuts must speak English.

One of the improvements in the new Home is the
establishment of a fire brigade among the boys.
Once a month they practise; then an alarm of
fire is sounded, the buckets are filled at the
river and passed up to the house in the shortest
possible time, and the boys in their firemen's
helmets (all made in the institution) are as busy
and earnest as possible; if they can help it, there
shall be no such disaster again in the Home as
the terrible fire of past time. The Shingwauk
Home is quite a little world, you see, all sorts of
trades being taught, and the boys being fitted
for any occupation which the necessities of life
demand.

They print books, pamphlets, and even a newspaper of the Home and mission doings; and Mr.
Wilson hopes to turn out by-and-by a little company
of grown men, with ideas beyond fishing, hunting,
and the making of maple sugar.

And then what is to be done with them? Mr.
Wilson has thought of that too.

He has already bought land at no great distance
from the Home, whereon he hopes to see a Christian
settlement, with village church, schools, shops, farms,

ay, and little homesteads, each with its civilized
red man at its head. To turn these lads out un-
guarded and uncared for into their native forests
would be to send them back to barbarism most
likely.

But what about the girls? Are they not a little
pushed into the background by their big brothers?
Perhaps so; at any rate there is a difficulty about
amalgamating school-girls and school-boys, and a
separate Home for the girls is one of the plans in
prospect. The boys are already hauling stone for
the proposed buildings, and till then the girls are
boarded out with the schoolmaster's sister. Mr.
Wilson came to England to ask for help in this
undertaking, and narrowly escaped shipwreck on
his return voyage. · In a certain degree he was
successful, but he still wants a great deal more
money. Let us hope that those who have the
power to help the spread of Christ's kingdom on
earth will think of this forest Home in Canada, and
do somewhat for those who are spending their very
lives for it.

The Home has but a small regular income, and
you all know what an anxious thing it is to have
little faces looking up to you for daily bread and
clothes and teaching when the purse is nearly
empty. Yet one would not for the world have a
single bright-eyed Indian child sent back to the
ignorance of its old forest life; rather, as Little
Pine does still (old man that he is), would you go
about from one Indian wigwam to another, praying

this and that ignorant brother to send his little ones to the pale faces' Home, there to learn how the Great Spirit would have them live on earth, so as to be fit to meet Him in heaven.

# BY THE QUAY-SIDE.

### TENBY.

MOST people know Tenby, or at least have heard much in praise of that pretty little watering-place on the Pembrokeshire coast, with its picturesque rock scenery, its yellow sands, and the almost Mediterranean tint of its blue sea.

Its four thousand inhabitants are amply content, not to say proud of their small seaport, and are apt to show off its beauties to the summer visitor with a "There, I defy you to match *that*" sort of air.

And it would be difficult, indeed, to find anything more lovely than Tenby in the sweet, soft haze of a summer sunset—the fishing-boats gliding gently away towards the cloud glories of the horizon, or hovering lovingly near the fairy islands of the coast, a part and parcel themselves of the fascination of the scene.

You stand and watch the glowing crimsons melt to tender lilacs, a thousand sweet and solemn thoughts coming with this fair evening-tide, when lo! a jar, slight, but still to be felt and resented, the echo perhaps of an oath from the sea-wall. "Only the Quay-men—a dreadful lot," says some one. And you turn homeward, feeling you owe these rough fishermen a grudge for having spoilt your sweet sunset, and you meditate choosing some other spot save the Quay-side for your next evening ramble.

Hundreds of times may and must such an incident have occurred before the rough word fell on an ear that heard it in all its sadness, and on a heart that longed to do somewhat to attune that harsh voice to something that should chime better with the sun-setting.

But the day came at last.

In the winter of 1871 some one began to ask where dwelt and how lived the seventy or more families of fisher-folk that Tenby was said to possess, and then, to those fisher-people's great amaze, some one was seen wandering among their cottages in the neighbourhood of the pier and sluices, bidding them good morrow, and inviting them on the following Sunday to a little cottage room on the Quay.

The townsfolk had had a habit of utterly ignoring the fisher-folk till then, so the invitation was strange, and to be brooded over before accepting; but the inviter being a lady, there was no bad language to grieve her that day.

Still, it was a question if any would go to the cottage gathering; the seafaring population were a thing apart in Tenby, living without regard to church or schools, or land-sympathy, and hardly feeling the need of anything of the kind.

So when five fishermen came to the front that Sunday on the Quay-side, the two ladies who had

taken on themselves to make this small beginning
felt amply satisfied, and the reading lesson and
Bible talk went forward with a will.  Before next
Sunday there was more visiting among the fishermen's homes, and one or another of the five great
scholars had bidden friend or brother come with
him to the cottage class, so that the room began to
fill in cheerful fashion.

And by-and-by as weeks went on it not only
filled, but brimmed over, and then what was to be
done ?

Here was, indeed, a difficulty.  It was of no use
going into the town and hiring there a good, wholesome, capacious room ; the blue-vested scholars could
on no persuasion have been coaxed from their own
special lair, the Quay and water-side, and the attempt,
however well meant, would have been a failure.

At last the desired spot came to light, if that
expression may be used when it was half under-
ground.  A dilapidated old room was found, formerly
used for storing lumber, the floor of broken and
uneven stone, the walls once coloured white, changing to deep brown with bands of mouldering green,
the wet running down from ceiling to floor.  The
approach lay through a long, chilly, dirty stone
passage, but it was situated on the Quay, and the
fishermen approved, so this grim mouldy room was
immediately secured, whitewashed, and decorated.

Yes, decorated with pictures and gay texts on
the treacherous walls, which, however, speedily
cracked, discoloured, and otherwise disposed of

these new-fangled adornments, and left the room
to find other means of attracting visitors.

These did not fail. From twenty to thirty
fishermen now regularly attended a Sunday class,
the strong desire of learning to read attracting them,
while, all unconsciously, they drank in at the same
time a better knowledge than that of mere A B C.

More teachers now became indispensable. What
were two ladies among a score and a half of
anxious, clamorous pupils, all demanding special
attention? This was a new and great difficulty,
for both teachers and pupils were fastidious. The
former would come once, and then withdraw,
appalled by the damp room—if ladies, pleading
terror of the rough fishermen; if gentlemen,
naturally depressed by the conduct of their charge,
who, accustomed at the outset to the sole tuition
of ladies, strongly objected to the sight of a black
cloth coat, and on the appearance of such would
vanish from their seats with scant courtesy and
disappear into the street, lost for that day. But
time and patience mended all this; order was
established, and teachers and taught became on
such good terms that the disagreeables of the Sunday quarters were forgotten in the interest inspired
by what went on within them. From the first,
indeed, a bad word or uncivil action found no place
among the rough scholars.

Not long after the commencement of the men's
classes, a boys' school was opened, to assemble
before their seniors. Here were collected together a

rough, barefooted little set, whose clothes, or rather
want of them, prevented their attending the parish
schools. The whole accomplishment of these small
imps was begging; of the three R's they were utterly
ignorant, and a day school three afternoons a week
was found necessary to supplement the Sunday work.

Such a day school as it was at first! Most of
the pupils had never been inside a school of any
sort before, and were utterly uncivilized, more like
cheerful young animals than anything else. Dirty,
noisy, and without the slightest idea of reverence,
they laughed, chattered, sang, whistled, and cut
capers, till a school of fresh-caught monkeys would
have been almost as hopeful to manage.

It was hard work keeping order in such a crowd;
but the blue guernsey harboured a little human
heart, and the mischievous eyes could soften at
entreaty, so love won a way in this difficult sphere.

Love and discipline. Some little lads were too
giddy and forgetful to be managed with a word,
and their noisiness and inattention naturally incon-
venienced the whole school.

How was this to be met? The boys themselves
suggested a remedy.

Like Topsy, they " s'posed they must be whipped,"
and a little stick was formally presented to the
teacher, with the suggestion to hit the knuckles or
curly heads of the unruly, a system weighted by
the administration of a " candy " to the industrious.

The plan succeeded; but a kind-hearted lady
visitor exhibiting great concern at the corporal

punishment, the boys were asked before her, " Well, which will you have—stick and candy, or no stick and no candy?" when the roar in favour of the good old system fully convinced her, and she was able to laugh at her own scruples. It may be stated here, however, that this was a discipline adapted only to the early stage of affairs; stick and candy have both been supplanted by a higher rule of self-control; and half-yearly small prizes are now the reward of industry and good conduct.

As soon as a boy became sufficiently tamed in this primitive school, and when, besides a glimmering of the alphabet and the ultimate design of pot-hooks, his clothes were reduced to something like decency, he was urged to attend the regular parish school. This was always a lion in the path; the stiffness and unfriendliness of the fisher-folk and their town neighbours was difficult to break through, but it had to be done. It was no part of the mission-scheme to rear as a sect apart these sea-faring brethren of all Christian men. So boys and elders were persuaded and harangued till a few crept into the church and schools, much abashed at first, but afterwards reassured by the comforting presence of one of their own teachers, who made it a system to go round on Sunday mornings and collect his timid flock. A necessary supervision was kept over them during service also, and in time a goodly show of about twenty boys and from ten to fifteen men regularly attended the services of the parish church. As yet attention had been

chiefly directed to improving the condition of the
men and boys of the fisher-folk, but as time went
on classes began to multiply, including, among
others, a weekly meeting of fishermen's wives for
Bible reading, a mothers' meeting, and a class for
little girls of the seamen's families.

The temperance cause soon took a part, of
necessity, in the work of the little mission; the
character for hard drinking held by the seafaring
population was found to be only too true a one,
men and women frequently being in slavery to this
terrible vice, wretched homes and neglected children
resulting therefrom. Temperance or total abstinence,
the latter often the only hope of the confirmed
drunkard, was urged with all the earnestness of
those who felt that they were pleading with the
man for his soul as well as his body.

It was uphill work, for years it seemed as if no
way could be made; pledges were taken and broken
again, the drunkard slipping backward into the
abyss out of which he had so painfully and carefully been lifted, to the grief of the mission workers.
But to despair would have been faithless and
cowardly, so the temperance lectures went on and
the young folks were got hold of. Almost all the
boys in the school are now non-drinkers, and at least
half the men. Care and thought has to be brought
into play in peculiar cases. Witness a stalwart
blue-eyed old fellow, the worst swearer and the
hardest drinker on the Quay, eleven years an
absentee from any form of public worship, and

yet withal maintaining a straightforwardness of demeanour and a certain rectitude in the midst of evil that marked him out as not altogether God-forsaken, if he was God-forsaking. If he could be brought out of the slough of drunkenness on to firm ground something might be done with him, thought the mission workers; so one made the attempt, reasoning, imploring, praying the old seaman to put out a hand and save himself. A long illness made the ground easier to work on—he looked with some sort of approval on the clergyman and the mission lady who entreated him to sign the pledge and give up the accursed thing; but still he hesitated, and at last came the somewhat plaintive cry, "How can I do it? What can I get but the drop of gin of a night to thaw the blood in my old bones after seine-fishing?"

There was somewhat of reason in the appeal, and it was met half-way. The old man signed a solemn promise in the presence of witnesses not to touch drink *except* when he came in from fishing in the middle of the night. This occurred seven years ago, and up to the present time he has manfully kept his word, nay, done more, for he has altogether and entirely abstained from the temptation of liquor at any time. With sobriety came a hankering after a better life and a knowledge of better things. He was seen in church, earnestly, and a trifle painfully, groping his way through the Prayer-book, losing his grip of affairs after the Psalms, and seeking to be righted by his ever-present friend and

teacher by a whispered query and a half-groan of
"I'd rather understand this book than have a pound
in my hand."

A different spirit in time began generally to
prevail regarding this great vice of drunkenness.
Instead of being regarded as in no way a sin, but
only a matter of amusement, pity, or ridicule, in-
temperance was now seen in its true colours, and
the self-denial of temperance respected in others,
even by those who had not as yet the strength to
embrace the same course.

Music was found to have a great attraction for
the fisher-folk, and for the purpose of keeping the
men away from the public-houses on the two nights
a week they were sure to be on shore, singing
classes were established on the Friday and Saturday
evenings. As a rule, however, the pupils were not
musical in the true sense of the word, and their
creed usually began and ended with the belief that
he who sang loudest at these classes sang best.
Still, however, the meetings flourished, and became
a favourite resort with the young fellows who
boasted a cheery seaman's voice.

Nothing would satisfy the lusty musicians after
a few months' practice but a concert, and in their
own room. The idea, though ambitious, was harmless. So the dismal vault was decorated once more,
a few ladies and gentlemen, friends of the project,
invited, and then the doors were thrown open to all
comers at a charge of twopence a head.

The concert, as a concert, could not be pro-

nounced a success; many of the men had carefully
studied their songs to the accompaniment of a
piano, but, either through nervousness or excitement, utterly forsook that trusty guide during the
performance of their melody, the result being per-
plexing to every one save the singer. In the un-
accompanied songs the false starts were numerous,
and met by roars of applause or derision from the
twopenny audience, according to the popularity of
the performer. In fact, the savage breast was anything but soothed by the music of that long-remem-
bered evening, and it required great faith and
courage to get up another such entertainment later
on, when provision was made against the failures of
concert No. 1, and a guarantee of good behaviour in
the listeners ensured by confining the distribution
of tickets among the mission men and their families.

A great improvement immediately showed itself
both in the music and manner of the rough throng,
and as half-year by half-year witnessed other and
better regulated meetings, the order and quiet of
those evenings now matches any philharmonic
gathering in the kingdom, even if the music be
still a little behind that of the outer world's gilded
and cushioned concert-halls. The false start or
nervous blunder now no longer excites the rough
jest or boisterous laugh; the fishermen and boys
who chiefly constitute the audience have learnt a
certain courtesy and self-control distinguishing the
Christian from the savage; they do not wish now
to disconcert Tom, or Jack, or Bill in his chosen

melody—they would rather help him out with it; so they sit patiently till he gets his footing again, and then at the close of the song get rid of their feelings in a burst of well-timed applause, thus relieving the promoters of the entertainment of much anxiety and the lurking fear that at first prevailed of giving the enemy occasion to whisper the word "bear garden" concerning these well-intentioned gatherings; such a fear now no longer exists, since the half-yearly concert is a well-conducted and agreeable musical evening.

When the Quay Mission had survived its second year, a desire began to be felt to put it on the footing of a recognized parochial institute, with suitable rules and proper buildings. The old room was then literally falling to pieces, and would soon have had to be abandoned, even if affairs had not been hastened by the owner hurriedly claiming it and ejecting the tenants. Hitherto the mission work had been a sort of stream under ground, carried on, of course, with the consent and approval of the parochial clergy, but in so quiet a manner that publicity seemed a thing to shrink from. Private means had hitherto almost entirely supported the mission, but if the welfare of the fisher population was to be seriously considered, the public must be invited to co-operate.

So, somewhat reluctantly, the facts were made known, the need of a good mission-room put forth, and after some trouble in telling the tale, public sympathy was roused to the extent of the needed

sum, *i.e.* £800. This took about a year and a half
to collect, during which time a site was secured for
the new rooms in the right quarter, close to the pier,
and the work of building and adapting was carried
on during the year 1874.

The edifice consisted of five rooms built over
some cottages, and taking the place of what had been
another story of cottage apartments. These rooms
comprised a class-room, two boys' rooms, a manager's
apartment, and the men's public reading-room.

On their completion the countenance of the
clergy of the parish, the Mayor of Tenby, and a
large gathering of friends, was secured, while the
Rev. Basil Wilberforce formally pronounced the
building open.

And then the Seamen's Mission-Rooms did in real
truth open wide their doors to the long-neglected
fisher-folk of Tenby. Let us look through them and
see what attractions they offer to the seafaring man.

Enter the men's room first: bright and airy, with
a good balcony hanging over their own old ally, the
tumbling sea, the room communicating easily with
the manager's by a window answering to a bar.
Here is sold tea, coffee, cocoa, ginger beer, and every
sort of non-intoxicating drink, with buns, bread
and cheese, sweets, and a sort of pudding called
"duff," dear to the stomach of Jack when young.
It was also found expedient to unite tobacco and
pipes with the other stock, since the want of these,
at first starting, occasionally compelled a visit to a
public-house. H

This bar always pays its way, even showing at the end of the year a small balance to the good. Papers are supplied to the men, with a good billiard-table, draught-boards, and dominoes. Gambling and bad language are strictly forbidden, and a certain number of members form a committee, and are in a measure responsible for the keeping of rules and the general good conduct of the inmates. Both the men's and boys' rooms are largely patronized, especially in winter, and it is rare for any rule to be broken, or for any disturbance to be raised. To any seaman, local or stranger, or to any member of the Sunday school, the reading-room is free, and it is found that stray sailors or steamer-men are glad to avail themselves of decent shelter and sociable company for the evening hours, even apart from the fascinations of the public-house.

Christmas Eve being discovered to be a season of the greatest temptation to the fisher-people, the idea of good fellowship at that time necessitating a meeting at the public-house, and consequent intoxication, a grand annual tea was devised for that night in the new rooms, which has proved a most useful institution. The most hopeful and sober of the flock had been found "wanting" so often on that day, that this effort to keep them together and in sight of those whose good opinion was much to them, has proved eminently successful. Then, again, Whit-Monday might more fully have been named Black-Monday among the Quay people, so given up was it to riot and drunkenness, till a project was set on foot bearing the aspect of a giant picnic on that day. The mission leaders, with as many followers as they could collect, started in sailing vessels for the neighbouring island of Caldy, about a mile and a half distant. The day's ticket, including passage and a famous tea on the island, is priced at one shilling; only one rule is enforced, every excursionist for the day is bound over to hold himself a teetotaller. The result of this arrangement is that though as many as seven hundred have been known to enrol themselves among the list of picnickers, and although the only police are the ladies of the mission, there has never been a jar nor a suspicion of ill behaviour.

Games and races amuse the holiday folk, and towards the close of the day no occupation has greater fascination than joining in the songs or hymns started by the fisher singing class. It is needless to remind the reader that this almost uncountable picnic party is landed in perfectly sober condition on their own Quay as near bedtime as practicable.

A bright era now dawned on the little mission in the shape of the advent of its own particular clerical overseer, the junior curate of the parish, himself formerly a naval officer, and therefore a well-qualified worker among his seafaring brethren. For some time previously mission services had been held on Sunday evenings (after divine service in the parish church), whenever one of the resident clergy or a visitor could be secured for the purpose,

but on Mr. Hastings' arrival the service became per-
manent and the attendance good and unvarying.

Such a helper greatly strengthened the hands
and cheered the hearts of the original workers,
enabling them in many ways to *do* what before
could only be planned and longed for, and though
after a time he left Tenby for another sphere, the
result of his good work remained behind.

There was still, however, much to desire in the
mission scheme, and chiefest of all was a chapel
needed, attached to the seamen's rooms, and capable
of opening, if need be, into the schoolroom.

A seamen's church is well known to be a necessity
among a fishing population; the rough fellows have
a not unnatural reluctance to mingling with the
silk and broadcloth crowd of a fashionable watering-place congregation, and here in Tenby, for the
want of such a building, the fisher-people have gone
nowhere, just idled away the Sunday hours on the
Quay, on the wall, or perhaps altogether lost the
meaning of the day of rest in Sunday evening
fishing. Then, again, neglect of church-going has
led to contempt of sacred things; the sacraments
are ignored, babes go unbaptized, and youths untaught and unconfirmed, young lads and lasses go
to the registry office for marriage instead of church,
and often the sole Church service attended by the
fisherman is one in which he takes no part, of
which the benefit can be no longer his—the service
of the Burial of the Dead.

The small chapel, then, needed to complete the

seamen's building in Tenby was made matter of immediate consideration. Funds were raised with some trouble, and a suitable building erected and opened on St. Andrew's Day, November 1, 1879.

The little church holds one hundred and thirty people, and has its comfortable and substantial benches (nothing gimcrack will do for Jack), its good harmonium, and, as there can be no east window, a pictured representation of the Good Shepherd on the east wall.

The services (three on Sunday) are very hearty and well attended. There are, of course, a good many hymns, for who likes singing so well as a sailor? The alms-bag is carried round by an old scholar, now manager of the rooms, and many a fitting and adornment of the chapel is pointed out as the gift of an old friend. Holy Communion is administered every Thursday morning at seven o'clock.

This is the story of the Quay Mission at Tenby. I think we may feel that they have tried to render the poor boatman's life happier who have struggled to make it holier; and that learning in his own house of God that God rules the storm and takes the life of poor Jack into His keeping, these rough, often thoughtless, men will go forth to their business in great waters better fortified to meet not only the waves of this troublesome world, but those more terrible billows of ignorance and evil which have hitherto threatened to make shipwreck of their souls.

# A BLACK BISHOP.

### VIRGINIA.

MANY years ago an American lady wrote a book which excited great attention. It was in every one's hands, every one asked " Have you read 'Uncle Tom's Cabin'?" The story was at once a striking and a sad one, a story of slavery under men of our own race—a tale of stripes and blows and cruel usage of the negro by the white man.

Thank God, the day of such things is gone by. Since the war between the North and the South in America, no savage overseer can beat an "Uncle Tom" to death, no poor "Eliza" be forced to flee for her life, with babe in her arms, over the broken ice of a half-frozen river; for slavery is abolished in all the States of America. The negro is as free as the white man.

But the abolition of slavery necessarily caused a great separation between whites and blacks. Until quite lately in America a white man would not sit at table with a negro, would not ride in a railway carriage with him, would not even kneel by him in church. And who can wonder if a great gulf seemed to divide the two races? If here and there the former servants of some good white master still hung about him, and seemed to regret their old state of loving dependence, there were not wanting stronger, bitterer spirits to whisper in their ears that they were acting foolishly and meanly, and that they ought to hate and shun the white man, who had lived so long on their labours.

Of one such fierce, bitter spirit I must tell you to-day. An old mulatto, or half-black man, he had been busy for long in the State of Virginia teaching the negroes to hate and stand aloof from their former masters. Negroes are like children, any one with a strong will may lead them; and when this strange deformed little man came among them, with his clever tongue and his strong feelings, they were all at his feet in a twinkling. His name was Howell. At his bidding the poor creatures cut down trees and built a rude church in the forest, accepting their leader for what he chose to call himself, their bishop, the founder of a new religion called Zion Union. And what was this new religion that bishop Howell took such an interest in spreading? I can tell you. Its great tenet was hatred to white men. No white man, it says, can enter the kingdom of heaven. " The whites have the Bible," declared this strange dark bishop, " but the Holy Spirit reveals Himself directly to us."

Sunday after Sunday the poor black people of the neighbourhood joined in this more than half-heathen worship, blessing God, and cursing their brother in the same breath! Sunday after Sunday

little negroes might have been seen gathering in
the forest for their Sunday school, that mockery of
better things, where was no Bible, no gospel of
love, only wild hymn-singing and wilder doctrines.

A white lady living near this rough church of
Bishop Howell's was possessed with a deep pity for
the poor, mistaken, childish negroes. She would
willingly have gathered a few little blacks together
and taught them herself the religion of love, but
none would come to her; negroes like stir and excitement, shouting and groaning and singing, and
these were to be had at the forest church, so there
they would go. Mrs. Buford was almost in despair.
Then a bright idea came to her: if she could not
establish a school of her own, she would ask this
strange powerful Bishop Howell to let her teach in
his. Very timidly she made her request. A white
lady asking a favour of him must have been pleasing
to the bishop. He received her joyfully, and she
took her place as teacher in his school. Such a
school as it was! No Bible, no books, no pictures,
no texts, but a wild hard doctrine of hatred of
white men everywhere. And yet out of this God
had minded to bring good, and Bishop Howell himself was to help;—at first only by kindly receiving
the lady teacher. She was a bold woman to venture
into his fold, but what else was she to do? There
had been no real clergyman in the parish for years.

Mrs. Buford's first act was to write to a kind
friend, the Secretary of the Bible House, New York,
and to ask him for books; the negroes were too

miserably poor to pay for them, they must come as a gift. They came, and a delightful parcel it was. A large Bible for the church was first unpacked, then Catechisms, cards, pictures, papers, etc. The bishop was as pleased as any one at the sight; poor man! perhaps poverty, perhaps ill treatment by the whites, had blinded him till now. Better times began from this day. The Bible was carried carefully into the rough church, and word went out into the plantations of the precious gift. Mrs. Buford soon after says in one of her letters, "The school is growing so rapidly that I am quite appalled at it. The little hut is crowded nearly every Sunday with grey-headed negroes as well as the little children, listening eagerly to the words of that blessed Bible, and handling it so reverently, and keeping it so sacredly that I never see it without a pang of self-reproach." The Catechisms, too, were taken possession of by the bishop; they were almost too precious for the children to have; they were wanted for his grown men, his preachers to learn from. Of course, Mrs. Buford gladly gave them up for that purpose. Very soon several of Bishop Howell's ministers were arranging their schools on the same principle as the one on which she taught. These ministers were all black men; indeed, there were hardly any whites in that part of the country.

After a while Mrs. Buford had a new stock of books sent her, amongst which were little books of the Church collects. These she handed over to the bishop's black preachers, asking them to use them

in their services. She told them how holy men
had written them long ago, and how they had been
preserved in the Church for ages. They promised
to use them devoutly in their public ministrations.
" God grant they may," says the anxious lady, who
was working so faithfully in the dark.

The children, of course, learned easily and pleasantly, like our English children, the Creed, the Ten
Commandments, and the Church Catechism, but the
old people it was who chiefly moved the gentle
teacher's heart. "If you could see, as I do every
Sunday, their poor old black faces as they listen so
thirstingly to the blessed words of the Bible ! You
cannot conceive how touching it is to see grey-
headed men and women, their faces withered and
black and old, entirely absorbed in the lessons,
repeating with the little children the Catechism,
the Creed, and the Commandments. Old Howell,"
she goes on to say, "who was more bitter in his
hostility to the whites than any one among them,
is now my truest friend and helper. He is wavering in his adherence to his own superstitions, and
I hope and believe and pray will connect himself
with our Church. He wields a greater influence
over the negroes than any other man in South Side,
Virginia."

One cannot but pause here to notice how gently
and wisely that servant of God, Mrs. Buford, entered
on her missionary work. Wrong as she felt Bishop
Howell to be, she never set herself in opposition to
him, nor roused evil feelings by denouncing him to

his ignorant followers. He was as much to be pitied and as greatly in need of tender treatment as the most ignorant negro, and God blessed her loving efforts to do good to him and his benighted flock.

So attractive did she make religion, that the bishop longed to connect himself with her Church. Zion Union numbered some two thousand members, governed by seventeen negro ministers, with Bishop Howell at their head. Twenty-five or thirty Sunday schools were under their care. Its gospel, as I said before, was for a number of years one of hatred to the white race. But now a change was to take place. Interested by Mrs. Buford's letters, a Church clergyman visited the settlement, and had a friendly interview with the Zion Union Bishop. Howell said he would like one of his ministers to be educated and ordained as a real Episcopal clergyman. Indeed, so softened had he become that he seemed to lean to a general union with the Episcopal Church. Knowing this, Mrs. Buford, her husband, and a Church clergyman, Mr. White, set out to attend an annual meeting of Bishop Howell's sect. There was a grand service in the forest church, strange wild prayers, and monotonous hymns were sung with much swaying of the body and many contortions of the face, but there was also much earnestness and a general craving for something beyond this rude worship. The Church clergyman was then asked to preach, which he did, and moans and groans and cries of assent testified to the interest his poor hearers took in his discourse.

Then came the great event of the day. Bishop
Howell, the poor old deformed white-hating mulatto,
rose and addressed his old enemy the white-skinned
clergyman. "We are children," he said, "who have
wandered far from home, and now, poor and blind
and starving, we come to you and beg you to give
us only one little corner in the poorest land of the
old Home Farm, and, if you will only let us in, we
will grub up the hedgerows and make some good
corn yet."

Such figurative speech pleases the negro; they
all fully understood that the Home Farm here
spoken of meant the Church of God on earth, as
established by the Apostles. Then he went on to
say that if some present objected to joining the
Episcopal Church, Mr. White would answer their
objections. And after that Mr. White rose and told
the black listeners that his Church had neglected
them once, but was seeking to atone for her fault.
"Now she comes to you and says, 'I am sorry for
the past; come to me, and I will help you and guide
you, and give you the light and knowledge which
I once withheld.'" A thrill of sympathy ran through
his hearers—the excitement was tremendous! The
old withered bishop asked, was any opposed to
union now? And the whole building seemed to
rise with the shout of "Not one, not one!" Perhaps the most hopeful part of the matter was the
coming of the better-educated negro preachers to
Mr. White to be allowed to be connected with his
Church, and to receive from him the Prayer-book.

The mass of ignorant people would shout and pray at any one's bidding, but to win over these better-educated black leaders meant real progress in that benighted little community.

There is a great deal more to tell about these poor plantation negroes, but I cannot make room for it here. One thing we may be sure of, that for the future the Church will never let them go : they have taken refuge in her bosom, and she cares for her black children as fondly as for her white ones.

*       *       *       *       *

I have given you a short history of one Negro Mission in the Southern States of America. Now for another, also in the South. The story is true, though no names are given. The difference between this effort and the last consists in the fact that here there was no wild sect to hamper the way, only dense ignorance. As before, the beginning was made after the war. A good old Church clergyman gathered a few black children together to be taught by his own family. This proceeding met with much ridicule. The world laughed at it. It was called "Dr. C.'s whim," and he was looked upon as a benevolent old gentleman might be in England who should begin to teach tricks to a set of rather troublesome and disagreeable poodles. But Dr. C. heeded neither laughter nor "faint praise." He went on teaching, preaching, praying, till God called him home, and a new clergyman came to take up his work. He found a large school of black children. Old negroes longing to be taught with the little ones. White men and women no longer scornful, but wishing to act as teachers. All very hopeful. Only where were the books and benches and chairs to come from for so large a party? Money never is plentiful among the poor blacks, and possibly the white people in the parish were not too well off, and not too willing to bestow of what riches they possessed. Matters were very simply conducted, however, in those regions, and the new clergyman merely gave out in church that he should be glad if every family would send a present of a chair to the school for the teachers, and then he borrowed hammer and saw and plane, and set to work himself to make fifty benches.

All the old spelling-books and hymn-books were hunted up, and when they failed old newspapers did for making out the alphabet. Some lads even brought bills they had torn off the walls to learn their letters from, and one little girl, a small teacher, was seen one day hacking away at a wall advertisement with a pair of scissors, to get the great A B C's for her class in school! School begins at two on Sunday afternoons, and by one o'clock the little darkies begin to arrive. It is a comical sight, says the clergyman, then to look out of the rectory windows. Between the houses and the church where school is held some hundred negro children are grouped about, tumbling on the grass, playing marbles even, and occasionally breaking out into wild shouts and wilder races up or down the road. Sometimes they stop short, afraid of injuring their

Sunday clothes; you see them dusting, rubbing, and brushing, till some one hits a little too hard, or something starts them off again with a rush and a shout. It is useless to try to keep them in order; they are bubbling and boiling over with spirits, infinitely fuller of life and mischief than white children, and a great thing has been done if they can be kept from fighting and swearing. About a quarter before two the black sexton comes to unlock the door. He is a staid, dignified man. He is greeted first with a shout of welcome; then with the quivering of fifty pairs of black legs in the air whose owners are standing on their heads! After this follows the dropping of numerous little darkies from all the trees in the neighbourhood, as if a blast of autumn wind had shaken down so many bouncing apples! Then while eyeballs begin to roll, and mischievous little tongues to wag, making fun of this respectable Uncle Tom, he solemnly moves on, utterly regardless of the fact that the youngsters behind him are marching in imitation of him, and copying his every movement! White children are often very troublesome in a Sunday school, what, then, must black urchins be? However, with these frisky little ones it is impossible to be much depressed. A good hymn is started to give the chattering tongues employment, and the feeble gaspings of an old piano are soon lost in the chorus of lusty voices.

Who teaches in this black Sunday school? Any one that can and will. The elder scholars from the white Sunday school close by are sometimes thus engaged. A white Sunday school is still a necessity. White parents in America are not yet willing that their little Evas and Clarissas should sit by and learn with the Chloes and Topsys of the neighbourhood, and so teachers and clergymen arrange to keep them apart. Children, however, shake off these prejudices more easily than grown-up people, and so many an elder boy or girl feels it now an honour and a pleasure to teach the little darkies whom their parents perhaps despise. The pretty little daughter of the churchwarden has a class of grinning, fidgeting black babies, and she keeps them in order beautifully, looking almost like an angel amongst them. Her golden hair, pale face, and sweet grey eyes are such a contrast to their shining black skins, round eyes, and woolly heads. And they do so listen and crowd round her when she tells them about the heaven in store for little black children.

Then Eddie, the clergyman's own boy, has another class of the worst boys in the school, who, under his charge, behave wonderfully well. Would you like to hear how he manages? Do not be surprised and think that would not do in England. I am not telling you about England and English children, but about the Southern States of America and little negroes. Well, Eddie's are big boys, and now and then one is troublesome, downright naughty. This one Eddie regards severely. "You must have a thrashing," he says to him; "come to me in the week for it." And if on Monday or Tuesday the lad does not come for his punishment, Eddie hunts him up, and gives him what he calls "a good first-class drubbing." Nearly every one of his class has, some time or other, gone through this process; but, somehow, they love their young master, run errands for him, wait on him, and especially learn his lessons, since they know what will happen if they do not.

They often bring him presents, and a queer little face grinning affectionately at a street corner is sure to be one of Eddie's boys waiting for a recognition. It is an odd way of managing a Sunday school class, but it seems to suit little blackies, and Eddie's father leaves him to it, for the boy teaches well, and is proud of his scholars.

Another teacher is an old lady of seventy; she is dearly loved by her black class, perhaps because she dearly loves them, for negroes are most affectionate creatures and will do anything for any one who cares for them.

Another teacher there is too, a gentle, quiet lady, very fair and sweet and refined. One day, during the singing of a hymn, the school-door opened and two grey-headed blind negroes fumbled their way into the room. They were poor, and old, and diseased, and, worse still, they were fearfully dirty. What was to be done—turn them out? The children looked at the superintendent, and he was in two minds what to do. Perhaps it would be best to gently put the poor creatures outside the door; they

I

were such wretched unpleasant neighbours in a
room. While he was wavering, the gentle lady
teacher stepped forward, took a hand of each blind
negro, and led them to a seat by herself. She
whispered them a welcome, and when the hymn
was over asked them where they lived, and what
they wanted, and promised to teach them. She
recognized the hand of God guiding these poor
miserable creatures to the light, and she would not
turn away from the work He had sent her to do.
The sight of her ready acquiescence made the other
teachers feel ashamed and yet glad. The next
Sunday the lady gave up her own class to teach
these poor old castaways, who brought with them
other companions; they became clean and neat after
a while, for the body can hardly remain defiled and
dirty where the soul is purified and enlightened.

Who can wonder after this incident that the
negroes began to have confidence in "white folks'
religion," and to believe that white people really do
care for them and mean well by them? What does
it matter that books are few, if the poor ignorant
souls can learn from acted lessons like these? Who
cares that benches and chairs are wanting, when the
little ones can sit literally at the feet of such a
sweet and loving teacher?

Of course, the clergyman has a beautiful dream
for this, his dear school and congregation. But
heavenly as the dream is, it requires earthly gold
to realize, and that he has not got at present.
This is the dream: to enlarge his church, which at

present is small, and only holds a few black people comfortably, without unduly crowding out the white; to have a white priest and a black one in the same chancel; a white choir and a black one answering each other in chant and hymn; a white congregation and a black one under the same roof, bowing together at the holy name of Jcsus, reciting the same Creed, kneeling at the same altar, looking forward to the same heaven.

Dear as this dream is to the pastor of his motley flock, yet he is not led away by it. He says of it, " When we reflect that all this might be to-morrow, had we a house of God large enough, we can hardly wait; and some of us propose to build and trust to the Church to help us to pay. But that would be to go forward, not at command, but at our own judgment. So we will not lay one brick until we have money to pay for it, and will try not to hurry faster than God leads. But surely some day God will hear our prayers."

## SICK AND SORRY.

### BOSTON, AMERICA.

In the year 1833 a sickly little child was born in the town of Boston, America. Years afterwards he wrote down the story of his childhood and youth. It was mainly a tale of suffering. Of his first years he chiefly remembered being carried up and down-stairs in some one's arms when other children were romping and dancing. As a school-boy he could not study on account of his bad health, and as a young man he had to give up business for the same reason. Just at this time a friendly doctor came forward, and asked the young fellow to go with him on his rounds; it might amuse him, the air might do him good, and perhaps if he liked the idea he might become a doctor too. But to this last suggestion Charles Cullis said no; he meant to grow strong, and to go back to business. God willed it otherwise, however. The lad still continued delicate, and, after a while, finding he should never be able to spend long hours at an offiee-desk, or bear much shutting up of any sort, he accepted his friend's suggestion, studied medicine, and became a physician.

All this, however, without much caring for the result personally, not seeing, as is often the case in this world, whither the hand of God was leading him.

And first there came a bright ray of sunshine in Charles Cullis's pathway—he married a wife whom he fondly loved, and held dearer than life itself. A few months of happiness and then that wife died of rapid decline, and the husband felt as if· for him everything in this world had come to an end.

Yet he had to live, and having no wife nor happy home on which to spend his earnings, he made a vow to give them all to God. "Lord, my wife is dead," he said aloud, "and I have no one now to make money for; I will give all that I receive over actual expenses for Thy cause."

It was a good vow, and he kept it; but he was not happy; his money went here and there, to this cause and to that; whoever came in the name of the Lord might have it.

By-and-by he began to doubt if all was well regarding this system; he did not wish to keep back one coin of his gifts, but he did want the money to do all the good that it could be made to · do. If people do not look after their charities, they often turn out ill.

Thenceforward he resolved to give thought and work to God as well as money. He had been serving God hitherto with a cold, dry sort of service, —thenceforth he would ask the Lord daily to mark him out a special work to do. The first idea he

had of this work came into his mind from seeing a
poor man who had been refused admission to the
hospitals because he was suffering from incurable
consumption. It cost Dr. Cullis a pang to send
the poor creature away without being able to point
out a home to him. At that moment a voice seemed
to say to him, " There, that is your work." And he
made it his work. Not all at once, not without
thought; months, even years had to pass before he
dared begin it, but still the care of poor consumptive
creatures was to be his work for life.

And it is this work, as much mission work, in its
way, as preaching to African negroes or caring for
South Sea Islanders, that I am going to outline
for you now—only to outline, and even that in an
unfinished manner, for, thank God, Dr. Cullis still
lives and goes on with his labours day by day.

This was Dr. Cullis's plan, if God willed that he
should carry it out—

To gather under one roof such poor consumptive
sufferers as needed tending during their weary sickness, or who perchance only desired a refuge in
which to lie down and die ; to make them happy
in that home, and to prepare them for another—
more blessed—in which the inhabitants shall no
more say, " I am sick."

Listen now to what may seem to us the strange
part of the doctor's scheme. He was not rich, not
able to support such a Home as he longed to institute out of his own earnings, though indeed he
meant to devote all of them to the purpose. What

was to be done? Should he apply to the rich people of his friends and acquaintances and press them to help him? Should he print appeals, and get up bazaars, and ask for sermons to be preached to obtain money? All these were means fair in their way, and likely to enrich him.

But no! Dr. Cullis was not of this way of thinking. God, as he felt, had led him to this point; had put into his heart the wish to help His sick and suffering ones, and he felt sure He would provide the way and the means for the undertaking. So he assembled no committee, got no great people on his list, and demanded no help save from God. To Him he prayed continually, asking first to be shown His will, and then for power, ay, and money to do it with. If it was time to set the Home on foot, he prayed God to send him a sign by putting it into people's hearts to help him with their alms. One day, after offering up this prayer most heartily, he received, without asking for it, a little gift of one dollar (four shillings) from a friend who had known of his desires for years, but who never thought of helping to advance them before.

Another small gift of money following this one, Dr. Cullis felt in his heart that God meant him to begin his work in right earnest. So the house was chosen, to be paid for within a certain time, and the preparations were begun.

Many kind friends came forward then with money and furniture and stores. Here is one of the first lists of gifts dotted down in the doctor's journal: "Six chairs," "a carpet," "a barrel of flour," "window curtains for the whole house," "two cot beds," "an extension table," "chairs and tables," "twelve husk pillows," "a stair carpet," "glass ware," "cotton cloth," "mattresses and boxes," "two floors painted and lettering done out of good will," "two contribution boxes lettered," "a clock *loaned.*" It sounds like getting on, this odd list of contributions. Well might the doctor write in his journal, "Blessed is the man that maketh the Lord his trust."

Of course, a great many people thought Dr. Cullis very foolish to begin such a work without a large sum of money in the bank, but then they were people who had not such strong faith in the goodness of God as our doctor. Certainly *they* would have fainted and failed in such an undertaking, but *he* did not. So the work went on till the 27th day of September, 1864, when all was ready for the dedication to God of this House for Poor Consumptives. People who had shaken their heads over the plan, and even blamed it, came that day with those who wished it well, and crowded into the comfortably if oddly furnished rooms to gaze and listen. There was a solemn service, dedicating all connected with that building to God—the House, the founder, the poor creatures that it was to contain. Many who came to scoff, remained to pray and to give of their abundance to the good cause. Those who had not money gave other things: a widow lady brought a towel, a pillow-case, and a sheet; and a little girl came with a gold piece she had had given to her as a baby and had treasured ever since. She was sure she should not be sorry nor want to have it back. So Dr. Cullis took it for God's work and for the comfort of his sick poor.

A week later and these sick began themselves to come; they were no more to be sent away uncured. First a man, then a woman, then more and more of all sorts, men, women, and children. For each the good doctor prays, "May the Lord be with him in the Home, and take him to Himself when his days on earth shall close." No one was refused; though this was to be a Home dedicated to God, and though Dr. Cullis earnestly desired that all his poor sick should rest in the Saviour's loving arms, yet he held open the doors to others, to the most miserable of God's creatures, to those even who denied and derided Him!

One poor man, talking with Dr. Cullis the day he came to ask for admission to the Home, was almost afraid to own that he had no religion, he was so afraid of being sent away to die in the streets. But Dr. Cullis was no hard judge, no strict rule-maker; this man was sick and suffering, and all the more to be pitied that he did not know or care for God; so the doors swung back, and the medicines and good food and kind nursing were all put at his service, and the poor fellow grew strong and well once more, and was able to leave the Home, not only blessing and thanking Dr. Cullis, but believing in a good God, who puts it into the hearts of His servants to be loving and merciful to their poor sick brethren.

A poor Irish girl was seen lying in one of those hastily collected cots. She had come to the doctor to tell him that they would not take her into the hospital because she had "got the consumption." Was it indeed so? she asked eagerly, hoping for a contradiction. And when he could not give her better news of herself, she began the sad cry, "What shall I do? I've no father nor mother nor home, and they won't let me into the hospital!" He turned all her sorrow into joy by telling her to go upstairs to the matron. This should be her home as long as she lived. Through the open door of her room this poor girl used to listen to the services in the chapel; she was too far gone to leave her bed, but the sweet singing and the "comfortable words" charmed her into a blessed dream that she was a little child in Jesus' arms, He loving her and promising to be always with her! "Is it true?" she asked the nurse when she woke, and she died with this happy new-born hope of rest with Jesus lighting up her face!

A French lad, a Roman Catholic, confessed the ignorant hatred he had always entertained for those of our Church, but forced by sickness and poverty into the Home, died there in love and charity with those around him, blessing those whom he had once despised.

Another prejudice, too, fell before the atmosphere of love that reigned in the Home.

A poor black woman was brought to Dr. Cullis; the rest had all been white. Now, in America there is generally a wide separation between the two races, even among the very poor and degraded, the white holding themselves very superior to the negro. So the doctor went to his white patients, three women lying ill in bed, to ask them if they objected to this new arrival being placed in their room. They immediately welcomed her, one saying, "I feel so thankful for so good a home, I would not keep any one out, black or white."

So the patients keep pouring in, filling the house to overflowing. It was necessary to have more room, and yet more. Money had never until now been actually wanting for the institution, though sometimes it had been slow in coming in. Strong, therefore, in faith that God would help, Dr. Cullis took first this house and then that (in addition to the original one), building a little, altering a little, till forty-four patients were housed. The work had now been going on for seven years, and much more had been accomplished than I have been able to tell you. Room was constantly needed for more patients. It is hard to turn from sheltering doorways those who are sick unto death. Dr. Cullis felt this most acutely. He thought seriously of the matter, and it ended in his resolving to buy land outside the town, in a pleasant, breezy situation, and there set up a roomier, more convenient Consumptive Home.

And in that place it now stands, on the Boston Highlands—a pleasant name to panting, breathless creatures. It is a cheerful roomy building, with this inscription in letters of gold over the porch, "Have faith in God."

The *seven* old houses in the town—for so many had the doctor acquired in the seven years of his work—were all merged in this new Home.

Come under the porch and glance around inside the building. A beautiful light reception-room, a reading-room, a comfortable sitting-room and dining-room, kitchens and laundries, and a large room below where a boiler sends out hot air over the whole house, making the atmosphere pleasant in the coldest weather! But chiefest among all the rooms of this beautiful new building is the one called the Home Chapel. It is in the middle of the house on the second story, with a gallery on a level with the third one, so that all the rooms on both floors open into it. Those who can walk have only to take a few steps and they reach the comfortable sofas in the chapel; those who are too weak to leave their beds may lie still, and through the opened doors join in the worship. Splendid stained glass windows cast their glow on the poor pale upturned faces, every one of these windows is a gift bestowed to make lovely this house of God, and to gladden the hearts of the suffering. Many a sick heart *is* made whole in this building, while the poor body that contains it is daily wasting.

There is another building within the grounds and close to the Home to which it is linked by very close ties. This is the Children's Home, for the care of the destitute little ones of those who die in the Consumptive Home. And besides this yet another Home is included in the cluster, a Home for Deaconesses, who assist in the tending and looking after this feeble community.

All these Homes are in the charge of Dr. Cullis, and the money to support them still comes unasked from great and small, rich and poor, babes and strong men.

It is a curious and a pleasant task to look back through the accounts and note the various givers, particularly the children with *their* little offerings: toys foregone, treasured gold and silver pieces yielded up, in favour of these poor sick.

In one great strait of early days the doctor had even to sell his gold watch; it was a trial, but it had to be done. You will be glad to hear that a friend of his, travelling abroad, and knowing nothing of this, returned with a present for him of a watch much more valuable. Sometimes the dollars come into the treasury in hundreds, sometimes it is only a few pence that arrive, but Dr. Cullis is equally calm. "The Lord will provide" is his motto. Where other people would have fretted, he prayed.

Two dollars came once in this fashion: a poor German woman with a husband sick in the Home pressed the money into the matron's hand, saying, "It is not for my husband, it is for the institution." The matron replied, "I cannot take it; you have yourself and three children to support by washing, and cannot afford to give away so much." The

poor woman insisted, and said, "Don't you know
if I give this to the Lord He will give me more
strength to work. You must take it for the Lord."
So the money was received.

Sometimes a patient that has been cured and
sent out of the Home comes back with an offering,
and this is always a cheering gift, however small
it may be. Once a sick man lying on his comfortable bed in the Home sent twelve dollars, his whole
substance, to the hospital-box. He told the nurse
"it ought to be given to the institution, for if he
got well he could earn more; if he should not
recover he would not need it."

There was another source, too, whence small
offerings frequently poured in; those who had lost
friends or relatives sent gifts of such things as had
belonged to the dead. It seemed a sacred manner
of disposing of them. Thus a widow contributed
the valuable gold chain that had belonged to her
husband; from another lady came the ring worn
by her dead mother, and the silver coin that
once hung round the neck of a baby brother long
since laid to rest! A box of money, the store-chest
of a child in heaven, containing gold and silver to
the value of forty-four shillings, was brought to Dr.
Cullis, as also a gold piece wrapped in paper and
treasured years ago by other dead hands.

Some people brought personal adornments, rings
and brooches, gold bracelets and buttons, and threw
them into the treasury of the hospital, to be sold
and turned into food and medicine for the sick.

Then again came thank-offerings, for a dear child restored to health, for a husband recovered from dangerous illness, and in one case came ten dollars —it seemed almost as a burst of gratitude—from parents blessed with a singularly happy and beautiful child. Once a gift of six dollars arrived very opportunely :—

Dr. Cullis had been much troubled in mind as to the propriety of admitting into his Children's Home other than the children of his patients. It seemed to him at first as if these latter alone would be a sufficient care ; but a poor widow dying in her own cottage pleaded so pitifully for the poor little children she was leaving destitute, that the doctor's intention was shaken. If he could only find out which plan was the wiser, which design, the larger or the smaller, the more according to God's will! He prayed for guidance, for a sign to know if God would have him undertake this extra expense. Half an hour later a note was brought to him enclosing six dollars *"for whatever object you last prayed for."* The doctor immediately, in his simple fashion, felt convinced that God would not have him refuse these orphan children, so the question was settled, and the Children's Home opened to all destitute babes that might apply.

And now you will like to hear something more of the poor creatures taken into the Consumptive Home. They know nothing of the straits that at times seem to distress the House ; the matron has orders to keep all that from them, and to deal out with liberal hand, as long as it is there, the food and comforts so necessary to these poor wasting bodies. As I said before, love and kindness are the rule of the House, and no stricter law exists. The candidate for admission need bring no good character to ensure the doors being held open to him; if he is sick and needs a physician, that is all that is required.

Of course, some bad characters do come, but it is hardly possible for them to do harm, hardly possible for them to escape learning some good. Here is an illustration—

A poor man died in the Home. A lady had given him ten dollars (two pounds of our money) shortly before he died, and he did not seem to have made any use of it. But as he might have given it to the relations who occasionally came to visit him, no inquiry was made regarding the money, and the subject was dropped. Some days afterwards an Irishman, sleeping in the same room which the poor man had occupied, called the nurse to his bedside and produced the sum. He had stolen it; "but," he added, "a man cannot keep that after reading the Bible."

A poor neglected child, deserted by his mother, and whose father had been lost at sea, spent the last three months of his life in the Home. He was just one of those Dr. Cullis loved to gather into his kind arms. He had suffered a great deal before he came, and was to suffer yet more, but he was carried as tenderly as possible down the path to the dark river, and beyond that stream his dying eyes had been taught to see his Saviour.

What recollection he could have had of the woman who had brought him into the world and then left him to struggle alone with its difficulties we cannot tell, but she must have cared for him once, for, leaning up against the pitying nurse in the last woeful night of suffering, he looked up in her face and said, "It seems as if you were my mother." And then the forsaken child asked to be kissed and held in her arms. Poor lad, he would need but little more such care! A few more broken words, a little childish talk of the children he would meet in heaven, a reiteration that he longed to go and was "Oh, happy, happy!" and all was at an end as far as earth is concerned.

One girl dying in the Home told a strange little tale. She was one of three orphan children. A maiden aunt kept them for a while, getting a place as nurse-girl for the eldest. This one, however, in lifting a heavy baby, over-strained herself, fell ill, and died. Then the brother got a place, and attended a night school. He wanted Katie to go too; but Katie knew nothing of books, or school, or God, or anything better than just slaving for bread, and told her brother she could not go. When she was twelve she obtained a place too, to take care of a baby. But she was so rude and saucy that the lady she served could hardly keep her, yet she bore with the rough little girl for two years, often talking to her and teaching her. Then Katie

K

wanted to better herself, and changed her place to
one where there were young ladies, who learned
history and arithmetic and other things.  This
made her wish to learn them too, and she often
pored over books when she ought to have been in
bed.  She wanted to be something better than the
ignorant little servant-girl that she was.  Then
came another change to new service, and a new
part of the country.  Katie was sixteen years old
and had never yet been in a church.  Something
made her go to one at this time.  But the preaching
seemed dull, she could not understand the Bible, and
she was not happy.  Then people who called themselves Christians, and thought themselves very
good, visited the house, and talked slander, speaking
unkindly of others, and Katie thought, " If these
are Christians, I do not care to be one."  So the
restless fit came on again, and the girl took to
working in a factory and afterwards in a shop.
And then she fell ill, and it pleased God to direct
a kind friend to the room where the wayward girl
lay.  The lady was one who had given herself up
to work among the poor and sick in New York;
no attic was too dark and dirty for her steps to
climb the stair, no cellar too damp for her to enter.
With her own hands she had got bricks to put under
the bed of one poor creature, and no service was
too degrading for her.  She had given herself body
and spirit to Christ and to His poor.  The little
servant girl's heart was touched at last; here was
the religion she was ignorantly longing for; some-

thing real, not mere talk. From that moment she, too, longed to serve Christ, and determined to be His servant. She kept her vow, but it pleased God that her time on earth should be short, and she died in the Consumptive Home not long after. The last words of this poor creature, who had never known father, mother, or earthly home, were those of sweet surprise, "Oh, I am going home!" she suddenly said, and immediately died.

The matron took down her story from her lips.

The Consumptive Home in its first eight years took in eight hundred and seventy-two sick people, and forty-five orphan children, and gifts were received to the value of a hundred thousand pounds of our money. All have been accepted as coming from God, since no means save prayer and the sight of His servant working in this good cause have been adopted.

Dr. Cullis is still alive, still at work, a physician for soul and body alike to the poor suffering ones to whom he has devoted his life. His remembrance of his sickly youth doubtless gives him a more real sympathy with his flock, although he now enjoys the strength and health denied to him in former days. It is not given to many to work, to dare, and to trust in the way that he has done, but to each God gives a special talent to use for Him, and I think we cannot but see that this Boston doctor has not hidden his away to rust in uselessness.

# NAVVIES IN INDIA.

## THE KOLS; INDIA.

In the year 1844 a German clergyman, called Pastor Gossner, sent out from Berlin four missionaries to Calcutta. They had no fixed place determined upon for their labours, no salary even promised them; they were simply sent out (as Christ's ministers to the heathen) to great wide India, to take up any work that God seemed to put in their way.

This might seem a rash enterprise to many; it is necessary to remember that these four men were brave and earnest followers of a brave and earnest master, for Pastor Gossner was well known in those days for his zeal in the establishment of Christian Missions—indeed, as a writer of his life says, " Wherever a people were living without God, there Gossner was waiting to step in."

So it was not, as we might term it, on a wild-goose chase that this devoted four left home and comfort for a distant land; they had a fixed purpose guiding them from the very day they landed in India, and that was to see who needed their services most, and then to give those services heartily, freely, wherever their lot happened to be cast.

To us living in England, India seems just India, nothing else, a hot sunny land, where the people are brown-hued, muslin-robed, turban-wearing; it takes reading and inquiry to find out that these brown people number many races, many sects, rich and poor, great and small, one as separate from another as our Queen and her Court are from the ragged street children and their wretched parents who cower in city alleys.

There is the proud Hindu with his caste and his ceremonies, as unapproachable as the Jew of old— the follower of the prophet Mahomet, with his mosque and his stated times of prayer; towards each of these two great classes Christian eyes have frequently turned, and Christian hearts have longed to influence them.

But our four sought beyond these well-known tribes, and their glance fell on a simple people whose home lay really among the far hills and highlands of the country, but who cropped up everywhere as labourers, road-menders, canal-diggers, the "navvies," in fact, of India. The four German evangelists were not deterred by the fact that these men, as a rule, were ugly in feature, with broad flat noses and thick lips; they looked further, and saw a promising earnestness in the way they digged the ground and carried heavy weights, while maintaining all the while a cheerful countenance. A merry, dirty set they seemed in truth, very much despised by the other dwellers in the land, and not the least depressed by their low condition. They did not even resent the name by which they were generally known, though it expressed the widest contempt—" Kols," or, as the meaning is, Pigs!

These Kols were the old early inhabitants of the country, and had only by degrees been driven back to the hills by new intruders, with whom probably they had fought every inch of ground. Now, however, they seem to have accepted their place in the land quietly, content to be regarded as servants or savages while working in the lowlands, and retiring a fifteen days' journey from Calcutta westward to reach their real mountain homes.

To that part of India, called Chota Nagpore, the new-comers, then, took their way—Pastors Batsch, Brandt, Schatz, and Janké—with the full intention of Christianizing this despised race, and making their home among them.

They had little pride, these poor Kols, and less religion, so there was not so much to undo as there would have been among other sects; but, oh! the amount there was to do!

The Kols had almost no religion. Bad spirits, indeed, they believed in and offered sacrifices to, but the idea of a loving, protecting Good Spirit was unknown to them. " Ghosts" they called the spirits that hid themselves, as they imagined, in trees and rivers, rocks and groves, coming out occasionally to worry or perplex one or another of the human dwellers around. Witches they

)ughly believed in and dreaded, and to kill
tch was thought to be a most praiseworthy

·inking, too, was universal amongst them.  Only
ιe particular did they seem even in their sins
ame more enlightened nations.  While in our
ts you may see the sad sight of a drunken
ιer, with a baby in her arms, staggering along,
› poor "Pigs" kept sober while they had
ɡ children—only when they were grown up did
 consider themselves entitled to indulge in
ɛing, the women as well as the men.  At
in festivals *every one* gets drunk; of a whole
ɟe not one is left in his senses.  Does this
ɕ you?  It well may; and yet how dare we
 one word of blame on these poor untaught
ɟes, while so many of our own people, warned,
'ated, dreached to, prayed over, fall into the
 deadly sin?
·inking always brings other evils in its train.
'ncing-place in every village was erected, where
hole nights young persons danced, belonging for
time *to the devil.*  No secret is made of this;
 by are two houses, one called the bachelors'
›, the other the girls' house, and parents may
:eep their children at home, but must let them
 one or other of these houses, there to belong
ιe devil, while their parents drink themselves
ɕtupefaction at home.
ιat a state of things for these four earnest
ɕtian men to witness!  What a sink of iniquity

to dream of cleansing! Many and many a time
must their hearts have fainted at the idea of the
work; but they never dreamed of giving it up.
They never despaired.

To settle down in the chief town of the district,
Ranchi by name, and to do what little work came
to their hand, was their simple mode of action. A
few orphan children were collected and taught in
the mission-house; or again, two of the missionaries
would go out, like the Apostles of old, into neighbouring villages, trying to get a hearing with the
rude people, but often driven out with stones.

The Kols, like ourselves, loved their sins, their
drinking bouts, their devil-feasts, and disliked the
idea of a purer faith. For five years the missionaries
toiled on, after a day of seemingly fruitless labour
trying to cheer themselves by the less ungrateful
work of planting their garden, building their houses,
and in all hope raising a Church for the good days
to come.

They had made up their minds in advance on
one matter—whatever teaching was to be given to
the Kols must be said or written in the Hindi
language, which the Kols naturally understood,
as it was that of their masters. But as yet they
had no one to teach save the few children they
had gathered round them. It was terribly dis-
heartening.

At length, however, a ray of hope broke on the
anxious teachers. In 1850 four men came to the
mission-house and asked to see the missionary.

see Jesus by faith, when they beheld the earnest
missionaries upon their knees.

Now, indeed, the poor teachers might venture to
rejoice, for the good seed, after lying so long in the
ground, had begun to peep forth in tiny shoots. By
twos and threes came other Kols to be taught and
cared for, and eleven years after the arrival of the
missionaries a goodly church, of which any Christian
people might be proud, was built and opened at
Ranchi.

It is grievous, however, to have to relate that the
Christian religion did not at first bring peace to
the poor Kol, rather persecution and distress. It
was not among themselves that this persecution
arose. As a rule, the heathen Kol looked quietly
upon his new-made Christian brother; if he did
not wish to follow his example, he did not annoy
the convert; they still worked side by side, and
lived in the same village, neighbours and friends.

But it was far otherwise with their masters, the
Hindu zemindars or farmers, and the Hindu
officials in the country; these greater folk were
strongly opposed to the Christian religion, and persecuted with cruel pertinacity the poor labourers
who embraced it.

We know, in olden time in our country, how
landowners and great farmers could make the lives
of their labourers and tenants uncomfortable if they
did not do as they wished with regard to elections
and such like matters; but few of us can realize
how these zemindars managed to plunder and

belonging to the district, and heart and soul tried
to root out the followers of Jesus from amongst
them.

The missionaries clung to their post to the last,
but when the officers of the station, bereft of their
men by mutiny, determined on saving their lives
by flight, they found they must fly too. On a July
morning they set out on their painful journey. In
the heat, over swollen streams, without an opportunity to save even the most valued papers, the
whole party was compelled to hasten off, and under
the protecting care of God they reached in safety
the railway station, where tickets to Calcutta were
procured through the kindness of a friendly stranger.
But they arrived without a single article of clothing
beside those they wore, and long ere their journey's
close their houses at their stations were in flames,
their church had been plundered, their faithful
converts seized or driven into the jungle, and the
Sepoys, after taking possession of the treasure, had
left the whole country to be ravaged by the treason-
able zemindars and the numerous prisoners whom
they had liberated from the gaols.

When at the earliest possible moment the missionaries returned to their old settlement, what a
scene of wreck and confusion presented itself!
Church, schools, and houses with broken windows
and wrenched doors, torn books strewn all over
the mission, the bells stolen from the church tower,
the organ broken, the congregation fled like themselves, and only timorously venturing back in

miserable starved groups. They had suffered too as sorely as their teachers; their huts were laid low, their growing crops seized or spoilt, and their chance of provision for the year destroyed. True, they had escaped with life, but their old, their babes, their sick had many of them perished in the jungle in their disastrous flight.

Some had not been able to escape in time from the Christian settlement, and these had another tale of woe to tell; they had been tortured, and mocked, and beaten. Taunting and scoffing, the cruel zemindars and others had asked them, "Where is your Father now? Where is Jesus? Where is He? Why does He not help you now?" And then, while smiting the poor creatures, they would say, "Now sing us something! Sing us one of your sweet hymns, and read us a little out of your books, and we will hear!" Verily these poor souls were early learning to take up their Master's cross. Yet not one denied his Lord, not one endeavoured to escape suffering by renouncing the Christian faith. Even the women and children were tortured, the head-man and Church elder of one village having his mother, wife, and daughters cruelly bound and beaten, while the savage tormentors put a price on his head, wishing, as they expressed it, to have the man's skin for a drum, and his young daughters for dancing-girls that they might be made to dance to its beating. One family owed their lives to a hole they had dug in the ground, into which they crept, covering the mouth with straw. Another man was beaten with an iron-bound stick, the zemindar asking between every blow, "Why have you become a Christian?" Such sad tales were poured into Mr. Batsch's ear as he endeavoured to collect his scattered flock.

Yet the main feeling was joy at seeing their old teacher again, and the salutation, "Jesus our help and protection," burst still confidently from all lips. Persecution had indeed only endeared the Christian Church to these poor converts. A hundred children were wonderfully restored to the mission, preserved in the jungle by a Church elder. So, by degrees, the remnants of the old flock gathered round the beloved pastor, and with them new converts, day by day more and more, for a feeling had begun to gain on the Kols that it was their *destiny* to become Christians.

No new-comer, however, was rashly admitted into the fold; a year of trial and waiting was insisted upon before any candidate could be baptized, and in this oversight the missionaries were greatly assisted by their system of elders and catechists. In any village where a few Christians lived an elder was appointed—a Kol, like themselves, but one better instructed, more advanced in Christian life and doctrine. Every Sunday the elder called his small congregation together in a house, or a little village church, as soon as it could be built, for prayer, Bible reading, and learning the Catechism. These men acted as fathers to the Christian communities, settling disputes, and keeping order in

see, in a great measure did what our godfathers and godmothers were intended to do.

After baptism the converts were brought to dwell on the Holy Communion as the next thing to be desired, and inasmuch as this could, at first for lack of clergy, only be administered in the head station of Ranchi, a building had to be run up called a rest-house, in which communicants could dwell at the time of the monthly Communion. Here mats and firewood were supplied to them, but they must find their own food. Such a place is very necessary when you think how far many of the people had to come, some sixty, some eighty, some even a hundred miles. One family living eighty miles distant never failed to attend the monthly Communion, which is always fixed for the Sunday next after the full moon. The rest-house was also needed at harvest homes and such like festivals.

A Sunday service among these poor Kols is interesting to witness. The church, with its good proportions and decent fittings, its organ and well-regulated music, has a very home-like aspect. Faces and figures, it is true, would be strange to us, and so would be the elders walking up and down the church to keep order and collect the alms of copper money in little baskets. When the sermon begins one or another stands up awhile. We should wonder what for, and then we should be told that it is the Kol way of keeping off sleepiness. When sufficiently roused the person sits down again and listens to the close. Sometimes an elder has to ask

in their wonted places and lead the prayers and praises of the flock.

Still, it was a great day when Bishop Milman arrived at Ranchi to receive, by confirmation, all these new members of the visible Church. Men and women, youths and maidens, knelt that day at the altar, following each other in continuous streams to the number of six hundred, every face wearing a devout yet joyous expression. These were they who had already been ranked as communicants. The next day, Sunday, came the Ordination Service, followed by the administration of the Holy Sacrament to six hundred and fifty worshippers. Then on the Monday forty-one candidates were admitted to baptism—babes in their mothers' arms, old men and women hardly able to totter to the font—all ages, whole families!

There was a general feeling of peace and joy among the poor Kols and their German pastors at the conclusion that they were now linked to a proteeting branch of Christ's Church on earth, whose bishops and overseers would be their loving guardians, whose festivals and holy days would spirit them on to a higher Christian life.

In this promising state we may now leave them with only a word or two more. Schools and churches are multiplying in the district. One headman of a village, finding the old little chapel of the place too small for the worshippers, with the assistance of his neighbours has built a neat brick church and enclosed a piece of land for a burial-ground,

. they call "The Lord's Garden." Another
nan, a heathen, established a school in his
e, which sixty children attended. The mis-
y, passing that way on one of his tours, was
ited to take the school under his supervision,
r sign how much the Christian profession is
ted even by the heathen. Still, though united
Church, the Kols are not English, and never
e. A glance at one of their harvest festivals
be enough to show this. The rice harvest
st been gathered in. A procession of brown-
open-mouthed children march solemnly up
urch, singing a hymn of praise, followed by
men bearing on their heads baskets of newly
e, which one by one they pour out before the
These are offerings for the poor and the
schools. At the festival held February 5,
the amount poured out amounted to ten
dweight, 1120 pounds of rice—not a bad
ution to the store-cupboard of the poor.
w clergyman and his wife have of late years
the Ranchi Mission. From a letter of Mrs.
y's we gather that a beautiful new church
en built at the head station; the Kols like
ouse of God to be well built and carefully
ed. She describes a Christmas-tide at
much enjoyed by little Kols as well as big
the Christmas tree as delightful to Indian
to English ones. English ladies had sent
iple presents for little Kol scholars, and the
ags and needle-cases, combs and hair-ties

among the gifts give one a good idea of the civilization spreading among a class who, not so long since,
looked on beads and a gay rag as their sole necessary apparel.   The little creatures were eagerly
examining their gifts when Mrs. Whelley asked,
"Well, have you nothing to say to the kind ladies
in England who made so many of these presents
for you?"   At which with one accord the small
voices piped forth, "We wish to thank them *very*
much."   As Mrs. Whelley says, "If our friends at
home could have enjoyed the sight, and joined in
our Christmas service, it would have filled their
hearts with thankfulness to see so many hundred
people rescued from heathenism, and praising God
for the birth of a Saviour."

I am glad to tell you that the latest accounts of
this simple people speak of the rapid spread of the
faith among them, large numbers of heathen
coming each year for baptism.

There are (1880) ten missionaries engaged in the
work, and under them is a large staff of native
helpers—priests, deacons, schoolmasters, readers, and
so forth.

and then acted upon it, and I am going to tell you something of her doings.

A Miss Robinson she was and is, from childhood fond of soldiering, sometimes with toy guns and sometimes with real ones, to the terror of nurse and quieter playfellows.

One of those healthy, noisy little girls do you picture her, with rosy cheeks and flying hair, " every bit as bad as the boys," as the mothers say in a voice they mean to be stern, but which really melts into loving pride ?

If Miss Robinson ever was like this, the rosy cheeks were soon faded, the active limbs soon quieted by sickness, and the days of childhood followed by weary hours on bed and sofa.

An invalid for life she was to be, the doctors said, a person to be pitied, one who could practise patience and submission to God's will, but not one to work in His harvest-field.

Doctors are for the most part kind and clever, but they cannot always tell what God will do for their sick, and they must have been surprised at what Miss Robinson attempted directly she felt a little strength given to her.

Though quiet and suffering and an invalid, she still loved soldiers, and while lying on her couch had often wondered what she could do to make their lives better and happier.

Her first beginning of real work amongst them took place at Brighton in 1865, with a cavalry regiment. She engaged a room outside the barracks,

a man wants to keep straight in the army, he meets with no encouragement. Most are listening as I say a little about the way to keep straight, and what God looks for in a soldier, and what His power can do. A man on the corner cot says he does not care about my papers. I may leave him one if I like. I say I would rather leave him something he does care about; and on finding that he writes home sometimes, I give him an illuminated text card to enclose, which pleases him very much. A man on the next cot says this reminds him of his Sunday school. I sit down by him while he tells his tale: mother dead, other friends lost through his own bad conduct—very unhappy—deserves it all—no use trying to be different—soldiers can't be religious, and so on. I have some earnest talk with him, and shake hands before passing on. The next man, preparing in haste for kit drill, calls out to me to put a tract *there,* and he will read it when he comes in; the bugle sounds, and he hurries out. Going into the next room, I encounter four men running out dressed for kit drill, so I leave tracts on their cots, and offer one to a man smoking in the corner; he nods rather contemptuously, but does not speak. Another tells me he has only seven months more to serve, and intends to think more about such things then. I speak faithfully to him, and he takes it well. Two others asleep; another pipe-claying. I offer him a small 'Pilgrim's Progress;' he shouts out, 'Why, if this isn't the book which my mother used to read to me!' and in answer to

"A most unpleasant thing in visiting the rooms of this regiment is the number of ill-tempered dogs they keep. Almost every day I had one or two fly at me; only it makes the men more civil afterwards and more disposed to listen. In one room I was giving papers round, when one man took his to a group sitting round the fire, and another snatched it from him and lit his pipe with it—an old soldier, who ought to have shown better manners, but he did not think I saw it, as I was talking to the men pipe-claying their belts at the other end of the room. Before leaving, I went up behind this man, and put my hand on his shoulder, while I said to all, 'Friend, I ask fair play for these papers. Read them first, if you use them for pipe-lights afterwards.' They all burst out laughing to see him so caught, and he did look so foolish."

After a little rebuke of this sort, however, Miss Robinson always tried to show some special kindness to the subject of it, and generally succeeded in making the offender into a friend. The sick are, of course, this kind lady's particular care—rough fellows, perhaps, who have nothing to think of as they lie on their weary beds but past sins and lost innocence. Of one poor young fellow, sick almost unto death with heart disease, she says: "I read with him every day, and I believe he was really converted, not so much from anything I said as from the old Sunday school teaching coming back to his mind. He had been a wild lad, and no doubt his teacher thought all was thrown away on

resist the desire to show Miss Robinson the usual
courtesy, and with a hasty bound he sprang out of
bed and held open the door. You may fancy how
the lady hurried out, fearful of giving the poor
soldier his death of cold!

As I told you before, Miss Robinson's great desire
was to get hold of what you would call the bad
men of a regiment. Like her Master, she had not
come to call the righteous, but sinners to repentance.
So when a pitiful message came from an old widow
woman in the country, asking her to find her son
for her, of whom she had not heard for three years,
she was ready in a moment for the search. He
had been a good lad, a kind son, yes, and a good
soldier too, for some years of his life; but the devil,
who never rejoices so much as when he can pull
down one of your sober religious men, had got hold
of him, and the first fruits of his influence was that
the lad left off writing to his mother, or sending her
money as he used to do, took to drinking, swearing,
and fighting, and at last got to be considered one of
the black sheep of the regiment. No use hunting
up such a man surely, he could be no comfort to his
poor mother. But Miss Robinson knew better;
mothers love their sons, be they sunk ever so deep
in sin, and she cared for the soldier, however bad he
might be. So she got a good fellow to go with her
to the barracks in Aldershot, and fetch the widow's
son out to her—*J. C.* she calls him. He came, a
wretched, miserable creature, his face swollen with
drink and blackened with fighting. A few kind

Then she spoke and asked him which life was best—that old happy time of serving God and doing his earthly work well, or this worse than slavery to sin and Satan? And she went on to assure him that the old place in his heavenly Father's heart was still open to him, that the love of God can never be tired out even by such sin as his.

Poor fellow! sobs came at this point, and broken questions of "Isn't it too late, too late? You don't know how bad I am." The hard heart was melting, and the stubborn knees fell once more into the attitude of prayer. Others prayed with him, and when they rose up a cavalry soldier came to him and said, "I was twelve years a drunkard after being religiously brought up, and Christ has saved me; trust Him, comrade."

This was comforting to the poor lad. He knew how deep is the sin of such as have seen the light and yet turned their eyes from it and preferred darkness, and this it was which made him fear that he had gone too far to be forgiven, so to find another in like case was hopeful.

Not many more words were said that day. One cannot talk much if one feels much, but J. C. went back to his barrack-room sure that a new day had dawned for him. God had called him once more; he had said once again, "Follow Me." Could the lad refuse? No.

Miss Robinson was not able to visit him again, but we hear that she had nice letters from him telling of a firm desire to forsake his evil ways and

English, and at last it came to be quite fashionable, if one may use such a word, for the Bibles to be brought out and read on Sundays without fear of annoyance from mockers. Miss Robinson was already recognized as a friend, and the worst characters dared to creep into the lecture-room, sure that love and not blame would be their share.

After a while Miss Robinson began to work also among the militia. This is by far rougher work for a lady than if she kept to the "regulars," who at least have proper rooms to receive her in, besides being under constant discipline.

But the soldier *is* a soldier, whether he wears a red coat for a month or a year, and Miss Robinson only felt she must work the harder for him if the time given to do it in was short.

We hear of her making her way among the Wiltshire Militia at Devizes. "The men, 700 strong, were billeted in twenty-eight public-houses, or any wretched outhouse into which the publican's conscience would allow him to thrust them, thirty-six messing in an old cow-house with an earthen floor and a great puddle in the doorway! They thought it wonderful any lady should come into such a place for *them*. After Miss Robinson's visit the sergeant would get a brush and brush her clean from the sawdust, potato peel, and cobwebs." Another billet was a loft over a donkey-stable, and very often the reading was disturbed by a loud hee-haw from the donkey below! But the worst billet of all was the Bear, where forty-three men

Since the quarters of this regiment were so bad, it was necessary to make the men comfortable somewhere else; so two schoolrooms were used as an institute for the men, where they were supplied with books, newspapers, periodicals, stationery, and coffee; while lectures, temperance meetings, readings, music, and singing classes went on every evening, with religious meetings on Sunday.

It was a pity that the last sight of these poor fellows should not have been more comfortable; but you all know what sort of a day it is on which a militia regiment is disbanded. A sad number of drunken men in the streets, a sadder number still of more sinful creatures, men and women, keeping sober to wile the money out of the pockets of the poor senseless fools, noise, confusion, and fighting! No place for a lady is such a scene, you would think. But Miss Robinson *was* there, passing by with a sigh the poor wretches lying drunk by the roadside, to earnestly entreat the more sensible to come out of the public-houses and go home quietly with the anxious mothers and wives who had come to look after them. A great many did obey her wishes, carrying the money they had earned carefully home in their pockets to buy comforts for the cottage or pleasures for the little ones, instead of throwing it all into that horrible clinking till at the public-house, and getting no good for it, only aching heads and smarting consciences. One of the recruits told a soldier of another regiment, with a certain pride, " That's Miss Robinson, the lady that

send some of it, at least, to the wife at home, but
the camp post-office will not give money-orders,
and so he puts it in his pocket, and from that unsafe
receptacle it often disappears before long.

The Autumn Manœuvres are not half the pleasant
"out" he thought they would be! In many cases
he ends by getting reckless, throws away his money,
forgets wife and babies, and joins the drinking,
shouting set around him! Poor fellow, it is more
his misfortune than his fault this time! We feel a
little sorry for him: Miss Robinson felt very sorry,
and determined to make an effort to help him.

She chose the Autumn Manœuvres at Dartmoor
for a beginning.

Dartmoor is a lovely heathery spot in Devonshire, where painters delight to linger and tourists
are enchanted. But it has a soil easily turned by
a shower of rain into thick black mud, and then
the mists creep up like a wet blanket, and there
is chill and wretchedness above, below, around.

This is very often the case in autumn, and so
it chanced to be at the particular time that Miss
Robinson decided to follow the fortunes of the camp
stationed there.

Dartmoor being deep in the country, far from
shops or stores of any sort, it was necessary for
this busy lady to make her own arrangements.

This was her plan: to attach a refreshment
and a recreation tent to one of the brigades, and to
furnish in them tea, coffee, eatables, newspapers,
books, games, and material and opportunity for

hastily rigged up to cover the most valuable of the stores; the poor men in charge, cold and wet, crept under the counters and slept there the first night. Miss Robinson gave her van up to the manager and his wife, and went back to Plymouth to inquire about the lost treasures, and such soldiers as came to the spot had to be content with bread soaked into a poultice, and coffee into which had found its way a great deal of fresh rain-water. Was ever anything more provoking? But at last the large tents came, and the work was really set on foot. At four o'clock in the morning the feeding tent was open, and the first customers for Miss Robinson's tea and coffee were the bakers to the force, who had been up all night making bread. They wanted a cup of hot coffee very badly. After that came the butchers, just as keen for their cup, and by-and-by there was a general rush on the supply. Meantime the waggon and horses went out with more coffee-cans to distant regiments, and a branch establishment a quarter of a mile distant was equally busy with the cavalry and artillery. Towards the middle of the day there was a lull, and only odd things were wanted from the tent, which was a sort of shop in that out-of-the-way place. Such were blacking, soap, hair-oil, the loan of a book, the sight of a time-table, pledge cards, an envelope and a bit of letter paper. Sometimes a soldier wanted a button sewn on, or he had hurt his hand and it wanted tying up, or he would like to send some money to his wife if he could get a

Of course, the fittings of the tent were not very grand; some rather rickety boards laid on two forms represented the reading-desk and pulpit, but the words spoken were just as well received as if they proceeded from the most beautifully carved erection. There was a real harmonium, however, one Sunday, and a real choir leading the hymns, for a village clergyman near kindly provided both these extras.

The soldiers enjoyed these simple evenings of prayer and praise, and did not at all mind when every now and then an overloaded form gave way and down they all dropped into the black mud or the soaked straw; they had come to rough it in all ways. They were very grateful to Miss Robinson for all her kind thoughts for their welfare, and even the commanding officers declared there was less crime and drunkenness in the camp that year than any other year. She had indeed given unwearied care and supervision to the whole matter, though she had not supplied the funds; those came from the National Temperance League. And also she had given bodily aches and pains to the same cause. For do you know to sleep in a yellow van on a sort of shelf is not the most comfortable matter in the world, the gipsies would tell you that; but a delicate lady used to a soft bed at home must feel the change much more. It is not pleasant, either, to sit up suddenly in bed and give your head a good knock against the roof of the van, nor to feel great chilly drops of real rain

barracks, he wants a little change, a little society, and there is none to be had in Portsmouth save such as is to be found in beer-shops and such like low places. In a very few weeks a regiment will have squandered all the money saved in India or other foreign parts, thrown it away as utterly as if they had dropped it over the side of the ship on the voyage home. And they will have not merely lost the money either, but have bought with it all kinds of wicked thoughts, evil habits, fatal tendencies.

What could be done to cure this terrible state of affairs? Miss Robinson was greatly distressed about her poor soldiers in Portsmouth. She thought and thought till the idea arose of getting up a building in the town to be known as " The Soldier's Home," and to be opened to all soldiers and sailors in need of a temporary refuge.

In two years she had collected the large sum of £13,000 necessary for the undertaking, bought the two or three houses in the High Street needed for the purpose, furnished them, appointed a manager, and, in fact, set going the "Portsmouth Soldier's Institute."

Now walk in and look. around. You will be quite welcome; the house is meant for soldiers' wives and daughters as well as for the men themselves, and there is every provision made for the comfort of all parties.

On the ground floor are two large rooms where soldiers can bring their friends or meet them; and who can tell the happy meetings as well as sorrowful partings that take place here!

moderate cost for as long as he likes, besides being
able to bring his wife or his mother there too. On
the arrival and departure of the great troop-ships
the house is generally full of soldiers' families, many
of them very poor indeed. One young woman
travelled all the way from Wales, with her baby
of five days old, to meet her husband there, and to
see a little of him before he sailed away again to
foreign parts. She did see him, and after the
good-bye Miss Robinson and her kind helpers
nursed the poor woman back to health and strength
before they would let her go. Another young
mother was not so fortunate; she had come also to
the Home with a tiny baby on the same errand;
but when the father sailed away he left her very
ill, and after fourteen days of pain and delirium
she died in the house, leaving her child, who would
have been quite friendless but for Miss Robinson.
She nursed it awhile, and then found out its old
grandparents in a distant corner of Ireland, who
were willing to receive and bring up the little
creature, but who had neither money nor strength
to go and fetch it themselves. To them she sent the
child, and they took it gladly. Their poor dead
daughter had married against their wishes.

Many a sorrowful heart seeks shelter in this
Institute, destitute widows and orphans and deserted
wives among the number, and each is, if possible,
relieved and comforted. One day a gentleman's
little son, who had run away from home with the
intention of going to sea, was brought there and

hospitable Home turns out no destitute soldier's wife nor babe.

Troop-ships going out are also visited by the ladies from the Home, and clothes are often provided for the poor women and children on board, besides good books, writing materials, and other little matters for the men.

It is pleasant to think of our soldiers leaving their native shores with a kind good-bye sounding in their ears, and some trifle or book or picture in their hands to make them remember that the name of Christ is no empty name, but that for His sake His followers have sought out and befriended their red-coated brethren.

Foreign ships visiting Portsmouth receive invitations to use the Institute. You remember the name of the *Grosser Kürfurst* in the papers, as associated with a sad collision in the Channel. The men of this vessel and of a sister ship, while in Portsmouth, were made welcome at the Home. Sunday services in German were held for them, and other entertainments given to them, so that relations in Germany wrote afterwards pleased letters of thanks to Miss Robinson.

On Sundays and Thursdays the Institute is full of life and stir, for the sailor lads from her Majesty's Training Ships are delighted to spend their half-holidays in the place. Where can they get such jolly hot coffee, such buns and cake as here?

Bowls and skittles on a week-day (the Institute has a capital bowling-green and skittle-alley) suit

momentary importance and ready to fall a victim to the old enemy.

No, her work goes further; she provides something instead of the drink, a shelter in place of the public-house. And when the man feels need not only of comfort and rest, but also of "something warm" too, she opens her well-lighted, well-warmed rooms, has her steaming coffee-cups ready, and there is his new public-house full of company and full of amusement—for music is sounding here, and jokes are cracking there, and only the sin and the shame are absent.

If there were but more of such places in all the big towns of England, ay, and the small ones too, how the mothers and the wives would rejoice, and the men likewise, when they came to realize the comfort of temperance, the misery of drink!

Miss Robinson lives in her great club—public-house—Soldier's Home—Institute, whatever you like to call it, and watches over its welfare day by day, hour by hour; it is the work of her life, and she does it well. But one thing hampers her, and that is the want of money to carry on all the different branches.

You cannot take in a poor soldier's wife and half a dozen children and keep them for days on nothing, and yet many such have to be kept occasionally when a ship comes home from India with soldiers and their families: neither can you supply books and clothes and little comforts to those about to sail away, for nothing. Neither can you build, and

# THE HOUSE OF BONDAGE.

## EGYPT.

"THE land of Egypt!" How easily the words fall from our lips! What do we know about the land, however? Let us pause a moment and think what recollections the words call up.

Did you ever stand in your childish days in a circle with other little learners, hands tightly clasped behind you, eyes downcast to keep thought from wandering, and lips carefully repeating words like these: "I am the Lord thy God, who brought thee out of the land of Egypt, out of the house of bondage"?

Words in the Catechism and in the Bible too. Calling up visions of poor prisoned, God-forgetting Israel, under the hard rule of Pharaoh and his officers, toiling day by day to make their tale of bricks without the necessary straw.

And then, before those exiles could leave that house of bondage, came the dreadful plagues all children know by heart. So stirring is the story in Holy Writ, beginning with the rivers turned into blood, and ending with the woeful death of the first-born. Even as a little child you must have

on that awful night when the destroying
swept through the land and carried away
him the breath of the king's first-born, as
is that of the beggar, unless he found the
blood on the lintel.

do we not see in our mind's eye yet another
and a very different one, regarding this land?

again, and a little company hurrying along
ndy track, not even tarrying beside the waving
trees or the precious wells; Joseph taking
oung Child and His mother by night and
ing into Egypt for safety from cruel Herod.

e is the story of the land of Egypt of our
ood. It was all we knew of it, and perhaps
s enough for our childish thoughts to
on.

now that we are grown men and women, is
nge that we should want to know more?—
ask of travellers and learned men, "Tell us,
hat have crossed the great sea and visited
lands, how fares the country whose stones
t of Moses and Joseph once pressed, on whose
plains the Babe Jesus learned to walk?"

y an Englishman and Englishwoman visit
nowadays, some for health, because its air
and life-giving, and it has scarcely any
cold; some for learning's sake, because there
ghty columns and temples of ancient days,
over in strange letters, full of instruction
h as can read them; some for curiosity,
there always are restless ones in the world;

and some for God's glory, to do His work, in the land out of which He called His Son. I shall presently tell you somewhat of the doings of one of these last in the country of the Pharaohs; but before I begin I should like to give you some idea of the land as it is now, its people and its daily life.

Surrounded by desert, Egypt itself would be nothing but a sandy waste too, if it were not for the river Nile, which, as you may have heard, overflows its banks every year, leaving behind it on the thirsty land a coating of mud, which produces the richest crops in the world. Sometimes it is a few feet on either side of the great river which shows these fair and quickly grown crops; sometimes it is a few miles, but beyond is always desert, with its burning profitless sands, its hot winds, and its long train of camels, taking the traveller hither or thither, but never tarrying longer than can be helped in the wilderness.

Neither will we linger there; come rather into the streets of some city, let it be Cairo, perhaps, and let us see what are now the customs of the land of Egypt.

As we walk along we overtake a whole Egyptian family: the husband, a big strong fellow, riding a donkey, the wife walking by his side, and carrying on her head a load that would make an English porter stagger, while the children, fat little comfortable-looking things, as soon as they espy you, begin deafening cries of " Backsheesh! backsheesh!" which

:rs to our "Give me a halfpenny!" and in
demand the elders are not a bit ashamed to
Not that these people are very poor, or at all
·y, but begging is so fashionable in Egypt that
ne of the greatest worries of a traveller. Other
es there are too, such as heat, mosquitoes,
as of flies; but these are of God's sending, and
)e borne more easily, even if in reality more
ıl. Perhaps the first thing that would strike
ımong the Egyptians is the fact that every
ın's face is covered with a veil, which hides
thing but her eyes; it is thought bold in the
ne to show the features as we do; even the
ittle girls of eight or nine snatch up a bit of
head-gear, and draw it over their faces when a
lraws nigh; by-and-by they will be properly
, but even now they like to pretend they are
ı up. And this custom prevails among the
as well as the rich, only I think the rich
n are worse off than the poor ones, for they
ghtly shut up in their houses, and only allowed
out at certain times, very closely veiled, and
riding on donkeys or more closely concealed
riages. They see nothing of the world, know
ıg of what goes on there; they can neither
ıor write, and spend their time in dressing,
ıg, and cither eating or preparing sweetmeats.
Egyptian ladies, they are badly off! After
:iled women, your eyes get puzzled between
slaves, Arab chiefs, water-carriers, blind
·s, priests, running footmen waving wands to

prevent their carriages running over people, donkeys and their drivers, and street sellers.

Perhaps the noisiest of all these are the last, and yet their cries are so curious that you must pause and listen—

" For a nail, O sweetmeat ! " screams one ; people say this man is a bit of a thief, and encourages children and servants to steal such things as nails or bits of iron out of their houses, which he exchanges for this treacle-sweet.

Then, " O comfort for the troubled, O pips ! " is the announcement of the toasted pips of a sort of melon, which must be a great favourite with the people to be so favourably spoken of.

A seller of sweet flowers shrieks out, " Odours of paradise ! "

A kind of cotton cloth, the machinery of which is put in motion by a bull, is cried as " The work of the bull, O maidens ! "  But sweetest of all the cries in the streets of Cairo is that of the water-carrier, " O ye thirsty, water ! " is one of his announcements, and for something like half a farthing, he will fill the brass cup he carries with him and present it to the parched buyer ; or he declares his business in another way, " The Gift of God ! " is now his cry. And at once the words of Jesus to the Samaritan woman at the well come to mind, " If thou knewest the *gift of God*, and Who it is that saith to thee, Give me to drink ; thou wouldest have asked of Him, and He would have given thee living water."

But enough of street cries, though I have not told you the half of them.

ı one important matter this country differs very
tly from our Northern lands, and that is the
tion of women.

he poor man's wife is his slave, the rich man's
prisoner, that is all the difference. Their very
;ion, that of Mohammedanism, supports this
ə of things, for women are hardly supposed to
ess souls. They are taught nothing; to propose
ı a thing would be to meet a contemptuous
ə or to rouse a mocking laugh. " What, instruct
women! they are as the beasts," said a son of
mother, one day, not meaning any special
ıt, simply giving expression to a belief of the
ɔle.

ı English lady spending a winter in Egypt was
ɔk with deep pity on hearing such a remark,
being one of that sort who strive to serve God
rever they find themselves, she determined, if
ible, to do something towards bettering the
ition of the Egyptian women.

ɔ begin with the little girls seemed the easiest
, and so she chose a house in Cairo, in a poor
ict, and determined to set up a sort of ragged
ɔl there. Her name was Miss Whately, and
her own account of her doings I shall choose
;omewhat to tell you.

ɩere were people of two religions living around
-the Moslems or followers of Mahomet, and
ɔopts, who are the remnants of the old Egyptian
stians, only greatly fallen away from the true
; the children of both sects Miss Whately was

anxious to teach and befriend, since both were
equally ignorant. Every one discouraged the willing
teacher. "You will have no pupils," they said;
"the men here do not wish their women taught
anything, and the women do not care to learn."

But Miss Whateley prepared a little schoolroom,
and nailed up pictures and texts as like as possible
to an infant school at home, and laid in a stock of
sewing materials, and then she was ready. Neither
tables nor chairs are needed in Egypt, since the
people prefer to sit on the ground.

Still the children did not come, and she had
to go out to fetch them, accompanied by a little
Syrian girl of thirteen, who was her only helper.
There were plenty of little girls in the streets, but
few willing to accept the English lady's invitation
to come to school; but presently, to her great joy,
she collected nine little Moslems. But it was with
great difficulty, for, as she says herself, " the project
of setting up a school for little girls quite made the
people laugh. It was as if in England some benevolent, but not too wise, lady should set on foet a
school for cats ! "

And something like the noise of cats were the
sounds produced by the first attempt at hymn-singing on the part of these little girls; that, and a
verse of Scripture, and the first few letters of their
difficult alphabet, was all that could be attempted
the first day.

The little Moslems did not care much for the
lessons, but the sewing was delightful. They threw

and pretty and nice, and, "*She* want *yours*, indeed,"
said this young champion, pointing rather scornfully
to the small Egyptians round, and flourishing her
hand in the air.

At this Miss Whately felt consoled, and told the
old woman that what she wanted the little girls for
was to teach them good things; but it was hard to
make her understand that a *fellow-creature* could
so love them and care for them, since one of their
notions is that God does not love women.

One of Miss Whately's troubles arose from the
early marriages which are the fashion of the country.
A girl of twelve or thirteen, just as she is getting
on nicely, will be missing from her place in school,
and a small sister will say that she is married. The
little wife has nothing to do with choosing the
husband, the parents do that, and whether she
wishes it or no she must accept their arrangement.

Sometimes the brothers of the little girls would
come softly to the school door and peep in, looking
as if they would like to learn too; but infant schools
in Egypt could not tolerate this, boys and girls
must be kept strictly apart. So, beyond the peep,
nothing more could be done by the wistful little
lads; a pity, since though *they* have native schools,
in knowledge of God and good things they are
nearly as ignorant as the girls. And English
people ought to teach them some good, since from
the English they readily pick up bad habits. One
little boy was swearing terribly one day in the
streets as he guided the donkey on which sat Miss

Whately. The broken words could not be mistaken, so the lady reproved him gently, and told him such language displeased God.

"That *Englis!*" replied the boy with a grin; he had thought himself very clever, no doubt, having picked up so much of a strange tongue.

It was a great triumph to Miss Whately when once she heard a boy of ten years old exclaim, in a piteous voice, as he leant against the doorway of her school, "I wish I were a girl." To wish to be that despised soulless creature showed he must earnestly have desired the care and instruction he saw them receive, and the English lady could not but console the poor lad and tell him some day she hoped there might be such schools for him too.

It was uphill work though, even keeping school for the girls; the mothers made many complaints. One Moslem sent word her child should not come to school if they kept pictures on the wall to worship; pictures of Adam and Eve, Cain and Abel, and of our Saviour they were, such as we have in every schoolroom in England, and very harmless we should think them, but Copts do really worship pictures, so the Moslems' terrors were half real. Then a little Copt girl would be seen really kissing and worshipping a picture. Once it was Cain, the wretched murderer, she was ignorantly kneeling before; so the pictures had to go. Then the marching, and clapping, and singing that we have at home, gave offence; both sorts of mothers sent word if school was to be nothing but play, they

should keep their children at home; in fact, they
wanted all sewing taught, to make their children
of use to them.  They had no sense to care for
better things.  How patient a teacher must be in
such a land!  But a work done for Christ's sake,
as was the teaching in this school, was not likely
to be given up for a few discouragements.

All work and no play would not please little
Egyptian children any more than English, so we
hear of a school treat given at this time, when the
little girls were taken to a lovely garden, and encouraged to play about, feasting afterwards out of
doors on cakes and coffee, whilst the Syrian girl-
teacher sat by and smoked a pipe.

Customs vary, you see, in different countries; the
English mothers would probably send in a complaint
if the governess who taught their children were
seen smoking, but in Egypt things are very different.
After the feeding the children sang hymns, and
then it was easy to tell them of another better land,
fairer even than this bright garden, where flowers
do not fade, and roses have no thorns.  "Take me
there—take me," said one and another of the little
ones, only half understanding, and yet pleased to be
told of the white robes, and the golden harps, and
the pleasant streets of the city of God.

This school treat was not like an English one in
one respect.  It began at six o'clock in the morning,
and ended at ten, when the heat became so great
every one had to hasten indoors.

There is very little cold weather in Egypt, but a

great deal of hot sun and dust, and sometimes troublesome winds. It is really dangerous when a strong wind rises in the desert, and all the hot sand is driven like smoke in the faces of travellers. The very camels are obliged to lie down and hide their heads, or they might be suffocated, and human creatures run a still greater risk. In Cairo, where there is no desert, it is yet so unpleasant that all who can, stay indoors during the hot winds.

As time went on, a ragged boys' class—the desire of Miss Whately's heart—was established, and after a while as many as a hundred and sixty boys attended a regular school, some coming on donkeys from a distance. In this school very good instruction was given in other matters than Bible learning, though that still kept the first place. Mere reading and writing would not now bring scholars, so languages, accounts, geography, history, and such things were taught, and the people saw the advantage, and sent their boys willingly.

The girls still required looking up frequently. It takes a long time to change the ideas of a country, and besides, in Egypt as in England, womenkind, large and small, are more wanted at home than the boys. And then the early marriages! I must tell you some more about them. Some mother of a grown-up son gets tired of carrying water and making bread, and doing her daily work, and so she encourages her son to look for a wife who shall help in these things; a girl of twelve or thirteen will do, and when she is brought home to her husband's house, in some pomp, under a sort of canopy, she is nothing but a little drudge or slave to the household, beaten by her mother-in-law if she does not exactly please her, strictly veiled, and hardly allowed to go out by herself. Sometimes she is even quite locked up for six months after marriage. For the least offence the husband beats his girl-wife, so unless he and the mother-in-law are really kind people, the little Egyptian bride has a poor time of it.

The women love their babies, it is true, but they let them grow up dirty and diseased, and they are in perpetual terror of "the evil eye," for no one dare praise a child, or an animal, or any possession of an Egyptian family, without saying afterwards, "The Lord keep it," or "The Lord preserve it to you." Good words these, but held in superstitious value by the ignorant people as averting the evil eye.

Some one asked Miss Whately why she did not take orphan children to educate, and so ensure keeping a few of these poor little things with her till a later age. The answer brings out one of the good points in the Egyptian character. "There are no orphans nor friendless children here; a desolate child is always adopted by some one who has no children. If a baby dies another is taken in its place, and made in every way a child of the house, be the parents rich or poor. If you asked an Egyptian on this point, 'Are you not afraid to undertake a charge that God did not lay on you?' he would answer, 'Oh, but He *did* lay it on me;

Perhaps it is this love of ease, of quiet, that makes them difficult of approach in matters of religion: firstly, they always object to change of any sort; and secondly, a religion which says, "Strive" to do anything, does not naturally find favour with them.

Curiosity makes them in the beginning lend a willing ear to a new doctrine, but afterwards it is difficult to keep up the interest. One old woman would say, "Good, good," as she seemed to listen to Miss Whately's readings, and all the while have her heart in her goats, which were galloping at will about the place, even to the upsetting of reader and book. At last she observed very coolly, "Let Aeeda listen to-day," meaning her daughter-in-law; she was quite tired of it all.

Then, so ignorant is the peasant in these lands, that Miss Whately's simple explanation of the gospel story was met in one instance by a poor old woman saying, "These words are so good, that I think if you would lend me your book to lay on my forehead, it would cure my headache, which troubles me all the day."

It will take time and patience and much zeal to teach these poor creatures how the Word must be applied, but if God grants the former, this English worker in an Egyptian vineyard has both the latter, and we may hope that her example will also influence others to help in bringing poor imprisoned souls out of the house of bondage in the land of Egypt.

to a seaman on board. He read it too, and gave it back with the remark that he would give anything to have such a letter himself. Did the soldier think the lady would write to *him?*

The soldier was quite sure she would, and promised to write and ask Miss Weston immediately. And now Miss Weston's work was cut out for her; first she must write to Jack, on board the *Crocodile,* and then to Jack's particular friend, and after that to a whole long list of sailors furnished by Jack, who all wanted letters.

Not just " How-do-you-do,-I-am-quite-well " letters, but a sort of comfortable sheet talking of Jack's troubles in this world, his leaving of his friends and family perhaps for so many long months, and Jack's happiness in the world to come, when families will be reunited, and there will be sorrow and crying no more.

One poor fellow on board a ship at Rio particularly enjoyed his letters, and answered them most punctually. His ship was coming home soon, and no doubt he looked forward with great pleasure to seeing the writer of them face to face. But alas! disappointment awaited him, he was transferred to another ship, and had to remain abroad. No seeing of his old father and mother now, no tramping down the village looking up old friends, no making acquaintance with the kind lady. " Do write to me again soon," he says sorrowfully, " my heart is almost broke at having to stay out here; but God's will be done. My old ship sailed out of

)our yesterday homeward bound ; we all manned
rigging to cheer her out. I could not cheer,
e was a big lump in my throat." Here is one
r's trouble, you see, and I make no doubt Miss
ton wrote back a comforting reply. But a
th or two later comes another letter from the
e foreign harbour in pencil, in a trembling hand.
sailor is ill, something tells him he shall have
ait still longer to see his dear ones on the other
his dear ones—and Miss Weston. He is bound
quite another country. She has written to him
od deal about that other country, and though
ould like to stay a little longer in the world in
h he has relations and friends, he is not afraid
). The last sentence in his letter tells that he
nding four shillings towards the expense of
ng more letters to brother sailors.
u may be quite sure Miss Weston quickly took
er pen to answer her poor sick friend, but
had distanced the mail steamer in the race
at foreign port, the bed in the hospital was
y.
m going home by a shorter cut than Old
nd," said the dying sailor to his mates around,
hen peacefully closed his eyes.
ss Weston's letter came home again to her with
ord " *dead* " written across it in red ink. And
lost one correspondent.
every day brought more. A man on board
hip would tell a friend on another of Miss
n's letters, and then there would be a request

that she would take the new ship on her list, such and such a seaman would dearly like a few good words from home now and then. " We never light our pipes with your letters," wrote a sailor, " because you thinks about and cares for us."

By-and-by a day came, however, when Miss Weston could not answer all her blue-jacketed writers, and so the idea came into her head of putting together a monthly letter for her friends, and getting it printed to send to them. Not stopping all the pen-and-ink letters, but adding this to them.

" Little blue-backs," these printed letters were called, because they came out in a blue cover, and four thousand of these messengers are sent out every month. The men prize them because they know the words are Miss Weston's, though they cannot trace the stroke of her pen in the clear print.

An officer stationed in the West Indies says that when he opened the monthly parcel of blue-backs on the lower deck of his ship, there were such cries of " Me one, sir ; me one," that he had to stand against a gun to keep off the crowd. And after the distribution there was such sitting about on the deck in odd corners, such rustling of leaves ! Here and there one was reading aloud the message to listening comrades : it was a message from home, a link with Old England. Yes, and a message from the home above, the better country. To all the ships of the Royal Navy go these kindly letters ; to the hospitals where sick sailors lie wearying

read in the dark days of an Arctic winter. I wish
I could copy out for you one of those blue-backs,
but I should not have space here; I can only give
you a general idea of one dated Devonport, May,
1878, and headed with this text, "Therefore be ye
also ready, for in such an hour as ye think not the
Son of man cometh."

It was the sad fate of the *Eurydice* which had
led to the choosing of that text. The vessel had
gone down close to home in a sudden squall one
Sunday afternoon at tea-time, as Miss Weston says
in her letter. She gives the story of that terrible
event, and then she reminds the sailor that though
our navy is a great and powerful one, God holds it
in His hand, able to destroy as well as to uphold.
Not armour plates, nor guns nor torpedoes, neither
brave men nor clever officers, can ensure victory,
she says, the sailor must look to God for that.
Miss Weston was to have visited the *Eurydice*
before it sailed on that last voyage; Captain Marcus
Hare invited her to do so, and she accepted. A
sudden gale, however, prevented her. "You must
come as soon as ever we return from the West
Indies," said the captain. But there was to be no
return, no anchoring at Spithead for that vessel.

Miss Weston writes in this blue-back, "I receive
heartrending letters from widows, mothers, and
friends, asking whether I knew their dear ones,
and, if so, what I can say about them. I am sure
you understand what they want to know: whether
their dear ones were trusting in the Saviour, whether

them, others make laws for them and try to hedge them in from their favourite sin, and others again endeavour by all means in their power to get hold of the daily life of each poor creature, and to make it complete and happy without the public-house.

Miss Robinson did this for the soldier, Miss Weston for the sailor. When she first had it in her mind to fight the giant Drunkenness, she asked to go on board some of the ships of the Royal Navy to talk to the men as a beginning, but it was not easy to get leave. At last, an admiral promised to help her on one condition—that she should first speak on shore to the dockyard men, while he and the chaplain listened to her, and then, if all went well, she might go on board the ships. You may fancy that there was nothing in what Miss Weston said to alarm or vex any one, and very soon she was able to pay a visit to any ship she desired.

First she went to the *St. Vincent,* and gave the boys there "a good talking to." It was a moonlight evening, and the young boy faces turned up to her in the pale light must have made her very earnest in begging them not to fall into so terrible a vice. The lads pressed forward at the end of her address ready enough, poor little fellows, to sign the pledge.

Then Miss Weston went to the *Vanguard,* lying in Plymouth Sound. The lady in her little boat noticed with some distress that the great ship was getting up steam for a voyage, and had already taken in the ladder that hangs over the side. The

niralty had telegraphed orders to leave port,
every one was in a bustle, but the moment her
le boat was descried she was so welcome that
wn went the ladder again and the boatswain's
te piped the notice, "Miss Weston's come aboard
give a lecture in the upper deck battery." Such
lattering of feet followed the words! All among
e guns gathered the crowd of brown-faced men
d boys.

The lecture was not a long one, but very earnest,
d at the end out came the book again, and down
nt the names of those who were going to deny
emselves the chance of ruin by drink.

On board another ship, the *Topaze*, there was a
od laugh over this part of the business; there
is no table handy to put the pledge-book on.
it close by Miss Weston saw a tub with brightly
lished bands that would do; it looked like a
ead-tub; might she have it? Oh, certainly, though
was the first time it had been put to such a use.
Now, men, a couple of hands to roll out the *grog-
b!*"

And, amidst cheers and laughter, it was rolled out,
d made a very good table for the purpose.

One young sailor, after signing his name, gave
e tub a good rap, saying, "There goes a nail in
ur coffin, old fellow!"

Perhaps the most remarkable instance of the
edge being signed and kept on board ship is in
e case of the *Alert* and the *Discovery* sailing for
rctic seas; it seems as if in those cold regions, if

anywhere, drink must be necessary. But no! Two
men in particular signed the pledge, and kept
faithful to it, and it was especially noticed that they
got through the hardships and privations of the
bleak Northern winter better than those who warmed
themselves now and then with "a drop of drink."

But all that I have told you yet of Miss Weston's
work has been done on board ship, either in person
or by letter. Now a time came when she wanted
to get hold of Jack on shore. It was young Jack
at first who touched her heart—young Jack wandering aimlessly in the streets—rough, idle, friendless,
homeless. Could she catch him, and say a few
kind words to him about matters a little above the
streets and the ship's deck? She asked some officers
the question. They shook their heads. Sailor-boys
were such restless things ashore, like birds let out
of a cage, nobody could collect them.

But Miss Weston thought she would try, so she
sent notices to different ships in port to invite the
boys to meet her in a large public hall in Devonport for singing and reading on Sunday afternoons.
How many boys came, do you think, that first
Sunday when Miss Weston sat anxious and ex-
pectant in her grand room? *One*, and he was two
hours late, and so frightened at finding himself
alone there that he would not stay! The next
Sunday not one came, though there were plenty
roaming the streets. And so it went on for four
Sundays. The plan was a failure.

Poor Miss Weston! She must have been dis-

)ointed, but she was not disheartened. She
1yed to be shown a new way to get hold of the
lor boys. And the new way certainly did better.
e friend in whose house she was staying promised
r kitchen for the meeting, backed by tea and
ke, and a dockyard man and a retired policeman
ered to go out into the streets and persuade the
ys to come in. A dozen were collected, and once
the bright kitchen, within smell of warm tea and
ke, there was no more difficulty. The lads felt
s was a real welcome, and very soon two and
ree dozen tramped in at the hospitable door.

There was always tea, of course, and then hymns
d talk, and a little Bible reading and prayer, just
1at the boys could understand and what they had
tience for. One lad told another of these com-
table Sunday afternoons, and before long there
re boys in every corner of the kitchen, boys on
2 window-ledge, boys among the cups and saucers
the dresser, and even boys inside the grate!

One of these kitchen visitors who became a regular
quenter of the meetings was a lad of seventeen,
med Arthur Philips. A merry, happy boy, he
joyed everything that went on, and, best of all,
entered fully into the better part of the enter-
nment. The hymns, the serious talk were to
n as much the precious food for the soul as the
1 and cake were pleasant to the bodily taste; his
e beamed over both. Every one was sorry when
2 day he gave out that he was drafted to a sea-
ing ship, and must say good-bye.

Young Philips had tears in his eyes, but his
voice strove to be brave, and his last words were
that as soon as ever he came into Plymouth Sound
again he would be up at the dear old meetings
"like a shot."

But he never came any more. He was killed in
that voyage by a fall on board ship, down an open
hatchway. A sad story the bare words convey;
but to Miss Weston's ears they sounded sweet and
comforting when fuller details came. His commanding officer reported him, "One of my smartest
royal-yards men, and such a good lad!" He added
that though he made no show of religion, it was
well known that he used to say his prayers in a
quiet place among the bag-racks, and it was supposed that he lost his life on his way there, through
some carelessness in leaving a hatchway open. He
had gained the respect of his messmates to such an
extent that they would not swear before him, or at
least they apologized for a bad word, if uttered.

The ship lay in the Mersey at the time of the
accident, and his shipmates erected a memorial to
him in a waterside cemetery, recording his fate and
their love and esteem, and adding the text, "Blessed
are the dead that die in the Lord."

As time went on the kitchen grew too small for
its visitors, and now Miss Weston being well known,
she was able to collect her boys in a large room
near one of the landing-places. Here an amusing
incident brought to mind the old saying of the
officer, that sailor-boys on shore are not to be de-

pended upon. About two hundred lads were present one Sunday afternoon, and had behaved themselves very fairly during the singing of the hymns. Then Miss Weston opened her Bible and began to look for her place. Her eye was off the fidgeting multitude. Their restlessness came to the top in a very marked manner. "I heard a slight noise," she says, "looked up, and the whole assembly was in motion, some running over the backs of the benches like cats, some slipping underneath. In less than a minute the room was cleared except for about a dozen on the front bench who had not been quick enough to fall in with the rest." Of course, she managed to keep these, but the incident taught her a lesson, never for a moment to take her attention off her restless young friends, but to have all places found and hymns chosen beforehand.

And now the men and boys themselves of whom Miss Weston had tried to make sober men and Christians raised a cry of their own needs. Would not Miss Weston try to procure for them a place where they might come in the week—a public-house without drink, a sort of home ashore for the homeless sailor?

It was a request the lady would dearly wish to grant, but, like most good things in this world, money was needed to obtain it, and where was the money to come from? Well, there are good souls in this world who think the best way of investing their money is lending it to the Lord, and when Miss Weston, in the columns of a newspaper, ap-

pealed to such people, they sent in their pounds
and shillings till in a few days she received enough
to pay a whole year's rent for such a building. So
in the autumn of 1874 was opened a good house
close to the great gateway of the Royal Dockyard
in Devonport. Others than rich people who read
newspapers contributed in after days to buy that
house, and to fit and furnish it. Officers and sailors,
boys in training ships, men on foreign stations sent
what they could save towards setting up a Sailor's
Rest; and amongst these sums a goodly number
were entered as "*grog money*," the money that in
other days had been spent in drink.

A sailor-boy's mother gave one shilling, a nameless person two hundred pounds, and so with many
tiny droppings and a few great showers of gold,
the house was completely put in order, and over its
portals in golden letters shone the inscription, "This
building was opened May 8th, 1876, for the glory
of God, and for the good of the Service."

Very much the same sort of place as the Soldier's
Institute in Portsmouth, so I shall not take you all
over it, as I did with that one. Dining-rooms, bedrooms, reading-rooms, smoking-rooms, all are here,
and a bar where all sorts of liquors are sold except
those that intoxicate. The sailors don't wish them;
they say plainly it would spoil the place. The bar
is open to any one in Devonport, not to sailors
alone, but the rest of the house is for Jack's sole
benefit.

On the walls of the refreshment bar are sea

:tures and coloured scrolls, while a parrot and a
1sical-box of lively tunes give an air of gaiety to
1at cannot be a dull place, for from 5.30 in the
)rning to 12 at night there is coming and going
hundreds through the swing-door.

There is a quiet writing-room, too, where letters
me can be composed, and there is no law against
tired sailor who has taken "the middle watch"
rhaps, stretching himself out on one of the sofas
re and enjoying a nap, soothed by the scratching
the pens and the groans of some "poor scholar"
10 cannot get his tool to stay comfortably between
s well-meaning but clumsy fingers.

The bedrooms are tiny cabins partitioned off so
at each man has a little space to himself, a great
ivilege. These wee rooms are sometimes called
er ships. You see the name outside—"Ruby,"
)iamond," "Undaunted," "Volage,"—the officers
d men of those vessels have collected the money
them. One, again, bears the name "Little
1n," another "Harry," in memory, perhaps, of
ne sailor's little one gone to its rest above.
hers again simply carry some text of Scripture
their frontal. These cabins, though simply
rnished, are thoroughly comfortable, and there
nothing the sailor enjoys after a rough voyage
much as the idea of a cosy night in such
arters.

The day before the building was opened to the
blic three men-of-war's men presented themselves
the door and asked to see Miss Weston. "They

had been watching the house for some time," they said, " and had made up their minds they would be the three first birds to roost there." " But the building won't be open till to-morrow," said Miss Weston, who no doubt was very busy putting the last touches to the rooms. "Couldn't you throw the red tape overboard for once, ma'am ?" they all answered, " for we've all three got leave from our captains on purpose to sleep here to-night."

And it was thrown overboard, and the men shown to their rooms. Just the men who would be glad of a quiet corner, for presently the low murmur from the tiny cabins told that one was reading his Bible before he lay down to rest, the others listening, till each knelt down to pray his nightly prayer in greater comfort than poor young Philips among the bag-racks.

The photographs of these " three first men " hang up now in the Institute, and they come back as often as they can to roost in the old nest.

Other than sober men sometimes find their way here. A half-tipsy sailor came in one night, demanding a glass of half-and-half, stiff, and throwing down a half-crown.

The barmaid was as bright as her coffee-cans ; she said at once, pleasantly, " We haven't your sort of half-and-half; but would you like to try some of ours ?" The sailor thought he would—a jorum of something hot.

Then the girl was ready with another question. " Are you a Devonshire man ? " He was.

"this beats all; the publican turned me out, and the teetotalers have taken me in; I shall go aboard and tell them about this."

This fellow, too, gave up drink in consequence, and was the means of bringing many other sailors to the Rest.

One of the pleasantest sights in the house is at dinner-time on Sundays, the tables crowded, one or two sailors carving, flowers making the board gay, and the beaming faces and expressions of pleasure at the decently ordered feast, "Well, isn't this nice? just like home!" This is the room where sailors on leave dine who board in the house; there are other arrangements for chance comers.

And now we come to the last but not least part of Miss Weston's design for the sailor's good: the hall for religious services. It is open every day, except on Sunday mornings when all the church bells are ringing, and the men may reasonably be supposed to go to their own places of worship. The sailors are not compelled to attend the meetings in the hall even if they live at the Rest, but they almost always do, they like the singing and the plain words spoken to them there.

A lot of little lads from one ship in port used to come to the hall, and one day an officer found them, as he thought, in mischief "on board," huddled together over a lantern. Little conspirators, no doubt. But no! they were having a meeting like the one in Miss Weston's hall, one reading, and then praying. The officer would not disturb them,

y were quite in earnest, and he walked away
self quite touched and thoughtful.

nother little lad, dying in the Naval Hospital,
l a nurse, "After I'm dead, go to the Sailor's Rest
tell the ladies and the boys how happy I was,
that I've gone to Jesus. I was as bad as other
s, but one Sunday I passed by the Rest; they
e singing; the hymn reminded me of the
day school at home. I went in, and there I
nt to love and trust Jesus."

want all mothers and Sunday school teachers to
e heart here and notice the beginning of good in
little lad; not Miss Weston's beautiful Rest,
only completed the work, but the quiet, hum-
m, little village Sunday school, where the children
et, and the teacher wonders, perhaps, if any good
eing done, there is so little excitement.

ying lips tell the truth, and this poor boy
inds us that the "Sunday school at home" was
guide to good at last.

meant to have said a great deal more about this
ilor's Rest and Institute," but I am obliged to
, my tale is growing too long already. I must
you to believe that I have only told you a small
of Miss Weston's arrangements for the benefit
he sailor. Meantime, it is past eleven o'clock,
Institute is shutting up, the best sort of men are
uading the noisy ones to go to bed, a rollick-
young fellow pops his head in at the door, saying,
st boat's just off; good night all!" and vanishes
is room upstairs, and so I say good night too.

# THE LAND OF GOLD.

## BRITISH GUIANA.

YEARS and years ago, about the time that our Queen Elizabeth reigned in England, there went a rumour throughout the world that in a certain part of South America lay a country rich in gold, of which the very houses of the people were golden, and whose king was gilded over each morning with fresh gold for clothing. From all lands set forth the curious or the greedy to seek this region of wealth. England herself was not behindhand in the search, but, as you may think, the golden province was never found. Men came back rich at times, it is true, from this journey, and it is also true that real sparkling bits of golden ore were in places gleaned from the common earth in those South American wilds, but the golden houses and the gilded king never dazzled the eyes of mortal man.

It is a common saying, however, that there is no smoke without fire, or, to speak more plainly, no rumour which has not a shadow of truth in it, and the story of the golden man may have taken rise from the fact that in Guiana it was a custom of

rtain savage tribes to cover their bodies with a
cky substance, turtle-fat, perhaps, on which they
owered bits of sparkling earth, which in the
nshine might bear the appearance of gold, on
eir naked bodies. It was not a comfortable sort
 dress, I should think, but it made a sensation
u see.

Crowds left home and comfort to meet danger
d disappointment in their search for that golden
rthly city; some dying in perils of land and
ter, some killed by the hand of the naked
vages whose country they invaded, some perish-
 of famine and fatigue, few reaping the least
ward for all their toils. After a long period of
pe unrealized, the gold-seekers began to tire of
ir enterprise, and then other people entered the
d with simpler views; they would fain settle
wn and cultivate the beautiful wooded, watered
ion of Guiana.

 cannot stay to tell you how the old inhabitants
the country, angered by a long course of injuries,
 on these new-comers, and slaughtered them
enever they could; but they did so, and one can
dly wonder at it. French, Dutch, and English,
h in their turn were attacked, murdered, and
etimes eaten by the savage Indians of the
rict.

By-and-by, however, the more civilized nature
n the battle, and a footing was gained in the
ired country. The strangers were fortunate in
aining a fertile soil and free space for themselves

and their children; but the poor Indian, what did he make by the bargain? Not much as money value goes, truly, and yet here and there, now and then, a boon above price fell to his share.

The Frenchman brought his priest, the Dutchman his Moravian pastor, into the forest and to the hut of his Indian neighbour, and by slow degrees those good men got a hearing among perhaps the very gilded savages of which we have spoken, telling them of things they never heard of before—of the life above, of the God who made them, of the Saviour who redeemed them.

But the history of the teachers of these early days is a sorrowful one; not only the Indians at times were their enemies, but the very civilized colonists often stood in their way and persecuted them. Then sickness attacked the missions, small-pox and fever, till, disheartened and sorrowful, the good fathers and pastors died off or left the country, and the poor savage too often forgot all he had learned of a better land beyond his supposed land of gold.

The last state of that man was indeed worse than the first.

All this that I have told you happened long before any of you were born, but about the year 1830 the Church Missionary Society, looking about it to see into what corner of the earth it should next send the good tidings, bethought itself of Guiana, which had once caught the echo of the sound and then forgotten it. No, not altogether

orgotten it either, since an old blind Indian somewhere, in some corner of that vast land of forest,
meadow, and river, was still heard singing a hymn
e had learned when a little child from the lips of a
Dutch missionary. The teacher was dead and gone,
ut his words lived. This was not a common case,
owever; utter ignorance was the condition of the
tribes in Guiana.

They had an idea, nevertheless, that the mis-
ionary was a man meaning no ill to them, and
hey favourably received the one sent to them by
heir English well-wishers. *One* among so many!
es, but there must be a beginning, and the little
ettlement at Bartica, on the great river Essequibo,
was the spot chosen for that beginning.

Mr. Armstrong was the name of the missionary.
He was not a clergyman, but as a catechist he did
ood service, for four years bearing alone the burden
nd heat of the day, teaching and preaching, warn-
ng and praying.

Dwelling when at home in a rude thatched hut,
e was not often in the same place, but travelled
bout among the people, breaking up the rough
round of their hearts.

While he laboured in far-off America, a young
man in Liverpool streets felt a burning desire to
ive himself up to the work of teaching the heathen.
fter a course of training at the Church Missionary
ollege, he was sent to help Mr. Armstrong in the
ttle mission at Bartica, reaching his destination
st before Christmas Day, 1832.

Some of you may know Liverpool, perhaps, and all of you know some of our large towns, with their busy streets, their crowd of human creatures, their carriages, their shops, their stirring life. Thomas Youd at home was, perhaps, not a rich man pampered with many servants, but at least I expect he had a mother, and possibly sisters, who cared for his comfort, and saw that he had a good bed and wholesome food. In England, even if we are poor, we seldom leave it to our men to see about such things. But all is changed when once the man becomes the missionary. Then home comforts, home service, are all left behind, and Thomas Youd in far-away Guiana must live in an Indian hut, sleep in a hammock, and eat the food the Indians ate, prepared by his own hands.

When one is young and strong this sort of life is almost pleasant, and Mr. Youd really liked it, solitary as it was, for Mr. Armstrong soon fell ill and had to return for a time to England. The new missionary was ready indeed for anything, whether it was teaching young savages in school or paddling in his canoe up the creeks of the great river searching for new pupils; no going home to bed in that case, but just slinging his hammock between two trees in the forest and lighting a fire beneath it.

But Guiana is a warm country, I know some one will say; why, then, does the Englishman need to make up the fire after he has cooked his supper? For one reason, to counteract the excessive dampness of the air after the hot day, and to scare

ay wild beasts, especially the tiger, or jaguar
iich is always lurking in those solitudes ready to
unce on the sleeping or unwary. Those great
ests abound in creatures dangerous to human
e, but only by degrees the English missionary
mes to know and guard against their attacks.

I have called the Indians of this land savages,
cause they were so utterly untaught, but those
io clustered round the young Liverpool teacher,
pecially the children, showed signs of an affec-
nate disposition and a gentle nature. True, there
re cannibals, poisoners, and sorcerers in the
tance, but they kept away from the Christian
iite man, even in their ignorance ashamed of
eir dark deeds.

Mr. Youd tells us that when he spoke of God to
s flock they stared stupidly at him—they had
ver heard of such a Being. He had to point to
e forest, the river, the sky, and the earth, and
rther ask, Who made all these? before a little
irk of his meaning entered their souls.

Twice he was asked if the God of whom he spoke
l not come from England.

On Sundays his congregation assembled some-
ies at one place, sometimes at another; and some
those who came for the first time, grown men
ough they might be, behaved as very little
ildren do when you send them to the house of
d with no one to look after them. Staring
out, sitting or lying with their backs to the
icher, talking, cutting sticks, laughing aloud.

The poor things meant no harm, but how could
their silly souls be reached? thought this earnest
young fellow out of Liverpool streets.

Pictures were found to be a good means for
attracting them. Coloured prints especially could
not be resisted; big men and little children would
alike crowd round the preacher to hear them
explained. Another missionary tells a little story
about this—you will like to hear it. He was
showing some pictures of Bible events to these very
Guiana Indians, and they were elbowing round him
greatly interested, all but one, the wife of the chief,
and she sat sulkily apart, perhaps ashamed of her
scanty clothing before the white man, and half angry
with him for bringing these new ideas into her
forest home. She could not help hearing the words
spoken, however, and by-and-by her eyes brightened
and her face lost its sullenness. There was talk of
a little baby in a cradle, soft and helpless. The
ah's! and oh's! over the pleasant picture roused her
motherly curiosity. She could sit apart no longer,
but quietly crept near the teacher to gain a glimpse
of the Babe of Bethlehem, and to listen to the tale
of His birth and early years. It was the very first
time she had heard of Him, and as it might be the
last, for the missionary was passing on to other
parts of the country, he took his listeners from the
manger to the cross, showing them a picture of the
Crucifixion, while they heard in rapt silence the sad
history of that dark day, which yet was to prove
so glad a day for them and all mankind.

I have said that the chief's wife was perhaps shamed of her scanty clothes, for indeed savages in ot countries hardly wear anything on their bodies, nd one of the first results of Christian teaching their desire to assume clothing. Different tribes ave different fashions: some roam about quite aked, their bodies tattooed in patterns, red and ellow, green and blue, great circles and startling ripes, women as well as men, creatures almost like ur pictures of devils to look at; others — the omen, I mean, and these are of the tribe the most vilized of the inhabitants of British Guiana— ear a white garment called a kimisa, doubt- ss the "chemise" of French settlers, who had erhaps long ago been murdered or driven out of he land, and have their long black hair carefully laited and hanging down their backs.

A congregation of Indians must always have ad some curious objects among them. One man rought five others to church, neatly dressed, as e thought, for service, in long red shirts, and tall arp-pointed caps made from the palm tree. These, f course, they kept on all the time, and it was most laughable to see them march up the little urch in such clothing, greatly satisfied with emselves. Another man came in a sky-blue ll hat, for which he had paid a large price while a a visit to the coast, and with which he was reatly delighted, till some busybody told him that o Christian minister would baptize or marry him such a gay garment. It was very hard on the poor savage, who thought clothing of any kind a sort of godliness, and who really liked his gay head-piece, and he was greatly relieved when the missionary assured him that God would not be angry with his coloured hat. You see how hard it is to teach poor barbarians, especially when meddling people interfere and confuse their childish minds.

And now I am going to tell you of a very remarkable custom which prevails among these tribes of South American Indians. On the birth of a baby it is not the mother who takes to her bed, and is waited on and congratulated, but the father. We should think this custom very laughable, but it is the fashion out there, and must be followed. The big man goes to his hammock, and is covered up, and fed, and nursed, and kept idle for weeks, while Mrs. Indian and the new-born baby hurry about and do the cooking, and think nothing of the event.

No one takes any notice of *them*.

So rooted is this custom that a young Indian, who had come to look on it with English Christian eyes, and so to see the silliness of it, yet dared not break through it; and when *his* baby was born he actually left home for three weeks, staying away where he was not known till it was the proper time for him to be up again. It was better than lying in bed, to be sure, but next time let us hope he was braver still, and stayed at home to help his wife and take a little notice of the baby.

None of you would like to change places, I think,
with an Indian wife. The husband does not
exactly ill treat her, unless she behaves badly,
but he considers her terribly inferior to himself.
When he comes in from his day's hunting, he drops
his game on the ground, puts his gun aside, and
throws himself into his hammock. His wife must
be at hand, but she dare not speak to him. When
he is in the humour, he asks what she has done
in his absence, who has called, and so on, much
as an English husband would do. But there is
no family dinner or supper, as would be in England, the master eats alone, the best of everything
prepared and served by the wife; after that she
may feed and the children. On a journey the
woman carries all the heavy baggage, as well as
the baby astride on her shoulder, her husband
walking on before with his gun, lordly and magni-
ficent.

It was a great surprise to these forest gentlemen
when Mr. Youd told them that women were not
so treated in the wonderful country from whence
he came. That there a man would be ashamed
to leave the hard work to the woman, and that
even the greatest chiefs would rather carry a
weight themselves than let it fall to their wives'
care. Mr. Youd did something better than talk
so; he showed them how to treat a wife by bringing back with him, after a visit to the island of
Barbadoes, a gentle white lady as his wife.

Mrs. Youd was, indeed, a helpmeet to him, as

well as an example to the mission station; she was
ready to face trouble and privation in the bush
with her husband, and not only to face it, but to
be cheerful over it.

She helped in the school; she called the poor
down-trodden women around her, and showed them
how to be neat and clean in their persons, and to
wear simple pretty clothing, besides giving them
some idea of making their huts pleasanter and
more comfortable. The growing girls she taught
to wash and sew, and do hundreds of things they
never heard of before, all of which, however, helped
to make their lives happier and brighter: and,
besides, she never lost sight of the main object
of missionary life, teaching all these poor creatures
how to love and serve God. So you may fancy
how dearly she was beloved, not only by her
husband, but by all these ignorant, affectionate
Indians.

How proud they were of this fair, white-faced
lady, all their own, living among them, and teaching them, and shedding such light on their dull
lives! And with what joy they must have welcomed the little white baby a year later, when it
came one December morning into the forest home!

But that joy was very short-lived. Little baby
Youd only lived three weeks, and the mother never
got strong again. Doctors and good food were not
to be had in that wild district, and, in spite of
much love and tender watching, the poor thing
sank and died a few months later, and was laid

her baby in the quiet forest shade, at rest for
er in this world.

She had seemed so useful, so necessary to the
le settlement, and, in spite of discomforts, so
ppy there, that it was hard to lose her; but God
lered it, so it must have been right.

Poor Mr. Youd had other troubles besides the
s of his wife; sickness often visited his mission;
ce it was almost destroyed by measles, seventy
dians dying of the disease, and the heathen
und took a dislike to Christianity in con-
quence; then twice he was driven from his
tlement by the Government of Brazil, who
clared that the land he occupied was *their* land,
d that the English teacher was trying to coax
er the Indians to believe they belonged to
gland. Of course this was all their own imagi-
tion. The only country the missionary tried
make them long for was the heavenly country.

Then Mr. Youd was in great danger once from
immense snake, which crept out of the forest,
d actually got into his canoe as he was paddling
wn the river Essequibo. The Indians themselves
re terrified at sight of the dreadful passenger—
rty-one feet long, and able to swallow any of
em at a gulp—and they jumped into the stream,
d left the Englishman to do battle alone with
e monster.

Happily he had a cutlass with him, and he aimed
well that the first blow killed the reptile, thus
ving his own life.

Another danger in these great rivers is from alligators, unwieldy creatures, who think nothing of making a meal of a human creature. A missionary dozing in a boat anchored to the river's bank for the night actually heard a number of these creatures sniffing under and about it, and lifting their ugly heads above the plank sides to try to see their probable prey. You may think he felt sleepy no longer, but jumped up and seized his cutlass ready for use. Some creature in the dusk came lumbering softly near him, and the white man's first impulse was to strike ; but he waited a moment and spoke, and it was well he did, for it was his faithful Indian servant, who had heard, and smelt the creatures too (they have a strong savour of musk), and he had roused himself to watch over his sleeping master.

Yet another white missionary was upset in his canoe, and had to remain clinging for hours to a tree half buried in the river, his body swaying to and fro in the current, till his Indian followers could right the boat and come to his rescue.

I tell you these perils by land and sea that you may realize a missionary's life and dangers, though really these attacks of wild creatures are nothing to be counted beside that worse trouble, the utter want of kind English friends, dear home faces in the strange land wherein Christ's follower must make his home. That is a real grief.

You will hardly believe that though Mr. Youd lived only to instruct and benefit the poor people

round him, there were some who watched perpetu-
lly to do him evil in return. Though many among
ie Indians liked his teachings, saying, " It is good,
, is good," and helped to build houses of God in
ie forest wilds, others were angry because he boldly
)oke against their sins of drunkenness and sorcery.
One man in particular was enraged because Mr.
'oud would not countenance a native feast, which
'as sure to be a scene of drunken revels; and
1ough he concealed his anger at the time, next
ay he sent the missionary a leg of venison as a
resent. Mr. Youd felt very ill after eating it, and
) did his second wife, to whom he was then
arried. He got better, but she died. It was
)isoned meat! Nothing could be done to punish
1e wicked Indian, who a second time and a third
peated the dose, putting the poison in different
ticles of food. Each time that Mr. Youd felt ill
) took an emetic, and so recovered for the time;
1t his death at an early age was attributed to this
use. He died at sea on his way back to England,
here he fancied he might recover his health.
[hen the sea gives up her dead, Thomas Youd will
ise, we believe, to hear the happy welcome, " Well
)ne, good and faithful servant, enter thou into the
y of thy Lord."
Most of his forest churches and mission settle-
ents have been given up now, and deserted; but
e do not think his labours were lost, though it
is not been found possible to continue to send
achers into the same regions, rather placing them

Q

nearer the coast, where they would be in less danger
of shipwreck on their long river journey, and more
easily protected from enemies on land.

Guiana is now under the care of a special bishop,
appointed the very year of Mr. Youd's death; he
keeps a watchful eye over all his wild diocese,
caring for the poor Indian as much as for the
civilized inhabitant of the towns.

The Society for the Propagation of the Gospel in
Foreign Parts also sends missionaries to Guiana.
So the land of gold is not yet deserted, though men
no longer speed to its shores for the sake of the
coveted earthly treasure. Rich people in the towns
of British Guiana are taking a great interest in the
spread of the gospel among the ignorant and un-
learned of their country; and the bishop writes
home—

"I had lately a very cheering visit to the
Pomeroon and Moruca Rivers with Mr. Brett."
(These were two mission centres established of later
years.) "There were about 1450 Indians assembled
in our two missions of Cabacaburi and Waramuri.
They are being well looked after by Mr. Heard."
And now I must end my scraps of mission story in
Guiana. They are only scraps; but they may serve
to convey an idea how much a man must give up
who takes up his cross and follows Christ to the
far wilds of a savage country. He really does renounce all this world holds dear to serve his Lord.

# AMONGST THE FOGS.

### NEWFOUNDLAND.

ſ King Henry the Seventh's account-book the
llowing item appears :—

"To him that found the new isle, £10."

Who was this nameless " him," and in what seas lay
is new-found isle ? are questions one naturally asks
ter taking the liberty of looking over the royal
penses. The man who received the ten pounds
ꞅ discovering on the coast of America an island
large as Ireland was one Cabot, a merchant of
istol, who had sailed forth by the king's per-
ssion in search of unknown lands.

He came home safely, reporting well of the new
ɔres; telling of innumerable fish to be caught
ɘre, of woods filled with game and fruit, of bright
1 and smiling sea, and of only a few defenceless
dians with whom to dispute possession.

The poor fishermen of the west coast of England,
d indeed men of other trades and professions,
ꞇened to the report, and longed to live in the
w-found isle, or at least to visit it, and enrich
ɘmselves with its spoil of cod and salmon, fox
1 marten skins.

Cabot had made his trip in the short summer-time of those regions, and the sunshine brightened his story.

The next visitors were not so fortunate. Sir Walter Raleigh and Sir Humphrey Gilbert, two English gentlemen of renown, started with four vessels for the new isle, carrying thither would-be settlers, masons, carpenters, blacksmiths, fishermen, ay, and musicians too. They landed them on the coast, taking possession of the country in the name of their English sovereign, and then they sailed away in search of more adventures. Alas! the smiling sea was now dark and troubled, a gale sprang up, and Sir Humphrey, on board the smallest vessel of the little fleet, was entreated to seek safety on a large ship. He refused, however, to leave his post. "We are as near to heaven by sea as by land," said the brave man, calm and steadfast on the deck of his ten-ton vessel, which was tossed about like a child's toy on the rough Atlantic.

They on the larger ship lifted up hands and eyes to heaven in supplication for their companions in danger; but in vain, their day had come, never more was the brave adventurer to sight home, to set foot on new-found isle—in that sudden gale the little ship went down with all on board.

So much for the first discoverers of Newfoundland.

Now let us visit it later on.

Many people had made the creeks and harbours of the island their dwelling-place; but they were

ll fishermen, some English, some Scotch, many
rish, some French, some of other countries, and
ifferent in nation these settlers were also different
a habits and ways of living.

The old inhabitants had long ago died out of the
and, as poor savages generally do when civilized
ations approach them, and the new settlers ought
ll to have been Christians, coming, as they did, of
Christian stock; but you know how easily people
lip downhill, and, when church and schools and
lergy are no longer there, how easy a thing it is to
orget the first day of the week, to let the children
un about untaught, and to give up by degrees the
ood customs of our forefathers. Yet still here
ould be a family abiding by the rule they followed
n some dear old English home, the Bible not only
n the shelf, but a book to guide their lives, and the
oung children taught the Creed and the Ten Commandments, and encouraged to say "Our Father"
t their mother's knee.

And then in only the next harbour, separated by
ust a few bare rocks and a stretch of waste land,
ould be the dwelling of another sort; the home of
ome runaway sailor, perhaps, whose coarse wife
nd neglected children hardly looked like civilized
eings, and certainly laid no claim to the word
Christian." Dotted up and down the coast were
uch settlers, all living by the produce of the sea,
o none caring to build houses far inland. New-
oundland, therefore, may be said to be only fringed
ith inhabitants, not filled.

Some fifty years ago there were only two clergymen in the whole island, which was nearly as large as
England, and so there was no one to help the greater
number of the settlers to remember God and strive
after holy living. The best of them always tried to
do what they could for themselves and their
children as regarded religion. Thus, as there was
no clergyman to marry people, and no church to be
married in, a man who was not willingly God-
forgetting asked the best reader among the fishermen to come and read over him and the girl he
wanted for his wife a bit out of the old Prayer-book
that came with them from England; and later, when
the baby was born and had to be named, he had to
be fetched again. Or perhaps the only good reader
was a woman, and she baptized the little new-
comer. It was a bad best, poor souls, to go by, as
what I am going to tell you will show. A mother
in one of those rough homes deserted her new-born
baby, and the grandmother in a passion took it and
christened it "*Cain.*" This was a cruel thing to do,
and when a clergyman did come near the place the
poor helpless child was carried with tears by another
relative to him and the question askèd, "Would he
give it a new name?" He thought deeply upon
the matter, and ended by baptizing it again by a
better name, first saying, "If this child be not
already baptized." So poor little Cain lost his
brand. You see things *must* be done decently and
in order. Though religion is of the soul, and not of
the body, if we do not keep up those outward guards

f church and clergy, rites and ceremonies, we are
ire to fall back—back into worse than heathen-
om, forgetfulness of the good which once we knew
nd loved.

I do not attempt here to tell you how the people
ι the new-found isle lived in those early days after
ie brave sailor adventurer died at his post, but I
ap some centuries and come to a time of which we
now more, and which, after all, is more interesting
ι us—the story of Newfoundland as it is, as good
en find it now, when they go out to their wide
arishes on its coasts.

As I said before, its summer is very short, and
ιe winters, oh, so long and cold! But the chief
sagreeable is fog. Newfoundland is known by its
gs. The ships dread them, and the inhabitants
slike them; but there they are at every turn,
ιick, wet, gloomy veils over the land, a frequent
ιuse of wrecks.

Then the cold; it is so intense that even the
·ead in the larder freezes. One missionary clergy-
an tells how a good woman cutting bread and
ιtter for him, hacked away at the loaf, saying she
ιuld not keep it thawed, *though she put it in the
ιys' bed directly they turned out.* This is not a
ιry pleasant idea, but it is very commonly done
nong poor people in those cold regions. Then the
ilk freezes solid in the jug, and you must cut it
ith a knife; and if your coffee or tea overflows
ιto your saucer, it freezes there, and the next time
ιu lift your cup, up comes the saucer too, glued
ι it.

The very ink freezes as you use it, and if you were writing a letter you would keep the ink-pot on the hob. But this is not the worst of the cold. You may get frost-bitten, or frost-burnt, as they call it, and lose fingers, toes, nose, or ears, as it happens. You do not feel the frost seize you, but any companion with you tells you that your nose or cheek is looking very white, and then you must rub it gently with snow, or in time you would lose the flesh of that part. Poor wrecked sailors suffer fearfully from frost-burn, and if they do reach land safely, often have to lose fingers or toes by the doctor's hand afterwards. One man, in consequence of frost-burn, had to lose both his legs, all his fingers, and one thumb. And sometimes poor old people are even frost-burnt in their beds at night.

So you see Newfoundland cold is no trifle.

Yet it has not deterred new settlers from leaving English homes to visit the land of rich fishing harvests, and for many reasons this has been good for the foggy island. Even if the new-comers were only poor fishermen, they brought with them the echo of church bells, the last words of the sermon heard in the old church at home; and if they were richer merchants, with God's grace dwelling in their hearts, they were not comfortable till they had done something for God in the new country: set aside a room, perhaps, where a sort of service could be held on Sundays; or opened their own dwelling on the first day of the week, that such as pleased might come in, and hear the Scriptures and the Church

prayers read to their own growing children. Here
and there the people actually built a church, though
they had no clergyman, and no hope of one. The
best reader then did his best, and any good man
passing by was entreated to conduct the service for
them. It was better than forgetting Sunday altogether, or only counting it as a day on which to
mend nets and lay in stores for the coming week.

But better still might be done, thought the overseers of Christ's flock, the bishops appointed by our
Church in these latter years.

I dare say many of you have seen an English
bishop in his robes in the cathedral, and know that
he works very hard consecrating churches, confirming children, and ordaining clergy.

But still you have no idea of the work of a Newfoundland bishop. To begin with, he is like a
master workman, overlooking every one labouring
under him; so if I try to tell you a little of the life
and labours of the last Bishop of Newfoundland, you
will have a good idea of how the souls, ay, and the
bodies too, of the poor fishermen in that foggy
island are cared for by the ministers of God.

Bishop Feild went out to his work straight from
a pleasant country parish in England, all among
green meadows, and when he landed in Newfoundland his first idea was to visit, if he could, all his
scattered flock. But they lived in seaport towns
and villages, on rocky cliffs and islands, with no
roads at all connecting them. What was to be
done?

Little open boats were not large or safe enough to carry the bishop for miles and miles along the foggy coast, and there were no steamers. Just at this time a present was made to the bishop, more welcome than anything else could have been—a beautiful little ship, called the *Hawk*, in which he could visit all his parishes and clergy. Such a useful little vessel it proved, not only to the bishop, but to other missionaries who needed to be taken to their churches. There was another use, too, to which the *Hawk* was put; it might well be called the "Church" ship, since Church service was actually held on its deck, in those places where no room could be had large enough to contain the congregation. Many a little baby has been baptized, many a couple married, nothing but sky above and waves around. The people were always delighted to see the bishop's ship nearing their harbour; word would go round instantly of his arrival, and if he stayed on shore the best bed, though only a hard wooden one, would be given up to him, the owner lying on the floor the while, and the bit of new bread or fresh butter would be brought out for his welcome. Nothing very much to place before a bishop, do you think? Wait till you hear what his chief food was in Newfoundland—dried fish and hard biscuit, sometimes no meat for days and days together.

Some one asked a good woman, who was bustling about after fresh butter directly she saw the flag of the bishop's ship in harbour, " Does he, then, require

put our money in the plate or bag, but it is the only plan for Newfoundland, where the men are away so much. Sailors out there, too, are very much like sailors on land. The money is spent directly they put their foot on shore, and badly the poor wives must want it, left to themselves for so many months.

One other duty our bishop took on himself, which was to get the fishermen to put money in the savings bank, while he took care of their books. But he would do a thousand other things very strange to him, and indeed to every English gentleman—jump out of his bed in the little cabin of the *Hawk*, with bare feet and scanty clothing, to help the steersman on a stormy night; sleep if need be on shore, in a mere wooden crib without sheets; and eat such food as you would hardly set before your children.

So long as he carried the gospel to these poor lonely fishing villages he cared for little else. It nearly broke his heart to go away and leave them, perhaps without church or clergyman, knowing it might be months or years before he could see them again, and very earnestly he wrote to England begging good men to come out as missionaries to this hungry land. The people were generally most anxious to have God's ministers among them; one poor sick man, who was rejoicing in the rare visit of a clergyman to his desolate corner of the island, prayed God to let him die while the good man was there; and he did die too, peacefully, happily, that

stiff and stark, dead on the frozen snow-field. And this was the tale they had to tell to his wife and daughter at home. Another earnest missionary was visiting his people in a boat, when what happened God alone knows, perhaps a gale of wind sprang up, perhaps the fog hid a treacherous rock, but the boat drifted shorewards bottom upwards, and no one to this day can tell where the body of the faithful servant of God lies.

You see, a missionary going to Newfoundland must be prepared for perils by sea as well as by land, and no wonder the bishop, amongst other things, used to hope that the clergy helpers sent out to him would be able to "manage a boat."

It is not the way a clergyman chooses his curates in England, but then, you see, we live in a very different climate. One cannot help feeling very much for these poor rough people with our English names and language, some of them even remembering the green homes of their childhood in Old England. It seems very hard that when they wish so sorely for teaching and guidance, no one should be found to live amongst them and serve their Church. Of late years there have been some additions to the stock of missionary clergy, but not nearly enough; it must still be our prayer that God will put into the hearts of earnest young men, willing to live for their faith, as well as die for it, to offer themselves for work in this Newfoundland. One such helper has given himself to the colony of late years, an officer in the Royal Engineers, Mr.

ırling, who first bestowed that valuable gift, his
.cht, to be used for Church work, and then on
e Day of Intercession for Missions, in 1872, was
l to give himself, asking to be sent to any station
here the people most needed a clergyman, and
king with him two schoolmasters and two mis-
mary pupils. Perhaps he felt, as we cannot help
ing, that these poor fishermen wanted guidance
d help even more than the heathen, since they
ew what they were losing when they lived with-
t Church services, without the Sacraments, with-
t holy teaching for their children; knew it so
ell that their cry was continually, "Come over
d help us."

The bishop of whom I have told you loved this
ugh and ignorant flock of his, and while he took
much pride in the ordering of his new New-
undland Cathedral as any English bishop could
of his time-honoured pile, he also delighted in
stormy voyages in the little *Hawk*, which flew
her and thither, in and out of creek and harbour.
herever men were, there it fain would be for a
son.

Old people need rest, one thinks, but this is what
r bishop did when sixty-six years of age. After
lding an ordination in the capital town, he set
l in his *Hawk* for a Church voyage. Twice in
fogs the little ship struck on the rocks, but was
off safely; then on reaching another chief town,
*Hawk* lay in harbour while the bishop in a little
it was out, for three days, visiting the different

settlements, confirming children here, consecrating a
graveyard there. At one town, where twenty years
before he could not get one person to receive the
Holy Communion with him, now nearly fifty pressed
forwards, anxious for the privilege. On again in
the *Hawk* for more confirmations, the ship again
getting fast on the rocks, this time so firmly that
the crew became very anxious. However, while
the bishop had morning prayer on shore, the tide
kindly lifted the good ship off the rocks and floated
her ready for more work. In the fisherman's house
where that service was held, was an English gentleman limping about on a crutch. He was a natu-
ralist, a collector of strange insects and flowers, for
which purpose he had visited Newfoundland, but
not being sufficiently careful of himself, he had got
his toes frost-burnt, and so lost the whole of those
on one foot—a great trial for himself, but a blessing
to the fishermen of the neighbourhood, since he
held Sunday services for them all the time of his
illness. You may fancy he was very glad to see
the kind bishop, who, however, soon moved on for
more confirmations, this time on deck, for at
Bonne Bay there was no church or schoolroom fit
for the purpose. Here the bishop left a clergyman
all alone amongst the poor fishermen to do his work
for God.

And then come records of bad winds for the little
*Hawk*, forcing it back into harbour continually, but
still the visiting went on, the bishop being no
fair-weather sailor. So stormy was it that the

eople on board the Church ship saw an abandoned
essel go down close to them, and the next day in
 squall a little schooner capsized almost by the
de of the *Hawk*, so quickly that the crew had
ily just time to scramble into their boat on the
eck, which floated off safely with them, though, as
iey had neither sails nor oars, they had a narrow
scape of drifting out to sea.

 This was about the last of the dangers of the sea
hich the Church ship witnessed during that
oyage, and you may think the good old bishop
as glad enough a little later to find himself in his
vn cathedral returning thanks for his safety.

 A few more years, and he was safely anchored
here there is no more sea. He died peacefully
id happily in his far-away diocese, a pattern of a
issionary Bishop.

# THE FORTUNATE ISLES.

## SANDWICH ISLANDS.

WHO has not heard of Captain Cook, the celebrated navigator, who first performed that feat of sailing round the world, which is now so common an exploit? In these days of maps and charts, compasses and ocean cables, the expedition only demands time, not special daring, but in the years gone by he was a brave man who faced the dangers of unknown seas, to land perhaps on islands or continents peopled with angry savages.

Our Captain Cook, as any book-loving child can tell you, fell a victim to his passion for travel and discovery, the ignorant natives of the Sandwich Islands first receiving him as a god, then doubting his divinity and slaying him on the shores of lovely Hawaii, the chief island of the group. The body of the murdered man was offered as a sacrifice to the gods of the land, then divided into portions, part being burnt with fire; and the heart falling to the share of some little children, they ate it, thinking it to be that of a dog, their favourite food.

I do not tell you of these horrors save with a

rpose, that of showing you the condition of the
ndwich Islanders not a hundred years ago.

The natives were, perhaps, not specially cruel,
t hopelessly evil-minded, but they were ignorant
d very superstitious, living under strange binding
vs, supposed to be made by their idols.  I can
rdly explain them to you, so different were they
anything we can conceive.  Every now and then
:ir heathen priests would pronounce this or that
.ng to be "ta-boo," and then woe to him or her
to transgressed their law concerning it.

Many things were always ta-boo, as, for in-
nce, for men and women to eat together, or to
at all of a certain berry specially belonging to
:ir gods.

Then these idols were bloodthirsty, and must
ve human sacrifices, so that their temples were
times horrible scenes of murder.  The beautiful
idwich Islands are full of volcanoes, some appa-
tly quiet for ever, but others perpetually burn-
and raging, sending up grey smoke and yellow
ne into the blue sky.  One of the great goddesses
the island was supposed to dwell in this fiery
lace; her name was Pélé, and her high priest
only to point to a native when he needed a
ifice, and he was instantly seized and strangled.
he first strangers that visited the Sandwich
nds in ships were looked upon with awe and
ze by the ignorant savages; they called the
els "floating islands," or "forests," from the
-like appearance of their masts; the clothing,

too, of the new-comers was most puzzling to the naked islanders. "They produce all things out of their bodies," they said when the new-comers brought this and that out of the pockets of their garments; the cigars they smoked were "fire in their mouths;" and the cocked hats the British seamen used to wear excited the greatest amazement. "Horned as the moon," these sharp-sighted islanders truthfully declared the queer head-dress to be. But English ships were, as you may imagine, shy of approaching these beautiful shores after the murder of Captain Cook. By-and-by, however, a good man called Vancouver, who had once accompanied his friend Captain Cook, dared to revisit the islands, and his gentle treatment of the natives gave them a love for our nation which yet exists among them. So deep was their admiration and reverence for distant England that the King of Hawaii desired to be placed under British rule And another request they made—that England would send them teachers of their religion, the religion of Christ.

But England was too busy, or too sleepy, to take any notice of the prayer; no Christian teacher left our misty shores for beautiful glowing Hawaii and the poor savage was thrown back on his false gods, his ta-boo, his murderous offerings, and his many superstitions.

And then all at once a strange thing happened— a thing that never has been before, and perhaps never will be again—the islanders rose up almost

one man, and cast away their idols from them.
ae of the first leaders of the movement was a
ieftainess of high rank, who descended the crater
the volcanic mountain to defy Pélé, eating the
rries sacred to that once revered idol, and amid the
irs and tremors of a watching crowd, returning
hurt from her awful errand. This doubtless gave
e first shock to idol worship; but what was to be
ne next? Could the people immediately become
iristiàns—instantly take on them the gentler
ke of Jesus? Oh no! they knew none of these
ings. Their false gods lay in the dust, hurled
her and thither, unable to content them, but their
solate souls had nothing else towards which to
rn—no stay, no comfort, no religion.
This state of things did not last long, however;
e Americans took pity on the islands, and, without
owing of this sudden renunciation of idolatry,
ey sailed across the seas to find the way prepared
their work, the people waiting for them without
owing it. A naked people, an ignorant people,
people not at first the least willing to receive
m, since they were not from the unknown but
oved England, but still a people with affections
be won, souls to be saved.
The good Americans settled down at once, work-
hard at the beginnings of all things, teaching,
ides the great truths of religion, the arts of
ilized life and the propriety of a little clothing
he lazy, good-humoured, courageous islanders.
hen, as years went by, the Roman Catholics

came, and tried in their way to win souls, building chapels and schools, and attaching to themselves a little band of worshippers.

And last of all England listened to the repeated cry of her distant adherents, and sent forth a bishop and clergy to these beautiful isles of the sea.

They are twelve in number, but only eight inhabited; they are called the kingdom of Hawaii, and possess a climate, perhaps the best in the world, neither too hot nor too cold. To describe them fully I must rely on the account of an English lady, who once spent six months there for the benefit of her health, and whose letters home sound almost like stories from fairyland—Miss Isabella Bird.

As she neared the harbour of Honolulu feathery cocoa-nut trees marked the shore-line; the sea was of a wonderful deep blue, fringed by white surf waves dashing over coral rocks; the sky was of as bright a blue; and the town of Honolulu—could there be a town, since all Miss Bird saw from the high deck of her steamer was a nest-like bower of greenery, from out of which peeped the roofs and windows of grass huts and lovely verandahed houses, with two church spires rising among them? Bright green lawns glowing with flowers almost running down to the sea-shore completed the picture. And this was the capital town of the Sandwich Islands. How different from London, or Dublin, or Edinburgh!

No wonder the people looked bright and smiling

oo in a land where there is neither frost nor fog,
where no fires are needed and no warm garments,
nd where men and women live as much in the
almy, soft water as on dry land. Nearly all the
miling women wore only one garment, but that
vas a very complete one, very much like an English
ight-gown, only here it was of all colours, and
ery bright ones—red, blue, green, yellow, or black.
'he men wore chiefly gay Garibaldi shirts and
)ose trousers, but all, men, women, and children,
ad wreaths of strange and glowing flowers round
heir necks, round their hats, trailing over their
rcsses.

We in busy England think children alone have
me to make flower-wreaths; but here the women
onsider it quite part of the day's duties, and are
ever seen without this beautiful ornament.
lowers are everywhere in these islands: the houses
e hidden in scarlet and orange, white and green
eauty; the air is heavy with scent; and our old
nglish favourites—geranium and fuchsia—grow to
large a size as laurel bushes.

You could not fancy this easy holiday-looking
ople ever doing much work. Why should they,
deed, when the cocoa-nut, the bread-fruit, the
m, the banana, and a dozen other good things
ow and ripen in their pleasant climate without
y trouble on their parts? To be sure there is
:alo" to be cultivated, a dish as necessary to the
ndwich Islanders as potatoes are to the Irish.
he men do that, however, when the root is grown,

making it into a sort of sticky but nourishing paste, the bread of the people. If any cooking is wanted, a hole in the ground lined with stones bakes the pig, chicken, or bread-fruit for the family. No cooks, no great kitchen fire, no washing day, for the one garment hardly can get soiled in this bright, clear climate, and if it did, it would want very little getting-up.

What, then, do the people do? I do not mean the foreigners, the gentlepeople, as it were, who form a good part of the town population, but the poor people, the working classes, as we should say in England. Well, you can easily see, for they are all out of doors, sitting on their mats, talking, laughing, singing, greatly amused by the appearance of the strange folk who land on their shores. These are their quiet moments; by-and-by one or another springs up, jumps on horseback, and gallops at wild speed down to the beach. The very poor even own a horse; once there were none on the island, and when a few were brought by ships in the year 1803, the natives fled in terror from the great unknown creatures; till then they had had nothing larger than a pig in their country. Now they are too common, for they are a wretched breed of lean creatures, the only uncomfortable-looking things on the islands; but still they go, and go well too, and every man, woman, and child has one, and will not trouble themselves to walk a step in consequence. Up they jump, the women like the men—their loose garment is not in the way—barefooted, but flower-crowned, and always smiling, they dash along.

Surely these are "The Fortunate Isles." We
egin to feel discontented and envious as we read
nd tell of these sunny, smiling, beautiful days in
he most perfect of all climates.

But stay a minute. If the mothers amuse them-
elves like this, where are the little children?
urely they must need some tending and care.

Ay, where are they? Of course there are some
omewhere, or have been, else would there have
een none of these smiling, fluttering yellow and
lue creatures on horseback; but now there are
ery few. Not many are born on the islands, and
hile there is no unkindness to complain of, yet
he mothers do not seem specially attached to their
ttle ones. They are fond of pets—puppies and
ttle pigs are their delight; but the babies—well,
hey cry and are a trouble, so the ease-loving people
ive them away to some one who has a special
aste for children, and are quite happy without
hem.

It is a strange state of things, and no wonder the
umber of the inhabitants diminishes daily. Some-
hing is not right in the land; these people, who
illingly cast away their false gods and called for
hristian teachers, have yet much to learn of Christ-
ke living. The little girls are the best hope here,
everal good, kind ladies have taken them in hand,
otably two English ladies from a sisterhood in
ngland, who have a happy little set of scholars in
shady nook of Hawaii. Such merry little souls!
he learning of cooking, sewing, reading, and

writing cannot sober them; they just compose their
faces for Bible reading and prayers, and then out
come the fun and frolic again. They must laugh,
they must dance, and as there is nothing wrong in
this last amusement, the sisters teach them graceful
English dances between the prayers and the lessons,
for it would be impossible to make prim, retiring
Englishwomen of these island maidens. Even in
school the scarlet blossoms brighten their hair as
the roguish smiles do their faces; but all the fun
the sisters try to underlay with good principles and
pure thoughts, things these little ones could never
learn at home from their ease-loving mothers.
Hawaïi children do not dislike learning; but going
to school is very different there to what it is in
England. You come to a glittering, shining river,
and see dark little heads bobbing in the stream.
It is little Tom and Jack, and Mary Jane of the
Sandwich Isles swimming to school, holding up
their scanty clothes in a bundle in one hand; they
learn to swim as babies, and on landing just shake
their little brown bodies, dry themselves a moment
in the sun, slip on that easy loose overall, and there
they are ready for work.

Fancy now, at a sort of boarding school for poor
little orphan girls, what the cry was when lessons
were over for the morning. "Go, children, and get
your horses!" And off dashed two small girls of
eight and ten, returning with their lean, unshod
steeds to enjoy a good scamper across country in
play-time. This sounds very delightful again; but,

las! I have not told you one of the chief troubles of this beautiful kingdom of Hawaii, a trouble that may, perhaps, account for the diminishing of the population in a great measure.

There is a terrible disease rife in this sweet land, a disease that it will make you shudder to think of, especially since in these days there are no great prophets, no loving Son of Mary treading our earth to take compassion on the sufferers. I mean leprosy. Yes, that is the name, not exactly the same sort of which Elisha cured Naaman, not exactly the same sort from which those lepers were cleansed of whom our Lord asked, "Where are the nine?" but a disease as fatal, as hopeless, as terrible.

For a time the signs of it can be kept secret, but by-and-by it must be found out—the puffed skin, the glassy eyes, will not be mistaken, and after that come the terrible sores, the devouring malady in all its horrors.

Day by day, of late years, the disease, which is very infectious, has taken firmer hold of the land, and the fear that in time the natives might be entirely swept away by it induced the king to take strong measures to put a stop to its inroads.

These measures seemed very terrible, but they were needed.

What do you think they were? No less than taking one island of the group and founding upon it a leper settlement, where the poor diseased wretches might be conveyed in ships to live out their miserable days, die, and be buried. No hopes of their ever getting better and returning to home and friends, they *must* die.

Of course, there was great grief and anguish when the Government made known its plan, and issued an order that all lepers should be given up by their families, and many of the poor things fled into hiding, or were concealed in their houses, only to be discovered by-and-by. Two officers of the Board of Health went round the islands repeatedly in their leper ship, collecting the poor victims as kindly and quietly as possible. But still it was a woeful business, many agonized partings taking place— husband from wife, child from its parents, friend from friend. Such wailing on the sea-beach, such kissing of swollen limbs and glazed cheeks as is not easy to forget. Rich people as well as poor fell under the strict rule of banishment. A half-white man, a lawyer, so little touched by the disease that no one knew he had it but himself, bravely gave himself up to the authorities, and was accompanied to the ship by a crowd of friends and acquaintances, all loudly weeping, for he was greatly beloved. The cousin of the queen, too, a man of property, was found to be another leper, and doomed to banishment also. In eight years' time more than eleven hundred poor creatures were sent to Molokai, the island set apart for them. It is an island of precipices, and between one very high wall of rock and the sea lies the leper village—a fearful spot, the home of the suffering and dying, " a community whose only business is to perish." Here husbandless wives, wifeless husbands, childless parents and orphaned children wait day by day for their only change, their only comfort—death. Ah! pleasant sunny islands!—we cannot call them fortunate now, cannot murmur in our hearts that to these laughing Hawaians God has given all the sunshine, all the pleasures, and left to us Northern folk the chills and labours of life.

The King and Queen of Hawaii are very kind and thoughtful over their poor afflicted subjects, who must be supported by the nation in their exile. They even paid a visit to Molokai, to tell the lepers how grieved they were at the necessity which drove them from their homes, and to see that they were properly fed and tended. A gentleman who went with the king describes the scene. Leper boys greeting their coming with drum and fife, joy in their poor disfigured faces; notwithstanding their dreadful condition, the whole community seemed, except in rare cases, to be possessed with the light, gay, careless natures of their happier brethren in the other islands. Many among the crowd did not seem stricken at all, but be sure the fell disease did lurk in their frames, one day to destroy them. All these poor souls came eagerly forward when spoken to, pleased to answer questions, pleased to talk of the homes they might never see again. It was sad to see them and realize their sufferings, but oh! sadder far to visit the hospital, where lay those literally sick unto death, who just glanced from out of the caverns of their poor sunken eyes at the strange healthful visitors, and then turned on their mats and withdrew into their own dreadful selves.

One sight is mentioned as most grievous of all. In the hospital ward, trotting about, looking to one and another for a word of love, was a little blue-eyed, flaxen-haired child three or four years old, much such a fair little creature as you might have at home; but this poor babe was a leper, glassy-eyed, shining-cheeked, exiled with the rest, born but to suffer and die.

But come from the close hospital air now into the balmy sweetness of out of doors; the place is not ill to look upon, with its pretty cottages for the few of the better class, and its grass huts, school-house, and churches for all.

Who serves the churches for these poor folk, do you ask? Alas! there are regularly ordained leper pastors for this stricken flock, leper schoolmasters for the diseased children. There is, however, one exception to this rule.

A small stone church near the landing, and another further on, tell of the devotion of a Belgian Catholic priest. I will give you his name, for it deserves to be remembered—Father Damiens. He, young, strong, untainted, an educated, refined man, has of his own will come to this terrible valley, and exiled himself, with this leper flock for Christ's sake.

"It was singular," says one on the spot, "to hear the burst of admiration which this act elicited from all." All sects, all branches of Christ's Church rgot differences, envyings, jealousies, when they eard of the noble act. Father Damiens is indeed terally following the example of his Master, by laying down his life for the brethren."

As we can no longer have the pitiful Jesus nongst us to say, "Be thou clean" to these poor eatures, we may be thankful that He has cast the antle of His love on some among His disciples ere below.

But we must leave this sad spot now, and perhaps ou will not be sorry to do so, since it is painful to atch suffering which cannot be relieved.

Back, then, for a while into the sunshine of com- on life, where the careless Hawaians are laughing d singing, riding and dancing in their flowing bes and flower-crowned heads.

As I told you before, the Americans were the first send missionaries to this island, and they were ost earnest in their endeavours to teach the people hristianity, establishing churches and schools in any places, living among them, rearing their hristian families in their midst, and earning spect and love everywhere. But "lightly come, ghtly go;" this dancing, singing, gay-hearted ople do not seem to take up willingly even the sy yoke of Christ. Though idols and ta-boo are olished in the land, though little children are no ore deserted by their parents, and though open i no longer flaunts on these green shores, there is t much to be done.

A pure and gentle religion must be ever kept in

sight of this childish, pleasure-loving people, and this we hope may be done by the efforts of Bishop Willis and his clergy, following on the labours of those gone before them.

A King and Queen of Hawaii visited England in 1824, and were received with honour by our King George IV. and the Government, but their visit ended very sadly. First one and then another caught the measles; the queen died first, her husband, with tearful eyes, saying over to himself the just learned comfortable words of the new religion, "She has gone to heaven," and then, saddened and depressed by the loss of one so beloved, he sank and died too. The Government sent their bodies back to their own green island in a frigate specially set apart for the purpose.

After this reigned a king who declared that "the religion of the Lord Jesus Christ shall continue to be the established national religion of the Hawaian Islands." And next came a monarch of whom much might have been hoped. The most accomplished and patriotic prince of his line, he had married a wife with English blood in her veins, and was the proud possessor of a little son, to whom our Queen promised to stand godmother. Great hopes were centred in this child, great and good plans made for the education of the little Prince of Hawaii, but all in vain; to the intense grief of his parents and the nation, the little boy died in infancy, shortly followed to the grave by his father

The present king and queen are amiable and

ell-meaning, though they have not yet been
ng enough in power for much to be said about
em.

And now we must bid good-bye to this interest-
g, frank-hearted island people. I should like
our last thoughts of them to be happy ones, so I
ust tell you that one of our clergy out there says:
There is one very cheering result of our labour:
believe we are making much progress among the
oung." And great pains they do take with the
ttle flower-crowned, careless creatures. Schools
d catechisings, children's services and choir
actices, all the well-known English ways of
aching and doing good are common to Hawaii
so. No one wants to stamp out the wreath-
aking, the singing, and the dancing. God made
is people beauty-loving and cheerful-hearted under
is beaming sky, and there is nothing wrong in
at, but we do want their souls to be as fair as
eir bodies, their thoughts as pure as the white
ies in their hands. And to effect this we must
y to make happiness and holiness join hands.

8

# RAGGED RUSSIA.

## RUSSIA.

In Russia, as in other countries, nay, perhaps, more
certainly indeed than in other countries, the hot
summer drives town-dwellers into the country.
Summer, however, is short and scorching in this
Northern land, and the winter consequently is a
long and a very severe one.  No rich person thinks
of allowing a little child to go out of doors in all
the long nine months of furs and frost; so you may
fancy what joy there is when the soft winds blow
the ice melts, and the trees burst into leaf.  O
course, the great people who live in palaces in the
towns, have their country homes as well, and hastei
to revisit them.  You may see them nodding her
and there to the old servants and tenants who com
out into the sunshine to greet their masters an
mistresses as the six or eight horse carriage rattle
by.  The town-dwellers, however, who have n
country house of their own, enjoy another pleasure
Every summer they are at liberty to go to som
different place, either to the seaside, to the moun
tains, or to the shady forest, just as they ma
please.

I who write this account am one of this last
ᵢss of citizens, and being free to choose my own
ound last summer, I took my daughters to a
etty country house in the neighbourhood of
oscow, which nestled among smiling corn-fields,
d comprised in the wide view that opened from
some half-dozen tiny villages. The sweet air
ᴐwing so freshly in our faces, and the perfect
ᵢet after the noisy town streets were delightful.
ᵣr a day or two time seemed to fly. We wandered
out doing nothing and praising everything. But
ᵢ were not really idle fine ladies; so by-and-by
me the feeling that all play and no work was
t complete happiness. What, then, should be
ᵣ holiday task here in the corn-fields and under
ᵢ shady trees ?

It must be work, but it must not be hard work.
ᵢe had left the city to enjoy ourselves and to gain
ᵢlth in the fields and lanes. Real work, good
ᵢrk it should be, or it would not satisfy the long-
ᵢs at our hearts. We considered a little, and then
seemed as if the work we wanted was lying all
ᵢdy to our hand, only waiting for us to begin it.
ᵢour walks through the neighbouring villages we
ᵢen met bands of ragged children as free and do-
ᵢhing as ourselves, bright-eyed and active they
ᵣre, pattering barefooted after wild flowers and
ᵣies, their only apparent occupation. Why
ᵢuld we not teach them something while we were
ᵢh them—set up a Russian ragged school, in fact ?
ᵢany rate it was worth thinking of, and the next

time we came across a group of these little people
playing in the lane we made a beginning by asking
"Children, do you know how to read?" A pause
a look from one to the other to see who would
speak first, and then a "No" from all. "Is there a
school near here?" This time a quicker "No.
"James can read a bit," said, bravely, a tiny boy
pointing to his big brother; "he learns from th
diatchek." (The "diatchek" is the reader in
church.) "And what do you read, James?" "
don't read any more," said Jemmy, importantly
"There is work to be done at home, and father can'
spare me." It didn't look much like work to fin
Jemmy playing in the lane, but it would not do t
seem unbelieving, so I went on: "What did yo
read with the diatchek?" "The Church books—
can only read them. It was very tiresome learnin
them, and besides he pulled my ears and my hai
and expected to be paid for that." "Well, childrer
shall I teach you something? I promise not to pu
your ears nor your hair, and I won't ask you
parents for any money. I shall only make tw
conditions—you must come to me every day exactl
at the same time, and you must have clean hand
and faces."

The last condition seemed to amuse the childrer
they looked curiously at their own dirty litt
hands, and one said, suggestively, "We could g
to the river and wash ourselves all over." It wa
a good idea, and the morrow was fixed for th
beginning of baths and lessons. "But whic

cottage' do you live in?" asked one of the boys.
We showed them our house; they all knew it well,
having often brought there wild strawberries to sell
to the previous owners. They were delighted to
think they might come again into the beautiful
grounds, and ran off in great spirits. And we too
made haste home to arrange for our new school.

We set aside a room for the purpose, the gardener
gave us a long table and two benches, and we
turned out of our boxes some pencils and paper,
making copies of letters for our scholars, and then
all was ready for a beginning. The next morning
the children came in high spirits, fresh from the
river, their hair streaming in little rivulets over
their shoulders. The boys wore ragged trousers
hanging in frills round their legs, and little faded
cotton shirts bound round the waist by a girdle, to
which hung a copper comb. Yet with all their
poor clothes they were straight, well set up little
fellows, pleasant to look at.

School began with seven scholars and three
mistresses; but towards the end of a week these
boys brought others with them, and the party had
to be divided into two classes. Seeing such numbers
coming to be taught, we could not bear to leave
them to themselves on Sunday. We longed to
gather the little flock together and teach them who
was their true Shepherd.

No one seemed ever to have taught them anything before, these poor little wild men, and their
parents were just as ignorant. Each little lad, to

be sure, could put a horse in the cart at need, could collect wood, guide the plough, and run and jump like a young colt, but that did not seem enough to satisfy us. The age of temptation was coming to each and all, and none of these accomplishments would help them through it.

So a Sunday school there was to be, a little different to the week-day school. The tables and the benches were now carried out under the trees near the house, and the children in gay-coloured shirts and well-oiled hair gathered closely together in the shade, wondering what was going to happen. Some women from the village, too, sat under the trees at a little distance.

I read a short prayer, the children accompanying it with much signing of the cross and bowing of the head. They had learned this outward show of reverence, poor little things, but knew nothing of what it meant. Then a New Testament was given to each child who could read ever so little. But that done, where should we begin with such ignorant little creatures needing to be taught everything, yet hardly knowing how to sit still? And there were only ten Sundays to do it all in.

There they sat, the poor little people, with their pleasant faces, and we thought how happy it would be for us if we could wake in some of these innocent hearts a desire to know God, and place some of these child feet in the narrow way to heaven.

"Dear children," I began, "I want you all to grow up good boys and honest men. I want to

elp you to be this, and to show you the only way
) become so. Do you wish me to do so?" "Yes,
es," said all the little voices. "I see, alas! every
unday your drinking shops full from early morn-
ıg, while in the evening the poor drunkards are
ʼing senseless in the dust, the laughing-stock and
:orn of even you little ones. Now I want you to
eep away from the drinking shop, to learn to be
ıdustrious, so that though you may be poor, still
ou may lead happy and respectable lives."

"I don't mean ever to be a drunkard," said
emmy, proudly; "my father never drinks, nor
ıy brother, although he has been a coachman at
[oscow more than a year. It is only fools who
ʽink."

"The lady isn't talking about fools, she is talking
bout us," said a big boy.

"Yes," I went on, "I am talking about you, and
want to talk to you about God who made us to
ıve Him, and who loves us, and takes care of us.
; is of Him I want to tell you every Sunday.
7ill you listen?"

"Certainly we will; only tell us about Him,"
ıid all the little voices, encouragingly.

It is not necessary here to repeat all our Sunday
:aching of those poor little fellows; we tried to
ıve them some idea of the life and work of the
aviour, and to warm their young hearts with the
ıle of His love; but the time was short, and so
ıuch had to be done in it. Generally we read them
gospel story or a parable, first explaining to them

the tale, and then applying it to their own lives as
village children.  Very difficult was this to do in a
country where religion is only taught as a lesson,
not as anything to do with daily life.

In Russia, amongst the poor, religion is for the
most part like a beautiful church, magnificently
decorated, while life is just a dusty road.  People
who enter the temple shake off the dust at the
doorway, and, coming away again, leave behind
them the impressions that may have been received
within.  To make the glittering dome of the church
the guide on the dusty road of life is what we
desired to do; or, to speak more plainly, to bring
holy thoughts and motives into every-day work.
And children might be taught to do this, we
thought, if only a beginning could be made.  As
a first step we always began Monday's lessons by
asking for a repetition of what had been learned on
Sunday.  The children would give their account in
their own way.  It sounded somewhat strange to
us at times, but did not much alter the Bible story.
Thus the tale of the rich farmer who made a feast
and invited Jesus to it, or the parable of the sower,
would be given with the addition of a few words of
their own, expressive of their experience in the
fields at sowing and at other times.  The story of
the Prodigal Son seemed a very strange one to
them.  They all felt for the *elder* brother, and had
plenty of hard words on their quick little tongues
for the younger one.  "That was a queer sort of
father in the story," declared James; "he ought to

and forks, kettles and saucepans, excited their
boundless admiration, so different were they to the
earthen cooking-pots and wooden bowls in their
own poor little homes.

As soon as our scholars could spell out a sentence, their pleasure was to carry their books
to the village, and there, surrounded by a group
of little admirers, to show off their learning.  The
listeners were never impatient, however long the
reader stammered over a word, and when the story
did dawn upon those who heard it, how beautiful
it seemed, and how clever the scholar with the
book!  But our lessons bore better fruit still.  One
day four little lads came hurrying to us, hot from
a wordy dispute.  "Madame," cried little Guerassime,
the brother of James, while he was still panting
in the distance, "we have found a fine penknife;
isn't it yours?" and he showed his lucky find
clasped in his hand.  "No, my boy."  "Well, then,
these boys here say we may keep it and draw lots
for it; but I say that isn't what you teach us on
Sundays.  We ought to make the round of all the
gentlemen's houses, and try and find out who it
belongs to.  What do you think, ma'am?"  You
may fancy what answer he got, and how pleased
we all were to find that one boy at least was trying
to act out what he learned.

Among our pupils were also some girls.  Two
of them, big girls, came to us in very touching
fashion.  Sisters, living in a distant village, they
made their appearance one Sunday morning.  We

the winter?" "Very sad," sighed Paracha, and
both girls lifted the corner of a coarse apron to dry
the tears that would come at the remembrance of
their dear lost ones. "We knit gloves in winter,"
she continued, "but we should so like to be able
to read the Gospels turn and turn about." "And
the distance? And the field work, which will
be very pressing soon?" "Oh, the distance, that
is nothing in summer," said Eudoxie, the youngest
sister; "and as to the field work, I can do it alone
at a pinch. I am the strongest, but my sister is
the cleverest; she shall learn first, and when she
knows how to read, she will teach me."

Of course, we were obliged to take into our ranks
these earnest scholars, and full of joy the two poor
girls turned homewards, leaving us to make two
resolutions—one to do our very best in teaching
them, the other never to judge by appearances
for the future. The sisters were, indeed, our best,
most attentive, most punctual pupils. They had
immense difficulties to overcome, it is true—their
stiff fingers would hardly close over the slippery
pencil, their memories refused to remember the
names of the letters, and their poor foreheads ran
down with perspiration over their new labours;
it was harder than working in the fields. Nevertheless, so great was their industry and perseverance, that at the end of three months they had
attained their end. They could spell out, so as
to understand them, the words of the Holy Book!
Every Monday, with loving exactness, they repeated

and that does it so much harm, and then, as a rest,
they send me on these errands."

This knitting takes the shape of woollen gloves,
which village boys and girls make for the Moscow
shops — coachmen, carters, and labourers buying
them at sixpence a pair. A child of twelve will
knit generally three gloves a day—that is to say,
a pair and a half—and all our little scholars work
at this trade with wonderful quickness. You may
also often see a white-bearded old man sitting in
the sun in front of his cottage, making the knitting-
needles fly over his gloves of grey or red. But
it was evident that this was quite the wrong sort
of work for poor Doreniacha, since it irritated her
wound terribly. "You ought not to knit," I said
to her. "Whatever remedies are applied they will
do no good if you go on wearying your poor arm
in this way." She smiled. "Not knit!" she
answered (it was such a ridiculous idea that!).
"Then who will knit for me? And how shall
I earn bread? The pence you have given me for
the eggs I shall take to the miller for flour; but
that won't last long." "Do you live on dry bread,
then?" "Ah, we are glad if we can always get
that; but we have the mushrooms too, when they
are not good enough to sell." Living on such food,
there was evidently not much chance of cure for
this poor child. "Have you no father?" I asked.
Her little face clouded. "Yes, I have a father,"
she said, "but he is no good; he drinks all he earns.
When he comes from Moscow for a holiday it is
we who have to keep him."

fresh wound in her arm, and that she knitted always in tears from the extreme pain it caused her. Surely some day the good God will grant her the comfort denied her on earth—give her the repose she cannot have here.

Children like this can easily understand death coming as a deliverer. One day, reading of the widow of Nain's son, we spoke of death in our Sunday school, and I asked the children if they wished to die. "I do," said a little voice in tones of deepest sadness. It was not Doreniacha who spoke though, but George, himself the only son of a widowed mother. He was thirteen, had a sweet sad face, and only came to school on Sundays, since he could already read well. "And why do you wish to die?" I asked. "Because we have no bread, and it is so wretched trying to live." At that moment there was a loud laugh in the class, a laugh certainly not caused by poor George's speech. I looked round, and soon saw the reason for it. A big, stupid-looking boy had shambled into the middle of my pupils, his clothes in rags, his head like an old door-mat. He cowered down at the foot of a tree, while the other children continued to laugh, poking him, and making fun of him in different ways. "Who is this boy?" I asked. "It is the idiot Nikita," said several voices contemptuously. "What, a poor idiot, and you are teasing him!" "Ah, he is a bad un, and so strong," they cried. "He would throw stones at you, and hurt you." "That is not to be wondered at," I said, "if you clamour after him

to his keepers. They had found him in the bushes, this poor little fellow of barely seven years; he had been there all night, all alone, only half clothed. "He has a stepmother crosser even than the other," said these little policemen in explanation; "and very often he stays out all night, hidden in a barn or garden, to escape a beating. No one cares for him at home; and if you are going to make any more shirts, here's the little chap that would be glad of one." The poor little man indeed bore in his face the traces of continued ill treatment. He neither looked up nor spoke, only waited silently the end of it all. Happily for him, his cottage was close to that of a big boy, and a very good boy, called Effime, whose parents were people of some standing, since the father was a good workman and did not drink, and the mother was—well, one of the best women in the village, with a kind, loving face, that explained why her cottage kitchen was always filled with poor neighbours, come either for sympathy in trouble or to borrow this or that article of domestic use. Her pity and her pots and pans were all at their service. This kind woman promised to give an eye to her unhappy little neighbour, clothing him as a beginning in a nice new shirt.

As for us, we were delighted to see our boys acting the policeman so cleverly in discovering the poor and wretched of the neighbourhood, and though many of the little fellows themselves were poor enough, we never found them begging for anything on their own account.

books. Even the children's parents, who at first hardly seemed to care for our school, began to show themselves grateful for our efforts, sending us frequent presents of mushrooms, and begging us to stand godmothers to their newest little ones. The godfather was always a peasant, one of their own friends; if we accepted the invitation we had to join the christening feast of tea, walnuts, and gingerbread, followed by omelette and cake.

In our country walks we were always accompanied by some of our scholars, and by Nikita the idiot boy, whose strong arm was often a welcome protection against dogs or cattle. One day as we were bidding adieu to our ragged escort, we stopped a moment to admire the lovely prospect spread out before us, the setting sun gilding the corn-fields, the river in the valley, the domes and spires and towers of beautiful Moscow, "the white-stoned mother of all Russia," as its inhabitants call the dear old capital of the kingdom. A cart heavily laden with sheaves of corn came along the road, drawn by an old peasant whose hair rivalled his shirt in its dazzling whiteness. He stopped when he saw us, and bowing to the earth, said earnestly, "God bless you for teaching our poor children." "Have you sons or grandsons among our scholars?" we inquired. "Oh no, I have no children," said the old man, "but it is all the same, they are our children these little ones whom you instrnct." This blessing of the poor old peasant cheered our hearts, coming as it did so willingly and unexpectedly.

sime, pushing back his hair all ready for his cap, declared decisively, " I shall go and fetch them." And off he went like an arrow. The others, fired by this example, rushed after him, and soon not a guest remained on the field. But it was all right, we could wait, and they had come so early there was yet a long afternoon before us. The tea-can was only just steaming on the table, the cake had only just been cut, when we heard in the distance the dull thudding of naked feet on the road; soon we caught glimpses of small red and blue shirts between the trees, and then we saw the whole troop of youngsters triumphantly conducting the two tiny ones, both gasping for breath, but smiling from ear to ear. Then we sat down to table. Our guests were neither shy nor greedy. Accustomed to drink tea as the Russians do, till every drop of water in the kettle is exhausted, they kept pushing forward their empty cups with a " Some more tea, please, Sophie dear," using the last little word to our maid in imitation of us.

But this feast of ours was unwittingly an occasion of much distress to poor little Guerassime. He had asked to remain till the last to help the servant to wash the knives and forks, an occupation which he always found very delightful. This time, however, there were two knives and forks missing, and our servant ran to tell us this great calamity. Of course, every one except ourselves threw the blame on the boys, and an old milkwoman living near delivered an address in our kitchen to this effect:

to have to leave my work so soon, and I told the
children so.  Then I paused to try to say something
more cheerful.  But a little voice at my elbow spoke
timidly, "*You* are going away," it said, "but still
the Saviour stays with us."  It was George who
spoke, the little man who had wished to die, because
to live was so sad.  This little speech did us all
good, it seemed like the fluttering blossom of the
fruit of our Sunday school.

Two days more and the children gathered round
the carriage which was to take us to the neighbouring station.  They would not play, they hardly
in fact exchanged observations on the horses, the
harness, the wheels, all those tremendously important matters in a boy's eyes.  They were thinking of their teachers, whom they were now to lose.
The good-bye moment came; how closely the little
arms pressed us!

But where was Guerassime, our little favourite?
We could not go without bidding him adieu.  "He
was here a minute ago," said the children, "he can't
be far off."  They called him, but no answer came.
Then I went back to the house, hastily glancing
through the different rooms till I arrived at the
kitchen.  There I found my lost lamb stretched by
the desolate hearth, his face in his hands, crying
bitterly.  God keep this poor little fellow, and all
the rest of the small flock of whom He is the
faithful Shepherd!  This is the story of our Russian
ragged school; there is no more.  God only knows
the end, and we leave the result to Him.

Besides the actual mission party who collected together in Liverpool Docks one March day in 1855, there stood by Mr. Mackenzie's side a favourite sister, whose delicate health it was hoped would be benefited by the African climate, and whose happy disposition, and thorough determination to help forward, as far as she could, her brother's work, was likely to make her a valuable companion.

I should like to tell you something of the after-lives of these two, this pleasant, frank brother and sister, full of love towards God, each other, and their fellow-creatures, black or white.

People soon show what they are made of on board ship, where every one is crowded very closely together, and a great many inconveniences of wind and weather have to be borne, willingly or un-willingly as the case may be; and so while Miss Mackenzie lay, as most ladies do at sea, sick in her berth, and only able to show the grace of patience, her stronger brother was very busy waiting on the poor passengers in the steerage, who were sick too, and withal strange and helpless. He made beds and helped to dress little fidgety children ; he com-forted the sick with cheerful words for their spirits, and nicely made arrowroot for their bodies. " I can make it famously now," he writes in a letter home, and, in fact, as his sister said, he was the life of the party, the sunshine of the steerage, and the director of everything, from the boxes in the hold to the preaching and teaching of all on board. Besides this homely work, he was steadily studying

the language of the tribe in Africa among whom he
hoped to labour—the Zulus, a poor ignorant race
of dark-skinned men.

Perhaps he was just a little bit disappointed
when, on landing, his charge was given him among
white people in a civilized town on the coast,
Durban, where the work and its little worries were
much the same as they would have been in a small
town in England, but this he would never confess
even to his sister Anne. He put his shoulder to
the wheel to do his best for his flock, while she
tried to get the house in order—not so easy in
Africa, where the white ants insist on living with
you and eating the lion's share of everything.
They, at any price, must be got rid of, since in a
night they will root up mounds all over the sitting-
room floor, and besides devouring food make a meal
of book-bindings or shoe leather. Miss Mackenzie
used arsenic to help her, but she says the only real
way to get rid of these tiresome creatures is to
dig till the queen ant is reached (a disgusting fat
creature, who seems to gather the rest round her),
and destroy her.

The Mackenzies were a year and a half at Durban,
working among the whites, but always with the
prospect in view of some day breaking new ground
and telling the story of salvation to the heathen
tribes. They made friends with a Scotch missionary, Mr. Robertson, who with his wife were
soon reckoned among their dearest friends, and
whose settlement some miles in the country was a

favourite resort of brother or sister when in need
of change.

Visiting in Africa, even among white people, is
so different to anything of the sort in England that
I must tell you something of Miss Mackenzie's first
visit to Umlazi, the Robertsons' settlement. Firstly,
her hosts built a house for her, or rather a hut,
and when the visitors were crossing the wide river
in sight of the dwellings, Mrs. Robertson called
hurriedly for a rake, to make the floor of the hut
quite smooth before the mats were laid down upon
it. This was supposed to be making things very
tidy and comfortable.

Miss Mackenzie, however, was not one to expect
English drawing-rooms in Kafir-land, and she made
herself very happy in the rough hut, spending her
day in teaching little black children and visiting
the natives in company with her friend. Mrs.
Robertson seems to have been specially fond of
little children, and the dark faces, wide noses, and
thick lips of the little Kafirs appeared to her as
beautiful as the blue eyes and golden hair of our
darlings at home. She was never tired of telling of
the pretty ways and pleasant sayings of Hali and
Billy, two small people whom she took into her
house as babies to educate and bring up in Christian
fashion. Plenty more followed to share her care,
but still these two kept their places, and seemed
quite her own children.

While Miss Mackenzie was staying at Umlazi, a
sister of hers who desired to join the missionary

sitting on trunks of felled trees, the psalms and
hymns rising straight through the clear air, the
earnest words of the discourse sounding so life-
like in that quiet corner of Africa. "Listen, my
children, the words I speak are not mine, but they
are the words of our Lord and Saviour . Jesus
Christ : 'He who believeth and is baptized shall be
saved.'" Oh, peaceful Sunday in far-away Africa !
Can we not all remember some such happy time,
when God seemed really present with us, and
trouble or even worldy fret far away ?

The three Mackenzies were now to be very busy
in their own quarters. A post was given to the
brother forty miles north of Durban, where each
and all would have plenty to do. The last comer,
Miss Alice Mackenzie, soon showed so great a
liking for and understanding of the natives that
Mr. Mackenzie used laughingly to speak of her as
his *black* sister, as distinguished from his *white*
sister Anne. On first taking possession of his new
charge, there was no house fit to hold the party,
so to each was allotted a round native hut, just
like a bee-hive. "Charles is indulging me with a
window of four little panes," writes Anne, the
invalid sister; but Alice, the stronger one, when
the weather is cold, hangs a blanket in her doorway,
and a shawl in the place where her glass window
ought to be, and is merry over it. And presently
Anne discovers a new charm in her future per-
manent apartment: it has an opening at the top
into the long room they use for a church, and

"Is not this a happy life?" writes one sister about this time.

And though we at home may think these gentle-people were often in want of the commonest comforts, far away from friends and most things the world thinks make life pleasant, we must own, when we come to look into the matter, that theirs might well have been true happiness. They were a loving family party, united in one common work, and that the best and happiest mortal man can undertake—the spread of their Lord's kingdom on earth.

But change is so much the order of the world that you will not be surprised to hear it found its way into this little African settlement. Circumstances made it necessary for the archdeacon to visit England, and his sister Anne was to go with him. She loved Africa and work, but still, as she said on hearing of the decision, "I am in a flurry of joy."

We do not need to say much about the English visit. All the while Archdeacon Mackenzie was only waiting for directions as to his future course, and when they came he calmly accepted them after consulting the dear sisters who formed part of his life.

And yet it was no easy work set before him. I will try in a few words to give you an idea of it.

Dr. Livingstone, the great African traveller, whose death all England has since deplored, had not long before come to England fresh from his travels in Africa, to tell a tale of heathendom and slavery,

ing, if need be, to give not only his work but his life to his Master.

So he sailed a second time for Africa, and was consecrated bishop in the cathedral at Capetown, leaving almost immediately for the scene of his future labours.

The arrangements made with the sisters were somewhat altered by circumstances. The white sister, Miss Anne Mackenzie, was in time to share her brother's labours, but at present she was left at the Cape till the ground could be a little smoothed for her; and the black sister—well, her lot was cast in her first quarters, Natal, by her becoming the wife of the Archdeacon of Maritzburg. This sister tells us of the joy of his old parishioners at seeing their beloved friend and teacher once more, and their bitter grief when he sailed for the new land.

Under Dr. Livingstone's directions, but with many drawbacks and tedious delays, the mission party made its way, first along the coast, and then up one of the great African rivers to the district where it hoped to form a settlement.

Of course, the travellers were struck down by fever, first one and then another; but the attacks were not severe, unfortunately giving the bishop an idea that the disease was not so alarming as was generally considered, and leading him to think lightly of precautions and remedies—a mistake which was to cost him dearly by-and-by. He was very hopeful ever, as he says himself, "always believing that things will go well." And when

Here was a perplexity. The bishop and his clergy had not left England to make war with any ignorant tribe, but rather to teach them the gentle doctrines of peace; yet were oppression and slavery to be allowed to go unpunished under Christian eyes?

It was a matter to be thought about and prayed over and not decided in a hurry, mused the bishop. But lo! while he mused Dr. Livingstone and his companions had come across a slave party, some eighty or more poor wretches tied together, with forked sticks round their necks to render them helpless, under the escort of half a dozen cruel masters with guns. It was the work of a few minutes to scare away the savage masters and to free the slaves, but it involved a great matter, that of stamping the missionaries as men of war as well as peace. Still, it was impossible to act otherwise; the poor chained creatures were full of gratitude to their new friends, and ready enough to tell their troubles to them. Two women who tried to escape, they said, had been shot as an example to the rest; and one poor woman, who could not carry both her babe and the burden allotted to her, had to see the child snatched from her, and its brains dashed out by the wayside. Dr. Livingstone, who spoke their language, addressed the slaves, telling them they were free, and might either go home or stay under the care of the English. They all chose to stay, so here at the very outset of his career Bishop Mackenzie found himself not only a bishop, but an

the Ajawas, and the conflict soon ended in their
flight, leaving many of their slave captives behind.
Of these the bishop took the very young children
to add to his flock, while those old enough to choose
for themselves went where they would. The
bishop's family, or tribe, whichever you like to call
it, was now growing very large; the little ones
were fed just like young birds in a nest, all placed
in a row while a woman went round with porridge
in a basin, giving to each a handful—of course
there were no plates or spoons as yet. The tiniest
baby of all was meantime perched on the woman's
back. She had adopted the little creature whom
war or misfortune had made motherless. This plan
of giving the children their meals was quite an
improvement on their first habit of scrambling for
the food as for nuts at a school feast. The food
itself was bought from natives who brought daily
to the settlement baskets of meal, bunches of nuts,
beans, big yam roots like potatoes, and goats or fowls.
For these the bishop paid in white or coloured
calico or beads. The boys were all marched down
to the river daily to bathe; they did not quite like
this, and some long faces were seen at the "off
clouts," which was the order given, but after a
while all ended in laughter. Then they came back
and helped to build the new house, and between
and after all the work there was plenty of singing
and dancing, native fashion. Morning and evening
there were Church prayers, at which all attended.

This is the sort of work the bishop had to do;

unwell and wearied in body and spirit by the late troubles!

In the last letter written by the bishop he describes this journey—first the walk across country, then the floating down the great river in a canoe to the meeting-place. All was going well till, by an unlucky accident, the boat grounded and filled with water. Out jumped the boatmen, out jumped the bishop and Mr. Burrup up to their waists in the river, trying to secure their baggage. They did recover most of it, but their greatest loss was their medicine, the packet of quinine, which in Africa is the only thing which puts a stop to the constant attacks of fever from which Europeans suffer. Mr. Burrup was already ill, and the bishop regretted deeply the want of medicine for him. They had ten days to wait before the steamer could arrive with the ladies on board, and this the bishop meant to employ in making friends with the natives round.

Meantime Miss Mackenzie was being brought daily nearer—brought, I say, for she knew little about her journey herself, lying as she did very ill of fever in the boat. She was wont to tell of this voyage that a kind sailor brought a spade with him on board "to bury the lady with," he afterwards owned, thinking it was impossible she could recover, and not liking to cast her body to the crocodiles of the African stream. But it was not the delicate woman who was to fall a victim to the terrible swamp fever; she lived to reach the appointed meeting-place, to find no brother there, and to pass on, told

by the terrified and untruthful natives that they
knew nothing about him. They were perfectly
aware that he had sickened and died at the waiting-
place ; but they feared, poor ignorant souls, that they
might be punished for this fever-victim, so they let
the sister and her party pass by his very grave, to
hear the fatal tidings higher up the river at the
next village.

It was almost impossible to believe that such a
dreadful calamity had occurred. When the first
shock was over, a messenger was sent to Magomero
for further tidings, and from thence he brought
word that Mr. Burrup had watched over the sufferer
till his death, able to do little for him, since there
was no medicine and no hope of getting any. After
that event he had buried him, and returned to the
settlement himself, so ill with fever that he lingered
but a short time after his beloved chief.

The bereaved ladies had now no one to meet, no
reason for going further towards the stricken band
in the wilderness, so they were silently taken back
along the great river, pausing awhile by that spot
near its banks where, hidden by long grass, was the
grave of the bishop. Miss Mackenzie was too ill to
visit this last home of her beloved brother, but a
cross of bamboo, supported by the staves of a ship's
tub, was erected on it by Dr. Livingstone, and a
description of the place brought to her by sym-
pathetic friends.

A wrought-iron cross has since been erected on
the spot by Lieutenant Young. Not that he whose

memory will be always fresh and dear in the hearts
of all who knew him needed a visible memorial,
but the sign of Christian faith rises not amiss from
the wild tangle of the African wilderness where
once he hoped to make that faith known.

And now what more is there to tell? You ask,
perhaps, if the sister, bowed to the very ground by
her awful trial, was taken home to die, or at least
to pine out the rest of her days in heart-broken
resignation.

Anne Mackenzie was not made of such stuff as
this. Her life, it was true, had come to a sudden
standstill; the light of her eyes had been taken
from her, but the world had still a path she was to
tread, and heaven was before her at the end of it,
with her brother among the "shining ones" therein.
Because his work on earth was done, was she to
neglect hers? Surely not. So back to England
came the bereaved woman, to set herself the task of
carrying on, so far as might be, the missionary plans
of her departed brother.

It was found impossible to continue the work in
the unhealthy region at first selected, and so for a
time it was agreed that that special tract must be
left altogether by the missionaries.

This must have been a grief to Miss Mackenzie,
but she directed her attention to collecting funds
for a new mission in memory of her brother. She
raised at once £5000 to endow a bishopric for the
superintendence and development of the work of
her brother's friend, Mr. Robertson, in Zululand.

And since then, year by year, her busy pen and
hearty appeals have raised a large sum of money
for the maintenance of the mission.  Thirty thousand pounds this untiring woman gathered!—still
an invalid, she maintained from her sick-room a
correspondence with missions in all lands, not alone
caring for her special charge, Africa, but sending
gifts, kind letters, and help in all forms to other
missionaries in other climes.  Death surprised her
—it may be pleasantly—in the February of 1876.
Dearly beloved in many lands, she sank peacefully
to rest, leaving behind her a vacant place it will be
hard to fill.

## NOBODY'S CHILDREN.

### NEW YORK.

"SUFFER the little children to come unto Me, and
forbid them not," said the gentle Son of God when,
as Son of man, He tarried awhile on that last
journey to Jerusalem to take the little ones in His
arms and bless them. There were those about the
Saviour who would have thrust away the thoughtless little ones as unworthy of His notice, but such
He rebuked firmly, showing Himself "much displeased with them." And what of the children
now? They linger on the "further side of Jordan"
as in the days when Jesus walked the earth, and
the words of invitation still remain as full of plaintive force as ever, "Suffer them to come to Me."

A strong desire to help the little ones to come to
Jesus stirred the city of New York, in America, in
the year of our Lord 1853. The number of vagrant
children and youthful thieves in its streets and
lanes had startled the decent citizens. In eleven
wards of the city three thousand of such small
offenders were reckoned, of whom two thousand
were little girls! Of these homeless female children
taken up by the police the numbers shortly in-

creased to nearly six thousand, while the boy-thieves amounted to about three thousand !

No wonder "The Children's Aid Society" sprang into being. Who could sit still with such a horde of childish wanderers waiting to be guided into safe paths ? The Society at the outset determined what ought to be done, and then steadily set to work and did it. The vagrant children were to be followed into their dens and alleys, their railway arches and cellars, and tenderly compelled to come in to the light and warmth of the industrial schools and lodging-houses prepared for them. Misery and wickedness and ignorance were only so many tickets of admission to the warm beds, good dinners, and loving care of these new friends.

In the great wide continent we call America there is a happy outlet for these friendless little ones, they may be sent "West," that is, to the roomy farms and cheerful cottages of a wide and not over-populated district. There many homes would be open to them, and people of all classes would welcome them, not as useful little slaves, but as members of their families. So agents were immediately established in the West, who received communications from families desiring the addition of a boy or girl into their circle, and then the desired article was brought or sent to their doors. After that, of course, the Society, you will suppose, shook itself free of the little waif. By no means. The work was only half done. By visiting the child occasionally the agent found out whether it was content and well treated; in cases where he judged such not to be the case the child was removed and another home chosen for it. In the quarter of a century or more in which the Children's Aid Society has busied itself in this work, over forty thousand homeless children have thus been provided with homes, and instead of filling the gaols and reformatories, are rapidly developing into respectable citizens and decent mothers of families.

As this is one of the greatest works of the Society, let us turn to the Resident Western Agent's report, and hear what he says. "My duties," he proceeds to tell us, "are so well known that it seems superfluous to mention them. . . . Wrongs to be righted, children to be visited and returned, new homes to be found, and places selected for the location of companies. In this way I am kept busy. But the happiest, brightest feature of our work is the very large number of little girls and boys whom it is quite unnecessary to visit or look after in any way (except, indeed, it be to encourage the visitor), for they have grown to be a part of the families in which they live, and have so entwined themselves about the hearts of their foster parents that nothing but death can separate them. . . . In placing out our children I am often amused at the anxiety of applicants to be fully and plainly assured that we will remove the children if necessary. But in a few months they invariably write for the most minute and particular information regarding their parentage, never for-

"I am ready to take your boy away now." And the answer comes, "Well, then, I guess you'd better take away the whole family, for we can't spare Joe. He has been away now just six weeks with my wife, visiting his grandpa in Ohio, and I assure you I want the boy as much as the wife. We all think the world of him." Joe is evidently a great favourite, and as the M.'s are well-to-do people, he doubtless leads an easy, happy life, as little children should do. Mrs. M. says she should not mind a boy of this sort every two years!

Pretty little Blanche, out of the cold streets, is now a smiling "parlour" child; she learns music, sews nicely, and speaks a little piece and sings a song for the agent when he visits her. She is taken in the earthly place of the real little daughter of the house to whom it has lately been said, "Go up higher."

Another city girl, Pauline, once pale and pinched and homeless, is now fat and happy in a country farm. When first she came she was very ignorant about common things. "You can't make me believe that chickens come out of eggs," was a remark of hers. But by-and-by she came to have a hundred chickens of her own, and knew all about them, and there is a whisper abroad, now that Pauline has grown tall and strong and womanly, that she is to be a Mrs. Farmer very soon, and have a home of her very own.

Henry Lindee writes that he has a good home in the country, and has raised nineteen pigs and eleven

thankful that your Society brought me out here, and found me so good a place to live. My intention is to try to be a good boy. I am very healthy since I left New York."

Charlie of twelve is also in clover. He has "a pretty pony, cutter (or sledge), and bells, an Elgin watch and chain, and good clothes." Fancy the change from being "nobody's child" in the grimy city streets to being the darling of a wealthy country home!

Willie Peters calls Mr. Peters "father," and has a more chequered tale to tell: "This is my second home since I left your place, and I like it better than the first. I have a little mule that I call my own, I have lots of fun with it; and I have a dog and his name is Penny, he is always with me. I am going to school now till the spring work commenees. I am now twelve years of age, as near as I can remember. I have been here two years only, and expect to stay till I am of age. I am a mean boy sometimes, and get a whipping when I need it. No more to-night." Willie evidently tacks on this last little honest confession somewhat unwillingly at the close of his letter.

And so the boys' letters run, nearly all telling of comfortable homes, and habits of industry, care, and independence, in spite of their beginning life as "nobody's children." The bigger lads speak of doing for themselves when they come of age or sooner, and many of them beg to have little brothers or sisters traced out and placed in similarly happy circumstances.

easy rules of the place. One rule is that, if they can, they pay a small sum towards their supper, bed, and breakfast; no boy, however, is turned out because he has empty pockets, but he gets to feel himself a "mean" boy if, by-and-by, when a run of good luck comes, he does not repay the cents he ought to have paid for his lodging in his poorer days. A horde of these tumble in towards evening; ragged, wet, tired, hoarse newspaper-boys; ragged, wet, tired, hungry boot-blacks; ragged, wet, tired, placeless errand-boys; all quite ready to brighten up at the long tables spread for supper. Tea and bread and treacle, as much as they can eat; that is the food, and very good it is thought too. After supper comes an hour's schooling, given in with the meal. Perhaps some of the boys are sleepy and tired with their long day's work, but still they struggle upstairs to the chapel and schoolroom combined, rubbing their eyes, and meaning to do their best.

The learning is going to be dreadfully hard work they are sure, and so those that have coats pull them off, and those that haven't push up their shirt-sleeves, and all buckle to with a will at the spelling and summing and reading. Little American boys know that education is a good thing, and worth money.

Round the schoolroom hang placards, "Always speak the Truth," "Boys who Swear and Chew Tobacco not allowed to Sleep here," and so on. There is an odd-looking table in one corner. It is covered with tiny steel squares or plates, each plate

this is all the Children's Aid Society can attempt to do. Besides which, if a little city boy looks weak and sickly, and cannot earn his living, and the superintendent finds out that he is friendless and unhappy, he asks him if he would like to go West or South among new people, and if the boy's eyes brighten at the idea, he hands him over to the emigration department, who straightway look out for a home for him where he may thrive and grow fat, and learn that there is love to be had on earth as well as love in heaven.

Every fortnight a little company of travellers leaves New York for the West, pinch-faced, yet smiling boys and girls, with new strong clothing; friendless creatures rescued from the gutter and the cellar, from prison and from death. The gentleman in charge never loses sight of his band till one by one he has given them over to the new fathers and mothers, masters and mistresses, who have applied for them, and who promise to render up an account to him shortly of their little people.

Of course you will guess that the Children's Aid Society has its girls' lodging-houses as well as its boys', since in New York there are even more girls than boys wandering homeless in the streets. These are managed much in the same way as the boys' houses. The girls go out to work in the day, and are comfortably fed and housed at night; such as desire it are assisted to emigrate, and for such as need work and cannot obtain it, machine-work and dressmaking are taught on the spot. A laundry also is shortly to be set up. No less than eleven hundred girl wanderers have made this Home a resting-place in the course of one year. Of these seven hundred have been provided with situations, one hundred returned to their friends, twenty-three were sent West, and the remainder otherwise accounted for. Hand-sewing is taught in this house while the girls are waiting for situations. They learn also to make button-holes, so as to be useful in shirt-making. At one of the departments of these schools the mistress has found a capital way of keeping order. For every breach of rules ten button-holes to be made; for a second offence twenty. The girls become wonderfully clever at such work, and after a time wonderfully clever in avoiding it.

A sewing-room for day scholars is kept open in one school; little girls come from the streets and from wretched homes to see curiously what is being done there. They are bold-eyed and dirty at first, often ragged and half-clothed. See, however, how their faces soften when the mistress proposes that they shall try to make for themselves some sorely needed article of under-linen! Perhaps threading the needle is an accomplishment hardly yet acquired; but never mind, they struggle fiercely with it, determined to master all difficulties in the way of decent attire. And then when that first garment of plain strong stuff provided by the school is really completed, what joy, what pride is awakened in the breast of the street-child! A vision of a whole set of tidy raiment rises before the pleasure-dimmed eyes, a desire to make sisters, brothers, mother, equally respectable-looking. Of course the school cannot give all its children this complete outfit at once ; but every girl is allowed to make herself one garment a month, the rest of her time to be spent in sewing for shops and factories.

The Children's Aid Society keeps up six boys' and six girls' lodging-houses, and no less than twenty industrial schools. Over a thousand of the pupils, are, or have been, professional little beggars, whining for "cents" at street corners, and pattering with small bare feet after soft-hearted-looking ladies or gentlemen. It takes time to turn such as these into self-respecting little learners, but it is to be done. Small match-sellers, boot-blacks, news-boys, and such like, are encouraged to come to school for half a day, and yet have time for their work ; and the poor little nursing sisters, whose arms are laden from dawn to dusk with that heavy perpetual baby, are allowed to bring it with them to school. The babies truly are not wanted in class, but they are a necessary evil, and so have to be endured. A kind lady has provided a nursery in connection with one of the schools, where a large provision of cradles, rocking-chairs, and playthings are collected, and the babies can be amused or put to sleep by one or two attendants at the most, while the elder sisters are busy in the school. When the very ignorant street-child has learned something, and appears in decent clothing, it is encouraged to go to the public schools,

But to speak of the most delightful department of all, the Summer Home for town children, the seaside dwelling where each year some two to three thousand children are built up into new health and strength by sea-bathing, salt breezes, and country rambles. These children are chosen from the various city schools and homes for this most pleasant of cures, and the progress they make from sickness or weakness to health and strength is surprising. As a rule, each child only remains a week at the Home, but what a week that is! The day is spent in fairyland, playing on the beach, bathing, digging in the sand, swinging, singing, exploring the green country. No need to amuse a child by the sea; nature does all that most thoroughly, and provides delightful playthings too. The week is a week of rapture, and the pale faces return to the city all brown and rosy, while the empty little minds are filled with stores of happy remembrances to be talked over in the long winter to come. Of course, this Summer Home cannot be made paying in the slightest degree; it must be dependent on the alms of those who consider the poor and sick as their especial charge, and the cost of their maintenance the investment they make who "lend to the Lord."

I have now pretty well run through the various channels of good designed by the Children's Aid Society. "The Flower Mission" in connection with it truly has escaped mention, which is hardly fair, as at all times and in all seasons flowers are such welcome visitors. Fruit and vegetables also not unfrequently form the groundwork of the flower hamper, and are much appreciated. Turning to the lists, too, at the end of the printed reports, a wonderful crowd of "acknowledgments to the public" appears for all sorts of welcome gifts, from clothing to candy, from Bibles to babies' toys. In the whole wide range of household and family requirements, there seems nothing but what some one has thought of and handed over to one or other of the twenty schools and six homes. Bedding, clothing, soap, candles, crockery, kettles, books, salt, ice-cream, rice, oatmeal, stockings filled with candy and popcorn, photographs, dressed dolls, turkeys, beef, an organ, Easter eggs, marbles, more ice-cream, post-cards, darning-needles, shoes, magazines, oranges, potatoes, chickens, oil paintings, and—hear it, ye poor little street-children—one kindly lady sends six hundred cakes! There are hundreds and thousands of other gifts equally varied. All are wanted, however, for the expense of keeping up so large and, in great part, so helpless a charity must be very considerable. Yet, wonderful to relate, the Children's Aid Society is now unfettered by debt. New York is a wealthy city, and apparently its citizens recognize the value of the work being done among their poor little ones. Long may they continue to give of their wealth to so good a cause!

And to those who give more than wealth, life itself to the work, what shall we say? Nothing;

it would be sheer impertinence. They will have
their reward in the great day to come, when the
little ones they have trained for heaven rally round
the steps of the great white throne, and the
triumphant words rise to their lips, "Behold, I and
the children whom the Lord hath given me."

# LITTLE ZULUS.

### ZULULAND.

I THINK you will like to hear something of the life of Mrs. Robertson, that dear friend of Miss Mackenzie, with whom such happy holiday seasons were spent in those African days of long ago. She —Mrs. Robertson, I mean—was something like Miss Mackenzie in the state of life into which it had pleased God to call her, both being delicate English ladies planted among the heathen, with spirit ever fresh for missionary work.

And at first both friends had their occupation in the same country, Natal; though, being only occasionally together, their friendship was chiefly carried on by letters—letters which best tell the story of Mrs. Robertson's doings. You will not quarrel with the writer that these letters are full of the little cares and joys of a true woman's life, just a home record chronicling the doings and sayings of her flock, the little African children she gathered around her.

Mothers everywhere can bear, we know, to hear a great deal about children. But Mrs. Robertson seems to have had a passionate love for the little things. When well she taught them, washed them, and dressed them; when sick she let them climb on her bed and nestle beside her, smiling amidst her suffering at their happy frolics.

Her first darling was the child of her own Kafir servants, "Boy" and "Mary."

I must tell you something about these two. Mrs. Robertson says in one letter she could not be better cared for by English servants than by them, they were so good and affectionate. When first they came to her they slept in the stable by their own special desire, and at night after they went to bed the sound of hymn-singing would rise from that humble sleeping-place. It is easy to fancy the hymns they chose; the Kafir Mary, taught so lately the story of the Babe born in a stable, must have liked the hymn all our children have by heart of "Royal David's City" and the "lowly cattle shed." This kindly pair had several children, and Hali, the youngest of them, was willingly given over to Mrs. Robertson's care to be her child, a Christian from its birth.

When Mrs. Robertson was first married she did not move into a quiet dwelling with just herself and her husband, but they had quite a little company of servants and dependents around them whom they gladly encouraged, feeling that here was a flock who might be brought by the daily influence of love into the fold of Christ. This is the list of their household: a Hottentot woman with her three children, Boy and Mary and their children, a Kafir

at which Mr. and Mrs. Robertson lived was Umlazi, and Mr. Robertson himself was always called in the Kafir tongue "Umfundisi," or "Teacher," a name by which his wife loves to call him in her letters. Here they settled down, building a house of one large room, divided by screens, and finding all troubles light in their strong desire to do good, and make the poor heathen around love and trust them.

Of course, schools were set up directly; it is always easiest and best to begin teaching the children, and then, when the little ones had learned a few joyful hymns and rounds and catches, Umfundisi took them out with him in the neighbourhood of the Kafir huts to sing them, which attracted attention and made many others send their children to the new teacher.

Only the tiny things came with a strange condition on their lips—they were not to be made to wear clothes !

But soon the force of habit caused these very children to ask for garments like the rest, and then the parents made no objection. The truth was, it was not the actual bright calico frocks and coats they disapproved of, but the rendering their little ones more like their Christian teachers than their heathen fathers and mothers.

These poor Kafirs sorely needed teaching, for one of the questions asked by an old man was, "Does God live in England ? "

When Mr. Robertson found the people specially

dull and careless of being taught, he used to ask them, "Where are your dead?" and then they would pause to consider, and at last consent to listen to the strange new truths that the Umfundisi had brought to them regarding this world and the next. Boy, the Christian Kafir servant, was a great help at the mission; he taught in the schools, and was very clever in keeping the children happy, his own little boy Hali being a member of his class. A heathen girl given to the Robertsons, whom they christened Christina, and afterwards married to the Usajabula whose baptism I have told you of, was a great help and a kind friend to the little colony. Mrs. Robertson says of her: "Christina is my nurse for the little children. She is so modest and earnest in her religious duties that I quite know if I am too tired to go to my little ones at night, she will not put them in their beds without hearing them say their prayers."

Such a number too of little ones as Mrs. Robertson gathered round her, beginning with Boy's little Hali, an orphan child called Billy, and a little heathen named Ujadu!

Very like the nursery tales of little English children are her records of Hali's and Billy's achievements; of their learning to read "I see an ox," of their thumbing of Sunday picture-books, and sorrow for Adam and Eve sent out of the Garden, and poor Daniel in peril of the lions. You can fancy her lying in bed in one of her many illnesses and smiling at her two adopted darlings

making a pretence feast with an empty biscuit-
box, singing their Kafir grace before and after
meat, though the play dinner consisted of smacking
their lips and saying, "Vely nice, excellent," over
the imaginary contents of the box.

These dark-skinned little ones were about three
years old at the time, and as teachable and clever
as any English boys of that age.

It was all pleasure to kind Mrs. Robertson
teaching and caring for these winning little people,
but there were many shadows over her path all
the same. Going into the school one day she found
three of the best and dearest of her children standing aside with red eyes and tear-stained cheeks,
the other scholars refusing to sit near them. What
had they done to be so treated ? Nothing at all;
but a chief in the neighbourhood had lost two
wives by death, and he chose to imagine that the
father of these poor children was a wizard, and had
brought about their death, so he sent witch doctors
to their hut to accuse the man and to search for
the medicine by which the bewitching or poisoning
had been done. The man was quite innocent, but
he could not clear himself of the charge, and so his
neighbours all shunned him as a wizard, and his
poor little children were in like disgrace. Do what
Mr. Robertson could, it was impossible to convince
the people of the foolishness of their fancies, and
the poor accused man at last left the neighbourhood
with his family, the only course he could pursue.

"It has all been so very sad," runs one of the

letters home, "so much that is horrible in heathen life has been revealed to us that Umfundisi had known before, but never realized. Can you believe that among this apparently kindly hospitable people the habit of secret poisoning is such a known thing, that the more nearly they are related, the more they dread each other, and that the custom of the host drinking himself, or tasting the food himself before he gives it to a guest, is really necessary to assure him that it is safe to take it; that the mere wish to have a neighbour's garden, or something that is his brother's, his cows for instance, is temptation enough to resort to poisoning, and then it is visited on a supposed umtakati or wizard, through the agency of these witch doctors?"

Of course, the wrong person is very often accused, and seldom manages to prove himself innocent.

Soon after the sad wizard interlude the Robertsons started to visit the Mackenzies at Umhlali;— do not imagine that only Mr. and Mrs. Robertson went to these dear friends: that is not at all the way in Africa. Early in December the party set off, consisting of the Robertsons, little Hali and Billy, and about nine other Kafirs, including Christina, and a certain Benjamin, who was engaged to Louisa, the girl who came to the Robertsons unclothed and miserable, but who now was a cheerful Christian girl.

This goodly throng spent some happy weeks at Umhlali, but as Christmas drew nigh they began to arrange for their return. Louisa's and Benjamin's

marriage must not longer be delayed. The Mackenzies, however, wished to keep their friends, and
proposed that the great event should take place
at their station directly after Christmas, Mr. Robertson going back meantime to Umlazi for his Christmas services, and also to bring back more guests
for the wedding !

On the last day of the old year he reappeared
with a large party ; he could not resist the tears
and cries of the many who wished to come, and
all were made welcome. Boy and Mary were with
this last arrival, and all were tucked somehow into
huts and schoolrooms for the time of their visit.
Would you like to hear what the bride wore ? A
white checked muslin dress, a little muslin handker-
chief on her head tied by a ribbon given by Miss
Alice Mackenzie, and a wreath of natural flowers.
There were four bridesmaids, Emily of course being
one, her companion of old days. After the wedding
came a grand feast for all—a whole ox cooked,
with vegetables, coffee, plum-pudding, and wedding-
cake !

Then home again and a letter back to Miss
Mackenzie to tell how happy Louisa and Benjamin
seemed, how bent on leading a holy life and keeping
a neat, pretty house, a good example for those
around.

The next wedding was Christina's, at home, also
a very happy one; only Christian people were
invited to the festivities, but the heathen poured
into the church also, curious no doubt to see this

new sight of a Christian marriage. They must have been very well-behaved during the service, for Mrs. Robertson specially speaks of the "quiet, holy time in the church," and such sights must have had a good effect on the poor wondering, untaught creatures. Wedding festivities were purposely designed to show how Christian feasting is managed.

And now the work of humanizing these poor people went quietly on, while the special group round the Umfundisi grew and flourished in the new faith. More little ones were brought to Mrs. Robertson. Boy and Mary had another little baby, there were more marriages, and every now and then some grown-up Kafir came out of the heathen throng and asked for light and teaching.

But sorrow came too, in the shape of a sad death. One of their boys had lately been baptized, going home first to tell his family; he met with great opposition and much cruelty there, returning gladly to the kind Umfundisi. But he only lived six weeks afterwards, and Mr. Robertson thought he had been secretly poisoned by the people, who objected to his becoming a Christian. He was a good, earnest lad, and it must be pleasant to those who loved him soul and body to remember that the night before his baptism he was found praying earnestly and secretly to his Father in heaven. That Father kept him peaceful and happy to the last, in the midst of intense pain; and lying in his coffin his beautiful countenance struck all who saw him. He was

indeed a Christian martyr, dying for the faith early
in his career, and deeply lamented by the settlement.

Another death grieved over by loving Mrs.
Robertson was that of the first baby of Benjamin
and Louisa; the parents loved it as you love your
babes, and when it was dying Umfundisi took the
opportunity of explaining to Louisa what he had
told her often before, that trouble is one of the ways
God takes to draw His people nearer to Him. The
little thing was only five weeks old, but being the
first baby, its loss was terrible to poor Louisa.

At one time, after several deaths had occurred in
the Christian settlement, Mr. and Mrs. Robertson
almost feared the ignorant natives taking a dislike
and a dread of their teaching in consequence, but
Mary, Boy's wife, set their hearts at rest by saying,
" We think this place must be very near heaven,
since so many go there from hence." It was a
pretty idea, and comforting to the anxious Umfundisi and his wife.

And now another anecdote of little Hali comes
in the letters. There was a cottage by the seaside
to which Mrs. Robertson used to go with her
children sometimes for a few days' rest; the little
ones enjoyed the change very much, but they were
a little frightened at the monkeys who, hidden in
the trees around, used at sunset to keep up an
incessant chattering; they had another terror too, of
snakes, who were supposed to haunt an unused
room in the hut. Once, however, in very hot

weather, Mrs. Robertson braved this last danger, and took her sewing into the suspected room, which was cool and quiet. When little Hali saw her there he was at first alarmed for her, then he thought it was only safe for *her*, the teacher's wife, their own God-fearing mother, and he remarked with awe, "Not even if you were to sleep in the bush would a monkey bite you "—his rendering of " Thou shalt not be afraid for any terror by night, nor for the arrow that flieth by day."

Perhaps this idea may have taken root when Umfundisi, hearing the little ones one day cautioning one another to talk low at night, for fear the umtakati, or wizard, should hear them, said, " Oh, he never comes where there is the house of an Umfundisi." After that they were always telling each other that neither lions nor tigers would harm their dear teachers. These children used to think that the wizard was a wild beast, perhaps in the same way that we describe the devil as a roaring lion seeking whom he may devour.

And now a new home was to be sought by the Robertsons. A mission station was to be established further north in Zululand, and thither, with many of their old friends and their baby children, they journeyed, a three weeks' sojourn in a waggon.

You could hardly fancy such a mode of travelling; the hooded heavy waggon, packed with boxes, household goods, women and children, the great gentle oxen harnessed to it in pairs, and the men walking alongside with whips; then the roads, or no roads, mere tracks over mountains and valleys, littered often with great stones a yard high, from one to another of which the waggon bounced and jolted till it was dangerous to remain inside it; then the rivers to be forded, often dangerously high, and always very trying to the poor oxen. Besides that, the weather was often changeable, the heat making the close waggon insupportable, and then the sudden heavy showers or fierce sun driving the feeble ones again under its shelter. During that three weeks' journey, Mrs. Robertson says she was always drying wet clothes, and struggling to keep the little pent-up colony of babes and girls good and happy. One knows how trying children often are when shut up a whole wet day in the house, and now think of them crowded into a waggon, not for one day, but many.

The arrival of the mission party in Zululand took place at a critical time in the history of the country. The old king was dying, and his sons and relations were fighting and murdering each other in the struggle for the next succession to the throne. Ketchwayo, the most powerful of the sons, held the first place, and though in his ignorant barbarism stained with the sins of murder and cruelty, he was kind to the mission party, and always willing to receive Mr. Robertson when he visited him.

Mr. Robertson was very anxious to win over some of the great men of the land, and when a rich and powerful chief, called Gaus, was thrown off his horse close to the station and broke his arm, the

Umfundisi took him in, set the arm—all missionaries
are in some sort doctors—and entertained him and
his servants for weeks. How many servants or
followers do you think Gaus had? Sometimes five
hundred, never less than fifty — rather a large
number of guests to entertain unexpectedly. Gaus
was very gracious and grateful to Mr. Robertson;
he was a kind man, and his people loved him, many
coming in tears to the station to ask after him.
One kraal sent an ox to the chief in his sickness,
with the message that "it was the ox of tears and
not of rejoicing;" it was sent to supply food for the
people, and was very necessary, as you may fancy.
Gaus got well in time, and went home much pleased
with the Christians, but those horrid witch doctors
were at work again, saying some one must be guilty
of bewitching Gaus, and causing him to break his
arm. So they fixed upon a man to suspect, and
executed him and two of his wives. One young
wife had a baby on her back, and they simply
threw that down by the wayside to die. Four lives
sacrificed for one man falling from his horse! It is
as senseless as it is terrible, but these are the laws
and customs the Christian teacher goes out to upset,
not the existing government of the country.

To enforce this idea Mr. Robertson meant, after a
time, to take all his Christian people to the king,
and introduce them as belonging to the monarch,
though followers of Christ.

But you will want to hear more about Mrs.
Robertson's pets and her Christian girls.

Hali was getting on nicely with his learning—
though he did once put Mrs. Robertson to the blush
by spelling "Cat" T—H—E, when desired to show
his cleverness to a visitor. He and Billy each kept
kids at the new station, and were very anxious for
them to grow up and have young ones " to give to
the offertory." Johnny, another boy who had no
kids, but a garden, meant to sell his produce and
buy a sheep, which was to have most beautiful
lambs, for the offertory too. I do not suppose these
children ever managed to accomplish such grand
gifts to their little Christian church; but the idea
was nice, and perhaps when they grew older they
might be able to carry it out. As it was, Hali
sometimes got a " pen " from his father—a three-
" pen "-ny piece to put into the plate on Sundays
and was as pleased to have such an offering to give
as any of our school-children would be.

You will be glad to hear that Louisa had another
baby to supply the place of the lost one. And now
poor Christina, still as good and faithful a Christian
as she had seemed before marriage, was called upon
to give up a darling—a fine little girl of sixteen
months old, called Jeanie. It died somewhat sud
denly, just after a terrible fire that had devastated
the poor Robertsons' huts, and it was difficult to
find a bit of wood even to make it a coffin. But
the mother was patient and gentle, and said, amidst
her tears, as she gazed on the little dead face, " I
know I have read that death which destroys the
body is nothing, it is sin only which really destroys.'

And she took pleasure in telling the signs of what she thought might have proved a holy disposition in her baby-girl: her putting her food aside while grace was said, her respectful awe of Mr. Robertson's books, placed in their hut after the fire. The poor natives take all books to mean *The Book*, and so hold all in reverence.

Christina showed her holy sorrow in another way too. She would have no witch doctor to inquire who had bewitched her little one—she recognized the hand of God in its death—neither would she have heathen weeping and wailing over its grave. The little child that was given on a Sunday, and taken away on a Sunday, should only be mourned as Christians mourn.

The fire of which I have spoken caused great alarm and loss in the mission settlement, the huts being built of such inflammable material that the least spark was destruction. Happily none of the Christian colony were injured, but a poor old heathen woman, seeking to save her little grandchild, was so badly burned that she died a few days after, the baby following her. It grieved Mrs. Robertson to see this poor woman laid in her unhallowed grave, as she says very truly there was something in the cause of her death so true and good, that to bury her like a dog was very painful. But she was not a Christian, and she was carried away and buried by her heathen relatives.

And now we come very near the end of Mrs. Robertson's life of love and quiet work. Yet there

wheels slipped on the dry grass, the oxen were overpowered, and the great waggon upset. A calm voice said, "Oh, remove the boxes," that had fallen heavily upon the occupants, Mrs. Robertson and Boy's youngest little one, and then all was quiet. One was taken and the other left. The little child—a care to every one, unable to do a thing in the world—was drawn out of the wreck uninjured; the busy labourer in the vineyard was dead. Such in this world are many of the hard things we have to bear without understanding. Mrs. Robertson was buried at a Norwegian mission station close by the scene of the accident, while her husband and the helpless flock went back to the desolate home.

You will be glad to hear that a great effort was made to keep the children together, and to continue the good work begun by Mrs. Robertson, even after her death.

## ANOTHER GIRL-MISSIONARY.

### SYRIA.

YOU remember the story of Mrs. Hinderer, who longed as a little child to be a missionary, and who at last obtained her desire, and amidst hardship and trial worked most happily in Western Africa till God called her to her rest.

Well, now, you must hear the life-story of such another devoted woman who, like Mrs. Hinderer, longed from childish days to do some work in Christ's vineyard. There are not many of such women in the world, so that I need not fear tiring you with such histories.

As a child even she loved holy things, this little Elizabeth, and one of the first recollections of a sister is seeing her curled up in a sunny window-seat, learning for her own pleasure parts of the Bible and Prayer-book. There are never wanting mockers in the world, and Elizabeth had quietly to bear the name, intended for a reproach, of "saint" in those early days.

When quite a tiny creature playing in the garden a bad woman stole her for the sake of her clothes, letting her loose without her pretty frock at last,

so that her anxious relatives were able to find **her.**
They asked little Elizabeth whether she had been
much frightened, and the answer came, " I did cry,
but I was not frightened; I knew God would take
care of me."

Like Mrs. Hinderer, Elizabeth did not wait for
great things to do at a distance, but when young
accepted the work that lay ready to hand—the
teaching little English children, the comforting
English sick and poor—but always keeping an
eye ahead for the prospect of serving her Lord in
other lands, where workers are few and hard to
be got.

And Syria was the land above all others to which
she trusted the hand of God would guide her.
Bible lands had great attraction for her from childhood. Her marriage with a Dr. Thompson, who
had been much in the East, was a step toward the
fulfilment of her wishes, since the newly married
pair soon set out on their travels, meaning to settle
near Antioch, where Dr. Thompson owned some
property.

Here, in the city where men first bore the name of
Christians, Mrs. Thompson began her first attempt
to make Christ's story known once more. All sorts
and sects clustered round the kind English lady—
Turkish, Jewish, and Armenian girls pressed into
her house to learn sewing and embroidery, and to
be taught the alphabet, and helped to stammer
through a Bible story. To the very poor children
who came to her schools she gave bodily food as

that their beloved mistress was going away from them.

Mrs. Thompson little guessed to what grief and trouble she was hastening with her husband. They reached Balaclava in safety, but Dr. Thompson had hardly begun his work when he was seized with the raging fever which prevailed there, and almost immediately pronounced to be in mortal danger. Only the careful treatment and quiet of the hospital at Scutari could save him, but that was for soldiers, and there had as yet been no letter from England with his appointment confirmed, so he was no army doctor yet, and might not have the privileges of such.

It was a bitterly hard case; he had been struck down caring for our soldiers, but he must die with the civilians. In vain poor Mrs. Thompson begged and prayed; rules must be kept, especially in war-time, and the sick man must toss and rave all night in the little steamer in the bay, knowing the while that his only chance of life was to be ashore in the hospital.

At last came the permission, and Dr. Thompson was carried carefully to the desired refuge, and laid on a cool, quiet bed. Roman Catholic nurses tended the sick, and Mrs. Thompson had once been apt to consider that their ways and hers lay far apart. Now she was to find that Christians have common ground. By the bedside of the dying she wrote of the kindness, nay, love, of these nursing sisters. But love and care could not save the precious life

z

Thousands upon thousands were butchered, their houses plundered and burnt, their widows and orphans put to flight, unless, as sometimes happened in savage mercy, their ferocious assailants fell upon the women and babes also.

The miserable remnant fled to the seaport towns, to Tyre, to Sidon, to Beyrut; such as reached those towns alive finding that Europe had sent out help in food and money to her oppressed brethren.

In the plains the villages were still smoking, and the murderers were still hunting their prey as if they were wild beasts, while the plunder of church vessels and household property was openly continued. It was a sad tale to reach the ears of any one who loved Syria.

Mrs. Thompson read the accounts in silence, and then made up her mind. Here were people needing comfort, homeless widows, destitute children. She would go out to them, and care for them body and soul, for Christ's sake and to make His Name known among them.

No sooner thought than done; leaving family and friends, once more Mrs. Thompson started for Beyrut, there immediately opening a home for poor fugitives.

Thirty women and sixteen children entered it on the opening day, but before the end of the week the number of souls swelled to two hundred.

And still more would press in, for there were thousands of destitute creatures in the neighbourhood asking for food and work. Yes, even road-

the wicked people who had slain their dear ones. One poor creature who had lost husband and sons drew from her bosom a cap stained with the blood of her dead child; she had seen him cut to pieces before her eyes by the cruel Druses, and she wanted to call down vengeance from heaven on them. Her fellow-sufferers sobbed around her while Mrs. Thompson told them of the best Comforter, and turned their hearts to the story of the Cross. Another widow of noble family told Mrs. Thompson how in the terrible day of murder she had stood up to her knees in the blood of her relatives while the Turks stripped her of her jewels —one attempting to cut off her finger the quicker to possess himself of her rings, another actually wounding her neck in his haste to secure a pearl necklace. And when food was brought to her in her need, behold, it was poisoned, making her very sick, and killing her mother and little daughter. Can you wonder that, as one mother bereaved of two sons declared, "We felt almost crazy, even to cursing God"?

But out of evil came good; this last poor woman, driven away from her devastated home, found shelter with Mrs. Thompson, there for the first time learning the things pertaining to her salvation.

"I am the woman who did not know anything," she says of herself. "I did not know that God had created the world. I did not know the Lord's Prayer. I thought it was enough to do the work of the house in Hasbeya, to go to the well and get

death, but I do not." She was a Mohammedan, you see. Mrs. Thompson had no time to say much, but as Lady Ikbar could read a little, she sent her a Testament with a velvet cover embroidered in gold, the pretty binding to take her fancy at first, the words within to sink deeply into her heart.

We hear no more of Lady Ikbar; she went far away that day, and perhaps Mrs. Thompson herself never heard whether she read that gilded book and learned from it that Christ died for the women as well as the men.

As months went by and the first terrible recollections of the massacre began to fade, Mrs. Thompson tells us that not only had she in her schools the orphans left by that sad time, but the very children of the murderers. She refused none; they, poor little souls, needed Christian teaching as much or more than the rest. On one bench might now be seen, with the so-called Christian orphans, Druse children, little Jewesses, Moslem girls, and even the daughters of a Greek priest, all recognizing the fact that from Mrs. Thompson they could learn nothing but good. Some of these children were of the richest families in Beyrut, and paid for their education, being brought backwards and forwards by their maids or in their carriages. Fancy little scholars decked in gold necklaces and bracelets as these were.

One Jewish child wore a head-dress, necklace, and brooch of pearls and diamonds. And the school-frock of a rich little Druse girl was of crimson satin

have known much about, only he saw it pleased them to do so, and next day he sent a purse of gold, and an order for embroidery. That short visit cheered Mrs. Thompson very much.

The people of Damascus now sent to beg Mrs. Thompson to set up a school in their town, greatly to her surprise.

This most ancient city in the world, the capital town of Syria, full of all creeds and all nations, would, she thought, have been the last to welcome a poor follower of Christ, coming without sound of bell, or gorgeous raiment. In the street, still called Straight, stands the great mosque or temple of the false prophet, once a Christian cathedral, it is said; and before that, the place whereon stood the house of Rimmon. Above its splendid doors the inscription still remains, "Thy Kingdom, O Christ, is an everlasting Kingdom, and Thy dominion endureth throughout all ages." Mrs. Thompson looked at these words, and was comforted: false gods might be lifted up for a time, and the very sanctuary be given up to their worship, but Christ would still be King.

St. Paul's School, Damascus, was soon firmly established and well filled with all ages and creeds. On the anniversary of the day on which Jerusalem was destroyed (in the year of our Lord 61) the little Jewish children, who usually shone in bright colours and golden ornaments, came to school with their hair uncombed, their faces unwashed, and their feet bare. It was a day of humiliation and fasting

Mohammedan gentlemen do not like their girls and women to be seen or spoken of, but they would let them learn to read and write, provided all is done very quietly.

These gentlemen found they could place perfect trust in Mrs. Thompson, who, when visitors came to see her schools, guarded her little gentlewomen from the public eye as jealously as if they were in the apartments in the harem at home. She did not want roughly to change the habits of a nation, she only wanted to rescue young girls from idleness and ignorance, and to give them an opportunity of hearing of Him who died in their land for them. It must have been a delightful green spot in her work when she was busy sending off a party of young Christian girls to Jerusalem, to be confirmed by our bishop there; these dear ones were really shut in the fold, not like the Moslem and Jewish children, to be lost sight of, perhaps, when they grew up and married and mixed with their own people.

But neither the pleasures nor pains of work were to be Mrs. Thompson's much longer. She fell ill, and after a while expressed her wish to return to England. There the doctors pronounced her to be in a dying state, and though when told of it she was perfectly calm and resigned, she still owned to a wish to live for her Syrian children if it should be God's will.

"Send a telegram to Beyrut," she asked; "gather the children to pray for me. . . . Pray without

# NOBLE SAVAGES.

### NEW ZEALAND.

I DARE say you all know very well that our Queen does not rule only over Great Britain and Ireland —those small islands which in a map of the world may be covered by the tip of a little finger, but in all parts of the globe she has colonies where the people of the land and the English settlers are also her faithful subjects.

We in little England have been multiplying so quickly of late years that the resources of our island would fail if some of our big boys and brave girls did not resolve to become emigrants, and seek a home in distant countries among strange people.

And if we thus take some of the land and the superabundant food of the foreigner, ought we not to do something for him in return ? It is, I know, a good deal the fashion among thoughtless colonists to drive the poor native into a corner, to despise him, and let him live and die like the beasts that perish, but such can never be the conduct of Christian settlers, who have been taught their duty towards God, and who feel in all its importance their duty towards their neighbour.

prising savages who chose to cross the sea to visit him. Once there was trouble and alarm in the parsonage in consequence. A number of the natives were staying in the house when a young lad, the nephew of a chief, suddenly died. Immediately, following the fashion of his land, the chief prepared to sacrifice a slave—to kill him, in fact, that he might go with the spirit of his nephew into the other world to wait on him there. What was to be done? Mr. Marsden was away from home, but his wife and children hid the poor slave for a few hours till he came back, and then with some trouble he talked to the chief, and tried to make him give up the cruel custom. He had to be very careful and gentle with the poor savages, for there were as many as thirty in his house at the time—all, like ourselves, very reluctant to give up the rules and habits of a lifetime.

But at last he prevailed, and the lad's life was saved, though the chief went away very sorrowful, saying he should be afraid to return to New Zealand and tell the dead boy's father that no servant was with his child in the other world.

Mr. Marsden did procure missionaries from England to teach these poor people, and they were kindly received, but I fear more because they belonged to the country which produced such treasures as beads and clothing, than from any real conviction of the truth of this new religion. The first question usually asked by the chiefs in answer to the message of the gospel was, "Will you give us

blankets if we believe?" and failing an immediate
earthly reward, they did not see the advantage of
becoming Christians.

Their own faith was so dark, so sad, and ferocious,
and their minds were so narrowed by it, that it
seemed impossible to make them understand the
first principles of a better one.

Their gods were demons, fierce and greedy, to
whom gifts must be made to secure their favour;
they appeared in the whirlwind and the lightning;
they spoke in the thunder; all connected with them
was fearful and terrible. Lesser demons were
supposed to take the form of lizards, moths, and
butterflies, and swarm around man to inflict evil
upon him. Could any religion be more horrible?
Rocks, stones, rivers, and fountains were prayed to,
while even eels were reverenced, and had daily
offerings made to them.

A story is told of a solitary turkey cock finding
its way to a small island in one of the New Zealand
lakes; it was a bird then unknown to those regions,
and doubtless its voice sounded very terrible to the
ignorant heathen around: it must be a god, and
they must make offerings to it, the ignorant people
thought, to prevent its harming them. So as canoe
after canoe fearfully paddled past the island of the
turkey-cock, a present of food was left on the beach
for it, and the bird grew fat on the fears of the
natives.

War, again, was a terrible hindrance to the Christian
faith in New Zealand; the tribes lived in a perpetual

state of conflict, and dreadful were the cruelties to
which this state of things gave rise.   The eating of
the victims after the fray was one of the worst
attendant evils; no wonder the first missionaries
often lost heart and doubted if ever they should be
able to make the smallest mark for good on this
benighted land.   Yet still they laboured on, content
if the people would only let them live in the land,
and tell their tale of a good God and ministering
angels in the place of the legends of the cruel New
Zealand demons.

A missionary's wife had need carry a brave heart
in those days.   Mrs. Williams, one of Mr. Marsden's
friends, writes of great alarms from a savage chief,
who for days together threatened her husband and
her household, sending her little child to her in an
agony of terror and cries of "Oh, mamma, they are
going to kill papa.   We shall all be burnt, and they
will kill poor papa.   I saw the men; I saw the
guns."   It was all too true; only, happily, "papa,"
the missionary, was able to stop the tumult, and to
calm the ferocious savage before great harm was
done.   The threats, however, of burning out the
missionaries were not light when we remember that
in those early days their dwellings were but of
interlaced branches of trees, which would burn to
the ground in ten minutes.

Amidst constant fears, these early missionaries
yet now and then had occasional gleams of comfort
when here and there a convert stepped forth from
the ranks of the careless and unthinking, and asked

2 A

to be told more of the new religion of peace and good will. A little nurse-girl, Lucy, who had been three years with Mrs. Williams' children, was one of the first; she became ill, and, dying, was not afraid, since Jesus and heaven would be hers, when the last summons came. No doubt in the three years of service she had learned how Christians live, and now she was fain to show how a Christian, young and timid, can die.

Soon after, another death occurred of a full-grown man; his had not seemed a very hopeful case, but one must not hastily judge of such matters as the work of the Holy Spirit in the heart. While seemingly unmoved by the teachings of the English, Rurerure was really alarmed and disturbed by what he heard. He was wont to pray secretly yet fervently that his soul might be washed clean in the blood of Christ, and that God would take him to Himself when he died. So, when the final moment came, though Rurerure had never openly allied himself with the little mission, he was able to turn to Jesus on the cross, and to hear that voice say once again the comforting words spoken of old to as great a sinner, " To-day shalt thou be with Me in paradise."

At that moment he was the only native whom Mr. Williams could be certain had been earnest in his inquiries after the new faith. Others might try to please the missionaries by listening to their discourses and attending their services, but beads and blankets and the riches that perish were too often

the motives which brought them forwards, and
great care had to be exercised in the treatment of
such.

Mr. Williams once paid a visit to a village, when
the native priest took him on one side and advised him to say nothing that day about the place
of punishment for sin, as he had a great chief
visiting him who might not like it; but, as you
may imagine, a Christian teacher could not be
terrified into delivering only half his message, and
the great chief had to hear the whole truth. He
was angry for a while, but it passed over.

Another chief, troubled in his own household,
declared that he could not be easy again till he had
killed some one; the missionaries hid away from
him the people of a strange tribe whom he longed
to make his victims, and so much did their dis-
appearance affect the old man, that he would take
no food and desired to hang himself. Holding up a
hatchet in his hand he exclaimed, " Sixteen persons
have been sent by this to the shades below, and
unless I can kill and eat some one now, I shall have
no rest." It was a long matter to dispel this cruel
madness, but Mr. Williams was very persevering,
and after a while the poor savage laid down his
weapon, saying, " I will use it no more."

These were the sort of people the missionaries
had to work among. Still, progress was made, and
in a very few years we read an account of a school
examination, which sounds very encouraging. To
be sure, the dinner afterwards was a specimen of

New Zealand manners. It consisted of pork, beef, potatoes, and bread, served in little baskets instead of plates. The guests had not been eating long when, with one consent, they left their seats and scampered off with the remainder of their food. They have not learnt, it seems, our rule of "Eat what you like, but pocket none."

I think I have already told you that the New Zealanders had no settled form of religion of their own, but, like many tribes of savages in other parts of the world, they believed in powers of evil, and had priests who were called upon at certain times, in war or sickness, for instance, and who were supposed to be able to bewitch people and also to free them from the bewitching of others. Children who were intended to be priests were brought up in strange and horrible fashion.

A remarkable account of the process was given by a young man whose father devoted him from infancy to the priesthood. When a tiny baby he had his food snatched from him by his father to make him angry, and the older he grew the more he was teased and tormented to excite his bad passions. All this was done before he could walk or notice what grew on the earth. When he could run about he was kept without food that he might learn to thieve, and he was taught to be revengeful and cruel. His father instructed him that to be a great man he must be a bold murderer and able to do all kinds of wickedness cleverly. "I recollect," says this young man, "while I was a child my father went to kill pigs. I tried to get a portion for myself, but my father beat me away because I had not been active in killing them. When the tribe went to war, and I was able to go with them, I endeavoured to fulfil my father's wishes by committing acts of violence, and when I succeeded in catching slaves for myself my father was pleased, and said, ' Now I will feed you, because you deserve it ; now you shall not be in want of good things.' "

Was not this indeed an education for the devil's service ? Yet this same young man, hearing afterwards of the very different teachings of the English missionaries, became attracted by them, and renounced the service of the evil one to become a faithful follower of the gentle Jesus.

As days and years went by in New Zealand, superstition and sin gradually retired before the new and better doctrine, some hundreds were received into the Church by baptism, and of this number many were communicants, while not only was the New Testament fully translated, but a knowledge of reading was very general. Only the love of war and fighting stood in the way of greater progress.

During all the troubles and alarms of the little Christian Church in New Zealand, Mr. Marsden had kept it well in mind, from time to time leaving his own home to visit and encourage the mission. Once he found war and tumult so rampant in the land that he could hardly make his way to the Christian settlement; and when he did arrive there, weary and footsore, stained with red mud, his clothes in rags, and for all covering an old nightcap on his head, he found the affrighted missionaries on the point of breaking up the mission, and leaving in the English ship *Dromedary,* then in the bay. The horrid scenes they had witnessed in the course of the war, the killing, the torturing, and the devouring of prisoners had so upset them, that hope of ever doing any good to the natives had fled from them, and their one desire was to escape to a more civilized country.

But this was no true missionary spirit, and Mr. Marsden rebuked and reasoned with his alarmed followers till he strengthened their faith and increased their courage to that extent that they gave up the idea of flight, and settled down once more on firmer ground than ever.

On his next visit to New Zealand Mr. Marsden was shipwrecked in company with some Wesleyan missionaries. For some days they were completely at the mercy of the natives, who might have robbed or murdered them with the greatest ease; but instead of that they behaved in the kindest, I had almost said most gentlemanly manner, bringing them offerings of their own food, while saying, " Poor creatures ! you have nothing to eat, and you are not accustomed to our kind of food."

Mr. Marsden's last visit to his beloved New Zealand took place when he was in his seventy-second year, his youngest daughter accompanying him. Though war was still raging in different parts of the country, he could not but be struck with the progress of the Christian Church, of which everywhere he was received as a father and a friend. Not only was he beloved by the Christians, but the very heathen flocked around him, anxious to do him service, and carrying him everywhere in a litter devised by themselves. At one settlement the entire native population came out to gaze lovingly on their dear old friend, some kept stead-fastly looking at him, and when told to give place to others, said, "Nay, let us still look upon our father's countenance, for this is the last time we shall ever see him here." They were right, the white-haired old man whose limbs trembled beneath him, but whose eyes yet shone with holy love for each and all, Christian and savage, would never again land on the beautiful shores of his beloved isles. He preached a last sermon on the love of God, and then sailed away to New South Wales, where he failed somewhat suddenly in the following May, " New Zealand " being the last words that fell from his lips.

So died this " Apostle of the South Seas," as a Roman Catholic gentleman, who witnessed his life and labours, aptly called him.

Very soon after his death New Zealand was made a British colony, and Bishop Selwyn was consecrated first bishop.

It was well that England should send out godly men to care for the new colony, since it is not always good that the ignorant native learns from

the bush fell upon them, killing one of the Christian teachers on the spot, and so wounding the other that he had only strength to give his Testament and papers to a comrade, saying he bequeathed him great riches, and then he calmly leaned his head against a tree and died. The Church's first martyrs in New Zealand!

Some years later another was added to the list.

Mr. Volkner, a clergyman who had lived for three years in the country, loving the people and trusting them, unfortunately fell into the hands of a body of natives who, having once heard the tidings of the gospel, had fallen back into a state of wild and savage heathendom. The last state of those men was infinitely worse than the first, in fact, they were almost mad, and utterly ungovernable.

Poor Mr. Volkner, quite unaware of all this, landing on their shores with medicine and nourishing food for the sick, was immediately seized and cruelly put to death. Their god willed it so, said a wretched chief, and his brother chiefs consented to the murderous deed. Following the example of his Master, the victim knelt down and prayed for his murderers, since in very truth they knew not what they did. They had sung and danced and talked themselves into a state of frantic excitement, and their master, the devil, had not scrupled to guide their hands to deeds] of blood. All the Christian dwellers in the neighbourhood, and indeed many of the natives, who at the time dared not interfere, were struck with grief and horror at this

they had sung long ago in England.   If in life they failed to acknowledge God, in death He was very present, and they were willing to bow down before His messenger.

When the service was over, the diggers gave the clergyman £10 for the church, collected among themselves.

Sad as that sudden death was, it might be the means of awakening many sleeping, yes, dying souls to a better life, a warning to them to lay up imperishable riches, treasure in heaven, while they dug and searched for the golden dross of this world.

a knot at the back of their heads when very busy, it is not thought full dress.

There are very few women to be seen in public in China; for one thing they cannot walk any distance, since it is the fashion there to bind the feet of baby girls, and so stop their growth that the boot of a little English child of three would fit a grown woman of their nation. It is esteemed a disgrace for a woman to have properly formed feet. Only the most neglected of children would be suffered to grow up with unbound and un-cramped feet, and no gentleman would think of choosing her for a wife.

Girl-babies have a poor time of it in China altogether. They are seldom welcome, and if a flock of these poor little things happen to come one after the other, the mother is in despair, and imagines her gods must be angry with her to send such an infliction. She takes the remedy in her own hands, however. She would not think of bringing up these small misfortunes, but, either by exposure or direct murder, puts an end to the little lives. This is not called murder in China, however, nor looked on as a sin.

One Chinaman, a little wiser and kinder than his fellows, wrote a book on education, and even advised that the women should be instructed, since " mon-keys may be taught to play antics, dogs may be taught to tread a mill, cats may be taught to run round a cylinder, and parrots may be taught to recite verses." He does not seem to imagine that

people on your mud-bank, England, dare to pity
our great, wise, ancient race! Do you not know
that our country is called the Celestial Empire, the
Flowery Kingdom, and that all who do not reside
within its limits we call barbarians? Are you
aware that the art of printing, the manufacture of
gunpowder, and the mariner's compass were known
to us long before you poor islanders ever dreamed
of them? Have you heard of our great wall of
China, built two thousand years ago to keep off our
northern enemies, so wide and strong that six men
could ride on the top? We are an ancient, wise
nation. We can't become wiser or better off than
we are already. No barbarian can do us any good."

Such a speech really came from the lips of a
Chinese gentleman; and true as the facts are, they
add to the difficulty of our making friends with his
country, and planting in it the one thing they do
not possess, clever and wise as they think themselves—a good true religion. Yet, hard as the task
is, we are trying to do it, and in time we hope we
may succeed. The greatest hindrance in spreading
the Christian religion is the necessity for learning
the difficult Chinese language; yet the missionaries
work very hard at this, and go out into the streets
and lanes to preach and teach directly they feel
they can make themselves understood.

From an interesting account written of the
mission work done in Fuh-kien, a territory on the
south-eastern coast of China, and in Fuh-chow, its
chief town, " the Happy City," as its name declares,

barbarian, the "devil," as they nearly all called the Christian messenger.

For ten years a few earnest missionaries scattered the good seed in the Happy City; but, alas! such thorns and weeds abounded in the soil that there seemed to be absolutely no fruit, not one poor Chinaman stepped out of the ranks of superstition, and at last the good people in England who sent out the missionaries seriously thought of withdrawing them to some less stony soil. The bodies of three good men and their wives were buried in the Happy City. Were more lives to be sacrificed in this vain endeavour?

There was one voice raised to plead for the stiff-necked inhabitants of the Happy City, and that one belonged to the missionary in charge. He could not bear to give up hope: let him tend this vineyard yet one year more, he entreated.

And that very year the reward came. Three men came forward really desiring to be taught, and one of them was a gentleman and a scholar. This was a real joy to Mr. Smith, their anxious teacher; it gave him a new impetus; he established fresh services, opened more schools, and finally Mrs. Smith set up a school for little despised girls. This was unsuccessful, however; the mission grounds were on the top of a hill, and the poor girls with their pinched feet could not waddle up the stony road. Very often women could not come to church for the same reason, and it clearly became, a little later on, the duty of Christian teachers to discourage the

crippling in women of the useful limbs giv
them by the Creator.

Riots against Christianity, in which chapel
schools were wrecked, and converts threatene
terrified, did not quench the little flame o
godliness; rather they did good, by makin
new doctrine better known.

One new convert reminds one very mu
Saul of Tarsus; he used to come to the Chr
services simply to interrupt them and to
the native believers, and once, becoming more
usually violent, he was turned out of the bu
For months Mr. Smith lost sight of him, bt
day he observed an attentive, quiet listener ε
his congregation. It was Ling the rioter con
be a Christian and worship Jesus." In
apparently dead months of absence the Holy
had been busy in his heart, the man had giv
idolatry and desired to know better things.
a period of instruction, his baptism was fix
Christmas Day, but now the man himself hes
"I am not worthy to be baptized on the dε
Saviour was born into the world," said the
noisy, self-important Chinaman. It was p
out to him that no better day could be
for a new follower to make his vows to his Μ
so Ling, with a baby daughter in his arms
to the font, and both were consecrated
service of Christ. Ling became a useful cat
bravely bearing much reproach and persecutio
his old associates.

At last it was possible to rear a real mission church in the Happy City, a solid building, with its font and harmonium, its reading-desk, and even bell to call the people to prayer. The bell had a story; it once hung at the forecastle of the ship *Childers*, which was wrecked that year, 1867, in the bay. The church was called All Saints'. The missionaries dared not name it after our Lord or one of His Apostles, because in China it is considered disrespectful to call a building after a person.

Soon a native clergyman was ordained in this church, a young man whose mother had violently opposed his joining the Christians, and then, won over by his gentle persistency, had become herself a convert. One of the oldest and most respected of Chinese traditions is the honouring of parents, and it must have cost this young man a hard struggle to disobey his mother. Little babes may be murdered and cast away to perish, but the aged father or mother must be respected until death, and after it. Disobedience to them is ranked in China as the worst of crimes. On the last day of the year all the children come and kneel before their parents to show their reverence, even the married sons and daughters joining in the ceremony. Nay, they go further. "Why," writes one of their teachers, "travel abroad to burn incense, when each man has in his house two living deities?" meaning his father and mother. After death this sort of worship continues, the Chinese believing that a person has three souls—one going into the grave,

one entering the spirit world, and one taking possession of a tablet, which they place on the wall of
their house.  Every house has these tablets; prayers
are said before them, incense offered, and the little
children are taught to bow down before them.

On the death of a relative paper money is burned
at the grave, as it is thought that these riches will
accompany the dead person to the other world, and
support him there.  So firm is the belief in this
superstition that money is even burnt to help the
friendless dead, who otherwise might, they think,
become beggar spirits and torment their better-
supplied neighbours.  A large sum is spent in China
every year in this way, and it is one of the
hindrances to Christianity, parents often forbidding
their children to join the Christians from the fear
that they themselves will suffer cold and hunger in
the spirit world for want of these offerings.

The neighbouring villages of the Happy City now
began to wonder what this new religion might be
that the " barbarian " had brought with him, and
a missionary writes as follows in a letter:—" At one
place I have been invited to perform the interesting
but novel ceremony of expelling the devil (*i.e.* the
idols) from the place.  We formed quite a procession.  Several Christians in front led the way to
the house of one of the inquirers.  An old man
came forward and at once brought the idols down
from the place which they had occupied for many
a year, with their incense-pots, sticks, etc., into the
large courtyard, and asked me to expel them.  I

desired the people to take them to the river close by, and after a short sermon on the folly and sin of idolatry, I smashed the pots and idols on the rock and threw the fragments into the water, and they were soon carried away by the rapid current amidst the apparent exultation of the crowd of bystanders. Many of the villagers looked on rather interested, and I could not help but feel that idolatry had received a severe blow in this village."

This was a good beginning. No wonder the missionaries took an exploring tour deeper into the country to see if other poor villagers were in a condition to listen to them. During this journey they suffered a good deal from the extreme curiosity of the country people. They had never. seen a European before wearing tight-fitting clothes and utterly destitute of pigtail; he was a most wonderful object to gaze upon. Wherever they stopped the whole population turned out, amazement depicted in their small eyes, cries of wonder on their tongues. The little children often fled alarmed at so new an object, but the grown people remained, behaving, we should think, like children themselves. They must touch the missionaries, fingering them all over, and specially struck by their eyes and noses. Every new set of people repeated the process, till at last the weary teachers would fall asleep after their day's journey, surrounded by hundreds of poor Chinese examining closely every article of their dress, every feature of their faces. Their questions, too, were equally childish with their

behaviour. But still they scoffed when they heard
of Jesus, saying, "What proof, what proof?" To
which the missionary replied, speaking of their
great prophet, "Who saw Confucius? What proof,
what proof?" which silenced them for a time. It
was actually an idol temple in which these messengers of the true God slept one night on this
tour; hundreds of idols were scattered around them,
some over nine feet high, and the priest waited
upon them. Before going to sleep the missionaries
sang the beautiful hymn, "Rock of Ages," and then
prayed for the idol priest, who, poor fellow! stood
watching them, lost in amazement.

Further on an old grey-haired man came to them,
asking them about their new doctrines. He was
quite satisfied himself with his great teacher Confucius, but since the missionaries persisted that
their Master Jesus was greater and holier he
listened attentively to their sketch of His life and
death. When they had finished, the old Chinaman
said, "Foreign teacher, you look young, but your
words are wise, your doctrine is good. It is deep
beyond the understanding. Who is the Holy Spirit,
and where is the kingdom of God?" He was
instructed in this matter as clearly as might be
in so short a time, and then he took from the hands
of the missionaries a Testament and some tracts,
bowed politely, and went on his way, possibly
never to meet Christian people again, since it is
rare for them to journey so deeply into the
country.

At another place a man observed to the missionary, "How can we live if we embrace your religion? You say we must not deceive, nor lie, nor swear, nor scold people; this is very strange doctrine." The religion, they all said, was good, but only too good for them. They did not wish to give up their sins. People in England often feel like these poor Chinese, though they are seldom so honest as to confess that they cannot and will not live without swearing, deceiving, or scolding. We often hear the saying in English villages, "I never profess to be religious." Which only means, "I never mean to take the trouble to live as Christ would have me live — soberly, righteously, and godly." Another saying too of a poor Chinese could easily be matched in our Christian country: "The doctrine is very good, but it will not do for me; I will do what my fathers did before me."

The travelling missionaries tell us that a Chinaman often bears three or four names, to cheat the devil, he explains, as he thinks if the evil one does not know his name he cannot torment him.

If parents lose two or three sons by death they often give a girl's name to the next, thinking thereby to deceive the evil spirit, who is supposed to take as little heed of girls as the Chinese themselves. Boys for this reason are suffered sometimes to grow up to manhood in girls' clothes, and are treated in every way as girls, all in order to outwit the devil. It must indeed be a release from bondage to leave this strange faith and to take a new name

The new teacher murdered her little scholars! Or, more ridiculous still, the rumour got about that since all little English children have blue eyes, the black eyes of the Chinese girls were wanted to send over to England! No wonder the poor little creatures with pigtails and crippled feet scrambled off their benches and waddled back to their parents in a desperate hurry after hearing these fearful tales whispered about their new teachers.

Yet it is chiefly among the poor and the ignorant that as yet the gospel in China has made its way. The rich and learned are too proud and self-satisfied to care for the doctrines of the meek and lowly Jesus. But still here and there when a great man or a scholar has embraced the truth, he has drawn many after him. Now the Bible is printed in the Chinese tongue we may hope that many of the upper classes may read it out of sheer curiosity, and so receive the new doctrines into their hearts.

I have not told you of one great obstacle in the way of Chinamen becoming earnest Christians. They will not give up the habit of opium-smoking, which is in their land as prevalent as drunkenness is in ours. You all know the hopelessness of a drunkard's condition. It is of no use talking to him, taking him to church, or trying to better his condition, if he will not give up drinking. It is just the same with the opium-smoker; the habit has as hurtful an effect upon him as drink on Englishmen — it stupefies him, ruins his health, beggars his family, and finally kills him.

We try what we can do to wean the Chinaman from his poisonous pleasure! but, as I said before, it is as hard as coaxing our men and boys from the public-house.

Christianity has been brought to China from many quarters; but it has not been thoroughly welcomed even yet. The American Church sent out missionaries before we did, who still labour in the land. The Roman Catholics are trying in their way to make Christ more beloved than Confucius, even clothing our Lord and His disciples in their church pictures in Chinese garb, and giving them Chinese faces, to make them seem better examples for the poor Chinese worshippers.

Whether their method will be more successful than ours we cannot tell; we must each go on in our own way, striving, hoping, praying very earnest in our own efforts, very thankful if, by our means, two or three are gathered into the Christian fold.

# DEAD AT HIS POST.

### PATAGONIA.

A MOTHER, going as usual into her children's nursery at night, to see that they were safe and happy before she herself retired to rest, found one, a little petticoated lad, asleep on the bare floor. On being awakened and questioned why he was not in bed, the child answered that when he became a man he meant to travel all over the world, and so he was preparing himself for any hardships he might have to endure.

Children often make great plans, and occasionally endeavour to carry them out, but generally years and altered tastes entirely change these youthful projects. It was not so, however, with this little man—Allen Gardiner; he kept his love of travel and adventure to his last day, and he did pretty nearly roam the whole world over, suffering the direst hardships and bearing them bravely, as he hoped he would the night he lay on the nursery floor.

Of course, he *must* be a sailor. Those were stirring days in which he lived: that great Emperor

of France was alive, with whose name English
mothers would frighten their naughty children,
saying that "Boney was coming" unless they left
off crying; and in very truth this Bonaparte was
carrying all before him, and looking at England
with so keen an eye that all her spirited boys must
needs be soldiers or sailors, and stand up in defence
of their country.

So Allen made baby plans of harbours on his
slate, and devised means for outwitting the French
fleet; and then, mindful that his travels would
possibly carry him into all corners of the world,
he copied out a list of words from the language of a
remote African tribe, which he found in an old
book of travels, and was happy in feeling he was
prepared for any emergency,

Few mothers but feel a pang when their boy
"will go to sea," and Mrs. Gardiner did what she
could to dissuade Allen; but his wishes were too
strong to oppose, and in 1810 the boy made his first
voyage, out of a peaceful, God-fearing home, plung-
ing straight into the then thoughtless, religionless
life of a roving sailor. In those days for a lad to
read his Bible and say his prayers on board ship was
to challenge mockery, and bring down upon himself
ill words and abuse, not only from his messmates,
but even from his superior officers.

Allen soon found that, brave as he was, he dared
not face ridicule and scorn, and when the good
mother died, who kept up, by her letters and loving
counsel, the teachings of his childhood, he left off

even the forms of religion, and believed it a sort of folly to read the Bible.

Now and then, however, the old feelings came back. When a friend was drowned, doing the very same work he had done the day before, Allen could hardly help, in the midst of his sorrow, thanking God that *he* had not been cut off in his present unsatisfactory state of mind. The good his mother had taught him as a child was not dead in his heart, it was only smothered for a while under the follies of a wild youth. But it was a very long time before the holy fire blazed up again in the young sailor's heart, and before the Spirit, long repressed but never quenched, urged the repentant youth to kneel and pray as of old and search the Scriptures for a light to lead him on his way.

Poor Allen! he did desire to amend his ways, but it was hard work. He had no Bible now; he had lost the one brought from home in the boyish days gone by, and he was ashamed to go to a bookseller's and buy another. Alas! in those careless days the very shopkeeper behind the counter might smile at such a request from a glittering young sailor. But he did do it, and on the next voyage we may fancy Allen Gardiner choosing quiet corners of the vessel, or perhaps waking in the still night to find out by Holy Writ how he could serve his God as well as his country.

I have not told you that Allen had already made a voyage to America, and was now journeying to India and China. Here cholera attacked his vessel,

and the sight of dead and dying comrades mad
him think still more of the world beyond. Abou
the same time came a letter from a friend of hi
mother's, full of tender, loving exhortation, an
enclosing a description of that mother's last day
written by his father.

It was impossible for young Gardiner to remai
insensible to these calls to repentance. While o
this voyage the young man attended a Sunda
service on the island of Tahiti. It was, perhaps, th
first time he had entered the house of God sinc
boyhood. He tells us of a large church built ther
by the king, so large that it held six thousan
people and had three pulpits, in each of which
preacher held forth. The natives were reveren
and attentive, and Allen Gardiner's interest wa
roused in the mission.

Perhaps here, too, he first felt the change dawn
ing in his adventurous disposition; hitherto he ha
travelled hither and thither, and done his dut
as a sailor bravely and gladly from mere love o
excitement and loyalty to his country, but nov
another motive was to sway him, a much highe
one. He *must* travel—he was not one that coul
sit still; but God should be his Guide and Captai
for the future, and His work should be the occupa
tion of his life.

But before this new period of exertion God gav
him a quiet time for consideration; the young sailo
fell ill and had to go home invalided. He wa
twenty-eight years old; he had been taught th

Holy Scriptures in his childhood like Timothy, and yet he had passed a careless, God-forgetting youth. Now the heavenly visitor was knocking again at the door of his heart. Should he open and let Him in? Yea, verily, and entertain Him there as long as life lasted.

From this point we may date the missionary life of Allen Gardiner. In his frequent voyages he had visited many a spot where God's name was not even known to the poor inhabitants, and his desire was now great to carry the news of salvation to such ignorant heathen.

South America was the first place on his list, and coupled with his longings to be a missionary was his further desire to take holy orders. But this was not to be. Allen Gardiner could work for God as well as a sailor as a priest, and he was ready when the first shock of disappointment was over to acknowledge this himself.

He returned, therefore, to active service, married, was gladdened by the birth of three little ones, and then lost his beloved wife in a lingering sickness.

Drawn again nearer to heaven and holy things by this new loss, he solemnly by the sick-bed devoted his life afresh to God, desiring no better for the future than to carry the gospel tidings to the most ignorant and degraded of His creatures.

To Africa he sailed with this intent, writing in his note-book on board ship his resolve and prayer: "Having put my hand to the plough, may I never turn back." He never did turn back. Many of

were glad to get afloat once more. To New Guinea, then, the party went; but after residing there some time Captain Gardiner could make no way, and with health impaired by fever, he sailed for the Cape on his way back again to South America. Another tribe of Indians might receive his teachings, he thought. He took a house for his family for six months, as near the province he meant to visit as possible, and then with Bibles and tracts in his hands he began his work. But no! the Indians could not believe he meant them only well; and he met with further discouragement from the Roman Catholics, who had been before him in the spread of Christianity, and who did not care to be friendly with one who was not of their fold.

Rebuff on rebuff. An ordinary man must have given all up in despair, but this was not our sailor's weakness. As a friend said of him, "The captain is iron-hearted as to difficulties, and almost incapable of fatigue; at least he will not yield to anything less than impossibilities."

As soon as one channel of usefulness seemed closed to him, this indefatigable worker hastened to open another.

Only a month from the time that the Chili Indians repulsed him, Captain Gardiner, his wife, and children were sailing southwards for the Falkland Isles.

These are a group of islands near the extreme southerly point of South America, and, being in the

2 c

rather signed towards the sea, and seemed to command them to depart as soon as possible. This being only a journey of investigation, Captain Gardiner did leave them, landing on the other side of the Straits, where some fires betokened an Indian encampment. Here the *Montgomery* left him with his tents and servant, while it proceeded further in search of wood, and the natives began to crowd round the strange settler. They were terrible thieves, and a watch had constantly to be kept over them, notwithstanding which they managed one day to steal the dinner of ship biscuit out of the kettle in which it was stewing.

Indeed, some poor American missionaries had long ago left the country in despair, since the Fuegians not only stole and ate their provisions, but cut up their books.

Captain Gardiner, however, determined to try and win them over, and the tobacco and gifts he bestowed made some impression on their hearts, for a chief promised to befriend him if he would come and live among them, and the natives seemed so peaceable that the captain quite resolved to bring his family and settle for a time in Patagonia.

He tried to tell the more intelligent natives of the good things he was bringing them, and he held one Sunday service in his tent, which was attended by the men of the *Montgomery* and an old North American negro called Isaac, and then he set out on his return to the Falklands.

When there the same difficulty, the want of a

ship, prevented his instantly carrying off his family
to the new ground he had chosen to occupy—he
would not risk their lives as he had done his own
in the *Montgomery*—so there was nothing to be
done but to wait, and meantime to try to get a real
missionary clergyman sent to Patagonia by the
Church Missionary Society.

This, however, was difficult to arrange, and in
the end Captain Gardiner thought it best to go
himself to England with his family to personally
plead the cause of the poor Patagonians. His
children, too, were growing up, and instead of the
desolate shores of South America, it struck him
that their education could be better conducted in
England. So from henceforth he made his mission
journeys alone, not forgetting his wife and children
at home, but writing them fond and wise letters as
he journeyed along.

During this visit to England he tried to make
people feel so much interest in the Patagonians as
should induce them to set on foot a mission there;
but again he was unsuccessful, and to fill up a
pause in his work he set out once more laden with
Bibles and good books to South America. Alas!
he found the country at war when he landed, and a
bookseller whom he supplied told him his Bibles
would not sell because they had *blue* edges, the
colour the enemy had adopted! Still he went on,
sometimes well received, sometimes threatened and
abused, but ever trying to do some good, and never
forgetting Patagonia. The larger towns of South

America promised to collect £100 yearly for a mission to those poor natives if Captain Gardiner would make a beginning, and back to England flew the eager sailor with the news.

Good people on this side the Atlantic took heart again, and at last Captain Gardiner and a Mr. Hunt did really set out for Patagonia, landing among the same people who had seemed so friendly on his first visit. But now things had changed; the chief who promised to protect them seemed sulky and unapproachable; he even threatened the lives of the English; and it was so utterly impossible for a couple of helpless strangers to make the least way without his help that they were reluctantly obliged to leave the land and once more to return to England with their tale of disappointment.

Still, Captain Gardiner was not cast down. He now asked more help from the Missionary Society which supported him before, but he added, with a firmness and heartiness none could doubt, "Whatever course you may determine upon, I have made up my own mind to go back again to South America, and leave no stone unturned, no effort untried, to establish a mission there."

And while they meditated he once more paid a visit to that continent, trying first in this tribe and then in that to establish a settlement for the spread of Christianity. But everywhere he was repulsed; sometimes one or another would listen to him, and his reception was generally a kindly one, but the main reply to his overtures was the same: "We do not want a Christian among us." One Sunday, under a broad forest tree, the undaunted captain knelt and prayed to his Master to show him some way which he could not mistake, as He had done unto Paul and Silas. Always patient, always enduring, he bore fatigue, disappointment, hunger, and thirst gladly in his one aim, the spread of Christianity. And still his mind turned ever towards those sullen, ignorant natives on that southernmost point of South America. Because they stole, and lied, and were ignorant almost as the beasts that perish, were they to be regarded as unworthy of interest, as beyond the pale of human sympathy?

Verily, no! Back again to England he fain must go after a while to organize a new expedition thither. And a little company really did set out, consisting of Captain Gardiner, a ship's carpenter called Erwin, and four sailors. They landed on the Fuegian coast, but the party was still too small and helpless for success; a handful of natives could overcome them, steal their possessions, and leave them to perish on that desolate shore. Captain Gardiner happily saw this in time, and dissolved the mission band once more, sending them safely home by different vessels before mischief had been done. If he had only always been as careful in his zeal, the pitiful close of his story might never have needed telling!

We cannot, however, blame this good man; he did according to the wisdom granted to him.

Another—the last—attempt was now made to establish the Patagonian Mission. Much thought was expended on the arrangement; large and small boats were selected, and a crew used to hardship was chosen of Cornish seamen. Joseph Erwin, the carpenter of the former expedition, begged to be again allowed to accompany Captain Gardiner, saying that "being with him was like a heaven upon earth, he was such a man of prayer." A surgeon (Mr. Williams) joined the party, as well as another good man, called Maidment. All these men knew they were going to face danger, and, if necessary, death in the cause of Christ, but they were cheerful and undaunted as they stood on the deck of the *Ocean Queen* in Liverpool docks on the eve of sailing.

They reached their destination safely, and landed on Picton Island in Tierra del Fuego; but the natives were again so troublesome with their thievish ways that they were compelled to take to their boats and put off from the land. The vessels got separated, however, and one ran aground; this was a signal for the Fuegians to crowd round it, possibly with no good intention. Captain Gardiner and his men had to arm themselves with guns, but trusting they might not have to use their weapons, they knelt down before the ignorant savages and prayed to God for help. The natives drew back awed by this proceeding, and a few presents diverted their attention till the other boat arrived.

A great blow now fell on the little company, in

the discovery that they had left all their powder
on board the *Ocean Queen*.  This meant that, should
provisions run short, they would have no means of
shooting the wild birds and animals which abounded
on the island, and which alone might keep them
from starvation.  They also would be utterly defenceless if attacked by the natives, who had already
begun to make ugly preparations in the way of war
spears and large stones, which they collected in
sight of the mission party.

Altogether matters began to look discouraging,
and Captain Gardiner and his friends soon came to
the conclusion that the readiest way to civilize
these poor unapproachable savages was to form a
mission settlement on the Falkland Isles, and
thither to carry over some of the young Fuegians
for education.  For this purpose a larger vessel
would be needed, and the size and fittings of the
craft were eagerly discussed by the poor missioners
in their perplexity.

Two calamities befell them now.  One of their
boats, the *Pioneer*, was struck by a heavy sea, and
so damaged that she could no longer be used save
as a sleeping-place when dragged higher up on the
beach; the other trouble was even more distressing,
*i.e.* the sickness which attacked first one and then
another of the party.  A relieving vessel was
anxiously looked for; but the mission party were
now in Spaniard Harbour, and it was most likely
that a friendly ship would seek them in their first
anchorage, Banner Cove.  So, before settling down

with their sick, they made a journey thither, plainly
marking in two several places on the rocks, "Gone
to Spaniard Harbour."

Then all were put on short allowance, and spent
weary days and weeks watching for a vessel and
tending the sick. A fox was shot once with a
spring gun, but other wild animals that might have
served for food they were forced to watch harmlessly
wandering near the caverns and disabled boats in
which they had taken refuge. Those were days of
trial, but the long-suffering captain and his faithful
followers never uttered a murmur. One brave
Cornishman after another sank and died under
disease and privation, prayer and praise on their
lips to the last.

Captain Gardiner, a man of iron constitution,
held out the longest, keeping up to the last a diary,
which recorded, along with the sad details of sickness and starvation, unfailing trust in the Master
he served. In those closing days of weakness he
even wrote a farewell letter to his son, advising
him on his studies and future life, and others to
his wife and daughter. Nothing was forgotten on
that desolate death-bed by the stormy sea.

When the relieving vessel at last did arrive it
was too late ; only lifeless bodies met the horrified
gaze of the searchers. Captain Gardiner, the last
survivor, was lying stretched by the boat, into
which he had probably been unable to climb through
weakness, a colder, stranger bed than the nursery
floor of long ago ! Other new graves and dead

bodies accounted for the remainder of the mission
band. A letter, found on the shore, stained with
sea-water, contained the last words of Allen Gardiner.
It referred to his comrade, Mr. Maidment, who had
left him the day before to seek food, and had not
returned. It ran as follows —:

"The Lord has seen fit to call home another of
our little company. Our dear departed brother left
the boat on Tuesday at noon, and has not since
returned; doubtless he is in the presence of his
Redeemer, whom he served so faithfully. Yet a
little while, and through grace we may join that
blessed throng, to sing the praises of Christ throughout eternity. I neither hunger nor thirst, though
five days without food! Marvellous lovingkindness
to me, a sinner!"

So perished the whole band, ten months after
landing on the hoped-for mission ground. A pitiful
story, indeed, but the lives of these brave men may
not have been spent in vain.

Who knows what effect their sufferings, their
patience, their trust in God, may not have had on
many a heart that grieved over their loss?

Neither did the mission to Fuegia and Patagonia
perish with its leaders. The plan for establishing
its head-quarters on one of the Falkland Islands
was adopted after Captain Gardiner's death, and a
schooner bearing his name was fitted out for the
purpose of maintaining safe communication with
Tierra del Fuego, and bringing over Fuegian boys
for education.

This was the plan devised by Captain Gardiner, and dear to his heart, and the realization of it formed, it was thought, the best memorial of so brave and zealous a missionary. The South American Missionary Society was formed to carry it out; and it has now a mission station on Tierra del Fuego itself. A clergyman and two catechists are living there, and already the thievish habits of the natives have been checked and many converts made. An English bishop has also been appointed to the Falkland Isles, who watches over and guards these infant missions.

ones of these regions became so painfully evident
that Sunday schools were set on foot for their
benefit. And inasmuch as Jesus Himself said of
the starving multitude, "Give ye them to eat," so
these poor hungry babes were fed with earthly
bread before the better food was set before them.

A hot breakfast of a currant roll and a cup of weak
tea is the delightful prelude to the work of instruction, and gratefully do the little creatures throng to
the school doors for both blessings. Their parents
lying late on the Sunday and preparing no food early
in the day, and the absence of all staying power in
the little half-nourished bodies, would otherwise
have rendered useless any attempt to fix their
attention on any higher subject than hunger and
wretchedness.

So out of the courts and alleys pour forth a tiny
"six hundred," sent all too soon into the battle
of life, noisy and quarrelsome among themselves,
their lips too apt at the language of sin, but with
hearts not yet hardened, lives not yet utterly given
up to the sway of the evil one. Poor little
people! no one has wanted them before; the
regular Church schools would admit them truly,
but the babes themselves hang back, a certain shyness of those more decent children, who have shoes
to their feet and gay Sunday raiment to shake
out on the benches, deters them. Here, in the
gutter schools (oh! they don't mind the name,
coupled with warmth and food and kindness), has
not the teacher been herself up their court or alley

to invite them to come ? And was not li
round the corner, with never a shoe to his fo
last Sunday, and had a hot drink, and a c
was showed pictures afterwards ? The
telegraph spreads quickly ; one child tells
of the new and delightful mission school ; 
in the districts where they are held the 
may be seen hurrying, Sunday after Sund
faces bright with the anticipation of their
treat, and nothing abashed that they are in
clothed in the flaunting motley garments
pawn-shop. But tea and bun are not all th
get ; the teaching comes later, chiefly in the
questions, broken small enough to reach the
comprehension ; stories from the Bible, 
home by striking pictures ; singing, plenty
and talking on all topics, but always w
object in mind, the conveying of, however
fragment of religious teaching.

To these schools used to come children v
you plainly they never said a prayer in the
never spent Sunday otherwise than "tearin
the streets," never heard of God, never ho
heaven.

One girl of twelve said her favourite am
was stopping out all night watching street
another, about the same age, was taken to tl
up, found "drunk and disorderly" in the
And the pale, sickly faces of many others
the complaint they make of wretched homes
in drink, mother sick, or perhaps drunk also.

The bits of creatures, whose legs dangle on the
school benches, are often steady workers for daily
bread, the monotonous labour of match and bon-bon-
box-making taking up all their week-day time.
They look on life with solemn eyes, and frequently
drop into an early grave. Still they too have a
smile for the buns and the tea and the pleasant
talk. One mother tells how her tiny child of three,
the youngest of seven, living in a cellar, woke her
up each day with the inquiry, "Ain't it bun-school
day, mother?"

These bun-schools still flourish, and in the
neediest and wickedest parts of London. The
Home sends out sisters on the Sunday to teach
in them. And such "Sunday" as it is in those
regions! Ragged children in the roadway, bigger
ones with the baby in their arms on doorsteps,
costermongers buying and selling, crowds thronging
the pavement, and in one district a Sunday bird
fair, where the shouting and bargaining concerning
the fluttering occupants of the cages really drowns
the voice of the teacher in the mission school. The
buyers and sellers cannot be driven with a strong
hand from the neighbourhood of this temple, but
the children's voices lifted up in their shrill sweetness, to the praise and glory of a God they have
just recognized, can in a measure deaden the outer
tumult.

And in connection with these schools are sick-
kitchens, whence go out portions of relishing food
to poor creatures laid low in their wretched homes,

and mission-houses available for classes in the week, centres of sympathy and help for all such as need them.

This is one, and a great work of the Home we are visiting.

But leave the East End now, and come back to our north-west corner again—back to the somewhat gaunt houses, and in at the wide hall door. A tiny maiden opens it, prettily clad in something dark, brightened by scarlet lines, a small round cap clinging to her brown head, but not hiding the hair.

As "one of the orphans" this small person announces herself, but with no sorrowful intonation; to be an orphan here is to be loved, cared for, to have home and friends. Upstairs, through passages and galleries, patters this very little door-keeper, till, if you follow, she leads you into the orphans' play-room, where some five-and-twenty children of much the same growth as herself are hard at work—playing. Yes, there are dolls and dolls' houses, Noah and his ark, cups and saucers for miniature tea-parties, and a real mock dinner going on in one window, where, in default of guests, a toy bust of Shakespeare has been pressed into the service, as host, at the top of the table. A pleasant sight. The little ones look very much as ordinary nursery-children do, in their second best frocks, holland pinafores, and legs warmly eased in winter stockings. No draggling drab garments, but trim short skirts in which to gambol, and a touch of colour here and there in the braid of pinafore, or

the blue ribbon in the hair—children clothed as
lowly born maidens well may be by-and-by,
modestly, economically, but not forswearing hue
of bluebell or pimpernel as if it were a sin.

But what orphans are these, then, so free with
their harmless cackle that no hush falls on them at
the approach of their guardians? It is difficult to
believe that they are all, or nearly all, workhouse
waifs, items out of that dull, stolid, monotonous
array that wind past one at rare intervals in the
streets, a procession as pitiful as ugly.

And no blame, perhaps, to the special workhouse
that contains them; the treatment there is probably
as kind as the law permits. No, it is the system
that is to blame; the herding together of a crowd
of poor little wretches, to whom no one owes love,
and who are cared for because for very shame the
country could not let them perish.

No one wants them; if they die, it is so much
saved.

The tiniest child seems to feel the ban and disgrace of belonging to such a flock—it soddens them,
stupefies them, gives them a dogged, downcast appearance. When they are older life is no happier; out
of a sphere where perhaps everything has been done
for them by machinery, they are turned all at once
adrift in entirely new regions. Some small shopkeeper applies for a girl to nurse her six children,
and act as maid-of-all-work in the house. With no
knowledge of cooking, no wiles to keep the baby
quiet, hands that break and let fall, and feet that

stumble, the poor girl is in disgrace directly.
Scolded and perhaps beaten, the workhouse orphan
has nowhere to turn, and becomes either an oppressed
drudge, or, taking the law into her own hands, runs
away to deeper degradation.

In this Kilburn Home the sad story of workhouse
life was so well known that at the first moment possible a refuge was opened for as many as could be
housed of these unloved little ones. The children
came at first without gladness or emotion of any
sort, their cropped hair and dull apparel stamping
them as paupers. Then a few days later small
smiles would steal to their faces at sight of the
new frock provided for them, or the delightful toy
allotted to their share, and by-and-by they would
drop a few words of pleasure. All told the same
tale: "Not enough to eat. I didn't like the workhouse; I wanted to get out." One little girl of nine
said very touchingly on her arrival, "I kept axing
the Lord to open a door for me, and He has opened
it." And another declared on the part of herself and
her little companions, "We don't feel like orphans
now, we feel like little girls as has mothers."

The workhouse clothing put on one side, the
stunted hair carefully attended to, and allowed to
develop a curl behind the round comb, what is then
done with this army of little maids from five to ten
years of age?

In garments the fashion of which shall carry
them quietly through the streets, and not separate
them from their own kind, they are sent to the

parish schools. There, seated side by side with little girls " as has mothers," they learn to read and write, in no way separate from other children to whom God has given natural homes and kindreds' love. After school, back they come to dinner, and *home*, play and prayers, and bed—bed in the dearest of little beds, facing the neat row of washing-basins, glittering with water for to-morrow's scrub. No turning out to the chilly lavatory in the early morning; these children are brought up as the tidy, cared-for servant-maids they hope to be some day. On one side stand small screens to draw round the bath on tub nights. Not too early can these poor little things be taught to do all things decently.

These children *are* naturally, honestly happy; not over-schooled, not overwatched—the very fearless way in which they flit about under the eyes of "sister" and "mother" is convincing of that fact; and the ready answer or quick smile in reply to notice from an outsider is as different as possible from the stolid silence of the small pauper when questioned by the "quality."

Yet all these little ones have their sad story, even though some may never have known them.

Workhouses are no paradise, but worse has often come before them.

Rescued at six months old from a disused sawpit, where it had been exposed, and its tiny arms gnawed by rats—that is the tale of one little pauper. Another was a foundling, taken, basket and all, from under the seat of a railway carriage, and so on. Such as these of course are friendless from the first, but there are others little better off. "Mother ill of fever and father run away," is an account of home life leading to the workhouse, very frequently given with variations. But a tiny mite among the Home orphans has its peculiarly sad background— a degraded father, a violent stepmother, passionate itself, the parents came from words to blows, and the child lost an eye under the cruel treatment of the woman that ought to have befriended it.

It was a child, too, that would have answered to kind treatment, since it first came under the notice of the Home through its gentle care of a poor paralyzed old woman. Not able to feed herself, the baby nurse, barely five years old, would carry the cup to the lips of the even more helpless creature, and, with enticing words, encourage the sufferer to drink. The poor woman died at last, and then the little nurse was sent to the Home by her care-nothing father. Such a haven of peace and rest the mutilated infant has never known before, and the one anxiety that fills her little soul is, whether *he*, the father she cannot think of without a shudder, will ever fetch her away. She hopes not, poor child, and so do we.

But leaving the orphans' playroom, which, by the way, little Belgravian children might well covet, with its low windows looking pleasantly out on the garden beneath, we come across children of a larger growth, yet withal not very large—girls of twelve or fourteen, who are flitting about with

a business-like air, evidently doing the household
duties. Who are they? Ah! there we come on
another branch of the Home work. These are
the industrial girls, forty in number, who are
received from all parts of England and trained to
become in future days good domestic servants.

Like the little children, many of them entirely
belong to the Home, being fatherless, motherless,
and friendless. These the sisters of the Church
speak of with peculiar pride and affection. "They
are entirely ours," say they. "This is their home
now; by-and-by we shall get them places as servants, but should they not suit, or be laid by with
sickness, they will return here, as to a natural
home, and be cared for by us as our children."
Some few are partially paid for by relatives; all,
however, are treated alike, taught to cook, sew, and
in every way learn the duties of a household. It
is hardly necessary to say that no servants are kept
in these five large houses; even the girls' washing
is done by themselves. Of course, there are many
mistakes made where the officials are so young, in
the kitchen especially; good food is occasionally
spoiled, and saucepans roasted out of bottom and
usefulness, to the tribulation of the young kitchen-
maids; but these are mistakes that will occur with
the most promising of juvenile cooks.

The demand for servants from this little band is
already great, and as years go on the supply will,
it is hoped, be in proportion.

Here, as among the smaller orphans, the girls

soon lose the trodden-down, stupid workhouse expression, and often brighten into really pleasant-
faced, happy young folks, though occasionally, as
will be pointed out, there is still a young thing who,
under less tender treatment, would be pronounced
stupid or idiotic, and who still requires the gentlest
consideration, the most cheerful encouragement.

"Are these girls never naughty, very naughty?"
asked one who knew something of workhouse
children and servant girls of a low class.

"Never very naughty," was the reply; "at least,
not so naughty as other children, we think. Some
are difficult to manage, but on our plan they work
round to try to please us in time."

"And what is the Home plan?"

"Well, part of it is this: there are three lists to
which all these bigger girls belong. Roughly speaking, they are the trusted list, the idle, and the un-
trusted. The trusted list are a happy set; they do
the errands, the little shoppings, are the helpers
and confidantes of the sisters and 'mothers.' Then
come the more unsatisfactory, but still hopeful, ones
—the idle girls, the chatterboxes, those who put
their pleasures before their duties, and so are not
to be counted on in time of need. These, and the
next class, are, happily, never content with their
position, and are always making the greatest efforts
to rise to the trusted list. To them the decree, 'I
cannot send Mary or Alice for this or that, they are
not to be relied upon,' is the most terrible form of
condemnation; they need nothing further to spur
them on to do better."

One of the great occupations of these girls is, under superintendence, cooking for the sick and poor. Come to a small room near the kitchen between twelve and one, and you will imagine yourself in a miniature cookshop. On a counter stand portions of meat, dumplings, Christmas pudding, all sorts of eatables, *sold* chiefly in penny portions to any poor customers, who are too glad to patronize the shop. I say "sold," and wish the word noted, since, though labour and firing is given by the Home, the food is disposed of at cost price to the poor of the neighbourhood; and very glad they are to buy it, coming with their cloths and covered dishes to carry it hot back to their often fireless homes.

Sometimes as much as a pound is taken daily at this dinner counter in penny portions, at other times less. On Saturdays very little is bought, the poor considering their children well able to subsist on bread and treacle, or bread and dripping, in consideration of the coming important Sunday dinner, which the poorest household endeavours to keep up. Monday, too, is a poor day for business here, what is left from Sunday having to do duty again; but on all other days there is a rush to the counter. Great is the demand for "Christmas pudding," a manufacture of batter and currants, sold in flat slices, and convenient for small hands to grasp.

Sick dinners are often provided and given in these regions, especially where the invalid is connected with the Home children or known to the establishment; and they do look most tempting, arranged, the bit of meat and the couple of potatoes, most carefully in a covered dish, safe for carrying into court or attic. No wonder languid eyes brighten and feeble pulses beat more strongly at sight and taste of them, for if the sick creature happen to be the mother of the household, as she often is, how could she otherwise obtain nourishing food, since she is too weak to stand over the fire or undertake the fashioning of the messes she requires?

But there is more to be told, so we must not fondly linger among these specially domestic matters.

The orphan little ones, as has before been mentioned, attend the National Schools of the parish, St. Augustine's, Kilburn, and here several of the sisters teach, having prepared themselves for the government examinations and gained certificates. Here, too, some of their girls are trained as pupil-teachers. So the influence of the home is brought to bear on seven hundred outsider children who belong to the neighbourhood, and are enrolled in one of the three distinct sections of the school— the ordinary National School, the mission or Ragged School, and one attended by children of the lower middle class.

Another agency for brightening and benefiting the little street children is the Children's Convalescent Hospital at Margate, opened two years ago by the sisters of the Church. Here are transplanted the sick and ailing, either of their own community or of other less favoured homes, and wonderful is the change three weeks' fresh air, sea-bathing, and good food will effect in the fading little city child.

In the first year seventy children were admitted to the Convalescent Home, returning to their families with smiles on their faces, their pockets full of shells and other sea treasures, and a stock of health to last them, it is hoped, for many a day.

One more work of the home must be mentioned, and that is, the grants of money, altar linen, or church fittings to poor or foreign missions. Natal, Newfoundland, the West Indies, New Zealand, Bombay, Cawnpore, and a dozen other names familiar to us, send grateful letters of thanks for benefits received in this way.

\*  \*  \*  \*  \*

You will like to hear the very last report of the Kilburn Home;—very pleasant news it is, too. The family in the five houses grew and grew till it overflowed the limited space. Yet children kept knocking at the door for admittance, pleading poverty and friendlessness and loneliness in this wide, wide world.

When the sisters had quite a long list of these sad cases turned away from their doors, on account of those two little words, "No Room," they and their friends thought it time to take a very bold step, and build a new large house to hold two hundred children. It cost a great deal to raise that house; cost not only money, but many prayers, many anxieties, and much labour; but, thank God, it was built, and eighteen months after the first stone was laid, it stood completed, and with songs of thankfulness the sisters and their adopted children took possession of it. This was in June, 1880.

And the same work goes on here day by day that went on in the five houses, only on a larger scale, for there are already one hundred and forty orphans instead of seventy—just double the number. Here are the same miniature cooks and housemaids, the same school-children romping merrily in the playground, the same round-faced babies in the nursery,—for this sort of work never ends. All are as happy and busy as ever, and will be as pleased to see any one who comes to visit the Home as they were in the earlier days of the Five Houses.

# TWO WORKING WOMEN.

## BURMAH.

I LIKE to tell you about women in these papers, and their connection with mission work, because their labours have been less frequently chronicled than those of their husbands and brothers, and yet have been equally valuable. Therefore I often pass by the names of men renowned in mission story to tell you of some perhaps humbler woman helper, who went out into the highways and hedges of the heathen world, and compelled the poor wanderers there to come in to the heavenly feast.

Two such women's lives are before me to-day; not Englishwomen, not even members of our branch of the Christian Church, but one with us in all else, sharing with us one Lord, one faith, one baptism.

Mrs. Judson, an American lady, with her husband, left a happy home and loving relations in her native country, early in the present century, with the desire to live and die among the heathen of the East, if only they might be permitted to teach them as Christ enjoined.

There were no steamers in those days, and the

missionaries were four months in reaching Calcutta by way of England. Very glad indeed must they have been to set foot on land; but imagine their disappointment and consternation when they received orders a few days afterwards to return immediately to America in the same ship in which they came. The East India Company, who ruled that part of India, were afraid of disturbances among the natives if teachers of the Christian religion were permitted to enter the country.

What were the missionaries to do? They would not (having put their hand to the plough) draw back, but they supposed they must choose some other country to labour in. A ship was sailing for the Isle of France on the coast of Africa, and though the captain, fearing the Government, durst not promise them a passage, he said, "There is my ship, do as you like with it." So at midnight they crept out of inhospitable Calcutta, followed by porters carrying their baggage, and got safely on board. Next morning the ship sailed down the river, and the new passengers began to think it was all right, when two days later the vessel was stopped, and the pilot was forbidden to proceed, as there were people on board who had been ordered back to England.

Poor Mr. and Mrs. Judson! Missionaries might have been thieves or murderers from the trouble taken to drive them away. The kind captain was very sorry, but he could do no more for them—he must think first of himself and his ship—and so he put them on shore with their baggage, sending word back by the Government officer that he had no such persons on board, and then he sailed away on his course.

The poor missionaries, left helplessly on shore, begged every ship that passed down the river to take them to some port; but the answer was always no, till a wonderful bit of good fortune came to them—no less than a permission to sail in the very ship from which they had so lately been ousted.

But that vessel must surely be far out at sea, for four days had elapsed since the Judsons had quitted it. Something might have detained it, however, at the port of Sangor, where it meant to touch, so the brave husband and wife set out in boats, rowing hard all night and all next day till they actually caught up the ship, safely anchored in Sangor Roads, waiting for its crew.

This was the beginning of Mrs. Judson's missionary life, and such a troublesome one, that one wonders she did not do as her family in America constantly begged of her—return to home comforts and loving friends, and leave the heathen and a missionary life to other stronger hands.

But no! She had made up her mind, and when later on Mr. Judson went from the Isle of France to Burmah, though the land was supposed to be full of murderers and robbers, and though there was not one woman in the whole country with whom she could speak, she quietly ordered her life so as best to help her husband and improve the poor natives.

They settled down at a place called Rangoon, and her first friend was a great lady, the wife of the viceroy. Mrs. Judson could not begin all in a minute to teach or preach to her Highness—a missionary must not be too bold, or he may spoil his chance of doing good—so she respectfully bowed down before her, and answered as well as she could the question if she was Mr. Judson's first or highest wife, as her Highness was first wife of the viceroy, with a great many lesser wives under her.

But Mrs. Judson did not have more to do with this great lady than she could help. She thought she could work best among the poor and lowly, so to them she directed her attention.

It was a land of theft and murder, but even more terrible than these crimes were the punishments inflicted on wrong-doers. They were hung on trees and their bodies cut open, shut up in prison with all their bones broken, and in all possible ways cruelly tortured. And yet the Burmese felt no need of the Christian religion; they had one of their own, with priests, and ceremonies, and temples, and drum-beatings, and prayer-makings. What did they want more? They simply told the missionaries, "Our religion is good for us, yours for you." It was very discouraging. But still Mrs. Judson set to work to learn the language, and make friends with the women. She got up a mothers' meeting almost directly, or at least as soon as she could make her party understand a word she said; and Mr. Judson, when he had reached the same stage, built a large shed with one side open to the road, under shelter of which he talked to all the passers-by, telling them something of his purpose in coming to Burmah.

The natives seemed to have generally behaved quietly and in an orderly manner when they attended the divine service established by Mr. Judson, and perhaps one reason for their gentle behaviour was the good example set them by the missionaries in this wise.

Mr. and Mrs. Judson used sometimes to go into one of the Burman temples and listen to the preachers there, and once the people said, " There come some wild foreigners; " but they were silenced when they saw the visitors take off their shoes and sit down after the fashion of the Burmese. The answer now ran round, "They are not wild, they are civilized." Of course, the Judsons did not join in any worship of the Burmese gods, but they felt as right-thinking people do in this day, that if we enter a place of worship, however different its services may be from what we approve, we owe it to the place to behave decently and quietly. So in Mr. Judson's zayal, or religion-house, the natives tried to follow the rules of the strange teachers, and at least to listen and sit still.

Mrs. Judson's mothers used to ask how they were to know when their hearts were changed under the influence of Christ's religion, and she gave them a very good answer. The Burmese are very quarrel-some, and she assured them if they refrained from hard words when scolded at, and instead . felt inclined to be sorry for their enemies, and to pray for them, they might certainly think that their hearts were changed.

Notwithstanding all the pains taken, however, by the American missionaries, only little progress was made in the establishment of the Christian religion for many years; the people came and listened, and seemed impressed, and then went away and forgot the teachings, or were too much afraid of their priests and rulers to dare to proceed further.

The better-disposed of the Burmese whispered to Mr. Judson not to talk more to common people, but to go directly to the lord of life and death; this was one of their names for the king. If he approved of the Christian religion it would flourish, but if not—and then the speakers dropped their voices and wore an ominous look. In vain Mr. Judson told them that his religion was not dependent on the will even of princes—they still held back. In the midst of doubts and fears news came that the king was sick, nay, some declared, under their breath, that he was dead. But a king of Burmah is supposed to be immortal, so none dared speak the news more openly, and presently a royal despatch boat neared the shore, and a messenger declared that "the immortal king, wearied with the cares of royalty, has gone up to amuse himself in the celestial regions." This is the way the Burmese announced the death of a poor mortal.

Mr. Judson now resolved to visit the young king,

and endeavour to obtain his countenance to the mission, and as a preparatory measure he asked permission to gaze upon "the golden face," and bow down before "the golden feet," the proper phrase for requesting to see the king. An audience with royalty was granted him, and as it is customary to go with a present in the hand, he took a Bible in the Burmese language, covered with a gilded cover. He saw the king, an imposing young man, with a golden sword and a lordly manner; he placed a petition in his hand, asking for protection while he taught the doctrines of the one true God; but the monarch took offence at the first line, and dashed the paper to the ground. As to the Bible, he was by no means ready for that, and would have none of it.

Unless the missionaries were also doctors and able to work marvellous cures, he would not have anything to do with them. The emperor laughed at the bare idea of their doing him or his people any good. It was very dispiriting, and Mr. Jndsou returned home full of perplexity as to his next move. If the Burmese found out that their king would not defend the Christian teachers, they were not likely to support them. A few converts, truly, there were, affectionately attached to the Judsons, but they were as nothing to the mass of unbelievers ready to join any party against them.

The Judsons felt as if they had best move to some more friendly region, where at least they might have liberty to teach and preach, and only the prayers and tears of one of the converts induced

2 E

them to remain a little longer in Rangoon. "If you go now," he said, "you will take with you the two other disciples, and I shall be left alone. I cannot baptize those who may wish to embrace this religion. What can I do?"

From which you see how few were the reliable converts, though the Judsons had been eight years in the country. Only three, and of these one had said "he would follow his teachers to any corner of the world;" and the other, in much the same language, had declared, "I go where preaching is to be had." No wonder the other poor man was in despair, and could neither eat nor sleep for fear of losing his beloved teachers, crying again and again, "Do stay with us a few months! Do stay till there are eight or ten disciples; then appoint one to be teacher of the rest." Of course the Judsons gave way—they only wished to be of use, and could not resist so pitiful an appeal. But I have not time to tell you of all the ups and downs of these earnest missionaries' lives. I must rather hurry on to a later period, when the greatest trial of all fell on the attached couple.

The English were at war with Burmah, and naturally enough Americans, like us in speech and appearance, were objects of suspicion to the Government. But surely the missionaries, so quiet in their demeanour, so humble in their aims, need not have fallen under the displeasure of the king, who had so long owned them as subjects. The dark day, however, did arrive, and before very long.

The Judsons were in Aoa, the capital town of Burmah, listening eagerly and anxiously to the talk of war around them. The Burmese were certain they would overcome the English force, and drive them out of the kingdom—soldiers, merchants, and settlers, every one of them. No, not every one; some were to be detained as servants, or slaves, of their conquerors. " Send me," said one of the great leaders of the court, "four white strangers to manage the affairs of my house, as I hear they are trustworthy." " And to me," said a gay young gentleman of the palace, " six stout men to row my boat." But lo ! instead of conquest came defeat, and Rangoon, the Judsons' old home, a considerable seaport town, fell into the hands of the strangers.

"Treachery !" was then the cry. The English living in the town had betrayed it, and the missionaries, as their friends, must be in the plot.

One day a band of ruffians, headed by a man with a spotted face (the sign of an executioner), rushed into the Judsons' dwelling at Aoa, demanding Mr. Judson. "You are called by the king," said the leader, and immediately he of the spotted countenance seized the missionary, threw him on the ground, and tied his hands behind him. In vain Mrs. Judson wept and prayed, and offered money to the cruel band; her husband was dragged away from her to the common prison, to the *death* prison. The poor wife meanwhile was closely shut in her house, though every now and then called from her prayers to answer the magistrate's questions. Next morning she was allowed to go out and visit her husband, who, with another missionary and three Englishmen, had been loaded with iron fetters, and fastened to a heavy pole in the prison. Of course Mrs. Judson had to bribe the officials to obtain this privilege, and to pay again for the removal of Mr. Judson and Dr. Price to a less horrible dungeon than the one she found them in. The next day she had an interview with the queen's sister-in-law, with the view of obtaining her husband's release, but all in vain. She returned home to find officers in her house demanding gold, jewels, valuables of all sorts. How should a poor missionary's wife possess such things! Her watch, however, she had to give up, and such money-offerings as Mr. Judson was treasurer of to build a church. But little did Mrs. Judson mourn over these losses, so occupied was she in besieging the court and the great people with petitions for her husband's release. All in vain. Only now and then could she tell her fears and perplexities to Mr. Judson, for it was rarely she was allowed to see him; but a woman has ready wit where her dearest affections are concerned, and Mrs. Judson devised two or three ways of sending him letters. Either she wrote on a flat cake and hid it in a basin of rice, or she rolled a bit of paper up and thrust it into the spout of the coffee-pot in which she was allowed to send him tea; Mr. Judson, in return, writing on a bit of tile, which when wet with water bore no marks upon it, but on being thoroughly dried displayed the words on its surface. To have been found communicating with a prisoner would have involved severe punishment, but Mrs. Judson dared everything in this case. Months passed in this heart-sickening suspense and delay; the hot season of Burmah had set in, and the poor prisoners, shut up in one windowless room with a hundred human thieves and murderers, were almost more dead than living.

The unwearied wife applied again to the governor of the city for a little relief for the wretched missionaries—just a little air, that was all; but the old man told her that he had orders to execute them quietly in the prison, and that therefore he dared not allow them to be seen in public. Touched by her grief, however, he did command that Mr. Judson should have a place near the grated door-way, and be led outside it to eat his rice. The breath even of the hot air of a Burman summer was sweet to the prisoners after the horrible close-ness of their over-crowded dungeon. Who can wonder that a terrible fever at last seized the unfortunate man, and reduced him to the brink of the grave? Mrs. Judson, permitted then to visit him, possibly thought herself passing through the deepest waves of affliction; but it was not so. She had her husband still near her; she could sit by his side and give him some poor tending amidst his sufferings, while the tiny baby, born during his imprisonment, lay on the floor at her feet. Her troubles only reached their height when one day

news was brought to her that the white prisoners
were gone, taken out of their prison, led no one
knew where, possibly to instant execution. Frantic
with terror and anxiety, the poor wife flew to the
governor—he who had once looked kindly upon
her—but he had no comfort for her. "You can do
no more for your husband; take care of yourself,"
said the old man. Had she indeed seen her beloved for the last time? thought the poor woman,
as she returned home to cast herself on the ground
in agonized prayer.

With evening came tidings, however, of the
prisoners, and next day Mrs. Judson was permitted
to take her baby and follow in their track. They
had been sent to a place where prisoners on a
long sentence were frequently confined. Here Mrs.
Judson came up with her poor weak husband,
whose bleeding feet and exhausted countenance
showed how much he had suffered in the hasty
march. He was still chained to another prisoner.
Mrs. Judson secured a little room near the prison,
suffering with her baby the greatest hardships
during six long months of waiting. At the close of
that time the English were advancing so near the
capital that they heard of the imprisoned missionaries, and demanded their release from the king,
who at last grudgingly gave up his innocent victims. Out of the "golden city" hurried the happy
travellers, their babe in their arms, hardly daring to
believe in their good fortune, since for two years
they had suffered close captivity among the very
people they had come to benefit.

The missionaries were very kindly received by the British force, and passed on shortly to their own beloved mission station, Rangoon. Their intention still was to cling to Burmah, settling down in one of the places under the protection of the English, and gathering round them a little Christian Church

And here we will leave them, sure that such earnest labourers would have their reward, if not in this world, in the one to come.

Years afterwards a little girl in New England read the story of Mrs. Judson's missionary labours, and was fired with a desire to follow in her steps. Her wishes were in time realized, and as the wife of Dr. Mason she spent her life among the Karens, a mountain tribe of Burmah, and the first person to meet and welcome her in the new country was Dr. Judson himself. Mrs. Judson was dead; the heats and damps of the climate, and perhaps the anxieties of her life, had worn her out before her time. We can hardly regret it, she must so sorely have needed rest; and besides, she had a little son in heaven to welcome her, a baby boy whose death had cost her some bitter tears in days gone by.

But to return to Mrs. Mason and the Karens; they were a very interesting people—"Mountain Men" she calls them—and though no one sought them out in the early days of Christianity in Burmah, they used themselves to visit Dr. Judson and ask him about his religion.

It seems that this people had a tradition that

God, the true God (whom they ignorantly worshipped), had revealed His will to men, and that the
"white man over the sea" had that will written
down.

So that when Dr. Judson, and afterwards Dr.
Mason, appeared among them they heard that Word
gladly, accepted the missionaries' God as the same
with their dimly worshipped Yuak or Jehovah, believed, and were baptized. Within three years there
were gathered into the fold of the Church three
thousand disciples, and there are now probably
more than fifty thousand Karen Christians.

The easier language and more open hearts of
these "Mountain Men" made them readier converts
to our religion. But Mrs. Mason—what part did
she take in the work? perhaps you ask. Why, the
true woman's work—teaching the children, her own
little ones among the number, nursing the sick,
taking cholera patients into her own house, reading
to the ignorant, begging for the poor and needy,
and in all ways helping on her husband's efforts.
She was a very bright, earnest, eager person, just
the sort to deal with simple, untaught natures, and
her Karen people were very fond of her. She
must have been a good mistress too, for she generally had good servants, and the little Karen school-
girls, two at a time, must have liked their mornings
in her house, learning cooking, washing, and tidi-
ness; it sounds almost like an English clergyman's
home. But I have not time to tell you in full of
the troubles and dangers this busy, happy woman

went through. As a specimen I may say, however, that once, when she was intending to settle in a new district, the surgeon called on her and asked her if she knew that she was probably going to certain death, new clearings being always very unhealthy. Mrs. Mason only smiled; her people were going there, and she would not desert them. So she went, and lived through it.

It is thought that the Karens received what religious ideas and traditions they possess from the Jews. They had no books, and therefore no written law of their God, and were prepared to accept the Bible as that declared will of God for which they had been taught to look.

Since these days of American labour in the great field of Burmah the English have sent out missionaries also, who have, thanks to the good men and women gone before, met with much success in their work. One who has lately died at his post gives us cheerful accounts of the very Karens among whom Mrs. Mason laboured. It seems that they have kept up the custom of assembling themselves together, for a sort of yearly festival, as she taught them to do; and Mr. Warren gives us a sketch of the last great meeting at which he was asked to officiate as chaplain. It differed a little from our Church gathering, since first the clergyman shook hands all round, which ceremony took some time, as there were over four hundred people present. Then a Karen hymn was sung to one of their own strange tunes; after that the Litany, which these

simple folk enjoy very much, feeling as if a part of
it really did belong to them. Then another hymn
and a chapter of the Bible, and two little sermons
from native teachers. After that Mr. Warren got
up and welcomed them into our own branch of the
Church, the Church of England, explaining to them
a few of the differences between our worship and
that of the Christian communion into which they
had first been received. And then he asked them
all, did they wish to come among us and be of
the bishop's flock? Up they rose as one man and
accepted the proposal.

And there we must leave them, under English
bishops and pastors now, but guided to this safe
fold by the loving care of an American woman.

# THE HOUSE OF CHARITY.

## EDINBURGH.

EDINBURGH, the capital of Scotland, is so beautiful, so picturesque, that we may well count it a queen among cities! Many an excursion train travels thither, and many tourists return from it, full of the praises of the noble castle, the quaint old streets, and the towering houses. They have seen the outside of things; shall we look further?

Better not, perhaps; the sight might only distress us.

"One half of the world does not know how the other half lives" is a saying eminently true of this great town. Is it well to tear away the veil, then, to shock the ears, and wound the heart of casual tourist, or of decent citizen, by letting daylight into these inner recesses of old Edinburgh, by telling their sad story, bit by bit, in broken fragments as it comes to us from those who themselves have looked and wept? I think so, since the tale concerns our fellow men and women, our neighbours, who, in these latter days, have fallen among thieves, ay, and worse than thieves, and whom we dare not (since reading the story of the good Samaritan) pass by on the other side.

Come, then, out of the sunshine and its glamour into this city court, past the squalid children in the gutter, up the crazy stairs of one of the picturesque houses you have admired from without, and when once your eyes have become accustomed to the darkness, see what you will see. Do not hesitate because the air is foul to fainting point, because your limbs are in danger from missing boards and uncertain railings, because the walls alongside of you are alive with that house-pest the decent poor will not name before you; come still on, on, and learn in what depths of wretchedness the creature whom God made and pronounced "good" can live.

Crowded into tiny dens, windowless many of them, and falling into ruins, poor Edinburgh folk, by no fault of their own, are compelled to live and die, the scrap of fire in the grate showing you here blinking, half-naked children, there dying wretches, or helpless age on the bare floor. The men and most of the women are out of the house in the daytime at work, but the sick and the babes are shut into the misery and darkness through all the long hours of the twenty-four. Those stately houses with their large chambers are divided and subdivided for the gain of their owners, till all hope of comfort, or even decency, is denied to the unhappy tenant, and all ages and sexes are huddled together in a pitiful heap of rags and wretchedness.

Good men, philanthropists, have stumbled through

these Edinburgh houses, and cried out in shame and anguish that no spot in sinful London was ever so defiled, so black for soul and body.

Take the body first, if you will. The whole water supply for a great stone storied house lies in the well down the street; every drop has to be carried in buckets up the steep stairs by the trembling hands of overworked women or weak children. Can you wonder that the babe goes un-washed? The clothes are wrung out but at rare intervals in the precious fluid, and the floors are utter strangers to the scrubbing-brush. Every drop is needed for the cooking or drinking, and that drop is often so hard to get. The waiting throng by the well-side must bide each its turn, the little ones some-times crying from sheer exhaustion as one, two, and three hours elapse before they can fill their pail; the elder girls and women, less easily depressed, but, alas! more hardened, lightening the weary moments by coarse jokes and unholy laughter.

That waiting by the well is a pitiful sight; the water of this world supplied in such grudging measure to these poor creatures!

And up those steep stairs, in the dark, close dens, who shall attempt to tell the misery this scarcity of water inflicts? One instance shall suffice.

On the *seventh* story of one of these great houses lay a sick man, down with fever for weeks, craving nothing, calling for nothing but water, water, and clutching continually the tin pannikin by his side. The sickly wife, with the idiot child at her knee,

had to carry every drop of that water from the
pump in the street below, and the pitiful tale came,
choked with sobs, from her lips, "I cannot carry
much; he drinks all I bring. He might be better
if we had things clean about him, but I can't
haul enough water for that. Last night a drunken
man pushed by me on the stair, and spilt the whole
pailful. God only knows what it is to slave after
the water; it's killing me and him too, and in the
glen we came from the bonnie burn ran by the
door."

Poor souls! they had come from the fresh air
of Perthshire, and by no fault of their own had
sunk thus low. Sanitary reform was not for them,
however; a speedier cure came for both very shortly
after, in the shape of a summons to the land where
they "thirst no more."

And the water of life,—does that flow less scantily
into these dreary pastures? Alas! as yet in this
wide woeful field the labourers are but few to direct
the purifying stream; still there are good men and
earnest women bent on the task of reclaiming for
God and heaven some part of this dark and dismal
tract, wherein it is still to be feared thousands of
persons live in less comfort and decency than the
beasts that perish.

Up on the hillside, behind the Castle rock, stands
the Church of St. Columba, and attached to it, in its
near vicinity and under its guidance, a little band,
whose motto is "Holy Charity," have made a Home,
not only for themselves as a centre for their mission

work, but also for other less happy creatures, struck down by age, or sickness, or infirmity, in the fight for life going on in the dark closes below. To win souls to Christ, and to succour the perishing bodies of the poor around, is the double aim of these true " Sisters of Charity."

The beginning was simple. An empty house was taken, and one stormy, windy evening a few earnest women moved into it, seeing by faith the ungarnished chambers filled in days to come with Christ's poor and suffering. The first effort seems to have been made for starving bodies. " At once," writes the head of the little mission band, " we began to dine the poor daily at our own table, and the first month between seventy and eighty dinners were given. Afterwards they rose greatly in number, but I was too much occupied to keep the dinner-book; all I could do was to see that the bills were paid; and they were paid. It is wonderful how God helped us at that time, and how He has con-tinned to do so, in His great goodness, since."

These dinners must have given them a welcome in many a wretched home. Night schools were next set on foot, Bible classes for grown men and women, a lending library, and a savings bank; and for each and all of these projects for the benefit of souls and bodies, the people had to be sought out and taught their need of help.

The great want of the district in those first days of the mission seemed to be a Home for the aged, infirm, and destitute. A special appeal was made for this, and through the kindness of a friend a second house was taken and the rent guaranteed for a year. But how to provide furniture, beds, comforts, food, for the helpless creatures? that was the question.

That God moved the hearts of His rich to pity His poor is not to be doubted. The first contribution to the Home for the aged came in the shape of two very handsome bracelets, the sale of which began a fund which gradually increased till the house was furnished, and the poor inmates collected, to be tenderly nursed and cared for till called to their eternal home.

This is the first great indoor work of the House of Charity. The second is a Home for little children, more particularly infants, who from any cause are deprived of that care and love little ones so specially need.

Very lovingly the mother tells the story of this dear branch of their House of Charity; of the bright rooms devoted to it, up at the top of the great house; of the pictured walls, showing the Good Shepherd with His tender lamb in His arms, and our Lord setting the babe in the midst of the multitude; of the text here realized and painted in large letters opposite the entrance, "When my father and my mother forsake me, the Lord taketh me up;" and, finally, of the babes themselves, often sick, crippled, and miserable, but always dearly welcomed into the loving arms held out to them.

Many of them come in nothing but the clothes they are dressed in, and for these wretched garments the relative who brings them has been known to ask afterwards, possibly to clothe some other poor little creature less happily placed. Some of the babes are orphans, of others the parents are woefully poor, while some have father and mother so steeped in sin that it seems only a Christian duty to snatch the infant from the pollutions of its natural home.

These children are nursed and trained in godly ways in the House of Charity, with the view of making them useful members of society as they grow older. All that are old enough are at once sent to school daily, but there are a nursery full besides of little ones, too babyish or weak to be anything but a care.

Willie and Alice, three years old, but with no strength in their small legs even to totter across the smooth floor; Minnie, not a year old; and Dickie, only "going on for two," are a flock to be tenderly guarded. Every fine day these wees are carried out of doors, placed in perambulators, and strengthened by the enjoyment of the fine air, for which Edinburgh is justly famous. Can you, reader, imagine the pride of the House-mother and sisters when this tiny procession blocks the way? The four perambulators, all gifts, crowded with small people in scarlet hoods and tippets, or in warm wraps of bright colour specially chosen out of the stores as suitable to the little folks, who ought to be so bright themselves. Shall I tell you a fearful

2 F

piece of extravagance the House of Charity was
guilty of once? It sent for a carriage with real
horses, and took these tiny pale-faced mites a drive
for a whole hour, probably the first time the little
souls had ever been in a carriage at all. You may
picture the crowing and exultation that went on
in that vehicle! Another day the elder children
were sent to the seaside for a day, and that was
more than joy, it was transport—a thing to dream
of, and to be spoken of with a sort of gasp of remembered joy for weeks and months to follow.

The little things dine every day with their care-
takers, the good sisters of the House, and have their
kisses and rewards like other more happily born
babies. But good food and human love are not
their best portion in their new home, though babes
must begin with these lesser blessings if they are
to live and thrive. Rather is it the love of God, in
the warm comfort of which these little ones are
shown they live, the Christian teaching which even
these small tottering darlings are not too young
to share.

Not all these poor children of wretchedness
recover their bodily strength even in such a
loving home; there are tender reminiscences in the
nursery of one or another fading away and going
at last, as the babes themselves would vaguely but
reverently tell you, "to Jesus." The picture of the
Good Shepherd is none the less real to infant eyes,
because "Jemmie" pointed at it and recognized
it as a friend the day he died. They like to think

that he got up in bed that last night to say his prayers for the last time; and the sight of snow-drops and such like fair winter flowers are in a small way hallowed to them by the recollection of the pretty wreath and cross the kind lady made for his coffin. Baby Rina, too, who, lying ill a few days of measles, presently left off crying and was no more seen,—where is she now.? Gone, the lispers will tell you, into the blue sky that, with children, seems so large and bright a heaven. It is difficult to tear one's self from the little ones, and come out of the light and brightness of their upper chamber into the haunts of sin and sorrow down in the dark closes below. But it must be done. The House of Charity would not carry out its name if it was not full of love for the sinful as well as the sinless.

Direct missionary work is undertaken by the sisters; there are no stairs too broken, no window-less den too vile, to keep them out. The girls and women are specially sought out and invited to attend evening classes, to join a guild, to attach themselves, in fact, by the link of this loving sister-hood to a higher life—the life of the Church on earth, the life that will be in heaven. The poor creatures are often too glad to seize the helping hand which draws them from their darkness and dirt towards the clean, well-lighted house on Sunday and Tuesday evenings, there to learn that life need not be so black, so loveless, as it seems to them in their poor homes. They are taught, very lovingly, the beauty of personal cleanliness, the evils of drink

—alas! a pitfall to women as well as men in these sad, over-peopled closes—and last, but not least, the lesson the babes upstairs are learning, the story of the Saviour's love for one and all.

But there are many that cannot be brought from their sad dwellings into daylight even for a moment; comfort must be carried to them. One such visit has been simply yet graphically described to me, and I shall give it as near as may be in the words of the visitor, the "Mother" from the House of Charity :—

"A poor woman I knew a little of was said to be very ill, so I set out to visit her at the close of a winter's day, taking with me neither lantern nor guide. The house was not difficult to find, but once within it, it was something like being turned in the dark into the ruins of an old Norman Castle, and there desired to single out the particular dungeon required. Only this old castle swarmed with inhabitants, and was, in fact, a human rabbit-warren. No light on the stairs of any sort, except where through occasional narrow openings or loop-holes in the walls, and under the various old doorways, streamed the feeble glimmer of fire or candle within. Up five sets of stairs to the fifth story, stumbling and falling, I made my way, lighting at last on the right garret-room. By a figure of speech my poor friend might be said to be in bed. There had once been a four-poster in the room, but the whole of the bottom of the bed was gone, and on a heap of rags on the floor, enclosed as by a wooden frame, lay the sick woman. No! not lay, for she was propped up against the hard fence, a candle in a bottle at her side, stitching for life and food while actually dying."

Three persons occupied that wretched couch at night, she told me!

Comfort for soul and body might be temporarily given to this poor creature; but one cannot but feel thankful that she was near the end of her troubles, and that there was only a step between that attic on the fifth floor and the home on high.

It is something that the sister walks unharmed among these " nests in the rocks," hearing, perhaps, bad language on each side of her, even shrieks and blows, but herself untouched, nay, treated with respect. Here and there, in the passage or on the stairs, is an obstacle—a poor drunken creature prostrate; to step over it is the only course, and to pass on. Drink here, like everywhere else, is the great drawback to civilization and Christianity.

In sober moments these very people will come forward with their small alms for the visitor of the poor, and are much insulted if it is not accepted. Probably they find the gift a salve to their conscience; they generally ask the sister at the same time to " pray for them." It may be that this very drink stupefies the poor wretches, and makes them oblivious of the horrors of their home; but be it remembered, at the same time, that necessity, not choice, drives them to roost in these dilapidated holes, without water or other necessary comforts.

In those better-fitted dwellings where spigots are on each landing, and decency is otherwise regarded, rents are high, above the means of the very poor. Back they must go to their smells and ruins.

But these are grievances for the landlord—the wealthy citizens of Edinburgh—to redress, it may be said; what can a few weak women do here?

Granted that property owners are the people to be looked to for great reforms in these terrible homes of vice, still there is much to be done that only one working for Christ's sake can effect.

Babes and young girls to be rescued and fostered; men and women to be watched and prayed over, who have promised to give up "the drink," but who, without constant supervision, must fall back into sin; sick-beds to be smoothed; the Church's ordinances to be brought to such as just feel their need of them, but know not how to grasp them in their low estate. The sisters of the House of Charity help the needy poor to defray the expenses of publishing banns of marriage, and, as they say themselves, are "very proud of their little weddings." The visiting sister as she goes along has been asked by anxious, yet ignorant, mothers to "baptize my baby, if you please," and then the way is open to seeing the poor little creature washed, and for once in its life dressed in fair raiment and brought into the visible Church of Christ. After that, the mother is seldom lost sight of, and so perhaps a family is won to desire something beyond their every-day wretchedness.

In one room of a common lodging-house, fireless and tenanted by several groups, the sister found a poor woman with three days' old twins by her side; neither mother nor children had clothes to cover them ; the father, who was no father, had deserted the poor creature in her trouble after living five years with her. Here, again, the missionary sister was to be found ready to help. Food and raiment were forthcoming from the House of Charity, and little Peter and Andrew were baptized by the mission priest of St. Columba, never, however, to grow up faithful soldiers and servants of Christ in this cold world of ours. First one little brother drooped and died, and then the other; and who could regret that the Good Shepherd reclaimed them so early for His heavenly fold ?

Our Church's funeral service has been found to touch in no ordinary degree the softened hearts of Scottish mourners; some among the very ignorant standing around an open grave have been moved to come and seek more teaching from a Church that can speak such "comfortable words" to sad hearts.

And these are brought by the sisters to the evening classes, and the cheerful services at St. Columba's, to be taught how to live under the Church's guidance, as well as to be buried with its blessing.

Such a work as this House of Charity does not stand still. Where there is life and energy, things must progress; and, thank God (for He has given the increase in labourers for the vineyard), it has grown.

A second Home has been opened, where, for eight months in the year, the delicate, both old and young, may enjoy the salt breezes with all the added pleasures of country life; for the Cottage is situated in a quiet open spot, and the kindest of neighbours give help and encouragement.

Little Alice, who for the first four years of her life could only crawl, found the use of her legs here, and every summer since she has had " all the time " at the sea (for most can only take their turn), and is now comparatively a strong, healthy girl, very bright and intelligent. Nor is this happy outlet reserved for the inmates of the Edinburgh Home; other weak and weary creatures may benefit by it, provided they have not been suffering from infectious diseases. Subscribers paying £2 may send a patient for a month, and the fresh air, sea-bathing, and good food seldom have failed in such cases to restore health; so that an enlargement of the seaside cottage is greatly desired.

One word now for old Edinburgh itself. The march of improvement has reached it. Better dwellings are now being provided, and water laid on in many of the courts and alleys where it was not formerly. It cannot yet be declared that literal parallels may not still be found to the wretched cases here noted down, but at least we may feel that they are fewer.

Greater efforts are being put forth against

drunkenness; yet, alas! Saturday nights are still sad eves of the coming Sunday, and Hogmany and New Year's Eve are only excuses for excesses carried to almost as great an extent as in bygone years.

This is a sad reflection, but it does not tend to the drooping of the arms in despair. They who work for the glory of God, as well as for the good of their fellow-creatures, remember that His blessing rests on perseverance to the end, and they will not pause or faint because, in their short lives, success does not seem to come in fullest measure.

## A ROYAL MISSIONARY.

### SARAWAK.

In the early part of this century a young English officer was so badly wounded in the Burmese war, that though he was but sixteen years old, he had to give up his profession and return to England, most people thought to die. But he did not die, neither did his severe wound crush out of him the activity and life for which Englishmen are famous; instead of that, by his own exertions he raised himself to a position few young men are called upon to occupy, that of a real king, with a beautiful kingdom of lovely uplands, noble forests, and fertilizing rivers.

You may never have heard of his kingdom, but there it lies at this moment, governed by his descendants, fertile and lovely still, and, we think, a thousand times happier and more prosperous for the wise rule of Rajah Brooke.

This was how he found his kingdom. After receiving his terrible wound, he was obliged for many years to do little but try to get well, and, as he came of wealthy parents, travelling about the world seemed the easiest and best way of accomplishing this. In one of his long sea-voyages he

saw for the first time the beautiful islands of the
Eastern Archipelago, and was grieved to notice how
poor and oppressed some of the inhabitants seemed,
and how little they knew how to till the fertile
fields which God had granted to them in those
sunny regions. It was not much use tilling them
either, and growing crops of rice or Indian corn, for
down upon the weak ones would pounce the strong
tribes of the island directly they heard of any stores
being collected, and all was robbery, confusion, and
distress.

The large island of Borneo especially attracted
the notice of Mr. James Brooke, so lovely and
desolate it seemed, so abandoned to ignorant barbarians and greedy pirates. The very name of
pirate sets an English boy's blood on fire now.
Who can wonder, then, that the young man sailing
past the very lurking-places of these treacherous
sea-robbers should long to do his best to protect
the innocent inhabitants of the island from their
attacks ?

But he had to be very cautious how he set about
so dangerous a task; it would be of little use dashing after one pirate vessel and destroying it; he
must begin at quite another end of the matter—get
hold, if possible, of some of the half-savage rulers
of the island and enlist them on his side, and then
perhaps real good might be done.

With such thoughts in his mind, Mr. Brooke
sailed back to England, and having come into more
money on the death of his father, he bought a

yacht and carefully chose out sailors to manage it, good men and true, as he hoped, who would be useful in helping him in his plans for making distant Borneo a happier and a more prosperous island. For three years he exercised these sailors in the Mediterranean, proving them, as it were, for the more difficult task to come, and then he sailed away for the almost unknown land which he had had always in his thoughts.

When the *Royalist*, as the yacht was called, drew near to Borneo, Mr. Brooke touched at Singapore, an English port near, and heard that there was a rajah, or governor, of Sarawak, one of the towns of Borneo, who liked the English, and who had kindly treated the crew of a merchant vessel wrecked at the mouth of his river. To this man Mr. Brooke immediately went, asking him about his territory and his people. "I am engaged in a little war with them," said the ruler in reply; "but it is only child's play." However, the child's play was so disagreeable that Rajah Muda Hassim was getting the worst of it, and in a little while he begged Mr. Brooke and his handful of brave sailors to help him. This Mr. Brooke did, soon conquering the rebels, every one of whom Muda Hassim ordered to be put to death. But now the Englishman showed his true colours. Such wholesale destruction was not civilized, not Christian; he implored the rajah to recall his order. There was a stiff argument; the rajah liked revenge, the Englishman loved mercy, and at last it came to this—Mr. Brooke got

up and threatened to leave the rajah and never help
him any more unless he pardoned the rebels. The
native governor was wise enough not to wish to
lose this clever white man, his men, and his guns,
so he gave way at last, and invited him to live at
Sarawak and help him to govern his lands.

Just what Mr. Brooke wished! But he only by
degrees found out what a difficult thing it is to
walk hand-in-hand with a half-civilized ruler. If
the pirates brought Muda Hassim a share of their
plunder, he winked at their doings, and only by fits
and starts could he be got to protect his more harmless subjects. Once a band of pirates actually got
his leave to go up the country and rob and murder
a tribe of innocent Land Dyaks, as the people of
the interior are called; and as speaking on Mr.
Brooke's part did no good, he left the grand house
in the town that Muda Hassim had built for him,
and went on board his yacht, ordering his brave
sailors to replace their guns for action. That sort
of talking even pirates and savages could understand, and sulkily enough they had to give up their
undertaking. In this way Mr. Brooke gained the
love of the peaceable inhabitants of Sarawak, and
after a while Muda Hassim, finding it impossible
to keep order in his way, gave up his governorship
to the clever Englishman, and Mr. Brooke became
Rajah of Sarawak, the province being made over to
him and his heirs for ever. And this is how there
comes to be an English king or rajah in the beautiful island of Borneo.

And now I must try to tell you the sort of people that Rajah Brooke had to govern in his kingdom.

The real old inhabitants of the island, the Dyaks, come first, divided into the Land Dyaks and Sea Dyaks; then the Malays, a stronger race, from which the pirates chiefly spring; the Milanaus, a wild hill people; and a large sprinkling of Chinese who have come over from the mainland of China, which is not far off.

The Dyaks are, perhaps, the most interesting of all these different peoples, being a gentle, kindly race, easily attached to such as treat them well. Rajah Brooke, however, had no favourites among his subjects; he tried to rule all with love, and believed that they would in return love him. He was sorry, it is true, for the Dyaks, who were in the position of slaves to the more lordly Malays, and he wrote after a while to England for help to raise them from their wretchedness. And this help came in the shape of a clergyman called Mr. M'Dougall, who afterwards became Bishop of Sarawak.

The Dyaks have many strange customs, and perhaps to our ears the strangest seems their congregating together as they do. How many houses do you think there are in a large Dyak town? Perhaps only two or three. But then one alone will hold as many as seven hundred people, divided into families, and each having a separate door. By the number of doors you may judge how many families live in the house, which does not stand on the ground but on raised posts. This may be most

likely designed to render the house more easily
defended from enemies, but sometimes it leads to
its destruction, the attacking force cutting down
the posts, when the whole house and its occupants
fall and are crushed together.

Another large house in the village is given up as
a sleeping-room to the young unmarried men, and
above, on the walls of this building, is hung a
dreadful decoration — a row of dried heads, the
heads of their enemies. It is an honour to have
many of these horrible ornaments, and sometimes
it is even the head of a friend that will look down
on a sleeping Dyak; for if a chief dies, or a beloved
relative, even, a Dyak rushes out vowing to kill the
first man he comes across, be he friend or foe. This
custom, as you may imagine, was the very first that
Rajah Brooke set his face against, and very soon
after his rule became established in Sarawak, the
head-hunting passion began to wane among such
Dyaks as lived near the seat of government. Head-
taking used to be fearfully prevalent among the
Dyaks. If a man was about to set out on a journey,
or sow his farmlands with seed, he must first go out
and seek a head with which to prosper the undertaking; and a woman's favourite wedding present
was a human head—it was to her a sign that her
husband was valiant and warlike. But perhaps the
real reason for so cruel a practice was that the
Dyaks believed that their evil spirits, whom they
hold in great awe, were fond of blood, and so they
shed it to satisfy them. They thought much more

of evil spirits than of the One Good One whom they believed to exist in the world.

I must now go to one of these missionaries' wives —Mrs. M'Dougall—for some account of Sarawak, as she found it in the early days of Rajah Brooke. As English missionaries must do in hot climates, she had sent her children to England to be educated, and to them in the dear old country she wrote from time to time letters from Sarawak, of which parts are very interesting to all readers.

One of the first things which struck this lady was the way the Malay mothers spoilt their children. A little Malay girl, in a passion, seized her mother's long hair and tore at it in her rage, while the mother only smiled when Mrs. M'Dougall released her, and kissed the naughty child as if she had done a very clever thing. Another tiny boy threw himself into the river in a pet, lying there, kicking and screaming and risking drowning, till his father dragged him into a boat close by. But no one reproved him, nor told him to control his temper. Who can wonder that when he grows to be a man he seizes a sword in his rage and runs out to kill any one he happens to meet? He calls this madness "Amok," or, as we might translate it, "running a-muck," and he is not the least ashamed of it. Of course, under Christian rule, this amok became unlawful.

Malay children are lively, busy little creatures, and Mr. M'Dougall once saw a little fellow spear and kill a fish in the river, which was so big he could not drag it into the boat, so he jumped into the water, clasped the fish round the body, and so waded with it to dry land. These children, in their warm island home, are indeed half fishes themselves, and paddle about on their rivers and seas in the most independent fashion; if the boat upsets, as it often does, with such restless occupants, they simply swim by the side till they manage to right it again. It is always warm weather in Sarawak, and there are no long days and short days, the sun always rising at six o'clock and setting at six o'clock, because it is so near the middle of the earth or equator. This sounds pleasant enough, but English people in time tire of the endless summer, and long for the change of weather which we have in England, the heat after a while making them feel sick and sorry, poor things!

Mr. M'Dougall soon set about building a church at Sarawak, and the laying of the first stone was celebrated by a grand procession of the governor, the English residents, and such officers of our navy as could be collected. I speak of the first STONE, but, literally, it was a block of wood; for St. Thomas' Church was built of wood, and a hollow place was cut out in it for the reception of some silver coins, among which Mrs. M'Dougall's baby boy slipped a silver fourpence sent him from England. This little fellow had not yet been sent home to his brother and sister, and indeed he was never to go, for not long after he fell a victim to the hot climate, and was laid down in his last sleep in the graveyard at

2 G

Singapore. But to the church. When the coins were put into the block of wood, the rajah, in his grand glittering uniform, lowered it into its place. Mr. M'Dougall read some prayers, and then the church was really begun, and day by day saw arch and pillar rise up as if by magic, the progress of building was so quick. The Chinese, as usual, were the chief workmen; they are an industrious people, and, wherever they are to be found, make capital servants and workers.

What pleased the Malays ˉmost of all in the church was the painted east window with the Sarawak flag pictured on it, a deep blue and red cross on a yellow ground, just such a flag as might float on any Sarawak boat. Wherever they saw it flying for the future it must remind them of St. Thomas' Church, and make them feel that somehow the God of the Church was the God of the fortress, of the palace, of the ship, of everything indeed in common life.

The font of this island church was a very large white shell, so large that a baby could be dipped into it. Besides the church, there was also a hospital for sick people, which Mr. M'Dougall attended, since he was a doctor as well as a clergyman. You know Jesus Christ when on earth healed the sick as well as pardoned sinners, so in humble imitation of Him our missionaries are often doctors, and when this is the case they are doubly welcome to the poor suffering heathen.

Schools, of course, there were in time in Sarawak,

Mrs. M'Dougall beginning them with an orphan school in her house of little Chinese and Malay boys and girls. Schools all the world over are pretty much alike, and we do not wonder that of this one the missionary's wife writes concerning the twenty-seven little pigtails and dark faces: "What peace reigns in this house when they are all asleep!" There is one arrangement, however, about sleeping in a hot climate which is unknown in England; all the beds must have their curtains safely fastened round them to keep out the mosquitoes, and the poor Dyaks sometimes describe the place to which they think good people will go hereafter as "a land under the earth where there are mosquito curtains."

The building of the church in Sarawak led all the people in the town to think more of religion, and when the Malay priests, who are Mohammedans, found that the church bell rang twice a day for service, they opened their mosques too, and insisted on the Mohammedans observing more strictly their hours of prayer.

Whenever Mr. M'Dougall made a journey in his boat to visit distant tribes he always had service on board, and preached to the few English who accompanied him, the natives watching him the while in solemn and respectful silence. The very putting on of the cassock was interesting to them, and when the little congregation broke out into responses they were evidently much impressed, though they could not understand the words said.

These boat services, held sometimes in strange rivers where English voices had never been heard before, sometimes in lonely nooks of the sea coast, formerly the haunt of robber-vessels, must indeed have had a strange and good effect upon the poor ignorant souls who witnessed them for the first time, and Mr. M'Dougall never lost an opportunity of so impressing them. Once in one of these boat trips he nearly lost his life: he was alone on deck in the middle of the night enjoying the cool air and the moonlight, and watching the rapid rush of the tide as he leaned against the boom of the vessel, when suddenly his support gave way, and over the side of the ship he went, to certain death as he thought, for, though he could swim, the water was rushing by too quickly to fight against, and, besides, he had seen a shark quietly swimming round the ship during morning service.

But God was watching over His servant, and provided a means of escape; the swing of the vessel at the moment of his fall brought the ship's boat right under him (it had been its whole rope's length away before), and into it he fell, escaping with a bruised arm and a thankful heart.

A missionary must be ready to meet danger in any form, but it is not wonderful that Mr. M'Dougall scrambled back into his ship, thanking God most heartily that He had preserved him from this solitary inglorious death.

It was very interesting to visit the distant tribes in their native homes of twenty or more families in one, and **Mr.** **M'Dougall** was very well received, partly because of his powers of doctoring, and partly because the Dyaks are a kindly, open-hearted people. They were very glad to be vaccinated also, for they dreaded small-pox greatly.

Rajah Brooke once questioned a chief as to his religious belief, and to show you how little religion they have you shall hear the conversation.

"Do you know anything of God?"

"No."

"Do your tribe believe that any one lives in the clouds?"

"Yes; Jupa lives there."

"Who sends thunder, lightning, rain?"

"Jupa."

"Do you pray to Jupa or offer sacrifices?"

"No."

"When a man dies, what is done with his body?"

"We burn it."

"Where do the dead go to?"

"To Sabyan."

"Where is Sabyan?"

"Under the earth."

"Where is your father gone?"

"To Sabyan. All the Dyak men and women who are dead are under the ground in Sabyan."

"How long will they stay in Sabyan?"

"Don't know."

"When you die, will you meet your father?"

"Yes, and my mother, and all my people."

"Are they happy in Sabyan?"

" Yes, very happy."

" If a man was wicked, would he go to Sabyan?"

" Yes, but to another part, and he would not be happy."

This is all they knew, poor souls! and kindly natured as they are it is no wonder that Rajah Brooke and the missionary teachers longed to give them a better belief, to direct their hopes to a better "Sabyan" than the "plank house with mosquito curtains" that bounds their fondest anticipations.

It was a strange flock the English clergyman came out to deal with—cool, unimpressible Chinese, Malay pirates, ignorant Dyaks, and a multitude of savage hill tribes, of whom little was known save that they hid themselves in fastnesses, building no houses and tilling no ground, living simply from day to day.

Very early in the mission history it was found that the terror of the pirates was so great as to hinder any real work, so the rajah determined to give them a severe lesson. With two English steamers and all the war-boats of friendly chiefs, he made an expedition up a wide river, meeting a pirate fleet on its return from plunder, defeating them after a fierce fight, and capturing eighty boats. After that there was peace for a while; the sea-robbers felt that their new English rajah was not to be trifled with.

But more troubles were to assail the mission. Mr. M‘Dougall had been appointed Bishop of Borneo, and more clergy were working with him, when a Chinese rebellion broke out, so terrible, that at one time bishop, clergy, teachers, ay, and the brave rajah himself also, had to fly for their lives.

At another time a Mohammedan plot created almost as great an alarm. It was very disappointing, when the missionaries dared return to the scene of their labours, to find their churches, schools, and homes plundered, and their hardly won disciples scattered, or perhaps relapsed into their old heathen ways; but there was nothing for it but for them to pluck up heart and begin again. They have done good, and they go on with their work, glad to be certain that year by year the people grow more civilized, and are loaded with fewer superstitions and cruel customs.

New missionaries from England still write home glowing accounts of the loveliness of this distant island—its splendid rivers, with their shadowy banks of great trees, creepers, moss, and ferns—and each new man that pushes his way up those watery highways means so much light and life to the ignorant tribes beyond. It is hoped, too, that of the children in the schools, and the Christian-born little ones of later years, some will be found to care for their less happy countryfolk in the wilds, and to go out to them before long as teachers and preachers of the better religion they have themselves been taught.

The promoters of Christianity in Borneo do not want it to be thought necessarily an English institution; they would rather see Malay, Chinese, and Dyak teachers and clergy, and have the Church make itself a home of its own in that beautiful island of the Eastern Seas. But till that good time comes Englishmen must help, and there is now a new Bishop of Sarawak and ten clergy sent out by the Society for the Propagation of the Gospel in Foreign Parts, all working hard to bring out the best parts of the Malay and Dyak character, and to bring them under the easy and light yoke of Christ.

# THE BARGEE'S HOME.

## CANALS OF ENGLAND.

IT must be now nearly fifty years since a country clergyman in Cheshire was called suddenly to attend a sick man, a canal boatman, struck down in a moment by cholera. It was a sad yet short business holding before the dying gaze the Christ it had never cared to look upon in life. Then by the side of the poor corpse the clergyman turned to the awestruck friends, urging them to prepare for another world ere it might be too late, and to live by the Word of God which he held in his hand. "Master," was the not disrespectfully meant answer of another boatman in that company, "we don't know naught about the Bible here, *we go by th' almanack.*"

This is a true story. The man intended no jest, he spoke out of the simple ignorance in which he and his fellows lived. They had an almanack on board their boats, and they knew how to interpret it, but they knew nothing of a Bible. Ah, well, that was fifty years ago; times are changed since then; good men have penetrated into the darkest corners of the world, and the heathen, be they white or black, have, in most places, had the gospel preached to them, the gospel of a pure life as well as of a happy death. No one could tell such a tale now, at least of Englishmen. Wait a minute; do not be too sure. I have something to say to-day on this very subject which will make thinking people—rich and poor—sad to listen to. It is the story of the canal boatmen of the present day.

I am not very fond of giving numbers, but how many canal boatmen do you think there are in England alone, living and working, week-days and Sundays, on our nearly 5000 miles of water highway? Something like one hundred thousand, and this, some say, without counting their wives and children. Who would have thought such a thing? Not you, cottage mothers and fathers, taking a walk in the fields on Sunday afternoons, and curiously watching the heavy black canal boat glide easily by, with the father smoking a pipe on deck, a little lad guiding the horse, and a woman, or another little head or two, peeping, like Jack-in-the-box, out of the tiny cabin. It seems to you as if these canal boats were mere occasional visitors, to be gazed at and talked about for a few brief minutes, and then to be forgotten.

Of course, people living near any of the great boat centres, where the lading and unlading go on, know more about the affair, but as a rule decent people on land know and care little about these water folk. Poor people pent in city streets have been found to envy them. Canal boat children must breathe pure air going through the fresh country. They have wide playgrounds on the towing paths and daisied meadows; surely they are not so badly off as children whose parents have but one room of a small house in a narrow street. Those who speak or think like this have possibly never looked inside the cabin of a canal boat, the one room of the bargee. I do not advise them to do so, it will be more for their comfort if they give the place a wide berth, but if they will listen I will describe one to them.

The size of the cabin is about two yards square, the height about five feet, even a fairly tall woman can never stand to her full height in it. One bed, a small one, is crammed into this place. Here the father and mother sleep. Two big girls of sixteen and fourteen lie on the table close by. A lad of ten and another lie under the parents' bed, whilst a little one is crumpled into a small cupboard above it. No doubt the air is very bad in these over-filled cabins, but it is a something much worse for growing children to be crowded together without a chance of learning decent ways, as they are in these places, where, in addition to what we have just mentioned, the wretched hole is further choked up with cooking-pots and other possessions of a family. Six children, and even seven, have been found crammed into these unsavoury nests, living just like little pigs, and receiving from their parents no greater care nor attention than the sow pays to her litter. This hole is moreover their home; in many cases they have no other, no parish, no neighbours, no teacher, no school, no clergyman, no church. "On board their craft not only 'father,' but 'mother' and all her brood habitually live. The barge is their home, and Mrs. Bargee is quite as much captain of the vessel as her husband. She can steer. She can hold her own with the man on the towing path. She can swear, and she does. Her children pass their lives within ear-shot of perhaps the most horribly foul language it is possible to conceive. They grow early familiarized with such spectacles as drunkenness, fighting, and gambling. They never go to school, their floating habitations are extremely filthy, and their manners savage and uncouth. They are, however, the most honest of all waterside characters. . . . The boys usually follow their father's avocation, and the girls marry bargees and continue to cook potatoes over the stove in the cabin, to take their turn at the helm, to smoke short pipes, and to swear at the man on the towing path, as their mothers have done before."

I quote this last statement from a newspaper. In the columns of another the case of a woman is mentioned who had twenty-one children born in one of these cabins. When questioned how they slept she said she could hardly say, but as time went on the elder girls got pushed out of the nest on to land to make the best shift they could, and the boys took to bargee work as their father had done before them. Another woman had not slept on land for twenty years. Can you see what that means? No quiet, no privacy, no cleanliness, no decency.

Of course, with so little possibility of keeping the cabin clean, the inmates are often much troubled with unpleasant insect companions. Any day along the canals you may see a whole family turned out on the towing path while the door, chimney, and cracks of the cabin are made airtight, and brimstone is burnt within to suffocate the intruders. This is called bug-driving, and it is such a common occurrence among the bargees that women talk about their last "bugging," much in the same way that ordinary cottagers speak of a house cleaning. Overcrowding on board the boats fosters disease. Small-pox and fever are frequently to be found on board the boats, and then sick and well must sleep together in the narrow cabin, and infection goes merrily on. The dirty water of the canal which they drink is also a fruitful cause of sickness. Who that thinks of the dead dogs and cats of these canal waters can help a shudder at the idea of such water being used for drinking purposes? The children incur other dangers too. Of course, they sometimes fall overboard and are drowned. That is a death which must always be awaiting them. But little George Millard, a baby of three months old, met with another fate. He, his three brothers and sisters, and father and mother all went to sleep one May night in their cramped little hole of a cabin, not so large as many a hen-house. At four o'clock the baby was warm and well, a little later, at getting up time, he was found dead. He had been overlaid by a young brother. Every one was very sorry. There was an inquest, and the verdict was, "Died from suffocation." Baby was buried, the boat moved on, and it seemed to be no one's business to interfere in the matter. Of course, human creatures ought not to be packed so closely together, but what is to be done? The cabin is small, the family is large, it is too poor to afford a home on land, and the children must sleep somewhere.

Then as to the education of the young ones. They cannot go to school, they are rarely long enough in one place to attempt such a thing, and besides they do not want to. So they play on the towing path or on the wharfs, leading the horse or helping with the cooking as they grow big enough, and meantime fighting, quarrelling, swearing, as they hear father and mother do. It is rare to find a boy or girl living in a boat who can read or write, or who knows anything about the world to come. Who can wonder at this when the terrible truth comes to light that in every two cases out of three the mother is no wife, and the only form of marriage gone through has been a day's outing, and a visit to the public-house? Of course, the bargee shakes off his wretched partner as soon as he is tired of her, or whenever the family in the cabin grows inconveniently large.

"Some time since a boater's woman died. An-

other woman, who had some grown-up daughters,
hearing of this a little time after the sorrowful
event, said to Jim, 'I understand thee hast no
woman; thee shalt have our Bess.' Away the
woman went to a neighbouring boat and fetched
Bess. The boater and the woman there and then
agreed upon terms, and Bess and Jim were instantly
married 'boater fashion.' Courtship and marriage
were all over within twenty-four hours; and to-day
they are floating about in their cabin home, with a
large family of children."

It can surprise no one to learn that the boaters
are often cruel to these miserable women, and that
the children are made to suffer in their turn.

Sunday on the canal is no different to other days.
The boaters will tell you that, even if they wished
it, they could not rest on that day. They say that
if they "tied up" on Sunday, a dozen boats might
pass them, and then, since all must unload and load
according as they arrive at the wharf, a great deal
of time would be lost by the boat that kept the
Sunday. The Sunday itself they could spare, say
many, but not the wasted week-day time they
would lose by keeping it. Almost the only exception to this rule of working on Sunday is that
of the boater who "ties up" abreast of a public-
house, that he may drink away the hours of God's
holy day.

As a rule, the female bargee as well as the male
drinks. A special temptation arises from the necessity of generally "tying up" at a public-house, as

stabling for the horses is difficult to obtain elsewhere. In this case the publican expects the
boater's custom, and the boater is only too ready to
give it.

Such is the sad story of the bargee's home; let
no one say that the picture is too highly coloured.
Certainly there are here and there bright exceptions,
tidy boats occupied by sober, steady men, whose
little children play on deck or on the towing path
with clean faces and decent clothing. But then if
you question them, you will generally find that
these people have a humble stationary home somewhere, and that the little ones occasionally attend
school and church. Ask these respectable boaters
to tell you the sort of character their comrades
bear, and they will most surely confirm what is
here said of them above.

And now what has been done, what is being
done for these brothers and sisters of ours who,
made in the image of God, are day by day defacing
that likeness, and working under the colours of the
Prince of Darkness? Has any one tried to reclaim
them? Have any of the good people who yearn
and pray for the conversion of the negro and the
South Sea Islander given a thought to these poor
savages nearer home? Well, the last two questions
can be answered with a Yes, even if it must be a
faint and feeble one. For the last forty years there
have been anxious hearts who now and again have
made an effort to get hold of the wandering boater,
have tried—alas! perhaps vainly—to humanize

him, to Christianize his little children; but the work was so dispiriting that it did not come to much. The barge whose occupants seemed most hopeful, the little children who listened so gladly to the kind visitor, at last moved on a stage further, and weeks must pass before the same party could be seen again. How was it possible to do any real good amongst them, or to talk of schooling for the young ones? A large remedy was evidently wanted for so large an evil.

So at least thought Mr. George Smith, who had spent much time in visiting these floating dwellings and studying the needs of the bargee. He brought the matter before the eyes of Parliament, and after infinite trouble, hard work, and disappointment, he got an Act passed by which every canal boat used as a dwelling was to be registered, only a certain number of people of certain ages were to inhabit it, and the children were to be compelled to attend school according to the education laws of the country. A very good Act, surely, and likely to benefit greatly the boater. Yes, it is a good Act, but it has to be carried out, and *there* is the difficulty. The ignorant, careless bargee cannot be got all in a minute to care for his children's education because Parliament has said they are to be taught. And so it will take months, and years perhaps, for the little ones to be drawn out of the mire of their cabin homes, and shown the beauty of light and goodness. You see I speak most of the children, not that their souls are of more value than those of

2 H

the grown-up people, but because their youth is
still here, fresh and soft and teachable, and because
it is so easy at this stage to train the tender branch
upwards. Besides, a hard, stubborn-hearted bargee
will sometimes learn good at second hand from his
little child, when he would turn away from a messenger sent straight to himself. Still messengers
are sent to the full-grown boater as well as to the
neglected child, and I may as well at once tell you
of a certain messenger that comes vividly before
my mind's eye as I write of these poor canal people.
Bishop Selwyn, of Lichfield, sent this messenger to
the muddy waters of the canal, and although the
Bishop was spared but for a short time to give the
work his countenance, the messenger is labouring
still in carrying good tidings to the ignorant and
neglected.

The messenger I speak of is a boat, a church
barge, in which the boaters can be collected for
Sunday and week-day services. In the centre of
the boat is the church, right and left are cabins for
the chaplain and the men who take charge of the
messenger, and at the extreme end is the stable for
the pony who tows the barge. The chaplain was
meant by the bishop to live on board and journey
in his church from place to place; but this plan
had to be altered for several reasons. The church
part of the barge will hold fifty people, and as some
one very truly said, if more come, there is the best
example possible for assembling the people on the
bank and preaching to them from the ship. Of

course, I cannot pretend to give you an account of
every voyage made by the messenger. I content
myself with telling you what was done in one year
by it.

And first I must ask, Do you remember the
January weather of 1879, the long hard frost which
turned our rivers and canals into firm ice, and put
a stop to all navigation? A bad beginning, you will
say, for the floating messenger. Not at all. Of course,
she could not move about, but her chaplain could,
and here was a splendid opportunity for visiting
the frozen-up bargee, who had nothing to do, no
cargo to load or unload, and who, left alone, would
probably be sitting in the public-house at the
"tying-up" stations, drinking to keep the cold out,
and to bring disease and poverty and misery in.
Once started on this work, the chaplain had need
be busy, for thirty-three boats were lying in one
long immovable line, at Stone, in Staffordshire, and
they stuck there for a whole month; thirteen were
lying a little further on, twelve again a stage beyond that, nine further on still, over forty at Stoke
and Etruria, and forty-seven at Wolverhampton,
the largest canal station on that line! Plenty of
parishioners to visit, and all at leisure, unless you
call drinking,] fighting, and swearing being busy.
The chaplain was not in a hurry to find fault, he
wanted to make friends, and the people were what
is called "at a loose end," and glad enough to talk
to a stranger who seemed civil and friendly. Just
at first, as poor folks will be, they were a trifle shy,

but after a while they would nod to their friend, and promise him their countenance at his services, and put down the pot of beer, or even postpone the fight just coming off to oblige him, and that was something gained in these early times. The chaplain was not afraid to rush in occasionally between combatants when an actual fight had begun, and he was generally able to calm his excited friends, assisting them in putting on their clothes, and encouraging peace in all ways. This reminds me again of the country clergyman of fifty years ago of whom I told you at the beginning of this paper. He was driving his newly married wife in her little pony-carriage, in those long-past days, when suddenly he pulled up, threw the reins to his wife, and sprang out. The next moment he was on the canal bank, thrusting aside two fighting bargees, to her intense alarm. Not much progress made in fifty years, you'll say: alas that such scenes should be repeated! The frost in 1879 at last came to an end, and early on February 21 the messenger set out on its journey to its head-quarters, Wolverhampton, it having been decided that that was the best place for the chaplain to reside in habitually. Not that he lived in the boat now; he had tried that plan, and the damp and cold of the canal had very nearly brought him to the grave, so it was settled that his residence should be on shore. The church, however, would be as useful as ever, and great attention it excited, as it was towed along that February day with its flags flying.

Of course, a congregation had to be collected for
it the very next Sunday. And the difficulty was,
not to get enough people, but to get them of the
right sort. The shore people all wanted to come
in their Sunday finery, with their Prayer-books in
their hands, but it was the bargee in his working
clothes that was really wanted. The way the
bargee was got at has been described to me by one
who helped in the work at another canal station.
"We take different sides of the canal," he says,
"starting an hour or more before the commencement of the service. We call at every boat and
invite them to come, getting as many as possible
to promise that they will. When we have visited
each boat we return, collect the people together, and
take them to the service. Many, of course, excuse
themselves, one of the most frequent pleas being
that they have 'to do their horses up.' Some,
indeed, may have arrived only just before our visit,
and so have reason for not coming. If we can get a
boater to attend once he is generally willing to
come again when opportunity offers. The ice is
broken, he has seen other boaters there in working
clothes, and he feels more comfortable about the
matter. Every Sunday, however, sees new boats and
new faces, and that makes the difficulty in our work.

" One evening, with a good deal of persuasion, we
got three young men to promise to go with us.
When we called for them on our return we found
that they had apparently already started, their
cabin being locked up; one of us, however, being

suspicious that all was not so fair as it seemed, got
in through the door at the back of the cabin, and
lifting up a lot of bags, found the lads concealed
beneath. They had a good laugh at our shrewdness
in not being deceived by their padlocking the front
door on the outside and creeping in through the
back door, and then they readily came along with
us. Does it not seem as if the right workers had
got to that canal-side, actually compelling the poor
neglected boaters to come in to the gospel feast?
When once a congregation is collected, it is not
difficult to interest it. However ignorant these
poor fellows may be they soon like to join in a
good stirring hymn, to listen to a few words addressed specially to themselves about their lives,
their children, their canal, their future, to join in
a plain confession of sin, and in the half-remembered
words of that 'Our Father' that some of the
happiest of them remember to have said long years
ago at a dead mother's knee."

When the church barge reached Wolverhampton
that February Sunday, about thirty-six boatmen,
their wives and children, came to the morning
service; in the afternoon a Sunday school was held,
and in the evening there was another service, when
the church was crammed, fifty attending, and a
harmonium being lent for the occasion. Wherever
there is a stopping-place on a canal there is urgent
need of a floating church or a mission-room, the
last perhaps being the most useful wherever the
church barge has already ploughed a way for the

gospel. The boater in his cramped quarters will always then be able to find a place of worship where Sunday clothes are not indispensable.

Do not suppose that the boat chaplain does nothing, however, but preach and pray, and give out hymns in his neat little church. Were it so, some boaters would be no whit the better off, since many would not conquer their .preference for a pipe and a sleep over a wash and a visit to the new-fashioned church. The chaplain has to be very busy in many ways; he has to make friends with his flock, to visit dirty close cabins, to talk to the women, nod to the men, and attract the little children. There must be no fault-finding—the boaters would resent that; by-and-by, when they get a little more light, a little more knowledge, they will find out their own shortcomings, and accuse themselves, but just now the utmost gentleness is needed. Even a wild beast can best be tamed by kindness, and these wild, fierce souls must be tempted into the gospel net by the fairest bait we can make use of. In this respect the children are easily attracted; a happy school-time, singing, pictures, pleasant books for the few that can read, —all these means easily win over childish hearts. Such bare and empty little hearts too ! Some not knowing there is a God, others never having been taught a prayer, and only recognizing Sunday as a day, perhaps, on which father and mother oftenest get drunk, and when, therefore, it is wisest to slink out of their way.

I began with a sad anecdote of the ignorance of the canal boatman; I fear I must end with another which speaks of worse than ignorance, of the most brutish cruelty and indifference, shown to a poor little lad. I take the paragraph as it appeared a little while ago in the London papers.

"The other day an inquest was held at the St. Pancras coroner's court, on a boy named Essex, who recently fell into the Regent's Canal, and was drowned. He would have been saved, but just as a man named Sadder was diving to recover the lad, a barge came along, and the bargeman declined to stop, though implored to do so. Several other barges followed, and all insisted on keeping their course. After they had passed, the lad was found firmly embedded in mud, having been pressed down to death by the slowly passing barges. There was much method in this otherwise strange conduct of the bargemen. It transpired in evidence that some of them had boldly said it was no good making a fuss about a drowning boy, who, if saved, brought them nothing, whereas, if fished up in the form of a corpse, he would be worth five shillings, or, as one of these savages put it, 'At least three gallons of beer.' Talk of savages! Surely our missionaries might find a good field among these heathen of our great water highways."

Beyond all doubt, it is clearly a duty to help on a mission work of this sort. Those who have not much money to give may yet be able to assist in another way. There is great need of books, pictures, old magazines, interesting tracts, and such like literature for lending out or giving to the boaters who can read. They must needs have a library of their own, since no church or school library could be asked or expected to trust their precious volumes to people who are "here to-day and gone to-morrow." I know one boater's friend (and I expect there are a good many more of the same kind) who would gladly welcome the smallest parcel of this nature, and it would find its way to him quite safely if addressed: "The Chaplain, Lichfield Barge Mission, Wolverhampton Station."

Do you remember the story of the Quaker who, when the grievous case of a poor man was being discussed in a large company, and many were loudly expressing their sympathy with him, got up, and quietly said to his neighbour, "Friend, I am sorry £5 for this poor man; how much art thou sorry?" Be sorry a few books, then, for the canal boatman.

## LADIES OF INDIA.

### INDIA.

THE ladies of India! What do you think I mean
by this phrase? Of whom do I speak? Not of
the fair-haired wives of our English officers and
civil servants who go out so smilingly with their
husbands in the great ships that continually leave
our shores, and come home a few years later with
a troop of baby children and saddened faces, because their father must stay behind in the hot
climate where he earns his bread. These for a
time, indeed, are ladies *in* India; but the ladies *of*
India are far, far different, and have a story all
their own. A story of a life dull and useless and
monotonous, but still a story good for us to read if
we only rise up from the reading to say thank
God for the brighter life He has given us, and
better still to read, if we have the wish and the
power given to us afterwards, to brighten and
amend these dull lives.

You all know a little of the daily life of a rich
kindly English lady. She has her pretty home,
her kind husband, her happy daintily clothed little
ones; she cares for these a portion of her day, and

in her intervals of visiting and entertaining grand
company, she has a thousand other little duties
crowding round her, many of them taking in her
poorer neighbours. Hospital tickets for which her
husband has subscribed to be distributed, or sent
to the clergyman to distribute; a letter of recommendation to be written for her steward's son or
her gardener's daughter; the village children's
school feast (for which her money has been previously furnished) to be overlooked, or the sick
girl at the lodge to be called upon and cheered
with a new sweet-smelling flower from the hot-
house, or something in a basket which my lady
has begged from her cook to please a failing appetite. Going down the village, my lady lets some
little Rhoda or Susan stop her with her wistful
face to tell about father's rheumatism, the needs of
the eight children, and her fourteen-year-old desire
for a "place," and she takes out her velvet note-
book to write down the particulars, for these con-
fidences are only one of a dozen she receives in the
course of her walk, and none must be forgotten.
Next month, too, she will go up to town, and be
busier still, with her own affairs and her husband's
talk of what goes on in the House, that large
House of Commons, where great people often sit
up through long nights considering the welfare of
the nation. Of course, there are foolish rich ladies
in England, and, sad to say, wicked ones too, but
as a rule it is, I think, fairly correct to allow that
the rich English lady leads, as far as she can, a

busy, happy life; clothed, it is true, in purple and
fine linen, but spending herself often in labours
for those who are not so blessed with this world's
wealth.

It is a pleasant life to look at and to think of.
Would that the rich ladies of India could lead such
lives! But theirs, as I said before, runs in widely
different grooves. I must try and tell you about
them. And first I had better count over what
advantages riches bring to a woman in India.
Beautiful airy muslins or gauzes for her clothing,
jewels of fairy-tale pricelessness to hang in her
ears and nose, and to clasp her arms and ankles.
The finest tobacco for her long pipe, or hookah,
scented waters to sprinkle her garments, and sweetmeats for her daily food. This is about the sum.
No money is spent on her education, and the richer
she is the more closely she is kept a prisoner in
her own apartments, denied even the pleasures you
enjoy when you snatch a day's out in the country
with husband and children. There are no "outs"
for the Indian lady, and she lives on dully, stupidly,
from day to day, never looking for change.

As a baby girl she has been taken from home
(with the red spot on her forehead, meaning "engaged") and carried to the dwelling of the husband
her parents have chosen for her. She has been
taught to desire marriage as the one thing needful,
and she has watched the heap of gold and silver
ornaments collecting for her dowry till perhaps she
fancies the new life is to be something fresh and

delightful, but the poor little wife is soon unde-
ceived. At home at least her mother loved her
and petted her and spoilt her, as mothers all over
the world do, but once taken from the old home it
is quite another thing. She passes instantly into
the charge of her mother-in-law, and is subject to
her; for one of the customs of India is that the
sons do not leave the father's house even when
they grow up, but each brings a wife or wives
home, and the new families live all together under
the headship of the old couple. To the sons this
is not galling; they go out into the world, do their
work, and have each their way; but the women
belonging to all are huddled into strictly barred
apartments at the back of the house, from whence
they may never come out, save in closely covered
palanquins, at the will of their various lords. Perhaps in those dull, unhomelike rooms may be found,
beside the child-wife, the mother-in-law, grandmother, and aunts of the young husband also.

" No books, no needlework, no pictures, except
the vilest daubed prints of their most vile my-
thology; no accomplishments except cookery, no
employment except smoking and playing with their
children, no knowledge of the grand past, of the
busy present or the eternal future. Yet this is
the life, these are the homes of the ladies of India ! "

I have copied this last sentence straight out of
an account of India by an English lady, who has
written a pleasant book of what she saw and heard
during a visit to that country a few years ago. It

is a miserable story, you will allow, that of a rich Hindu wife, but there is a more miserable chapter to come, containing the story of an Indian widow.

You have perhaps all heard, and yet hardly taken the trouble to believe, that not so very long ago it was the custom for Indian widows to allow themselves to be burned alive with the dead bodies of their husbands. Foreigners could hardly credit the fact that the poor creatures willingly accepted the fate, but they did so; perhaps they were stupefied with drugs, perhaps they were filled to rapture with the idea of the bliss beyond that blazing pile, anyhow there was rarely the least reluctance to face the dreadful death.

The friends cheered them on, the dead husband lay there, and they went to their fate calmly, unhesitatingly. But this sort of self-murder could not be permitted under our rule, and the English law forbade widow-burning some years ago. The woman's life was preserved, but for what? She was condemned to an existence of misery, neglect, and discomfort. She might not marry again, and she was looked upon as a burden and a disgrace by every one belonging to her. Never to her dying day might she adorn herself with the jewels she had been taught to love so well, never wear anything but coarse, plain clothing, never sleep upon a bed, never eat anything but the very simplest food.

No one threw her a word of the commonest kindness, for by Hindu law she ought not to be in the world at all—she was a monstrosity, a living widow. So the poor soul, who might be in her teens, for young husbands died occasionally, took her fate sullenly and silently, and lived out her life—one of the most miserable of the ladies of India.

But English rule has abolished widow-burning, say‾some; cannot it also abolish the ill treatment of the widow? A slow business this. One may make laws against murderers, but evil-speakers and the unkindly are difficult to deal with. Still, very slowly a change may come, and once there seemed to be a bright example of this good change.

I will tell you the story.

Not so very long ago an Indian gentleman of high rank and education, a judge in one of the Bombay courts, lost his wife, and having mixed much in English society and learned Christian ways of looking at the matter, he resolved in process of time to marry again, not a little child, as his nation and custom demanded, but a full-grown woman. Of course, a single woman was not to be found, all those were mated long ago, but a widow of five-and-twenty, of suitable birth and position, was only too glad to accept his offer. Of course, he knew the cost of marrying a widow, loss of caste among his own race—loss of caste being to the East Indian what excommunication once was in Christian countries. No one looking upon him save with horror, no one eating with him, none meeting him in friendly intercourse, marked in life, accursed in death, and the same penalties descending on his children. A few friends this judge had, however, who were

nearly as enlightened as himself, and who promised
to support him in his new life; so, full of hope, the
newly married pair began their career. They loved
each other, and that was happiness. There came a
little son, and both rejoiced again; but, alas! the
clouds were already gathering that would make
wreck of their lives.

The grown-up sons living in the house (as, you
know, was customary) threatened and wearied their
father with lawsuits and contentions, the daughters-
in-law and aunts and other women of the house
made the life of the new wife miserable, because
she had neither died with her former husband nor
lived a pleasureless, colourless, single life, as was
her next duty; every day and every hour the poor
creatures, half-Eastern, half-English in their minds,
were tossed and turned and buffeted by friends and
foes till heart and hope left them. They were not
strong enough to live down the breaking of old
customs, the loss of that precious thing to a Hindu
—caste. And they had no Christian faith to fall
back upon for comfort. So the end of the tale is a
sorrowful one.

Out into the still moonlight night went the pair,
leaving their babe asleep in the dwelling; they
must have sat down on the parapet of the wide
well, and there deliberately tied themselves together
with the husband's scarf and cast themselves into
the deep water, for there they were found next
morning clasped in each other's arms out of reach
of human taunts. The wife was arrayed in her

jewels and her costliest apparel as she would have been had she sacrificed herself on the pyre of her first husband. What became of the poor little one accursed by birth, we are not told.

After hearing all this, can you wonder that some Christian people long to better the condition of the women of India, and that a mission of English ladies to Indian ladies has now been on foot for some years? Ladies only can avail in this case, since no man would in any case be admitted into the zenana, or women's apartments, of an Eastern dwelling. And so particular are Indian husbands that their ladies shall not even be gazed upon by the opposite sex that, if a change of residence has to be made, or some necessity arises for a native lady to pass through the streets, she is shut up closely in her palanquin, the sliding doors are fastened, and then over all, to close every chink, a thick red cover is thrown. The box, for such it is and nothing more, is then carried by four servants through the public ways and planted down in the women's apartments of the new house, when the poor creature inside is released. The richer and grander the lady the more strictly she is hidden from the world.

Several such crimson-covered boxes were seen by an English lady in the bottom of a boat approaching her steamer at Madras. She leaned over the ship's side and watched the process of lifting the poor ladies on board. A stout rope was tied round each box, and into this a hook was inserted, by which the box was lifted, dangled in mid-air, and finally placed on deck, to be instantly carried, still closed, to a private cabin.

Fancy the feelings of the poor ladies inside, in total darkness, half stifled with the heat, first tossed in the small boat, and, secondly, enduring the extraordinary swing on board at the end of the hook. They were the wives of a rich nabob on a journey, and by-and-by he came on board and went downstairs to see how his poor ladies fared. However long a sea-voyage may be, Indian ladies can never stir out of their close little cabins to sit in the larger saloons for fear of meeting men. Once in a while, however, the husband, if he is kind, asks the captain to clear the saloons and passages of all man-kind so as to permit his wives the pleasure of seeing these apartments, and greatly do the poor shut-up things enjoy this. They are then like babies or very little children out for a treat, touching this pretty bit of gilding, admiring that picture or ornament, and very much pleased if English *lady* passengers take notice of them and show them their trinkets and toys.

But perhaps I have told you quite enough about the hedged-in lives of the ladies of India, and you will now like to hear of a few who have dared to let a little light into the chinks of this terribly dull existence.

It is not an easy thing to do. Indian gentlemen are very suspicious of allowing any visitors to their wives; but somehow the English lady manages a first visit, generally with a bit of pretty gay wool-work in her hand, which she shows the zenana ladies how to execute. They all crowd round her with questions and chatter, which she meets as best she may, and by-and-by she must go amid general lamentation, leaving perhaps the work behind her.

She comes again, however, and this time the cross-stitch has been mastered, and the shut-up wives want more work, and the Indian husband is perhaps pleased that his pet wife is pleased with so innocent an amusement, and the English lady is welcomed and asked to stay longer.

And now the talk is not all about cross-stitch, but about better things, and the poor zenana ladies are astonished to hear of how English wives live and work, teaching their little ones, making their clothes, and so on. Perhaps the visitor takes the opportunity of a pretty little child being brought to her to tell the company of our God coming to earth as an innocent babe also, and then the interest is great, though it takes many visits really to teach these poor souls anything, they are kept so ignorant and foolish. It is almost impossible, too, to make them understand our religion till they are a little raised out of their apathy and sloth. So zenana visitors try to get the rich ladies to learn to read and write and do tiny sums, just as we teach our little children, as a preparation for better things. Some schools have actually been set on foot for high-class children; but as quite tiny girls are soon removed to be married and shut up in their husband's apartments, the teacher, who really cares for them, has to follow them there.

"In some houses," says the lady from whose book I have already quoted, " the mother of the family, two or three of her daughters-in-law, and some of their children were all pupils together, besides others crowding into the room to listen and look on; and one can fancy what a beam of light from the outer world the coming of the English lady must shed on these secluded rooms."

Here is another bit :—" I asked one of them (the wives) how they used to pass the time before their teacher came, and she replied, ' We used to bathe, and plait our hair, and cook, and eat, and sleep, and smoke, and play with our jewels and eat and sleep again.' I believe they all cook for their husbands, though they do not eat with them; and they make a great variety of sweetmeats, some of which, made of cocoa-nut, are very nice."

Here is a visit to another house described :—" In this one house there are upwards of fifty souls, including the old grandfather and grandmother, great-aunt, etc., all the sons and sons' wives, and all their children and grandchildren. Of course, we saw none of the men except casually outside the zenana; but the women were very glad to see us, and some of the little children were the dearest little brown things you can imagine. Under five or six years old they go perfectly naked, except perhaps a heavy silver girdle and large silver rings on their ankles,

and the plump, sleek creatures, with their splendid
eyes and pretty demure ways, were most droll and
winning. . . . The young wives and mothers read
and repeated lessons in Bengali and English, did
sums, and showed their fancy work, repeated
hymns, and asked us to sing to them. They were
reading a Bengali translation of 'Daybreak in
Britain,' which you may have seen in the *Sunday
at Home*, and the less advanced ones read 'Line
upon Line.' They then talked and asked us
questions in very simple, childlike fashion; and
when I made some remark about the children's
silver girdles, they fetched out all their jewellery to
show us. You would expect that with all this
profusion of jewellery they would have at least
comfortable furniture, but this by no means follows.
I cannot say what the men's apartments were like,
but the poorest people in my old district (in England) would think themselves ill off indeed if they
had no more of the conveniences of life than these
Hindu ladies. The floor was cement, without mat
or carpet: there were no glass windows, only
wooden shutters, and the only article of furniture
I saw was the rough wooden bench we sat on.
Their religion forbids these people to wear any
dress that is sewn together, so a piece of cloth, fine
or thick, cheap or dear, as suits the means of the
wearer, is all that is wound round the person. The
richer the lady, the thinner her drapery; sometimes
it is a mere gauze veil thrown round the body, but
the extreme heat of the climate and the entire

seclusion in which the Hindu lady lives prevents this very slight apparel from appearing immodest."

This account of the interior of a zenana represents that of hundreds of others, the poor ladies lost in sloth and ignorance, and only waking up like babies to find that there is such a thing as a better life in this world, to which such small matters as learning to read and sew lead up in time. Some few Hindu gentlemen, however, are beginning to wish to have better-instructed wives, and so cast about them how to obtain the teaching without the necessity of changing their religion. Into some houses the English lady is invited on the understanding that the wives and daughters may learn reading and fancy work but not the " good tidings " which she most longs to bring to them. Here, of course, she is obliged to be very upright and truthful, or the Christian religion might suffer blame: we may not do evil that good may come, and to teach a wife to deceive her husband would be to break one of our strongest Christian laws. So the spelling and the stitching go on, and it is a beginning; meantime the English visitor must have patience. There are even schools where little high-class children attend, who may have lessons in everything but Christianity; and there are others far less bigoted, who may be taught how the Christian's God loves these dark-eyed children of His; but all these schools have to be most carefully watched over and regulated, since if a little veiled girl met a man anywhere on the premises, were it only a workman passing by to his work, she would be instantly taken away as disgraced, and the school would suffer in consequence.

That thing called caste in India is the bar in the way of education and improvement, one class of people may not touch or come near another without being defiled and losing caste; and this, as I told you once before, is the most dreadful thing that can happen to a Hindu. We have nothing like it in England; to say that such and such a person is so bad that no one will notice him or her, gives no idea of the horror and disgust with which an Eastern looks upon one who has "lost his caste."

A poor ayah, or nurse, coming home with little English children, may not eat of their food or she would lose caste; she must prepare her own food with her own hands. I knew one who threw up a good engagement to bring an English lady's little baby to England, because at the last moment it was decided to take the overland route instead of coming all the way by steamer. On board ship the ayah was sure of being able to respect her own religion and prepare her own food; but overland, at hotels, and travelling quickly in trains, she could not hope to do so, and so she preferred to lose her appointment to risk her religion.

This difficulty creeps into all classes, and must be done away with before the Hindu can become a Christian, before the Eastern lady can lead a busy happy life, a little like her rich English sister's.

At present she could not give alms to a poor person, since the touch would defile her; neither could she go to church for fear of sitting next a person of some other caste, and so losing hers; in fact, if she had liberty to go about the world, it would be of no use to her.

There is a great deal to be done, you see, in this vast India of ours, of which our Queen is Empress, before we can feel we have done our duty by the land, and there are a great many opinions as to what is wisest to attempt.

The gradual teaching of the rich ladies to sew and read seems the best way of beginning: they must be roused out of their likeness to animals sleeping in the sun before their hearts can be reached. And this rousing is what is now going on in India, a work taken up by English ladies under the title of the Zenana Mission. I have only tried in this paper to give you an idea of the very beginning of it; but you will see how it is growing when I tell you that in the four great towns in India where it has taken root, it has altogether more than a thousand scholars, some of them rich men's wives and little daughters, only permitted teaching in their own homes, others pupils at school under the constant care of English ladies.

Surely we may hope that before long the ladies of India may lead happier, busier, holier lives; this world brightened for them, and the next shown to them in purer, truer colours than their own faith ever could employ.

# A MORNING IN ITALY.

### A LONDON ALLEY.

HAVE you ever been to London? Some of you smile: you " live there." Others have " never been so far from home as that." Well, in any case, there are many parts of this huge city which you certainly would not know. I am nearly sure, for instance, that you have never visited the particular spot I want to take you to to-day. It is almost in sight of St. Paul's Cathedral, that is to say, the great round dome peers over the tops of the houses, and is only distant some ten minutes' walk from it; it lies within two minutes' walk of Smithfield, celebrated for its market, and, alas ! for its terrible burnings also, since here, in the dark times gone by, men thought to enforce the religion of the loving and pitiful Saviour by putting to a cruel death such as did not think exactly with them in religious matters. My alley lies in this closely populated heart of London city; but you English mothers, London mothers, have most probably never trod its rugged stones, not even as the chance visitor of a single day. How can I be so sure of this? Ah, there comes the telling of my story. This is the

Italian quarter of London. Every house, every shop, every garret, every cellar is tenanted by Italians. I dare say you are surprised to hear that the Italians in London need a special quarter of their own. Surely the boy with the monkey, the girl with the piano on wheels, and the two or three men with plaster figures on trays one meets in a morning's walk, could find a corner in some ordinary lodging-house amongst our own poor. Perhaps they could, but they naturally like to be amongst their own people in a foreign land, and when I tell you that there are said to be something like ten thousand Italians in London, you will perhaps hardly be surprised at their making a sort of home for themselves in the great city.

That home is in the neighbourhood of Hatton Garden, and here I found myself one bright, sharp morning in autumn, come for the purpose of paying some visits to the inhabitants. You will like to hear how I was received; it is always the most interesting sort of story, that of real people, their ups and downs, joys and sorrows, and I can assure you the lives of these black-eyed wanderers from home and fatherland are often very interesting. But, before I give an account of my morning calls, I must tell you what I know concerning the appearance here of these Italians. This takes me for a while into Fleet Street, where a splendid new pile of buildings rises on the north side, close to Temple Bar. "The New Law Courts," a policeman tells me, and he goes on to say, "Don't you know there was a strike among the masons some while back, and they got over a lot of Italian workmen to go on with the building? We had to look after them a bit at first, for the roughs had a fancy for molesting them, but after a while they got used to seeing them, I suppose, and now we've no more trouble." Yes, I had seen all that in the newspapers long ago; yet it set me wondering where those strange masons lived, if their families were with them, and if any one cared for them beyond the masters for whom they worked.

By-and-by I got to know that some one did care for them—a countryman of their own, an Italian gentleman who had been a clergyman in his own country, but who had been guided by God to come and work amongst his poor brethren in London. The masons of these new Law Courts were his first charge, but by degrees Dr. Passalenti discovered other large colonies of Italians in that same favourite neighbourhood of Hatton Garden, who were living, strangers in a strange land, striving for daily bread, with eyes fixed solely on the streets in which that bread could be made—hearts never uplifted to the Giver of all good.

They are not a people difficult to deal with, they are friendly and affectionate, grateful for interest taken in them, and the mass of them are by no means the idle creatures they appear to those who judge solely by the organ-grinder and monkey-boy specimens of the tribe. There are two distinct races of Italians to be found among these settlers—those from North Italy, a hardy, industrious class, furnishing us with labourers, masons, cabinet-makers, etc.; and the Neapolitans from Southern Italy, who are by nature an easier, idler race, preferring the wandering trades of organ-grinding, ice-selling, and the furnishing of models for artists. No one sees more clearly than the Italian himself the difference between the two classes; the north-country people, indeed, rather look down on their southern brethren, just as here you will find the English poor holding themselves above their Irish neighbours. The Neapolitans are indeed the Irish of Italy—easy, happy, not too particular about cleanliness, but impulsive and affectionate. They, as well as the northerners, are a frugal people, not given to intoxication and content with far fewer luxuries, or even comforts, than we English.

To these transplanted families in Hatton Garden, then, came Dr. Passalenti, with an ardent desire to do them good in any and every way that God should point out. Of course, the first thing to be done was to make his face familiar to them, to show himself their friend, in fact, and then to invite them to attend a Church service in Italian, held specially for them, and to open a free mission school for their children in their midst.

A church was now lent by a neighbouring clergyman for afternoon service. It is a dull, old City church, going by the name of St. Thomas, Liberty of the Rolls. Little did the English worshippers of long ago think that such a congregation as I saw

there would ever be gathered within its walls, such
dark eyes and brown faces, or that the aisles would
ring with such a new song as burst from the eager
lips of the Italian congregation. Dr. Passalenti
belongs to our English Church; he holds a licence
from the Bishop of London, and uses our service
translated into the Italian tongue. It seems now
familiar, now strange, to see our words in their new
dress, the little children in the centre of the church
joining their voices uncertainly in some responses,
but bursting out with new energy as the Lord's
Prayer begins. They all know that. Yes, and many
of the hymns too. The Italians love music, and
sing very well.

After a while we English catch the name of
*Victoria* in the prayers; they are praying for our
Queen; and then comes a new name—*Umberto
Primo*—and we know they are asking God to bless
and keep their Italian King, Humbert the First.
It must bring religion very near to these wandering
children of Italy when they are taught to pray for
this far-away monarch, who yet belongs to them,
and to whose beautiful country many of them hope
to return some day.

After rising from our knees, a very well-known
hymn is given out; and here the children have it all
their own way, running off with the melody now and
then in sheer triumph and enjoyment. They can be
very quiet, however, as they testify in sermon-time,
when the story of Samuel is told them with more life
and movement than is usual in an English sermon.

The school is much like an English school. The children, arranged in orderly fashion in classes, might be so many little Tommies and Janes in our Board Schools, we think for a moment; but then the dark eyes are upturned, and the brown cheeks warm with a shy flush, and we feel that these are really little Antonios and Angelinas, Pietros and Josephinas. One little boy, indeed, is called Dante, after the great poet of Italy, and there are many names that would strike you English parents as very odd indeed, notably Veranda, Palma, Raffaella, and so forth. The children are taught thoroughly all such subjects as are required by the education laws of our land; and they are taught more than that, for Dr. Passalenti holds that his task is only half done when he is giving his scholars such instruction as shall carry them comfortably through the world. He wants to do more, to fit them for a better country beyond this fleeting one. It is all very well to learn reading, writing, and arithmetic, to acquire a good trade, and start well in this world; but who knows how long the young boy or girl will be allowed to remain here below, and then, if called away, will all they have learned be of any use to them in the new life?

Stop and think of this, and then you will feel with Dr. Passalenti that it is a poor school that does not try to fit us for the *beyond* of this world. There are fifty-three children on the books of this school, and they learn Italian and English. There is a mission service held in the room on Friday evenings, when many Italians attend, and seem much interested in the teaching given.

A mothers' meeting is also set up in just the same fashion as for English mothers. After all, there is not much difference between one sort of mother and another—they all want to know how to get a little sewing done for their growing families, and to talk about those families, the trouble they have with John or Battista, Maddalena or Mary; how tiny Giovanni has never a tooth yet, and screams all night; or how Luigi is growing a big lad, and talks of following his father's trade. But you will hear more of this talk when I come to the house visits I paid that autumn morning.

A few more words first about the Italian mission. Some English gentlemen and ladies are helping Dr. Passalenti with his flock; the ladies especially go in and out of the houses, and are received with delight. The simple-hearted Italians like to be talked to, and to talk and show their white teeth in ready smiles at sight of a visitor. The husbands are not often at home, but when they are, off goes the slouch hat at sight of a lady, the very chair the man is sitting on is pushed forward for her accommodation, and he makes it plain that he is pleased too.

"Ah! that's always the way of foreigners," do I hear you say, "they are very polite, but——." No, I don't think there is a *but* in their politeness; the Italians have faults, of course, but I do not think there is a shadow of humbug in this pleasant welcome of theirs; it is quite real. And just as they are easily moved by kindness, so are they as easily roused by the opposite treatment, which may account for the ugly stories we see occasionally in the papers of Italians stabbing each other in sudden fury.

These poor Italians, however, are very ignorant, and all instruction is so new to them that they take the liveliest delight in such Bible stories as we should narrate to our children. Sometimes when a visitor is reading in some tiny room such portions of Holy Scripture, the door will softly open, and with a nod and a smile the neighbour from next door, or the lodger from below, will step in, and so by degrees the congregation will almost overflow the apartment, and questions will be asked and ideas exchanged about the reading in most interested fashion. Once when a lady was reading to a number of Italians one man began suddenly to dance and sing; he was speedily taken by the shoulders and turned out of the room by his better-behaved comrades. By-and-by, however, the man came again, and again tried to disturb the little company. Now, however, the women interfered, and forced him to go away, entreating the lady, who was putting by her book, to remain, and pardon the offender. It is pleasant to add, that when the lady did leave the house a little later, the man came up to her and asked her to excuse his rude behaviour. There is a soup kitchen opened in winter for these Italians, who are often very badly off at this time. Among the school children also a Band of Hope has been instituted, that they may not fall into the drinking habits of the nation among whom they have taken up their abode.

And now, having heard something of what was being done for the bodies and souls of these so-journers in our London streets, I was ready to visit them in their homes, and hear from their own lips how they fared in our country.

I need not describe more particularly the alley I first entered; it was just like many London courts, lined with poor, not too-well-kept houses, and paved with uneven stones, over which wandered queer little boys and girls, with handkerchiefs wound round their heads, and quaint bright garments, of which full linen sleeves seemed the main feature. At one house-door we knocked, proceeding upstairs into a tidy room which seemed all bed—a large bed on one side, a small one under the window, a sofa-bed beside it. Mrs. Palla, her husband, and three children lived here. She was at home with baby on her knee, dressed in a nice little scarlet frock. Her pleasant face beamed at sight of us; she was ready to talk or answer questions as might be, and this was the way her story ran. Yes, they had had a good summer, a very good one, and now it was over, and she had time to breathe, for the eight young men left for Paris yesterday. You might see their rooms empty below. Eight of them, and she had done for them all. What was their trade? Same as her husband's, the ice-trade—selling penny

2 K

and halfpenny ices from the carts. Ah! they had
all had work enough. Who made the ice? She
and the young men. How was it made? Of good
milk and eggs; four eggs to a quart, boiled together,
and sugar put in, and left to cool till morning, when
the young men got up early to freeze it. It wasn't
light work for any of them, made in such quantities; what with the standing over the fire, and
the freezing, and then all that tramping about with
the cart. And the trade was being spoilt by those
Neapolitans (a jerk of the thumb over the way at
the dwelling of the offenders). They didn't care so
long as they got customers, and they would under-
sell the ice horribly, give a penny ice for a half-
penny. They did it at London Bridge, and then of
course the boys found it out, and wouldn't come to
the old carts. How the Neapolitans do it she doesn't
know, for to use good material you can't price the
ice as low as that; and Mrs. Palla hints darkly at
water adulteration. Why have the young men
gone to Paris? For work in the winter. Italians
don't mind what they do so long as they make a
living. Sugar-baking, that's what they are after
now, and then next spring they'll come back to
London for the ice-season. Mr. Palla—Paul—he
thought he'd go too, but she didn't like to be left
with the children in England, so she begged him to
stay, and now he's working at odd jobs. Ah, yes!
the baby does look pale, he's been out in the street
all summer, his mother's not had a minute for him,
but now he's getting a bit of nursing, and Mrs.

Palla looks at the white face surmounting the red frock with a loving gaze, which cannot be mistaken. How well she speaks English! Why yes, she *is* English, only she has lived among the Italian colony all her life, and married into it, so she knows all their ways, and is more Italian than English herself. The children are at school. Carlo is ten; writes English and Italian beautifully; see, here is his copy-book and his prize-book. He is one of Dr. Passalenti's good scholars, and Josephina, the best little creature——. But the mother's tongue is stopped by the appearance of Fina, a little black-haired, black-eyed Italian girl of six, with the good look in her soft eyes. A word more from us. Has she been able to put by out of this good season's earnings? A smile and a shrug. Yes, a little, but it is hard work; it costs a great deal to keep the five of them.

We can hardly believe that Mrs. Palla is English; she has quite the look of an Italian woman; but we like her frank ways, to whatever nation she belongs, and we are sorry to leave her, and grope cautiously down the steep stairs into the alley again, where the ice-carts stand or are piled up housed for the winter by dozens.

Now for a Neapolitan house. Ah, one might be in Italy here! A stone-floored hovel, darkened by wet clothes hanging across it. Under the shadow of the clothes, seated on a low stoel, is a large, calm, brown-eyed woman, with three tiny children and two cats softly crawling round her. She is a new-

comer, and all alone in her out-of-the-way home she
wears the clothes we should think put on for show
if we saw her in the streets, the full skirts, the oddly
cut bodice, the square of linen on the head, and a
large gold bead necklace and earrings.  The babies,
too, are queerly dressed, like little women, and all
(even the mite of eight months old), wear earrings
too, quite large showy ones, in the ridiculous little
ears.  Her people go out with pianos on wheels, but
she does not like the street, so she goes as seldom as
she can, and stays ordinarily with the babies.  Well,
but the piano season is just over.  Yes, she knows
that.  What will be done now?  Will she return to
Italy?  She doesn't know; she shakes her head,
and goes on with her sewing.  The mite with the
biggest earrings, her sister's child, rolls over, and
the large calm woman picks her up with a purring
noise.  Then we notice that the tiny thing looks
like a grown-up person seen through a diminishing
glass, her plentiful hair screwed into a knot behind,
her little face perfectly formed and sensible.  She is
the image of a dressmaker I once knew in Naples.
Only eight months old!  She looks as if she could
handle a needle already, and fit on a dress, though
it would have to be for a fairy certainly.  Sometimes
these little foreigners, with their dark eyes and
clearly defined features, do give us this idea of
completion, particularly when contrasted with a
bald-headed, colourless English baby.  It was of no
use lingering here; our new friend seemed amiable
and gentle, but reserved and shy of visitors.  She

dared not come to the mothers' meetings yet; she clung to the babies and the washing, and there we left her. .

Upstairs again into another dwelling, another room full of beds, and damp wash fluttering about them. One inmate only, but she is delighted to invite us in. She talks too. Ah, yes, the piano business is over now the sharp days have come. Indeed, she and her mother are off by to-morrow's boat. Where to? Across the sea to Piacenza— their home. Have they saved money enough for that long journey? Ah, well, a little. But only for the crossing. And after that? Do they play the piano as they go along to make money? The piano! That is only hired, two shillings a day. It goes back to the shop. No, no, they procure some small instrument, accordion perhaps, and play little tunes at houses on the way, and so get sous, and at farms people give them beds or let them lie in outhouses. Oh, most people are kind. And your face; how have you hurt it so badly? The girl's countenance clouds. "Oh, that was Friday night," her voice assumes a crying tone; she was playing in the road, and two men come out of what we call "public-house," and, without one word, throw piano over and her beneath it. Policeman comes, takes her to hospital, men run away.

The girl seems to be telling the simple truth, and has been the victim of a sudden outburst of brutality from half-tipsy men, excited by a foreigner. Happily the piano was not hurt, she tells us, since it fell

upon her.   And then we hear more about Piacenza.
Her old grandfather lives there; he is ninety-six,
and owns a vineyard.   She and her mother will be
in time for the grape-gathering.   That will be
charming.   The poor thing with the scarred cheek
smiles.   But the grapes are going off.   Grandfather
is too feeble to attend to them, and father, who has
come to England every year since he was eleven
years old, does not understand vine-tending.   We
wonder he can find the heart to leave the blue skies
and purple grapes of his own Italy for our land of
fogs and frost, but then we remember that ripe
grapes are only for a certain portion of the year,
and the rest of the time the Italian peasant is
miserably poor.

I quite envy the girl the tramp across France
and Northern Italy in the bright autumn days; but
yet I dare say her feet will ache long before she
reaches grandfather and father; and certainly poor
mother, going of seventy, will be terribly tired, and
perhaps hungry, with only an accordion to depend
upon for daily bread.   Let us hope that what they
have learned in St. Thomas's Church, and those
talks at the mothers' meetings, will go with them
to Piacenza, and be a little seed of good among
those vine-clad hills.   It is a strange life, this
tramping between Italy and England, but it goes
on to a larger extent than we stay-at-home people
imagine.

To another dwelling.   Ludovico is a tailor, he
has been long in England; he too comes from

Northern Italy, and still remembers the bright sun there. "It made a man feel strong." But then he only got one franc for stitching a pair of trousers there, and he gets three in England, and so on with all the work, and he has ten children. No, he never thinks to return to Italy. He is quite content evidently, and talks cheerfully to us for some time. The next beautiful sight his eyes will see must be heaven, for his windows look on a gaunt, ugly London street, and he has given up all thoughts of bettering the prospect in this world.

After bidding adieu to our contented friend, we betake ourselves to a piano factory, where the barrel-organ pianos are made, and mended, and hired out. Here, again, we are kindly welcomed by a woman and a girl in a back parlour. We can't talk much because "drum—whirl—rattle—run"—one of those very pianos is careering at full speed in the next room, so we accept the invitation to go and look at the thing. We take the bull by the horns, as it were, and a very noisy bull it is, shut up into a small front shop. It is a sick piano come to be cured, and very nearly well it seems. A very jolly, pleasant Italian, in a bib apron, the master of the shop, tries to make us understand how many tunes it can play. He takes infinite trouble in pulling off its side and revealing its cylinder to our ignorant eyes, while the owner stands, we think, a little impatiently by, not a nice-looking man at all, but a fellow with a downcast countenance and thick lips, just the sort of

person one fancies to tyrannize over the poor girls
that hire his organs, who, wet or fine, good day or
bad, must pay their two shillings to him.

We would fain have paid more visits after this
one, but time failed, and we had to make our way
out of these Italian streets, among more old women
in gay head-dresses, more men in slouch hats, more
shaven-headed or black-haired children, all smiling.

One old crone dandled a wee-wee child in our
faces, a creature to make any mother's heart ache,
a thing no bigger than a small doll, with sad-mean-
ing eyes in a face not so big as the palm of one's
hand.  Two years old?  Impossible!  Yes, the old
woman laughed and held up two fingers.  Small!
Ah, no wonder! the mother had not wherewith to
feed it, and it did not thrive on other nourishment.
The wan thing, however, is beloved.  One of the
slouch hats comes up to listen, and passes a great
brown hand round the baby's face and in amongst
its plentiful dark hair.  It smiles at its father, a
smile that glorifies its sad little face.  If love (without proper food) will save it the baby will live, but
more likely it will follow its four-year-old countryman, who died the other day in one of these hovels,
singing to the last its infant school hymn—

"*Sicur' in man di Christo.*"
"Safe in the arms of Jesus."

It is a good thought that those arms are wide
enough to take in all—rich and poor, babes and
full-grown men, Italians and English.  Does it not
teach us to be wider in our love?

# MURDERERS AT SCHOOL.

## BRITISH COLUMBIA.

BRITISH Columbia, a tract of land in North America, shall be the corner of the world to which you shall now be introduced. Here for many years a traffic with the Indians for the valuable furs of their country has been established by the Hudson's Bay Company, who have forts and stations scattered along the coast; but a quarter of a century back the red men learnt little better from their association with their white brethren than drinking and swearing.

Sins of their own they had in plenty, poor souls, but that we should teach them new wickedness was a thought to trouble good men in their beds at night, and set them thinking how to remedy so crying an evil.

With the intention of sowing good seed in ground already covered with rank and clinging weeds, one Mr. Duncan was chosen and sent out in the year 1857, by the Church Missionary Training College, to Fort Simpson, in British Columbia.

Did he half guess the work he had before him? I think not; at any rate *you* would hardly believe the sort of people he had to deal with. It was not only that he had to make men into Christians, but he had to convert murderers, and cannibals, and doers of all kinds of wicked deeds, into human creatures, with hearts to be softened. Imagine this one man gazing pitifully at his flock of red men and their children, numbering 25,000 souls, of one tribe alone, and realizing that their very religion was sin.

They believed in a great God, it is true; but when their worldly affairs went wrong they would rail even at Him, gnashing their teeth and heaping abuse upon Him. And he who was most respected by his tribe was the man who could most like a wild beast tear and devour the body of a fellow-man to the sound of drums and rattles, and shouts of an admiring crowd. Dog-eaters came next in rank— wolfish creatures with streaming black hair and naked bodies, who worried and shook the carcase of the poor brute that was more human than them- selves, to the delight of the bystanders. Hopeless material out of which to make Christian men! but Mr. Duncan meant to try, and in one case his labours were signally rewarded. You must hear the story of his convert.

Legaic was his name, the head chief of the whole tribe, a passionate man, a murderer, a drunkard, and one of the strongest upholders of the "medicine rites," heathenish ceremonies which the whole tribe held in awe. The first act in his life which fell under Mr. Duncan's notice was the murder of a

helpless and innocent stranger. Being irritated by
some other chiefs he went out and shot a man, any
one, he did not care who, so long as his angry feeling
could find vent. And death and destruction might
not end here; according to the laws of these Indians,
the chief under whose rule the murdered man was
living must now send out and kill some one else,
some, perhaps, utterly guiltless creature living under
the care of Legaic. And so like links of a chain
one wretched deed clung to another.

Like one-tenth of the population, Legaic was a
"medicine man" too, and strange rites and deeds of
darkness went on in his hut on the beach. Mr.
Duncan had not thought of this when he caused his
school-house at Fort Simpson to be built on the
shore in a central situation for the community, and
close to the great chief's dwelling, but he was soon
to feel the inconvenience and danger.

At a certain season of the year the medicine men
have their solemn meetings, when they admit new
followers into their ranks with all kinds of secret
ceremonies and awe-inspiring mysteries; and when
this season drew nigh for the first time after the
new white teacher's arrival, the great chief found
the sharp sound of the school bell and the tramp of
the scholars past his door disturbing to his dark
doings. He was reluctant, also, perhaps thus to
attract the notice of people who were taught to
think shame of these heathen rites, so he waxed
angry and sent an imperious message that the
school must be shut during the great month of

medicine work ; but Mr. Duncan, after deep thought, refused to give in to heathen ceremonies, and then the great man sent still more pressing demands for at least a fortnight's respite of bell and book, then for four days, then for one day.

And still the follower of Christ refused to clear the way for the devil's work, though Legaic declared he would shoot any scholar who dared to attend in spite of his wishes. It might, probably, be no empty threat, as the teacher and the scholars knew ; but still they came, the bravest of them, at the sound of the bell struck that one terrible day by the master himself that it might send forth no uncertain sound. And in amongst the little throng burst, after short delay, the chief and seven of his followers, mad with rage and drink, demanding the school to be closed.

Mr. Duncan answered him gently but plainly, telling him his works were evil, and that he could not in any way help them on; that threats were useless, since he feared only His own Master, God, not Legaic, and was bound alone to obey Him. For an hour the parley went on, the chief drawing his hand across his throat and saying he knew how to kill people.

Then he turned to the benches of scholars— not alone containing simple children as in our country, but grown men, sin-stained heathen in the ranks—observing, contemptuously, to his followers, "I am a murderer, and you are murderers, what good is it for us to come to school?"

It might seem useless to answer such a question to the infuriated chief, but Mr. Duncan did so, telling him gently that Christ would pardon even murderers. And then, to the surprise of every one, Legaic withdrew and school resumed.

Mr. Duncan writes in his journal that day, as if amazed, "I am alive; I have heartily to thank that all-seeing Father who has covered and supported me to-day."

In the knowledge of man that heathen chief had never before been so thwarted without laying his opponent dead at his feet, and God alone could have held back his blood-stained hand from slaying Mr. Duncan.

The school flourished in spite of opposition, and many chiefs and great men attended it, promising to give up their own medicine mysteries in favour of the new faith; and of those who did not come, Mr. Duncan found one chief learning his alphabet at home under the guidance of one of the best scholars.

Still murder and crime raged freely in the settlement, and notwithstanding that the Indians listened to his teaching and frequented the school and the Sunday services, the missionary felt disheartened for the young children, and the timid converts living and breathing in so sin-laden an atmosphere.

While that horrid drum beat, and the cannibals ran unchecked, nay admired, among the people, how could he keep his flock undefiled? nay, there was actual bodily danger to them. One day he saw the people flying in all directions, taking refuge in their

canoes and putting to sea; and why? A cannibal
had failed to find a dead body to devour, and was
seeking a living creature for his prey. So all were
in peril of their lives. But despond as Mr. Duncan
might, some good had been wrought by him in the
midst of prevailing evil, and a certain and remarkable proof of this was now forthcoming.

Five days before Christmas Legaic had threatened
teacher and scholars alike in the Christian school
with death if they dared to continue to assemble.
In April of the next year the murderer chief crept
into the school, humbled and somewhat ashamed, a
learner himself. Five months of school and Church
services, of children coming home with hymn tunes
and Christ-like words on their lips, had unconsciously worked on the heathen chief; he would
fain learn, too, these new things, and see if perchance
they were better than the old.

"The head chief," writes Mr. Duncan, "was at
school to-day. His looks show that he well remembers his past base conduct; but I try to disregard
the past, and show him equal kindness with the
rest."

And so the school went on and prospered, Legaic's
example drawing other great men after him.

On New Year's day, 1861, a school feast was
given, the red men and children enjoying their soup
and rice and treacle as much as our young ones do
their tea and buns, games following in the old
country fashion, and giving great satisfaction. We
do not, however, hear of any outward coming forth

from the heathen among the converts to the new religion till the month of July, 1861. Then twenty-three people were baptized, and others came forward, but were hardly thought fit for admittance to the rite.

No Legaic's name is on that list. And now once more an old longing of Mr. Duncan's broke forth,— the desire to form a Christian settlement away from the contamination of heathen surroundings, where children and weak followers of the new doctrine might grow up in a freer, purer air.

The place seemed prepared for such a project— a deserted village some twenty miles distant on the coast, Metlahkatlah by name, a beautiful spot, and one which the Indians as well as Mr. Duncan deemed suitable to the purpose. Mr. Duncan visited it two or three times in a canoe before making up his mind, and then framed a set of laws, the observance of which should be compulsory on all who would join the new settlement.

These were his rules:—1. To give up their mysteries, or Indian devilry. 2. To cease calling in conjurors when sick. 3. To cease gambling. 4. To cease giving away their property for display. (A common habit among the Indians, and by no means proceeding from generosity. The richer chiefs could easily recover themselves after such an outburst, but among less important people it caused great distress and poverty.) 5. To cease painting their faces. 6. To leave off intoxicating drinks. 7. To rest on the Lord's day. 8. To attend religious instruction.

9. To send their children to school. 10. To be cleanly. 11. To be industrious. 12. To be peaceful. 13. To be liberal and honest in trade. 14. To build neat houses. 15. To pay the village tax.

In May, 1862, a little band, headed by Mr. Duncan, set out from Fort Simpson, literally bound for the Better Land, about fifty souls in all, many of them having come out from heathenism by a mighty struggle; the giving up of the "mysteries" they had been born among, and the surrendering of national customs being to them as the cutting off of a hand, the plucking out of an eye.

All day they spent building their houses, and re-erecting their school and church, of which they had brought the materials with them, while every night they assembled, these exiles for Christ's sake, for a service of singing and prayer.

These souls snatched from destruction were very dear to their leader; but he still mourned over many left behind, and great was his joy when a cluster of canoes a few weeks later darkened the horizon, and three hundred people, with two chiefs, joined the settlement.

They brought news of small-pox raging at Fort Simpson, and, alas for the backslider! of Legaic, in the thick of heathen ceremonies and superstitions, endeavouring by means of drums and rattles and incantations to ward off the dread disease.

Thoroughly beaten down at last by the death of many in his tribe, and alarmed for himself, he virtually gave up his position as a chief, and, bring-

ing his wife and daughter with him, settled down
at Metlahkatlah, becoming one of Mr. Duncan's
chief upholders. The fear of small-pox spreading
in the new settlement gave Mr. Duncan much
anxiety, but it seems to have taken no great root
there, only five deaths occurring. One of the first
baptized, Stephen Ryan, is described as dying in a
wretched hut away from everything he held dear,
but with all the heart-comfort of a Christian man.
"I am quite happy," said this poor sufferer, on his
uneasy bed. "I am not afraid to die. Give my
thanks to Mr. Duncan; he told me of Jesus. I
have hold of the ladder that reaches to heaven.'
And more to the same effect, with loving messages
to his mother to seek the same way in which Mr.
Duncan had placed his feet.

Later on another death took place in the colony,
that of a man named Quthray, who had for some
time been an earnest and regular attendant at the
instruction class for baptismal candidates, and who
had expressed in the clearest terms his repentance
for his past sins and his faith in the Saviour of
sinners. You will shudder, doubtless, when you know
what this man's past career had been. Mr. Duncan
himself, in the terrible, early days of his Mission,
had witnessed him kill a poor slave woman, tear
her limb from limb, and then, aided by a brother
cannibal, devour her as she lay on the sea beach.
And now this man lay sick unto death, but clothed
and in his right mind, at the feet of the Saviour,
weeping for his sins, but believing that Christ

2 L

would pardon and save him. He desired baptism
so greatly that, though no clergyman could be summoned to the dying bed, Mr. Duncan administered
the sacrament in full conviction that the deed was
pleasing to God. The barbarous cannibal Quthray
was signed with the sign of our salvation, and
breathed his last the penitent Christian, "Philip
Atkinson."

Good days now began to dawn on Metlahkatlah;
the little settlement was steadying down into comfort and prosperity. A yearly tax of one blanket,
or two dollars and a half, for every grown man, and
one shirt, or one dollar, for youths, formed a little
fund for carrying on public works. The first year
this levy amounted to one green, one blue, and
ninety-four white blankets, one elk-skin, seventeen
shirts, and seven dollars. Money, it thus appears,
was not so plentiful as goods at Metlahkatlah.

A church and school combined, capable of holding
seven hundred people, had already been built, so
the proceeds of the tax went to purchase a trading
vessel for exporting to Victoria fish, salt, furs, etc.,
the *Carolina* being entirely at Mr. Duncan's orders,
and adding another item to his cares. But he saw
the necessity of advancing his flock in all ways if
he would see them emancipated from heathenism.

In 1863 the Bishop of Columbia arranged to visit
the settlement, to baptize, to marry, and generally
to encourage the little Christian Church. He was
deeply touched by the earnestness of the poor
Indians, some of whom, however, had to endure a

longer probation before he could receive them into
the Church, one or two reversing his decision by
their eager entreaties.

One child of fourteen, who had been thought too
young, wept and prayed so for baptism that the
bishop dared not continue to refuse her. Another
man pleaded he might not live till the next visit of
a clergyman. A third brought a friend with him,
the two promising that if the wife of the former
might only receive baptism, they would answer for
it that she should live as the new God would have
her.

And among these anxious creatures stood Legaic,
the man who had been so long almost persuaded
to be a Christian, desirous now to put away his
evil deeds and to hold fast on God. As "Paul"
he was christened, a name singularly appropriate
to one who had so often and so fiercely persecuted
the earlier converts. But with his baptism his
troubles did not cease. Though he said to the
bishop during his examination, "If I turn back it
will be more bitter for me than before," the temptation to return to his old friends and the haunts of
heathendom seemed to visit him even more strongly
now that he had promised to renounce the devil
and all his works. On one occasion he actually
gathered his friends at Metlahkatlah together, and
told them he *must* go away and resume his former
position of chief to his tribe. Stepping into his
canoe, he said that he was "pulled away." He
knew that he was doing wrong, and would perish

for ever, but he must go. And so, amid general
tears and mourning, his canoe disappeared from
sight, but not for long.

Something induced the poor backslider to pause
before he had gone very far, to put in shore, and
there in sobs and anguish to ask the pardon of God
for his want of endurance.

Back he came next day to Mr. Duncan, who
received him coldly at first, but afterwards became
convinced of his real penitence and desire to
amend.

And now the poor Indian's face seemed indeed
set for heaven. He was very industrious in the
calling he had chosen, that of a carpenter, and he
never failed to second Mr. Duncan in all his under-
takings. He was earnest in his endeavours to
retain and encourage other wavering souls, and he
constantly confessed Christ before the unbelieving
or uncertain. His child, a modest-looking girl of
fourteen, three years back a howling naked savage,
tearing and devouring bleeding dogs, was at this
time in the first class of the mission school, obedient
and gentle.

But Paul Legaic was not long to be left in Metlahkatlah, a proof of the power of the gospel on a
ferocious savage; he was soon to be where none
can " turn back," where all are safe. He was taken
seriously ill when away from home, in 1869; he
instantly wrote to Mr. Duncan, begging him to visit
him, and saying that he was already on the ladder
that reaches to heaven. To his great grief Mr.

Duncan could not obey the summons, and the tidings of his death followed a few days later, together with an unfinished letter to the effect that he was very happy and not afraid to meet God. Such was the end of this once-dreaded murderer and sorcerer, by the power of the gospel converted into a faithful soldier and servant of the Lord Jesus Christ.

The story of the beginning of the mission at Metlahkatlah is now pretty nearly told; at any rate, in its most important points. Steady progress has been made of late years; more and more grown men have come forth out of heathenism, and with their young children have asked for Christian baptism. Other holy deaths have proved the power of the new faith to comfort in the last hour, as well as render life happier. The schools are filled, and the people troop to the sound of the church-going bell. The careful earthly shepherd is still with his flock, teaching, watching, guarding, full of hope for the future, full of thankfulness for the past, his dearest ambition to say one day, in the words of his Master, " Of them which Thou gavest me have I lost none."

## LITTLE MAIDS AT HOXTON.

### LONDON.

WE are all meant to work, and even hard work, it not too hard, is no bar to happiness. Only there must be in the case of "Little Servant Maids" a home and a mother, as a rule, in the background, to make the worker perfectly happy. God has made us in such fashion that we *must* have love of some sort. I knew a little boy who had neither father, mother, kith nor kin, and who, brought up in the workhouse, nearly cried his eyes out when he had to leave it for a good situation in a gentleman's family. The workhouse people had been good to him, and afterwards, whenever he had a holiday, he started for "the House" with as bright a face as if he were making for the snuggest cottage home.

I am not going, however, to speak of boys in this paper. "Little servant maids" are to be the subject, and the very saddest class of those little maids, too,—London children, obliged from earliest infancy to earn their own bread, and who, through poverty, sin, death, or disgrace, have no homes, or worse than none, no relatives, or worse than none. It is pleasant to watch a neat little maid hurrying along with her market basket, and perhaps a baby in her arms, careful of the one and tender of the other. And it is a most pitiful sight to see another girl, hardly older, a little maid, too, swinging an empty beer jug in her hand, and bandying rough words with rougher lads at street corners, rude, dirty, and degraded. Most people pass such girls as this last with a look of disgust. One good person was found to pity them, and she determined to try and do something for the homeless, loveless, little servant maids that she came across in London streets. She had an idea that what they wanted was not so much wise teaching and training, as home-care and love. So she started a Home a few years ago, in a busy part of London, and called it " The Hoxton Servant Girls' Home," and she filled it with friendless little maids wanting places, and loveless little maids wanting homes, and she watched over and cherished her children for two years and then died. But her work lived and prospered, quietly yet steadily, and the other day I set out to visit this London home for little maids, and to gather for myself its story.

A large roomy old house belonging to the Haber-dashers' Company is now the " Home." It stands well back from a busy London street. A neat little maid opened the door, and after summoning the Lady Superintendent, returned to her chair in the hall, a very composed little hall porter.

I asked many questions as we sat in the wide, lofty class-room, with its three great windows look-

ing on the court and the street beyond, and I was
answered with all possible friendliness. Yes, this
was the Girls' Home, and the girls were upstairs in
the work-room, twenty-three of them. They were
under the superintendent (now speaking) and one
matron; no more officials of any sort; the girls did
everything in the house for themselves, washing,
cooking, sewing, scrubbing.

Many were friendless, others had been taken
from bad fathers or sinful mothers, and all were
sheltering here till fit places could be found for
them. Hoxton keeps many little servant maids, so
at the end of three weeks or a month a place is
generally found.

These girls, whose helpless condition is often
discovered by a district visitor or a mission woman,
come to the Home on the recommendation of some
trustworthy person, who pays a sovereign as
entrance fee. By this means no thoroughly bad
children are admitted. When a place has been
found for a girl, and she leaves it for any reason,
she may come back to the Home, because it really
has become her very own, and no more desires to
shake her off than a good parent would do. But
as changing places is not a thing to be lightly encouraged, the girl must now pay for her board out of
her wages, 2s. 6d. a week at first, afterwards more,
if she returns a second, third, or fourth time; 9d.
a day being the limit.

Though there is no over-petting nor spoiling,
there is a great deal of kindness, and the girls feel

that it is a real "home," and not just a charitable
institution. As they are not meant to remain for
more than three or four weeks, there cannot be a great
deal of teaching given; it is more the spirit of the
place that they are supposed to take in, the spirit
of love and of honest work, of cleanliness and
diligence.

Every girl has to do her share of house work.
The whole house is scrubbed down thoroughly
every day. It is an old house, and it stands in
smoky London. On rising, a certain number of
girls are told off for the stairs, so many for the
passages, and so many for the rooms. Then come
prayers and breakfast, and more house and kitchen
work till eleven o'clock, when all the scrubbing and
bed-making is over, and most of the girls can
assemble in the work-room to make and mend
according to their powers. Many of the poor little
maids have hardly handled a needle before. Some,
again, are quite clever. There is always a great
deal of work to be done, for the superintendent
takes a pride in turning out her girls as decently
as possible to their new places.

In the afternoon a book is read aloud, a story
generally, one that the girls can understand, and
that will do them good. They enjoy this immensely,
and have very clear ideas about the sort of tale
they like, and about what is "just nonsense and
nothing else," which was the verdict they pronounced some time ago on a book that did not take
their fancy. In play hours they may romp to

their hearts' delight at the back of the house, in a fair-sized garden, which they have dug and tidied with their own hands, and where now and then a few flowers spring up, as if to remind them of the sweet country beyond these London streets. There is a swing in this garden, which is much favoured, and the girls may romp until they are hungry if they like, for capital meals are set out in the great old-fashioned kitchen, and three times a day they may eat without stint, not to speak of the good slice of bread and jam, or bread and treacle, at bed-time.

The bedrooms are all very pleasant. Every girl has her red or white-covered bed, according as it is summer or winter, and takes a pride in her room looking nice. There are texts on the walls, and sometimes ornaments on the mantelpiece, sent by grateful little maids of a bygone day. One room is particularly pretty, with its two little beds, its bit of carpet, and its nicely coloured walls nearly covered with pictures and texts. This is the sick-room.

Coming away from this room, we stop on the stairs to notice a short passage leading nowhere, unless it be to a window looking out on the garden below, and the green trees in it. Beneath that window stand two chairs. This is the "quiet corner." What does that mean, do you ask? All the girls know, and it is a great treat when some Sunday or holyday afternoon two girls are told, " You may go to the ' quiet corner.' " Off they set, with books and smiling faces, a delightful half-hour before them, the elder girl reading to the other one, or teaching her her text or verse : no worries, no harsh voice to mar the peace, and just that delightful sense of liberty and of being trusted that makes the joy of most young hearts. The pleasant little gushes of talk, when the chapter has been read or the text learnt, the sight of the passing clouds, of the chattering birds, and of the waving branches, as seen from that "quiet corner," will all be remembered later on, as so many moments spent in a kind of paradise.

Sunday is a very great day at the Home, by reason of its being the visiting day of all the little maids in place within walking or even riding distance. Morning church and dinner over, tea for any number almost is laid in the pleasant three-windowed room facing the front court, and then all the afternoon the girls come pouring in, ready for the Bible-class, the pleasant chat, and the good tea. Now, indeed, the Home is a home ; the girls come to the superintendent as to a mother, telling her their various trials and perplexities, and learning from her what is best to be done in each special case. One girl is advised to be patient and take quietly the rebuffs of a hasty-tempered mistress, while another, seemingly perhaps better treated, gives such an account of her place as leads the superintendent to resolve that she shall be removed if on inquiry her statement is found to be true. Sometimes these poor children are unwittingly placed

with drunken masters or mistresses, who perhaps
offer them drink.   As soon as this is known they
are as quietly and quickly as possible fetched home,
and another situation found for them.

There is lying on the superintendent's table a
gift to her from the girls.   It is a handsome photographic album full of little servant maids.   Undo
the broad clasps and look in.   Such nice-looking,
respectable young women meet your eye : pretty
pictures even when the faces are not absolutely
pretty.   Many of them are dressed with real taste,
no finery, but their pleasant faces appearing beneath
a neat cap, and the muslin apron lighting up the
stuff dress.   One girl is carrying a tea-tray, looking
the very picture of a tidy little maid, as indeed she
is, and living in a place where she is valued.
Another girl has her mistress's pretty baby in her
arms; she, too, is the good servant of a good mistress.   The girls used to bring their photographs to
the superintendent, taken in all the finery they
could muster, the feathers and flowers and flounces
so dear to many girls' hearts, and so dear and
useless to buy too!   But they know better now;
their kind friend told them at once how pleased
she was to have their likenesses, but how much
more she should value them if they represented
them as she knew them—neat little maids—not
mere finery pegs.   And the girls not being stupid
have taken the hint.

To turn from the book to real life, however, there
are two tiny children in the group of girls who

seem to be much too young to entertain the idea of being little servant maids. Six years old, no more! How did they come here? It is a sad story. One little creature was brought by its sister, a girl in the Home, saved from neglect and ill usage, one parent dead, the other cruel and drunken. It was impossible to send the child away, so it was taken in for the moment, and then it fitted into a corner and could not be turned out. And much the same story attaches itself to the other baby girl. These tiny ones are not allowed to trench on the funds of the Home. Kind friends have risen up to find them their small beds, their bit and sup, and to send them to the National Schools hard by. The bigger girls wash and dress them, and are proud of the little pair, and it softens their hearts, we think, to have this other ingredient of a home furnished them even in their temporary quarters.

But it would be impossible to tell everything there is to be told about this Home in London streets, its arrangements, and its working. Indeed it seems to me that most people would be more interested in hearing about the girls themselves and their stories. Of course, they are of all sorts, and many have led a hard life before they found their way to this kind refuge. One girl, for instance, a motherless creature, was deserted by her father when "down with fever," and left to the mercies of the workhouse. "I never want to see *him* no more," said this poor thing resentfully of her father. The Home got her a place, and she

turned out honest and hardworking when overlooked, but at other times she behaved more like
an untamed savage than a civilized creature; the
instant the mistress's eye was off her she was away
like an uncaged wild bird down the street, followed
by the dog of the house, just such another wild
spirit as herself. When found talking to any idle
boy or girl she chanced to meet she would regret-
fully return to her work, to escape again at the first
moment possible.

This is an instance of the difficult sort with
which the Home has to deal, the ignorant, untaught, half-witted creatures, born of want and sin.
Poor Emma always spoke affectionately of the
Home, and would bring out the Bible she had had
given her there with an air of pride, adding, "And
I'm to have a new waterproof cloak when I've been
a year in my first place." It is hardly necessary to
say that she did not remain a year in her first
place. The cloaks are given as rewards by a kind
friend and supporter of the Home, and sometimes
there will be quite a festival on the occasion of a
dozen or so of steady little women claiming the
prize.

Poor Polly, some thirteen years old, passed through
a time of trouble after the Home had found her a
place. She was brought back one day by her mistress, crying bitterly, accused of having stolen her
master's gold stud. It was of no use her protesting
her innocence, the mistress would "not keep such a
bad girl a moment longer in the house." So there

she was, for the superintendent to do what she liked
with. Guilty or innocent, there was no doubt that
Polly must be taken in, and tucked up in one of
the white beds, shaking the bedclothes with her
sobs, and still asserting that she knew nothing
about the stud. The superintendent could not
judge of the case all in a minute, but she could
not help feeling glad she had leaned towards
Polly's statement of affairs, and been very gentle
with her, when next morning there came a note
from the mistress to say the stud was found, and
Polly might come to tea with her that evening.
Not much of an apology after the hard words and
cruel suspicions of the night before. But little
servant maids do not often bear malice, and Polly
was quite ready to go, even before she opened a
tiny note slipped into the mistress's letter. It was
from the little daughter of the house, a girl of
eleven years old, and was as follows:—"My dear
Polly, I am so thankful God has heard our prayers,
and has not allowed father to lose his stud in the
street." The superintendent asked Polly, "Did you
and this child, then, pray that the stud might be
found." "Yes," said Polly, simply, "we both knelt
down in the bedroom, and prayed that it might be
found." Polly, you see, was not quite so friendless
as she seemed, she knew she had a Father and
Friend in heaven.

Marianne is another little girl with a trouble.
She has bad parents, so bad that they would hinder
her, if they could, from being a respectable servant.

They find her out when she gets a tidy place, and take her wages away for drink; nay, once they took her boots. Of course the mistress, if she is at all a decent one, cannot do with this sort of people about the house, and so Marianne first gets a caution and then a dismissal, and comes back at last sadly to the Home. Another place is got for her, and the same thing happens again, till the superintendent manages to procure the poor little thing a place at some distance, where the cruel parents cannot find her out. And what makes it harder for Marianne is that she is so very, very small for her fourteen years, that it is very difficult to get her a place, though she earnestly protests, "I know I'm small, but I'm a first-rate hand at scrubbing and cleaning for all that; you'd say so if you saw me at work."

Nelly, again, has suffered from a bad father, a drunkard and a cruel man. He beat and ill-treated wife and children, till the one died of decline, and the other he thrust into the street with a baby sister in her arms! Nelly did her best, getting odd jobs of work to keep herself and the child, but naturally enough she could not manage it altogether, and deep down in her poor heart she must have felt that there was love and tender care to be had somewhere in the world for desolate children, for she asked many people did they know of a Home anywhere that would take in herself and the little one? Luckily for her, her questionings carried her to the parish 'clergyman, and he passed her on to the

Hoxton Home. There she was taught what the poor lost child sadly needed, the duty of keeping herself clean and checking her temper, and then she went out into the world as a general servant, to rise afterwards into a respectable housemaid in a gentleman's family.

There are numbers of such stories to be heard in the little Home at Hoxton, and consequently there must be numbers of poor little maids who owe life and health of soul and body to the kind treatment they receive there. It must shed on their souls, one would think, a glint of holy light, to find that there are people in the world, neither kith nor kin of theirs, who for Christ's sake will take them in and cherish them. Poor little London servant maids, it is well they have one such refuge to come to when homeless and placeless they plod drearily through the cold and heartless streets! I cannot tell you exactly how many girls have been cared for by this one institution, but I know they can be numbered by hundreds, and every day brings more to its doors. Happily every day brings mistresses, too, rapping busily for the neat young hall porter to open, and asking, "Have you a little maid that would suit me?"

This is a wicked world, people are very fond of saying, but it is pleasant day by day to find how many people are employed in trying to mend it.

# A MARTYR BISHOP.

## MELANESIA.

WHO among you does not recollect with pleasure a day spent at the seaside, when sea and sky were one brilliant deep blue, when the grass and trees wore their freshest, brightest green, and when it seemed impossible to be other than glad and happy, full of praise of God, full of love to man!

Try now to imagine such skies, such seas, such green things of the earth, hundreds and thousands of miles away from England; but picture to yourself the sun always shining there, shrubs, ay, and fruit trees, always feathering down to the water's edge, and the crystal waves always so warm and pleasant that the very babies learn to swim almost before they can walk, making the sea their happy play place. Does it not sound like paradise?

Scarcely any work to be done in these pleasant islands, just a few fish to be caught, a few cocoa-nuts or bread-fruit to be knocked off the trees, and there is breakfast and dinner and supper of the nicest kind, all ready to hand.

What can be wanting in these islands of the Pacific to hinder their being a very garden of Eden?

So much, that bright and beautiful as the country is, men tremble to land on its sparkling shores, since not long ago the whole population of these isles were heathen and cannibals.

Has any one been found, then, who dare take his life in his hand and set sail for these fairy islands, determined to teach Christ-like doctrine in so heaven-like a field?

Yes, many a one, whose very name has never reached us, good men and true, who for their single reward will have their Lord's "Well done!" said to them. No other praise, for men have scarcely noted their labours, and their graves are just green hillocks in those Pacific isles.

But for our edification the footprints of one man, one missionary to those far-off islands, are left plain and unmistakable before us, and to trace these out is almost to tell the story of the Melanesian Mission. So let us note to-day how John Coleridge Patteson lived and died for his island flock.

It was a curious congregation, a strange parish that of his in Melanesia, scattered literally among the winds and waves, for the islands among which he worked were many of them widely distant from each other, and some of them lay so near the Equator that a European could not live and labour in their intense heat.

The question was how best to teach and preach in this great field with all its dangers and difficulties. Bishop Selwyn, the Bishop of New Zealand, had thought it well over before he asked Mr. Patteson

to come out from England and help him, and he had
come to this conclusion, Do what is possible for the
grown men and women; but at all hazards get hold
of the children, the boys and girls with soft hearts,
and minds not stubbornly fixed on old customs and
evil ways of living.

So he chartered a ship, and went from island to
island, begging the bright-looking children from
their heathen parents, and taking them back with
him to his head-quarters in New Zealand to be
educated.   Sometimes he met with refusals, sometimes with threats, but still the mission ship sailed
on, gathering on its deck a happy little party, all
bound for their pleasant school-home in a less
scorching climate.

It was just like going to school, for when the cold
weather came on in New Zealand the ship spread
its sails and carried its young passengers back to
their own lands, lest they should shiver and die in
the unaccustomed winter season.

Then the heathen fathers and mothers would rush
down to the water's edge to greet their children,
and another question would trouble the minds of
their teachers.   Will these little ones sow again the
good seed we have tried to plant in their hearts,
and so all unconsciously help to spread the gospel,
or shall we find them, when we come again, fallen
back into heathenism, not strong enough to resist
old ties, old associations?

Many an anxious voyage back had Mr. Patteson,
after dropping his promising scholars in their heathen

homes; but on the whole the plan was successful, and the year following he was gladdened by the sight of the same young faces waiting on the beach for their school ship, the *Southern Cross,* to carry them away again.

Mr. Patteson loved children—black, white, or brown. He writes of them lovingly, too. " Numbers of children and boys playing in the water, or running about on the rocks and sands. . . . There was no shyness on the part of the children. Dear little fellows of from six to ten clustering around me, unable to understand my coat with pockets, and what my socks could be. I seemed to them to have two or three skins."

With all his heart he longed to carry off these unclothed, frolicsome creatures out of the huts, whose ornaments were human skulls, away from their fierce fathers, whose sole occupation was fighting, whose sole pleasure eating and sleeping, to make them children of God, heirs of eternal life. It grieved him sorely to leave them alone in their heathen homes for so large a part of the year, and so after a while he decided not only to teach them in New Zealand in the summer months, but to go back with them when the winter set in, and live with them on one of their islands. It does not sound much to write of such a plan, but this is what it meant.

To live for four whole months, the only white man on a distant island in the ocean, never sure that life even was safe, without a friend save such as could be made of the ignorant people around, without letters from home, without a soul whom he could address in his native tongue. But our missionary was no grumbler; he only remarks on all this, " Of course, I shall like to have a good talk again in English with some one."

The reason that even good men's lives were not safe in these scattered islands is not difficult to divine. The natives could not all at once distinguish them from those other white men who also came occasionally in ships, but with no good purpose, taking away with them the strongest of the young men as labourers for distant lands. These traders, or kidnappers as they almost were, occasioned Mr. Patteson much trouble. When first he asked the islanders for their children to take away with him, they looked upon him with the greatest suspicion, and not till the first batch of young lads had been safely returned to their homes could they entirely believe in his good faith. Then the excitement and joyful confusion of the poor islanders was pleasant to witness, and they gladly listened not only to the account of their children's lives in distant lands, but to the story of the gospel as it had been taught them, simply but plainly declared by one of the young scholars. And so for six years Mr. Patteson toiled on; sometimes teaching A B C in school; sometimes setting a sum like this, "Four cocoa-nuts for three fish-hooks, how many for fifteen fish-hooks?" sometimes working with broom and scrubbing-brush, showing native lads what cleanliness is; sometimes preaching, always praying, and in his mission ship journeying from place to place, a busy guardian of his scattered flock.

In the year 1861 he was consecrated Bishop of Melanesia, and surely never before had bishop so beautiful, so wild a diocese. In one of his letters home at this time our bishop says: " Those nights when I lie down in a long hut among forty or fifty naked men, cannibals, the only Christian on the island —that is the time to pour out the heart in prayer and supplication, that they, those dark, wild heathen about me, may be turned from Satan unto God." "How I held tight," he goes on to say, speaking of his consecration, "the Bible my dear father gave me on my fifth birthday with both hands! and the bishop held it tight too, as he gave me that charge in the name of Christ, and I saw in spirit the multitudes of Melanesia scattered as sheep amidst a thousand isles."

And then from his knees our bishop rises to build his house at Mota, one of the islands under his charge, missionaries being workers in all ways. It was the house for the winter school, which had to serve for everything—the stores of flour and biscuit stowed away on shelves, and the floor cleared for teaching in the day and sleeping on at night. Ague and sickness visited this little settlement that first year; both the bishop and his scholars fell ill, and one young lad died. But there was comfort even here. "The boys were patient and good," said their kind guardian, "and I verily believe that Henry died trusting in the mercy of God, through Jesus Christ, for pardon and peace. After an interval I went and talked to the Mota people, who were crowding round the little bit of a house, of the resurrection of the dead and the life everlasting."

More sickness fell later on Bishop Patteson's charge, and this time not in their island homes, but in the New Zealand school settlement, the college at Auckland. The bishop was now the nurse of his young scholars; he alone could speak the language of many of the sick, so he alone could whisper words of comfort to the suffering, of peace to the dying. For of the fifty-two Melanesians who drooped under this sickness, six died. The poor boys were patient and gentle, obedient and thankful for the love with which they were tended. Their bishop sat by their bedsides, anxious to find out and gratify their wishes, sometimes hardly stirring for hours, fearful of disturbing the sleeping. On one such occasion going to the bed of one of the patient sufferers, he found him dead. A sad ending to his watch, but better to lose this baptized scholar by death than by a relapse into heathenism.

It caused the bishop some anxiety, however, to know how he would be received by the parents of the boys who had died when he came back without them. He was now, however, so generally known and trusted, that no harm followed the sad announcement on his return to Mota.

Bishop Patteson was not a man who feared danger from his half-civilized flock, and as yet he had passed wonderfully through the risks of visiting new islands, and making friendly advances to tribes generally thought to be fierce and ill-disposed to white people, but now he was to find out how real are the perils a missionary has to encounter.

The island of Santa Cruz was always looked upon by navigators as suspicious ground, that is to say, its people were a strong, fierce, untamed race, difficult to make friends with, and not to be trusted. But for all this our bishop must try to beg its tribute of little ones to be Christianized, and on one such expedition the natives attacked the boat's crew of the mission ship, and suddenly let fly their poisoned arrows among them. Happily the bishop was untouched, but three others were wounded, and of those, two died an agonizing death from the effects of the poison.

You should read the story of their death in their loving teacher's own words. Here the account must necessarily be short. The sufferers, not Melanesians, but the descendants of an English crew wrecked in their vessel years ago in these latitudes, were God-fearing, pure-minded youths, just such as could now help their bishop in his missionary work, just such as he grieved to spare. Not one word of complaint broke from their lips during their terrible sufferings, but when the pain was worst they could always be calmed and soothed by a word concerning that greater sufferer, the Lord Jesus; then even

a smile would cross their poor faces, a holy smile,
for were they not soon to be at peace on His breast?
"I am glad," said one dying boy, "that I was doing
my duty. Tell my father that I was in the path
of duty, and he will be so glad. Poor Santa Cruz
people!" Then he begged the bishop to kiss him,
and asked, thinking of the angels in heaven, "They
never stop singing there, sir, do they?" And so,
full of pure and holy thoughts, he fell asleep. The
other lad lived longer, a few days, and he too
literally spent his whole time in unwearied prayer
and praise, though for the five last days and nights
he could not sleep one instant, his spasms were so
violent. Lovely and pleasant in their lives, in their
death they were not divided.

Bishop Patteson writes of them with wet cheeks,
for to him the sorrow was very great. "Dear, dear
Edwin and Fisher! Their patient endurance of
great suffering, and simple, loving thoughts and
prayers about their poor Santa Cruz people are, and
ever I trust will be, a holy example before my eyes."

But sorrow must not hinder work, and back
again went the teacher to his New Zealand school
—a different one in many respects from an English
school, and yet conducted with the greatest strict-
ness. One thing would strike you on entering the
room, and that would be the seeing the scholars
seated on the floor instead of on chairs or benches;
but they liked that best, it was most natural to
them, and they would have to do it when they returned to their own huts, so it seemed useless to

make a point of their acquiring a different custom.
Then, again, girls were to be seen learning with the
boys, and it might surprise you to hear that many
of these were the young wives of the Melanesian
scholars, brought over with them and taught Christian truths and civilized habits. What was the use
of taking great pains with the lads, if they were
only to go back to their own islands and marry
heathen wives? It is not the father who dandles
the babies, and sings them to sleep with hymns
about the Babe of Bethlehem—so the mothers had
to be thought of too.

The boys, however, made the best cooks, so they
took that part of the house work, while the girls
stitched and washed and ironed, and acquired orderly
habits and neat ways.

There was a dairy of thirteen cows at the college,
which, besides supplying the whole mission party,
enabled them to sell considerable quantities of butter
and milk; and considering the rat is the largest
animal really belonging to New Zealand, the islanders
learned very quickly how to manage these new
creatures. Cocoa-nuts had been their only cows
hitherto.

Then printing was another occupation of the
scholars. The Scriptures had to be translated into
many different tongues, the Psalms too, and the
Church service, and there were catechisms, hymns,
and all sorts of little matters that could hardly be
taught without the printer's assistance.

Yet through all the daily work and drudgery the

main business of the mission was never lost sight of,
to Christianize these few stray islanders, and then
send them back to their people, each one to be a
centre of life and knowledge in days to come.

In 1867 the head-quarters of the mission were
moved to Norfolk Island, which was more convenient than New Zealand, as being nearer to the
other islands, and also as possessing a climate
better suited to the Melanesians. There sprang up
quickly the buildings needed for the work—the
school-house, the chapel, the rooms for the bishop
and clergy, and a few cottages for native married
couples.

And still the bishop sailed round his diocese, here
and there collecting scholars to join his flock.

A certain honesty seems to have existed amongst
these poor heathen, for one young lad having been
given to the bishop's care by his father, and afterwards slipping away and swimming ashore, the
father sent back the axe which had been given him
after he offered his son.

The change to Norfolk Island was doubtless a
good move on the whole, but to Bishop Patteson it
brought a still greater isolation from the world, a
parting from such friends as he had made in New
Zealand. But he was not one to murmur at this;
he had given up home and kindred long ago to
devote himself entirely to the heathen, and a little
more or less self-denial did not distress him. In fact,
he says at this time, "I don't know when I have
felt more happy. . . . What a happy, happy life

mine is! so full of blessings, so free from cares on the whole."

Trouble came once more, however, in the form of sickness; fever broke out in the school, and twelve died, besides six others lost in whooping-cough.

The parents of these children spoke of them sadly yet gratefully to the bishop on hearing of their death. "It is good perhaps; if he had stayed here," said one, speaking of his son, "he would have died. We know that you take care of them, and do all you can for them." Words true enough, and consoling to the spiritual father who cared so tenderly for his flock. Sickness softened the hearts, too, of those who were left; the boys would talk seriously together of those who were gone, and the conference generally ended in a visit to the bishop, two or three of the lads together, with a request to be taught more, to be baptized, to stay a long time with him. And in truth there were many more baptisms in the months that followed that outbreak of fever, and a sensible turning to God and holy things of the poor Melanesians.

The little colony gathered round it by degrees all it needed, as it had done in Auckland. Kitchen, printing-office, carpenter's shop, stores, cart-shed, and dairy. Horses and cows, pigs, sheep, and poultry were among the live stock; but the wild cats on the island were too fond of dining off the cocks and hens.

Here took place the first Christian wedding,

making as usual a pleasant stir in the little community. There were three couples. The chapel
was decorated with evergreens and lilies, and the
brides were beautifully dressed. The whole school
was present, and the bridal procession chanted the
Hundredth Psalm. The wedding rings were made
out of fourpenny pieces, and the Marriage Service,
which had been specially translated and printed for
the occasion, was well pored over by the attentive
congregation.

And next event, the first native clergyman was
ordained by the bishop, one George Sarawia, one
of the bishop's first pupils. Years before, the bishop
was visiting one of the islands. As he returned,
wading through the sea to his boat, a good deal
depressed because of the refusal of the natives to
lend him any of their children for education, he
suddenly spied a little black boy crouched at the
bottom of the boat, and begging to go with him.
The people on shore, however, had seen the runaway; and as they showed signs of anger,
threatening the boat with their spears and other
weapons, the bishop lifted the little fellow in his
arms and held him out to them, to show he would
not take him without leave. Thereupon the child
began chattering vehemently to his friends, and
though no one understood his words, the end was
that he was allowed to stay with the bishop. And
so this little wilful creature came to grow up the
first convert, and afterwards the first native clergyman in the Melanesian isles. He proved a most

useful helper to the bishop, since he was able to leave him at Mota with a branch school there, and a model settlement growing up around it. The Rev. George Sarawia was married and had one child at this time, so that the heathen around had the advantage of seeing the daily life of a Christian household among their own race.

Mota was indeed growing into a Christian community. The bishop spent seven weeks there later on, and baptized 291 persons. Some old enemies who had even shot each other came together to the font, as did often husbands and wives. And the people said, " We don't know how it is, but we feel quite different now. Before we did not attend, and went on in many of the old ways; now we think and talk of nothing else, and the old ways we see to be wrong, and we have put them away."

But all was not brightness around the mission party. At some of the islands of late the people had shown considerable shyness of the bishop's visit.

It seemed that traders' vessels had called at various places, and carried off many of the people to work in the plantations of Fiji. These vessels the poor heathens aptly called thief-vessels or kill-kills.

" Is it the bishop, or another kill-kill vessel ? " they would ask, half tremblingly, half angrily, of each other when a sail hove in sight. And small wonder that they trembled and raged, for in one island alone eighteen people were known to have been murdered in cold blood by the men of these so-called labour-vessels, while fifty others were taken away from their homes, either by force or false pretences.

In many cases the captains of these ships would pretend to belong to the mission, and even dress up to resemble the Bishop and his clergy, so it is not strange that the poor natives could hardly distinguish friend from foe, the dreaded slave-ship from the peace-bringing *Southern Cross*. Bishop Patteson well knew the danger he incurred of being confused by the half-informed islanders with these dreaded enemies; but still he went his way, avoiding no path, however dangerous, where his duties led him.

Still he experienced much uneasiness when he heard that a labour-vessel was about to visit Santa Cruz. That island, though fairly friendly towards him personally, had never given him one child for his school, and was not likely willingly to spare young men for less known regions.

In case of force being used or outrages committed, the natives would hardly stay to inquire from whence came these white men to disturb their peace, but revenge themselves on the next comer of that race. So, as the Bishop was brave, not rash, he resolved not to land at Santa Cruz on his next cruise till he heard whether any traders' vessels had really been there; as a wiser course putting in at a small island near, called Nupaka, where he had been in the habit of calling to obtain an in-

terpreter for Santa Cruz. Some canoes were lying
off this island, and the bishop, with another Englishman, Mr. Atkin, and three Melanesians, put off
in the boat to speak to them.

In years before the islanders here had always
come out in a joyful haste and curiosity to meet
the bishop, clambering on board his ship without
fear or reluctance. Now all noticed a sullen silence
and calm among the canoes which lay behind a
coral reef at a little distance. The bishop's boat
could not cross this reef, so, wishful to converse
with the people and restore confidence, he entered
a native canoe, on board of which were two chiefs
of his acquaintance, and was taken ashore.

No one knows what the bishop did there; suddenly a volley of arrows was let fly on the mission
boat, wounding every one on board. Here was war
proclaimed without doubt. The boat was hastily
rowed back to the vessel, and nothing being seen of
the bishop's canoe, a strong party well armed was
sent out to ascertain his fate. In spite of his
having been wounded, and of the danger of the
poison working into his system, Mr. Atkin bravely
volunteered as guide to the expedition. The tide
would not yet let the boat cross the reef, but they
lay close alongside, watching the island with a glass.

At half-past four there was water enough to float
them over, and then for the first time they saw an
apparently empty canoe drifting near them. They
rowed towards it, and beheld a silent heap in the
middle of it.

It was the body of the bishop.

A yell of triumph rose from the beach as the mission crew recognized their leader, but the islanders attempted no further revenge.

Swiftly and silently the awe-struck crew rowed back to the *Southern Cross*, murmuring as they gained its sheltering side, "The body." Yes, that was all they brought back, not the brave, considerate, active leader of Christ's army, but his helpless, silent body.

The bishop had been wrapped in native matting, and a palm branch thrust into his breast, with five knots tied in it. The explanation of this was imagined to be, that the murder of the bishop was in revenge for the death or capture of five natives of the island by white men.

This might be the case, but the palm branch, that symbol of a martyr's death, was strangely applicable to the dead man's case, even though laid on his breast by savage hands. He had evidently been killed by a sharp blow on the head, his body was pierced by many arrow-wounds, but the sweet face still smiled, and there was no sign on it of suffering or terror.

The slave-vessel *had* visited the island a few days before, and this was the result of their visit.

There is not much more to tell of this sad voyage. The *Southern Cross* sailed to the mission settlement at Norfolk Island, with her ensign half-mast high. Who was dead? What had happened? questioned the anxious stay-at-homes. When the boat put off and neared shore they called out from the land, "All right?" But the answer chilled all hearts, "No; sad news."

The bishop was gone, Mr. Atkin was dead, and also a sorely wounded Melanesian. The deepest grief fell at once on the community; it was as if each had lost a father or a brother.

It was indeed a sad blow to the mission. Who could supply the place of so kind and loving a teacher, so brave a leader, so tender a father to all his dark children?

Death to the man himself could have had few terrors; he had faced it often before.

Once, indeed, as he told a friend, he was being led by natives to a secluded spot for the purpose of putting him to death there and then, when he begged a few minutes' rest in a deserted hut, where he knelt down and committed himself into God's hands, to do with him as He would. On rejoining his would-be murderers, he noticed a change in their behaviour towards him, and after consulting together, they turned and led him back safely to his ship.

Afterwards he learned that they had watched him at prayer, and decided from his peaceful and holy looks that *he* could not be the man who had lately killed a relation of theirs, and so should be spared their vengeance.

But now his time had come.

There was a passage in his well-worn Bible scored and underscored, and blotted with tears. It was this: "There is no man that hath left house, or brethren, or sisters, or father . . . for My sake, and the gospel's, but he shall receive an hundredfold now in this time, houses, and brethren, and sisters, and mothers, and children, and lands, with persecutions; and in the world to come eternal life."

The man whose story is written here had experienced all this. His island children had been to him the dearest of ties, and now had come the life everlasting—the good and faithful servant had well earned his rest.

The Melanesian Mission still goes on; other good men have arisen to carry on the work, but the name of the martyr bishop will always be associated with it, and the dearest wish of those who come after him will ever be how best to tread in his footsteps.

THE END.

PRINTED BY WILLIAM CLOWES AND SONS, LIMITED, LONDON AND BECCLES.

# Society for Promoting Christian Knowledge.

---

# THE HOME LIBRARY.

*A Series of Books illustrative of Church History, &c., specially, but not exclusively, adapted for Sunday Reading.*

Crown 8vo., cloth boards, 3s. 6d. each.

**GREAT ENGLISH CHURCHMEN; or, Famous Names in English Church History and Literature.** By W. H. DAVENPORT ADAMS.

**MILITARY RELIGIOUS ORDERS OF THE MIDDLE AGES; the Hospitallers, the Templars, the Teutonic Knights and others.** By the Rev. F. C. WOODHOUSE, M.A.

**NARCISSUS: A Tale of Early Christian Times.** By the Rev. W. BOYD CARPENTER, M.A.

**SKETCHES OF THE WOMEN OF CHRISTENDOM.** Dedicated to the Women of India. By the author of "The Chronicles of the Schönberg-Cotta Family."

**THE CHURCHMAN'S LIFE OF WESLEY.** By R. DENNY URLIN, Esq., F.S.S.

**THE HOUSE OF GOD THE HOME OF MAN.** By the Rev. Canon JELF.

**THE INNER LIFE, as Revealed in the Correspondence of Celebrated Christians.** Edited by the late Rev. T. ERSKINE.

**THE NORTH-AFRICAN CHURCH.** By the Rev. JULIUS LLOYD, M.A. With Map.

**BLACK AND WHITE.** By H. A. FORDE.

**CONSTANTINE THE GREAT.** The Union of the Church and State. By the Rev. E. L. CUTTS, B.A.

**THE LIFE OF THE SOUL IN THE WORLD; its Nature, Needs, Dangers, Sorrows, Aids, and Joys.** By the Rev. F. C. WOODHOUSE, M.A.

## Prayer.
For the Use of the Sick ; based on short passages of Scripture. By the Rev. F. BOURDILLON, M.A., Author of "Lesser Lights." 12mo. ..........................*Cloth boards* 1

## Being of God, Six Addresses on the.
By C. J. ELLICOTT, D.D., Bishop of Gloucester and Bristol. Small post 8vo. ..........................*Cloth boards* 1

## Bible Places ; or, The Topography of the Holy Land.
By the Rev. Canon TRISTRAM. With Map and numerous Woodcuts. Crown 8vo. .............................*Cloth boards* 4

## Christians under the Crescent in Asia.
By the Rev. E. L. CUTTS, B.A., Author of "Turning-Points of Church History," &c. With numerous Illustrations. Crown 8vo. ....................................*Cloth boards* 5

## Church History, Sketches of,
During the first Six Centuries. By the Rev. J. C. ROBERTSON. Part I. With Map. 12mo. ...*Cloth boards* 1

——————————————————— Part II. From the Seventh Century to the Reformation. 12mo................*Cloth boards* 1

Parts I. and II. in a volume ..................*Cloth boards* 2

## Daily Readings for a Year.
By ELIZABETH SPOONER. Crown 8vo. .........*Cloth boards* 3

## Englishman's Brief, The,
On behalf of his National Church. New, revised, and enlarged edition. Small post 8vo. ..............*Cloth boards* 2

## Gospels, The Four,
Arranged in the Form of an English Harmony, from the Text of the Authorized Version. By the Rev. J. M. FULLER, M.A. With Analytical Table of Contents and four Maps. Post 8vo.... ............................*Cloth boards* 1

## History of the English Church.
In Short Biographical Sketches. By the Rev. JULIUS LLOYD, M.A., Author of "Sketches of Church History in Scotland." Post 8vo. .............................*Cloth boards* 2

## History of the Jewish Nation, A,
From the Earliest Times to the Present Day. By E. H. PALMER, Esq., M.A. With Map of Palestine and numerous Illustrations. Crown 8vo. .........................*Cloth boards* 5

### Land of Israel, The.

*s.*

A Journal of Travel in Palestine, undertaken with special reference to its Physical Character. By the Rev. Canon TRISTRAM. Third edition, revised. With two Maps and numerous Illustrations. Large post 8vo..........*Cloth boards* 10

### Litany, The.

With an Introduction, Explanation of Words and Phrases, together with Illustrative and Devotional Paraphrase. By the Rev. E. J. BOYCE, M.A. Fcap. 8vo. ......*Cloth boards* 1

### Narrative of a Modern Pilgrimage through Palestine on Horseback, and with Tents.

By the Rev. A. C. SMITH, M.A. Numerous illustrations, and four Coloured Plates. Crown 8vo. .........*Cloth boards* 5

### Paley's Evidence.

A New Edition, with Notes, Appendix, and Preface. By the Rev. E. A. LITTON. Post 8vo..............*Cloth boards* 4

### Paley's Horæ Paulinæ.

A New Edition, with Notes, Appendix, and Preface. By the Rev. J. S. HOWSON, D.D., Dean of Chester. Post 8vo. ..............................*Cloth boards* 3

### Peace with God.

A Manual for the Sick. By the Rev. E. BURBIDGE, M.A. Post. 8vo. ...............................................*Cloth boards* 1

### Plain Reasons against Joining the Church of Rome.

By the Rev. R. F. LITTLEDALE, LL.D., &c. Revised and enlarged edition. Post 8vo. .......................*Cloth boards* 1

### Plain Words for Christ.

Being a Series of Readings for Working Men. By R. G. DUTTON, B.A. Post 8vo. ...........................*Cloth boards* 2

### Prophecies and Types of Messiah.

Four Lectures to Pupil-teachers. By the Rev. G. P. OTTEY, M.A. Post 8vo. ...........................*Cloth boards* 1

### St. Chrysostom's Picture of his Age.

Post 8vo.................................................*Cloth boards* 2

### St. Chrysostom's Picture of the Religion of his Age.

Post 8vo..................................................*Cloth boards* 1

Places mentioned in the Bible, beautifully executed, with Descriptive Letterpress. By the Rev. Canon TRISTRAM.

*Cloth, bevelled boards, gilt edges* 7

## Seek and Find.

A Double Series of Short Studies of the Benedicite. By CHRISTINA G. ROSSETTI. Post 8vo. ...........*Cloth boards* 2

## Servants of Scripture, The.

By the Rev. JOHN W. BURGON, B.D. Post 8vo.

*Cloth boards* 1

## Sinai and Jerusalem; or, Scenes from Bible Lands.

Consisting of Coloured Photographic Views of Places mentioned in the Bible, including a Panoramic View of Jerusalem, with Descriptive Letterpress. By the Rev. F. W. HOLLAND, M.A. Demy 4to.

*Cloth, bevelled boards, gilt edges* 7

## Some Chief Truths of Religion.

By the Rev. E. L. CUTTS, B.A., Author of "Pastoral Counsels," "St. Cedd's Cross," &c. Crown 8vo. *Cloth boards* 3

## Thoughts for Working Days.

Original and Selected. By EMILY C. ORR. Post 8vo.

*Limp cloth* 1

## Turning-Points of English Church History.

By the Rev. EDWARD L. CUTTS, B.A., Vicar of Holy Trinity, Havistock Hill. Crown 8vo. ...........*Cloth boards* 3

## Turning-Points of General Church History.

By the Rev. E. L. CUTTS, B.A., Author of "Pastoral Counsels," &c. Crown 8vo. ......................*Cloth boards* 5

## Under His Banner.

Papers on Missionary Work of Modern Times. By the Rev. W. H. TUCKER. With Map. Crown 8vo. New Edition ......................*Cloth boards* 5

## Ventures of Faith; or, Deeds of Christian Heroes.

By the Rev. J. J. HALCOMBE. With six Illustrations on toned paper. Crown 8vo. ......................*Cloth boards* 2

### Depositories:

NORTHUMBERLAND AVENUE, CHARING CROSS, W.C

43, QUEEN VICTORIA STREET, E.C.; 48, PICCADILLY, W.; AND 135, NORTH STREET, BRIGHTON.

Lightning Source UK Ltd.
Milton Keynes UK
UKOW01n0833090218
317603UK00003B/137/P